The Curse of the Silver Goat

Alleyn bowed, stooped...and pounced.

His hand shot along the floor and under the hem of the heavy skirt. She made a short, angry noise and tried to trample on the hand, but Alleyn stepped back neatly and extended his arm, keeping the hand closed.

"A strange egg, Madame Blanche," he said, "for a respectable hen to lay."

He opened his hand. Across the palm lay a tiny silver goat.

"You have one chance," he said. *"Where is the boy?"*

SPINSTERS IN JEOPARDY
NGAIO MARSH

A BERKLEY BOOK
published by
BERKLEY PUBLISHING CORPORATION

Contents

Cast of Characters

Roderick Alleyn........ Chief Detective-Inspector, Criminal Investigation Department, New Scotland Yard

Agatha Troy Alleyn.................... his wife

Ricky .... their son

Miss Truebody.......... their fellow-passenger

Dr. Claudel............... a French physician

Raoul Milano .... of Roqueville. Owner-driver

Dr. Ali Baradi........... a surgeon

Mahomet .... his servant

Mr. Oberon............... of the Château de la Chèvre d'Argent

Ginny Taylor
Robin Herrington } his guests
Carbury Glande
Annabella Wells

Teresa .... the fiancée of Raoul

M. Dupont................ of the Sûreté. Acting Commisaire at the Préfecture, Roqueville

M. Callard .... Managing Director of the Compagnie Chimique des Alpes Maritimes

M. and Madame Milano.................... the parents of Raoul

Marie .... a maker of figurines

M. Malaquin............. proprietor of the Hôtel Royal

P. E. Garbel.............. a chemist

Prologue

I

WITHOUT moving his head, Ricky slewed his eyes round until he was able to look slantways at the back of his mother's easel.

"I'm getting pretty bored, however," he announced.

"Stick it a bit longer, darling, I implore you, and look at Daddy."

"Well, because it's just about as boring a thing as a person can have to do. Isn't it, Daddy?"

"When I did it," said his father, "I was allowed to look at your mama, so I wasn't bored. But as there are degrees of boredom," he continued, "so there are different kind of bores. You might almost say there are recognizable schools."

"To which school," said his wife, stepping back from her easel, "would you say Mr. Garbel belonged? Ricky, look at Daddy for five minutes more and then I promise we'll stop."

Ricky sighed ostentatiously and contemplated his father.

"Well, as far as we know him," Alleyn said, "to the epistolatory school. There, he's a classic. In person he's undoubtedly the sort of bore that shows you things you don't want to see. Snapshots in envelopes. Barren conservatories. Newspaper cuttings. He's relentless in this. I think he carries things on his person and puts them in front of you without giving you the smallest clue about what you're meant to say. You're moving, Ricky."

"Isn't it five minutes yet?"

"No, and it never will be if you fidget. How long is it, Troy, since you first heard from Mr. Garbel?"

"About eighteen months. He wrote for Christmas. All told I've had six letters and five postcards from Mr. Garbel. This last arrived this morning. That's what put him into my head."

"Daddy, who is Mr. Garbel?"

"One of Mummy's admirers. He lives in the Maritime Alps and writes love letters to her."

"Why?"

"He says it's because he's her third cousin once removed, but I know better."

"What do you know better?"

With a spare paintbrush clenched between her teeth, Troy said indistinctly: "Keep like that, Ricky darling, I *implore* you."

"O.K. Tell me properly, Daddy, about Mr. Garbel."

"Well, he suddenly wrote to Mummy and said Mummy's great-aunt's daughter was his second cousin, and that he thought Mummy would like to know that he lived at a place called Roqueville in the Maritime Alps. He sent a map of Roqueville, marking the place where the road he lived on ought to be shown, but wasn't, and he told Mummy how he didn't go out much or meet many people."

"Pretty dull, however."

"He told her about all the food you can buy there that you can't buy here, and he sent her copies of newspapers with bus timetables marked and messages at the side saying: 'I find this bus convenient and often take it. It leaves the corner by the principal hotel every half-hour.' Do you still want to hear about Mr. Garbel?"

"Unless it's time to stop, I might as well."

"Mummy wrote to Mr. Garbel and said how interesting she found his letter."

"Did you, Mummy?"

"One has to be polite," Troy muttered and laid a thin stroke of rose on the mouth of Ricky's portrait.

"And he wrote back sending her three used bus tickets and a used train ticket."

"Does she collect them?"

"Mr. Garbel thought she would like to know that they were

his tickets punched by guards and conductors all for him. He also sends her beautifully coloured postcards of the Maritime Alps."

"What's that? May I have them?"

". . . with arrows pointing to where his house would be if you could see it and to where the road goes to a house he sometimes visits only the house is off the postcard."

"Like a picture puzzle, sort of?"

"Sort of. And he tells Mummy how, when he was young and doing chemistry at Cambridge, he almost met her great-aunt who was his second cousin once removed."

"Did he have a shop?"

"No, he's a special kind of chemist without a shop. When he sends Mummy presents of used tickets and old newspapers he writes on them: 'Sent by P. E. Garbel, 16 Rue des Violettes, Roqueville, to Mrs. Agatha Alleyn (née Troy) daughter of Stephen and Harriet Troy (née Baynton).'"

"That's you, isn't it, Mummy? What else?"

"Is it possible, Ricky," asked his wondering father, "that you find this interesting?"

"Yes," said Ricky. "I like it. Does he mention me?"

"I don't think so."

"Or you?"

"He suggests that Mummy might care to read parts of his letter to me."

"May we go and see him?"

"Yes," said Alleyn. "As a matter of fact I think we may."

Troy turned from her work and gaped at her husband. "What can you mean?" she exclaimed.

"Is it time, Mummy? Because it must be, so may I get down?"

"Yes, thank you, my sweet. You have been terribly good and I must think of some exciting reward."

"Going to see Mr. Garbel frinstance?"

"I'm afraid," Troy said, "that Daddy, poor thing, was being rather silly."

"Well then—ride to Babylon?" Ricky suggested, and looked out of the corners of his eyes at his father.

"All right," Alleyn groaned, parodying despair. "O.K. *All right*. Here we go!"

He swung the excitedly squealing Ricky up to his shoulders and grasped his ankles.

"Good old horse," Ricky shouted and patted his father's

cheek. "Non-stop to Babylon. Good old horse."

Troy looked dotingly at him. "Say to Nanny that I said you could ask for an extra high tea."

"Top highest with strawberry jam?"

"If there is any."

"Lavish!" said Ricky and gave a cry of primitive food-lust. "Giddy-up horse," he shouted. The family of Alleyn broke into a chant:

> How many miles to Babylon?
> Five score and ten.
> Can I get there by candle-light?

"*Yes! And back again!*" Ricky yelled, and was carried at a canter from the room.

Troy listened to the diminishing rumpus on the stairs and looked at her work.

"How happy we are!" she thought, and then foolishly, "Touch wood!" And she picked up a brush and dragged a touch of colour from the hair across the brow. "How lucky I am," she thought, more soberly, and her mood persisted when Alleyn came back with his hair tousled like Ricky's and his tie under his ear.

He said: "May I look?"

"All right," Troy agreed, wiping her brushes, "but don't say anything."

He grinned and walked round to the front of the easel. Troy had painted a head that seemed to have light as its substance. Even the locks of dark hair might have been spun from sunshine. It was a work in line rather than in mass, but the line flowed and turned with a subtlety that made any further elaboration unnecessary. "It needs another hour," Troy muttered.

"In that case," Alleyn said, "I can at least touch wood."

She gave him a quick grateful look and said, "What is all this about Mr. Garbel?"

"I saw the A.C. this morning. He was particularly nice, which generally means he's got you pricked down for a particularly nasty job. On the face of it this one doesn't sound so bad. It seems M.I.5. and the Sûreté are having a bit of a party with the Narcotics Bureau, and our people want somebody with fairly fluent French to go over for talks and a bit of field-work. As it *is*

M.I.5. we'd better observe the usual rule of airy tact on your part and phony inscrutability on mine. But it turns out that the field-work lies, to coin a coy phrase, not a hundred miles from Roqueville."

"Never!" Troy ejaculated. "In the Garbel country?"

"Precisely. Now it occurs to me that what with war, Ricky and the atrocious nature of my job, we've never had a holiday abroad together. Nanny is due for a fortnight at Reading. Why shouldn't you and Ricky come with me to Roqueville and call on Mr. Garbel?"

Troy looked delighted, but she said: "You can't go round doing top-secret jobs for M.I.5. trailing your wife and child. It would look so amateurish. Besides, we agreed never to mix business with pleasure, Rory."

"In this case the more amateurish I look, the better. And I should only be based in Roqueville. The job lies outside it, so we wouldn't really be mixing business with pleasure."

He looked at her for a moment. "Do come," he said, "you know you're dying to meet Mr. Garbel."

Troy scraped her palette. "I'm dying to come," she amended, "but not to meet Mr. Garbel. And yet: I don't know. There's a sort of itch, I confess it, to find out just how deadly dull he is. Like a suicidal tendency."

"You must yield to it. Write to him and tell him you're coming. You might enclose a bus ticket from Putney to the Fulham Road. How do you address him: 'Dear Cousin—' But what is his Christian name?"

"I've no idea. He's just P. E. Garbel. To his intimates, he tells me, he is known as Peg. He adds, inevitably, a quip about being square in a round hole."

"Roqueville being the hole?"

"Presumably."

"Has he a job, do you think?"

"For all I know he may be writing a monograph on bicarbonate-of-soda. If he is he'll probably ask us to read the manuscript."

"At all events we must meet him. Put down that damn palette and tell me you're coming."

Troy wiped her hands on her smock. "We're coming," she said.

II

In his château outside Roqueville, Mr. Oberon looked across the nighted Mediterranean towards North Africa and then smiled gently upon his assembled guests.

"How fortunate we are," he said. "Not a jarring note. All gathered together with one pure object in mind." He ran over their names as if they composed a sort of celestial roll-call. "Our youngest disciple," he said, beaming on Ginny Taylor. "A wonderful field of experience awaits her. She stands on the threshold of ecstasy. It is not too much to say, of ecstasy. And Robin too." Robin Herrington, who had been watching Ginny Taylor, looked up sharply. "Ah, youth, youth," sighed Mr. Oberon, ambiguously, and turned to the remaining guests, two men and a woman. "Do we envy them?" he asked, and answered himself. "No! No, for ours is the richer tilth. We are the husbandmen, are we not?"

Dr. Baradi lifted his dark, fleshy and intelligent head. He looked at his host. "Yes, indeed," he said. "We are precisely that. And when Annabella arrives—I think you said she was coming?"

"Dear Annabella!" Mr. Oberon exclaimed. "Yes. On Tuesday. Unexpectedly."

"Ah!" said Carbury Glande, looking at his paint-stained fingernails. "On Tuesday. Then she will be rested and ready for our Thursday rites."

"Dear Annabella!" Dr. Baradi echoed sumptuously.

The sixth guest turned her ravaged face and short-sighted eyes towards Ginny Taylor.

"Is this your first visit?" she asked.

Ginny was looking at Mr. Oberon. She wore an expression that was unbecoming to her youth, a look of uncertainty, excitement and perhaps fear.

"Yes," she said. "My first."

"A neophyte," Baradi murmured richly.

"Soon to be so young a priestess," Mr. Oberon added. "It is very touching." He smiled at Ginny with parted lips.

A tinkling crash broke across the conversation. Robin

Herrington had dropped his glass on the tessellated floor. The remains of his cocktail ran into a little pool near Mr. Oberon's feet.

Mr. Oberon cut across his apologies. "No, no," he said. "It is a happy symbol. Perhaps a promise. Let us call it a libation," he said. "Shall we dine?"

I

Journey to the South

I

ALLEYN lifted himself on his elbow and turned his watch to the blue light above his pillow. Twenty minutes past five. In another hour they would be in Roqueville.

The abrupt fall of silence when the train stopped must have woken him. He listened intently but, apart from the hiss of escaping steam and the slam of a door in a distant carriage, everything was quiet and still.

He heard the men in the double sleeper next to his own exchange desultory remarks. One of them yawned loudly.

Alleyn thought the station must be Douceville. Sure enough, someone walked past the window and a lonely voice announced to the night: *"Douce-v-i-ll-e."*

The engine hissed again. The same voice, apparently continuing a broken conversation, called out: *"Pas ce soir, par exemple!"* Someone else laughed distantly. The voices receded to be followed by the most characteristic of all stationary train noises, the tap of steel on steel. The taps tinkered away into the distance.

Alleyn manoeuvred to the bottom of his bunk, dangled his long legs in space for a moment, and then slithered to the floor. The window was not completely shuttered. He peered through the gap and was confronted by the bottom of a poster for

Dubonnet and the lower half of a porter carrying a lamp. The lamp swung to and fro, a bell rang, and the train clanked discreetly. The lamp and poster were replaced by the lower halves of two discharged passengers, a pile of luggage, a stretch of empty platform, and a succession of swiftly moving pools of light. Then there was only the night hurrying past with blurred suggestions of rocks and olive trees.

The train gathered speed and settled down to its perpetual choriambic statement: "What a to-*do*. What a to-*do*."

Alleyn cautiously lowered the window-blind. The train was crossing the seaward end of a valley and the moon in its third quarter was riding the western heavens. Its radiance emphasized the natural pallor of hills and trees and dramatized the shapes of rocks and mountains. With the immediate gesture of a shutter, a high bank obliterated this landscape. The train passed through a village and for two seconds Alleyn looked into a lamplit room where a woman watched a man intent over an early breakfast. What occupation got them up so soon? They were there, sharp in his vision, and were gone.

He turned from the window wondering if Troy, who shared his pleasure in train journeys, was awake in her single berth next door. In twenty minutes he would go and see. In the meantime he hoped that, in the almost complete darkness, he could dress himself without making a disturbance. He began to do so, steadying himself against the lurch and swing of this small, noisy and unstable world.

"Hullo." A treble voice ventured from the blackness of the lower bunk. "Are we getting out soon?"

"Hullo," Alleyn rejoined. "No, go to sleep."

"I couldn't be wakier. Matter of fac' I've been awake pretty well all night."

Alleyn groped for his shirt, staggered, barked his shin on the edge of his suitcase and swore under his breath.

"Because," the treble voice continued, "if we aren't getting out why are you dressing yourself?"

"To be ready for when we are."

"I see," said the voice. "Is Mummy getting ready for getting out, too?"

"Not yet."

"Why?"

"It's not time."

"Is she asleep?"

"I don't know, old boy."

"Then how do you know she's not getting ready?"

"I don't know, really. I just hope she's not."

"Why?"

"I want her to rest, and if you say why again I won't answer."

"I see." There was a pause. The voice chuckled. "Why?" it asked.

Alleyn had found his shirt. He now discovered that he had put it on inside out. He took it off.

"If," the voice pursued, "I said a sensible why, would you answer, Daddy?"

"It would have to be entirely sensible."

"Why are you getting up in the dark?"

"I had hoped," Alleyn said bitterly, "that all little boys were fast asleep and I didn't want to wake them."

Because now you know they aren't asleep so why—?"

"You're perfectly right," Alleyn said. The train rounded a curve and he ran with some violence against the door. He switched on the light and contemplated his son.

Ricky had the newly made look peculiar to little boys in bed. His dark hair hung sweetly over his forehead, his eyes shone and his cheeks and lips were brilliant. One would have said he was so new that his colours had not yet dried.

"I like being in a train," he said, "more lavishly than anything that's ever happened so far. Do you like being in a train, Daddy?"

"Yes," said Alleyn. He opened the door of the washing-cabinet, which lit itself up. Ricky watched his father shave.

"Where are we now?" he said presently.

"By a sea. It's called the Mediterranean and it's just out there on the other side of the train. We shall see it when it's daytime."

"Are we in the middle of the night?"

"Not quite. We're in the very early morning. Out there everybody is fast asleep," Alleyn suggested, not very hopefully.

"Everybody?"

"Almost everybody. Fast asleep and snoring."

"All except us," Ricky said with rich satisfaction, "because we are lavishly wide awake in the very early morning in a train. Aren't we, Daddy?"

"That's it. Soon we'll pass the house where I'm going tomorrow. The train doesn't stop there, so I have to go on with you to Roqueville and drive back. You and Mummy will stay in Roqueville."

"Where will you be most of the time?"

"Sometimes with you and sometimes at this house. It's called the Château de la Chèvre d'Argent. That means the House of the Silver Goat."

"Pretty funny name, however," said Ricky.

A stream of sparks ran past the window. The light from the carriage flew across the surface of a stone wall. The train had begun to climb steeply. It gradually slowed down until there was time to see nearby objects lamplit, in the world outside: a giant cactus, a flight of steps, part of an olive grove. The engine laboured almost to a standstill. Outside their window, perhaps a hundred yards away, there was a vast house that seemed to grow out of the cliff. It stood full in the moonlight, and shadows, black as ink, were thrown by buttresses across its recessed face. A solitary window, veiled by a patterned blind, glowed dully yellow.

"*Somebody* is awake out there," Ricky observed. "'Out,' 'in'?" he speculated. "Daddy, what are those people? 'Out' or 'in'?"

"Outside for us, I suppose, and inside for them."

"Outside the train and inside the house," Ricky agreed. "Suppose the train ran through the house, would they be 'in' for us?"

"I hope," his father observed glumly, "that you don't grow up a metaphysician."

"What's that? Look, there they are in their house. We've stopped, haven't we?"

The carriage window was exactly opposite the lighted one in the cliff-like wall of the house. A blurred shape moved in the room on the other side of the blind. It swelled and became a black body pressed against the window.

Alleyn made a sharp ejaculation and a swift movement.

"Because you're standing right in front of the window," Ricky said politely, "and it would be rather nice to see out."

The train jerked galvanically and with a compound racketing noise, slowly entered a tunnel, emerged, and gathering pace, began a descent to sea-level.

The door of the compartment opened and Troy stood there,

in a woollen dressing-gown. Her short hair was rumpled and hung over her forehead like her son's. Her face was white and her eyes dark with perturbation. Alleyn turned quickly. Troy looked from him to Ricky. "Have you seen out of the window?" she asked.

"*I* have," said Alleyn. "And so, by the look of you, have you."

Troy said, "Can you help me with my suitcase?" and to Ricky: "I'll come back and get you up soon, darling."

"Are you both going?"

"We'll be just next door. We shan't be long," Alleyn said.

"It's only because it's in a train."

"We know," Troy reassured him. "But it's all right. Honestly. O.K.?"

"O.K.," Ricky said in a small voice, and Troy touched his cheek.

Alleyn followed into her own compartment. She sat down on her bunk and stared at him. "I can't believe that was true," she said.

"I'm sorry you saw it."

"Then it was true. Ought we to do anything? Rory, ought you to do anything? Oh *dear,* how tiresome."

"Well, I can't do much while moving away at sixty miles an hour. I suppose I'd better ring up the Préfecture when we get to Roqueville."

He sat down beside her. "Never mind, darling," he said, "there may be another explanation."

"I don't see how there can be, unless—Do you mind telling me what you saw?"

Alleyn said carefully, "A lighted window, masked by a spring blind. A woman falling against the blind and releasing it. Beyond the woman, but out of sight to us, there must have been a brilliant lamp and in its light, farther back in the room and on our right, stood a man in a white garment. His face, oddly enough, was in shadow. There was something that looked like a wheel, beyond his right shoulder. His right arm was raised."

"And in his hand—?"

"Yes," Alleyn said, "that's the tricky bit, isn't it?

"And then the tunnel. It was like one of those sudden breaks in an old-fashioned film, too abrupt to be really dramatic. It was there and then it didn't exist. No," said Troy, "I won't believe it was true. I won't believe something is still going on inside that house. And what a house too! It looked like a Gustave Doré, really bad romantic."

Alleyn said: "Are you all right to get dressed? I'll just have a word with the car attendant. He may have seen it, too. After all, we may not be the only people awake and looking out, though I fancy mine was the only compartment with the light on. Yours was in darkness, by the way?"

"I had the window shutter down, though. I'd been thinking how strange it is to see into other people's lives through a train window."

"I know," Alleyn said. "There's a touch of magic in it."

"And then—to see that! Not so magical."

"Never mind. I'll talk to the attendant and then I'll come back and get Ricky up. He'll be getting train-fever. We should reach Roqueville in about twenty minutes. All right?"

"Oh, I'm right as a bank," said Troy.

"Nothing like the Golden South for a carefree holiday," Alleyn said. He grinned at her, went out into the corridor and opened the door of his own sleeper.

Ricky was still sitting up in his bunk. His hands were clenched and his eyes wide open. "You're being a pretty long time, however," he said.

"Mummy's coming in a minute. I'm just going to have a word with the chap outside. Stick it out, old boy."

"O.K.," said Ricky.

The attendant, a pale man with a dimple in his chin, was dozing on his stool at the forward end of the carriage. Alleyn, who had already discovered that he spoke very little English, addressed him in diplomatic French that had become only slightly hesitant through disuse. Had the attendant, he asked, happened to be awake when the train paused outside a tunnel a few minutes ago? The man seemed to be in some doubt as to whether Alleyn was about to complain because he was asleep or because the train had halted. It took a minute or two to clear up this difficulty and to discover that the attendant had, in point of fact, been asleep for some time.

"I'm sorry to trouble you," Alleyn said, "but can you, by any chance, tell me the name of the large building near the entrance to the tunnel?"

"Ah, yes, yes," the attendant said. "Certainly, Monsieur,

since I am a native of these parts. It is known to everybody, this house, on account of its great antiquity. It is the Château de la Chèvre d'Argent."

"I thought it might be," said Alleyn.

II

Alleyn reminded the sleepy attendant that they were leaving the train at Roqueville and tipped him generously. The man thanked him with that peculiarly Gallic effusiveness that is at once too logical and too adroit to be offensive.

"Do you know," Alleyn said, as if on an after-thought, "who lives in the Château de la Chèvre d'Argent?"

The attendant believed it was leased to an extremely wealthy gentleman, possibly an American, possibly an Englishman, who entertained very exclusively. He believed the ménage to be an excessively distinguished one.

Alleyn waited for a moment and then said, "I think there was a little trouble there tonight. One saw a scene through a lighted window when the train halted."

The attendant's shoulders suggested that all things are possible and that speculation is vain. His eyes were as blank as boot buttons in his pallid face. Should he not perhaps fetch the baggage of Monsieur and Madame and the little one, in readiness for their descent at Roqueville? He had his hand on the door of Alleyn's compartment when from somewhere towards the rear of the carriage, a woman screamed twice.

They were short screams, ejaculatory in character, as if they had been wrenched out of her, and very shrill. The attendant wagged his head from side to side in exasperation, begged Alleyn to excuse him and went off down the corridor to the rear-most compartment. He tapped. Alleyn guessed at an agitated response. The attendant went in and Troy put her head out of her own door.

"What now, for pity's sake?" she asked.

"Somebody having a nightmare or something. Are you ready?"

"Yes. But what a rum journey we're having!"

The attendant came back at a jog-trot. Was Alleyn perhaps a doctor? An English lady had been taken ill. She was in great pain: the abdomen, the attendant elaborated, clutching his own in pantomime. It was evidently a formidable seizure. If Monsieur, by any chance—

Alleyn said he was not a doctor. Troy said, "I'll go and see the poor thing, shall I? Perhaps there's a doctor somewhere in the train. You get Ricky up, darling."

She made off down the swaying corridor. The attendant began to tap on doors and to enquire fruitlessly of his passengers if they were doctors. "I shall see my comrades of the other *voitures*," he said importantly. "Evidently one must organize."

Alleyn found Ricky sketchily half-dressed and in a child's panic.

"Where have you been, however?" he demanded. "Because I didn't know where everyone was. We're going to be late for getting out. I can't find my pants. Where's Mummy?"

Alleyn calmed him, got him ready and packed their luggage. Ricky, white-faced, sat on the lower bunk with his gaze turned on the door. He liked, when travelling, to have his family under his eye. Alleyn, remembering his own childhood, knew his little son was racked with an illogical and bottomless anxiety, an anxiety that vanished when the door opened and Troy came in.

"Oh golly, Mum!" Ricky said and his lip trembled.

"Hullo, there," Troy said in the especially calm voice she kept for Ricky's panics. She sat down beside him, putting her arm where he could lean back against it, and looked at her husband.

"I think that woman's very ill," she said. "She looks frightful. She had what she thought was some kind of food poisoning this morning and dosed herself with castor-oil. And then, just now she had a violent pain, really awful, she says, in the appendix place and now she hasn't any pain at all and looks ghastly. Wouldn't that be a perforation, perhaps?"

"Your guess is as good as mine, my love."

"Rory, she's about fifty and she comes from the Bermudas and has no relations in the world and wears a string bag on her head and she's never been abroad and we can't just let her be whisked on into the Italian Riviera with a perforated appendix, if that's what it is."

"Oh, damn!"

"Well, can we? I said—" Troy went on, looking sideways at her husband—"that you'd come and talk to her."

"Darling, what the hell can I do?"

"You're calming in a panic, isn't he, Rick?"

"Yes," said Ricky again turning white. "I don't suppose you're both going away, are you, Mummy?"

"You can come with us. You could look through the corridor window at the sea. It's shiny with moonlight and Daddy and I will be just on the other side of the poor thing's door. Her name's Miss Truebody and she knows Daddy's a policeman."

"Well, I must say..." Alleyn began indignantly.

"We'd better hurry, hadn't we?" Troy stood up, holding Ricky's hand. He clung to her like a limpet.

At the far end of the corridor their own car attendant stood with two of his colleagues outside Miss Truebody's door. They made dubious grimaces at one another and spoke in voices that were drowned by the racket of the train. When they saw Troy, they all took off their silver-braided caps and bowed to her. A doctor, they said, had been discovered in the *troisième voiture* and was now with the unfortunate lady. Perhaps Madame would join him. Their own attendant tapped on the door and with an ineffable smirk at Troy, opened it. "Madame!" he invited.

Troy went in, and Ricky feverishly transferred his hold to Alleyn's hand. Together, they looked out of the corridor window.

The railway, in this part of the coast, followed an embankment a few feet above sea level and as Troy had said, the moon shone on the Mediterranean. A long cape ran out over the glossy water and near its tip a few points of yellow light showed in early-rising households. The stars were beginning to pale.

"That's Cap St. Gilles," Alleyn said. "Lovely, isn't it, Rick?"

Ricky nodded. He had one ear tuned to his mother's voice which could just be heard beyond Miss Truebody's door.

"Yes," he said, "it is lovely." Alleyn wondered if Ricky was really as pedantically mannered a child as some of their friends seemed to think.

"Aren't we getting a bit near?" Ricky asked. "Bettern't Mummy come now?"

"It's all right We've ten minutes yet and the train people know we're getting off. I promise it's all right. Here's Mummy now."

She came out followed by a small bald gentleman with waxed moustaches, wearing striped professional trousers, patent-leather boots and a frogged dressing-gown.

"Your French is badly needed. This is the doctor," Troy said, and haltingly introduced her husband.

The doctor was formally enchanted. He said crisply that he had examined the patient, who almost certainly suffered from a perforated appendix and should undoubtedly be operated upon as soon as possible. He regretted extremely that he himself had an urgent professional appointment in St. Céleste and could not, therefore, accept responsibility. Perhaps the best thing to do would be to discharge Miss Truebody at Roqueville and send her back by the evening train to St. Christophe where she could go to a hospital. Of course, if there was a surgeon in Roqueville the operation might be performed there. In any case he would give Miss Truebody an injection of morphine. His shoulders rose. It was a position of extreme difficulty. They must hope, must they not, that there would be medical man and suitable accommodation available at Roqueville? He believed he had understood Madame to say that she and Monsieur l'Inspecteur-en-Chef would be good enough to assist their compatriot.

Monsieur l'Inspecteur-en-Chef glared at his wife and said they would, of course, be enchanted. Troy said in English that it had obviously comforted Miss Truebody and impressed the doctor to learn of her husband's rank. The doctor bowed, delivered a few definitive compliments and, lurching in a still dignified manner down the swinging corridor, made for his own carriage, followed by his own attendant.

Troy said: "Come and speak to her, Rory. It'll help."

"Daddy?" Ricky said in a small voice.

"We won't be a minute," Troy and Alleyn answered together, and Alleyn added, "We know how it feels, Rick, but one has to get used to these things." Ricky nodded and swallowed.

Alleyn followed Troy into Miss Truebody's compartment. "This my husband, Miss Truebody," Troy said. "He's had a word with the doctor and he'll tell you all about it."

Miss Truebody lay on her back with her knees a little drawn up and sick hands closed vise-like over the sheet. She had a rather blunt face that in health probably was rosy, but now was ominously blotched and looked as if it had shrunk away from her nose. This effect was heightened by the circumstance of her having removed her teeth. There were beads of sweat along the margin of her grey hair and her upper lip and the ridges where her eyebrows would have been if she had possessed any; the face was singularly smooth and showed none of the minor blemishes characteristic of her age. Over her head, she wore, as Troy had noticed, a sort of net bag made of pink string. She looked terrified. Something in her eyes reminded Alleyn of Ricky in one of his travel-panics.

He told her, as reassuringly as might be, of the doctor's pronouncement. Her expression did not change and he wondered if she had understood him. When he had finished she gave a little gasp and whispered indistinctly: "Too awkward, so inconvenient. Disappointing." And her mottled hands clutched at the sheet.

"Don't worry," Alleyn said, "don't worry about anything. We'll look after you."

Like a sick animal, she gave him a heart-rending look of gratitude and shut her eyes. For a moment Troy and Alleyn watched her being slightly but inexorably jolted by the train, and then stole uneasily from the compartment. They found their son dithering with agitation in the corridor and the attendant bringing out the last of their luggage.

Troy said hurriedly: "This is frightful. We can't take the responsibility. Or must we?"

"I'm afraid we must. There's no time to do anything else. I've got a card of sorts up my sleeve in Roqueville. If it's no good we'll get her back to St. Christophe."

"What's your card? *Not,*" Troy ejaculated. "Mr. Garbel?"

"No, no, it's—hi—look! We're there."

The little town of Roqueville, wan in the first thin wash of dawnlight, slid past the windows, and the train drew into the station.

Fortified by a further tip from Troy and in evident relief at the prospect of losing Miss Truebody, the attendant enthusiastically piled the Alleyns' luggage on the platform while the guard plunged into earnest conversation with Alleyn and the Roqueville stationmaster. The doctor reappeared fully clad and gave Miss Truebody a shot of morphine. He and Troy, in incredible association, got her into a magenta dressing-gown in which she looked like death itself. Troy hurriedly packed Miss Truebody's possessions, uttered a few words of encouragement, and with Ricky and the doctor joined Alleyn on the platform.

Ricky, his parents once deposited on firm ground and fully accessible, forgot his terrors and contemplated the train with the hard-boiled air of an experienced traveller.

The station-master with the guard and three attendants in support was saying to the doctor: "One is perfectly conscious, Monsieur le Docteur, of the extraordinary circumstances. Nevertheless, the schedule of the Chemin de Fer des Alpes Maritimes cannot be indefinitely protracted."

The doctor said: "One may, however, in the few moments that are being squandered in this unproductive conversation, M. le Chef de Gare, consult the telephone directory and ascertain if there is a doctor in Roqueville."

"One may do so undoubtedly, but I can assure M. le Docteur that such a search will be fruitless. Our only doctor is at a conference in St. Christophe. Therefore, since the train is already delayed one minute and forty seconds..."

He glanced superbly at the guard, who began to survey the train like a sergeant-major. A whistle was produced. The attendants walked towards their several cars.

"Rory!" Troy cried out. "We can't..."

Alleyn said: "All right," and spoke to the stationmaster. "Perhaps," he said, "M. le Chef de Gare, you are aware of the presence of a surgeon—I believe his name is Dr. Baradi—among the guests of M. Oberon some twenty kilometres back at the Château de la Chèvre d'Argent. He is an Egyptian gentleman. I understand he arrived two weeks ago."

"*Alors*, M. l'Inspecteur-en-Chef..." the doctor began but the station-master, after a sharp glance at Alleyn, became alert and neatly deferential. He remembered the arrival of the Egyptian gentleman for whom he had caused a taxi to be produced. If the gentleman should be—he bowed—as M. l'Inspecteur-en-Chef evidently was informed, a surgeon, all their problems were solved, were they not? He began to order the sleeping-car attendants about and was briskly supported by the guard. Troy, to the renewed agitation of her son, and with the assistance of their attendant, returned to the sleeping-car and supported Miss Truebody out of it, down to the platform and into the waiting-room, where she was laid out, horribly corpse-like, on a bench. Her luggage followed. Troy, on an afterthought, darted back and retrieved from a tumbler in the washing cabinet, Miss Truebody's false teeth, dropping them with a shudder into a tartan spongebag. On the platform the doctor held a private conversation with Alleyn. He wrote in his notebook, tore out the page and gave it to Alleyn with his card. Alleyn, in the interests of Franco-British relationships, insisted on paying the doctor's fee and the train finally drew out to Roqueville in an atmosphere of the liveliest cordiality. On the strangely quiet platform Alleyn and Troy looked at each other.

"This," Alleyn said, "is not your holiday as I had planned it."

"What do we do now?"

"Ring up the Chèvre d'Argent and ask for Dr. Baradi, who, I have reason to suppose, is an admirable surgeon and an unmitigated blackguard."

They could hear the dawn cocks crowing in the hills above Roqueville.

III

In the waiting-room Ricky fell fast asleep on his mother's lap. Troy was glad of this as Miss Truebody had begun to look quite dreadful. She too had drifted into a kind of sleep. She breathed unevenly, puffing out her unsupported lips, and made unearthly noises in her throat. Troy could hear her husband and the station-master talking in the office next door and then Alleyn's voice only, speaking on the telephone and in French! There were longish pauses during which Alleyn said: "'*Allo!* '*Allo!*'" and "*Ne coupez pas, je vous en prie, mademoiselle,*" which Troy felt rather proud of understanding. A grey light filtered into the waiting-room; Ricky made a touching little sound, rearranged his lips, sighed, and turned his face against her breast in an abandonment of relaxation. Alleyn began to speak at length, first in French, and then in English. Troy heard fragments of sentences.

"... I wouldn't have roused you up like this if it hadn't been so urgent.... Dr. Claudel said definitely that it was really a matter of the most extreme urgency.... He will telephone from St. Céleste. I am merely a fellow-passenger ... yes, yes, I have a car here.... Good.... Very well.... Yes, I understand. Thank you." A bell tinkled.

There was a further conversation and then Alleyn came into

the waiting-room. Troy, with her chin on the top of Ricky's silken head, gave him a nod and an intimate family look: her comment on Ricky's sleep. He said: "It's not fair."

"What?"

"Your talent for turning my heart over."

"I thought," Troy said, "you meant about our holiday. What's happened?"

"Baradi says he'll operate if it's necessary." Alleyn looked at Miss Truebody. "Asleep?"

"Yes. So what are we to do?"

"We've got a car. The Sûreté rang up the local commissioner yesterday and told him I was on my way. He's actually one of their experts who's been sent down here on a special job, superseding the local chap for the time being. He's turned on an elderly Mercedes and a driver. Damn civil of him. I've just been talking to him. Full of apologies for not coming down himself but he thought, very wisely, that we'd better not be seen together. He says our chauffeur is a reliable chap with an admirable record. He and the car are on tap outside the station now and our luggage will be collected by the hotel waggon. Baradi suggests I take Miss Truebody straight to the Chèvre d'Argent. While we're on the way he will make what preparations he can. Luckily he's got his instruments, and Claudel has given me some pipkins of anaesthetic. Baradi asked if I could give the anaesthetic."

"Can you?"

"I did once, in a ship. As long as nothing goes very wrong, it's fairly simple. If Baradi thinks it is safe to wait he'll try to get an anaesthetist from Douceville or somewhere. But it seems there's some sort of doctor's jamboree on today at St. Christophe and they've all cleared off to it. It's only ten kilometres from here to the Chèvre d'Argent by the inland road. I'll drop you and Ricky at the hotel here, darling, and take Miss Truebody on."

"Are there any women in the house?"

"I don't know." Alleyn stopped short and then said: "Yes. Yes, I do. There are women."

Troy watched him for a moment and then said: "All right. Let's get her aboard. You take Ricky."

Alleyn lifted him from her lap and she went to Miss Truebody. "She's tiny," Troy said under her breath. "Could she be carried?"

"I think so. Wait a moment."

He took Ricky out and was back in a few seconds with the station-master and a man wearing a chauffeur's cap over a mop of glossy curls.

He was a handsome little fellow with an air of readiness. He saluted Troy gallantly, taking off his peaked cap and smiling at her. Then he saw Miss Truebody and made a clucking sound. Troy had put a travelling rug on the bench and they made a sort of stretcher of it and carried Miss Truebody out to a large car in the station yard. Ricky was curled up on the front seat. They managed to fit Miss Truebody into the back one. The driver pulled down a tip-up seat and Troy sat on that. Miss Truebody had opened her eyes. She said in a quiet, clear voice: "Too kind," and Troy took her hand. Alleyn, in the front, held Ricky on his lap and they started off up a steep little street through Roqueville. The thin dawnlight gave promise of a glaring day. It was already very warm.

"To the Hôtel Royal, Monsieur?" asked the driver.

"No," said Troy with Miss Truebody's little claw clutching at her fingers. "No, please, Rory. I'll come with her. Ricky won't wake for hours. We can wait in the car or he can drive us back. I might be some use."

"To the Château de la Chèvre d'Argent," Alleyn said, "and gently."

"Perfectly, Monsieur," said the driver. "Always, always gently."

Roqueville was a very small town. It climbed briefly up the hill and petered out in a string of bleached villas. The road mounted between groves of olive trees and the air was like a benison, soft and clean. The sea extended itself beneath them and enriched itself with a blueness of incredible intensity.

Alleyn turned to took at Troy. They were quite close to each other and spoke over their shoulders like people in a Victorian "Conversation" chair. It was clear that Miss Truebody, even if she could hear them, was not able to concentrate or indeed to listen. "Dr. Claudel," Alleyn said, "thought it was the least risky thing to do. I half expected Baradi would refuse, but he was surprisingly co-operative. He's supposed to be a good man at his job." He made a movement of his head to indicate the driver. "This chap doesn't speak English," he said. "And, by the way, darling, no more chat about my being a policeman."

Troy said: "Have I been a nuisance?"

"It's all right. I asked Claudel to forget it and I don't suppose

Miss Truebody will say anything or that anybody will pay much attention if she does. It's just that I don't want to brandish my job at the Chèvre d'Argent." He turned and looked into her troubled face. "Never mind, my darling. We'll buy false beards and hammers in Roqueville and let on we're archaeologists. Or load ourselves down with your painting gear." He paused for a moment. "That, by the way, is not a bad idea at all. Distinguished painter visits Côte d'Azur with obscure husband and child. We'll keep it in reserve."

"But honestly, Rory. How's this *débâcle* going to affect your job at the Chèvre d'Argent?"

"In a way it's useful entrée. The Sûreté suggested that I call there representing myself either to be an antiquarian captivated by the place itself—it's an old Saracen stronghold—or else I was to be a seeker after esoteric knowledge and offer myself as a disciple. If both fail I could use my own judgment about being a heroin addict in search of fuel. Thanks to Miss Truebody, however, I shall turn up as a reluctant Good Samaritan. All the same," Alleyn said, rubbing his nose, "I wish Dr. Claudel could have risked taking her on to St. Céleste or else waiting for the evening train back to St. Christophe. I don't much like this party, and that's a fact. This'll larn the Alleyn family to try combining business with pleasure, won't it?"

"Ah, well," said Troy, looking compassionately at Miss Truebody, "we're doing our blasted best and no fool can do more."

They were silent for some time. The driver sang to himself in a light tenor voice. The road climbed the Maritime Alps into early sunlight. They traversed a tilted landscape compounded of earth and heat, of opaque clay colours—ochres and pinks—splashed with magenta, tempered with olive-grey and severed horizontally at its base by the ultramarine blade of the Mediterranean. They turned inland. Villages emerged as logical growths out of rock and earth. A monastery safely folded among protective hills spoke of some tranquil adjustment of man's spirit to the quiet rhythm of soil and sky.

"It's impossible," Troy said, "to think that anything could go very much amiss in these hills."

A distant valley came into view. Far up it, a strange anachronism in that landscape, was a long modern building with glittering roofs and a great display of plate glass.

"The factory," the driver told them, "of the Compagnie Chimique des Alpes Maritimes."

Alleyn made a little affirmative sound as if he saw something that he had expected and for as long as it remained in sight he looked at the glittering building.

They drove on in silence. Miss Truebody turned her head from side to side and Troy bent over her. "Hot," she whispered, "such an oppressive climate. Oh, dear!"

"One approaches the objective," the driver announced, and changed gears. The road tipped downwards and turned the flank of a hill. They had crossed the headland and were high above the sea again. Immediately below them the railroad emerged from a tunnel. On their right was a cliff that mounted into a stone face pierced irregularly with windows. This in its turn broke against the skyline in fabulous turrets and parapets. Troy gave a sharp ejaculation. "Oh, *no!*" she said. "It's not that! No, it's too much!"

"Well, darling," Alleyn said, "I'm afraid that's what it is."

"La Chèvre d'Argent," said the driver, and turned up a steep and exceedingly narrow way that ended in a walled platform from which one looked down at the railway and beyond it sheer down again to the sea. "Here one stops, Monsieur," said the driver. "That is the entrance."

He pointed to a dark passage between two masses of rock from which walls emerged as if by some process of evolution. He got out and opened the doors of the car. "It appears," he said, "that Mademoiselle is unable to walk."

"Yes," Alleyn said. "I shall go and fetch the doctor. Madame will remain with Mademoiselle and the little boy." He settled the sleeping Ricky into the front seat and got out. "You stay here, Troy," he said. "I shan't be long."

"Rory, we shouldn't have brought her to this place."

"There was no alternative that we could honestly take."

"Look!" said Troy.

A man in white was coming through the passage. He wore a Panama hat. His hands and face were so much the colour of the shadows that he looked like a white suit walking of its own accord towards them. He moved out into the sunlight and they saw that he was olive-coloured with a large nose, full lips and a black moustache. He wore dark glasses. The white suit was made of sharkskin and beautifully cut. His sandals were white suède. His shirt was pink and his tie green. When he saw Troy he took off his hat and the corrugations of his oiled hair shone in the sunlight.

"Dr. Baradi?" Alleyn said.

Dr. Baradi smiled brilliantly, swept off his Panama hat and held out a long dark hand. "So you bring my patient?" he said. "Mr. Allen, is it not?" He turned to Troy. "My wife," Alleyn said, and saw Troy's hand lifted to the full lips. "Here is your patient," he added. "Miss Truebody."

"Ah, yes." Dr. Baradi went to the car and bent over Miss Truebody. Troy, rather pink in the face, moved to the other side. "Miss Truebody," she said, "here is the doctor."

Miss Truebody opened her eyes, looked into the dark face and cried out: "Oh! No! No!"

Dr. Baradi smiled at her. "You must not trouble yourself about anything," they heard him say. He had a padded voice. "We are going to make everything much more comfortable for you, isn't it? You must not be frightened of my dark face. I assure you I am quite a good doctor."

Miss Truebody said: "Please excuse me. Not at all. Thank you."

"Now, without moving you, if I may just—that will do very nicely. You must tell me if I hurt you." A pause. Cicadas had broken out in chittering so high-pitched that it shrilled almost above the limit of human hearing. The driver moved away tactfully. Miss Truebody moaned a little. Dr. Baradi straightened up, walked to the edge of the platform, and waited there for Troy and Alleyn. "It is a perforated appendix undoubtedly," he said. "She is very ill. I should tell you that I am the guest of Mr. Oberon, who places a room at our disposal. We have an improvised stretcher in readiness." He turned towards the passageway: "And here it comes!" he said, looking at Troy with an air of joyousness which she felt to be entirely out of place.

Two men walked out of the shadowed way onto the platform carrying between them a gaily striped object, evidently part of a garden seat. Both the men wore aprons. "The gardener," Dr. Baradi explained, "and one of the indoor servants, strong fellows both and accustomed to the exigencies of our entrance. She has been given morphine, I think."

"Yes," Alleyn said. "Dr. Claudel gave it. He has sent you an adequate amount of something called, I think, Pentothal. He was taking a supply of it to a brother-medico, an anaesthetist, in St. Céleste and said that you would probably need some and that the local chemist would not be likely to have it."

"I am obliged to him. I have already telephoned to the pharmacist in Roqueville who can supply ether. Fortunately, he lives above his establishment. He is sending it up here by car. It is fortunate also that I have my instruments with me." He beamed and glittered at Troy. "And now, I think..."

He spoke in French to the two men, directing them to stand near the car. For the first time apparently he noticed the sleeping Ricky and leaned over the door to look at him.

"Enchanting," he murmured, and his teeth flashed at Troy. "Our household is also still asleep," he said, "but I have Mr. Oberon's warmest invitation that you, Madame, and the small one join us for *petit déjeuner*. As you know, your husband is to assist me. There will be a little delay before we are ready and coffee is prepared."

He stood over Troy. He was really extremely large: his size and his padded voice and his smell, which was compounded of hair-lotion, scent and something that reminded her of the impure land-breeze from an eastern port, all flowed over her.

She moved back and said quickly: "It's very nice of you, but I think Ricky and I must find our hotel."

Alleyn said: "Thank you so much, Dr. Baradi. It's extremely kind of Mr. Oberon and I hope I shall have a chance to thank him for all of us. What with one thing and another, we've had an exhausting journey and I think my wife and Ricky are in rather desperate need of a bath and a rest. The man will drive them down to the hotel and come back for me."

Dr. Baradi bowed, took off his hat, and would have possibly kissed Troy's hand again if Alleyn had not somehow been in the way.

"In that case," Dr. Baradi said, "we must not insist."

He opened the door of the car. "And now, dear lady," he said to Miss Truebody, "we make a little journey, isn't it? Don't move. There is no need."

With great dexterity and no apparent expenditure of energy, he lifted her from the car and laid her on the improvised stretcher. The sun beat down on her glistening face. Her eyes

were open, her lips drawn back a little from her gums. She said:
"But where is—? You're not taking me away from—? I don't
know her name."

Troy went to her. "Here I am, Miss Truebody," she said. "I'll
come and see you quite soon. I promise."

"But I don't know where I'm going. It's so
unsuitable.... Unseemly really.... Somehow with another
lady...English...I don't know what they'll do to me.... I'm
afraid I'm nervous.... I had hoped..."

Her jaw trembled. She made a thin shrill sound, shocking in
its nakedness. "No," she stammered, "no...no...no." Her arm
shot out and her hand closed on Troy's skirt. The two bearers
staggered a little and looked agitatedly at Dr. Baradi.

"She should not be upset," he murmured to Troy. "It is most
undesirable. Perhaps, for a little while, you'll be so kind..."

"But of course," Troy said, and in answer to a look from her
husband, "of course, Rory, I must."

And she bent over Miss Truebody and told her she wouldn't
go away. She felt as though she herself was trapped in the kind of
dream that, without being a positive nightmare, threatens to
become one. Baradi released Miss Truebody's hand and as he
did so, his own brushed against Troy's skirt.

"You're so kind," he said. "Perhaps Mr. Allen will bring the
little boy. It is not well for such tender ones to sleep over-long in
the sun on the Côte d'Azur."

Without a word Alleyn lifted Ricky out of the car. Ricky
made a small questioning sound, stirred, and slept again.

The men walked off with the stretcher, Dr. Baradi followed
them. Troy, Alleyn and Ricky brought up the rear.

In this order the odd little procession moved out of the glare
into the shadowed passage that was the entrance to the Château
de la Chèvre d'Argent.

The driver watched them go, his lips pursed in a soundless
whistle and an expression of concern darkening his eyes. Then
he drove the car into the shade of the hill and composed himself
for a long wait.

II

Operation Truebody

I

AT FIRST their eyes were sun-dazzled so that they could scarcely see their way. Dr. Baradi paused to guide them. Alleyn, encumbered with Ricky and grouping up a number of wide, shallow and irregular steps, was aware of Baradi's hand piloting Troy by the elbow. The blotches of non-existent light that danced across their vision faded and they saw that they were in a sort of hewn passage-way between walls that were incorporated in rock, separated by outcrops of stone and pierced by stairways, windows and occasional doors. At intervals they went through double archways supporting buildings that straddled the passage and darkened it. They passed an open doorway and saw into a cave-like room where an old woman sat among shelves filled with small gaily painted figures. As Troy passed, the woman smiled at her and gestured invitingly, holding up a little clay goat.

Dr Baradi was telling them about the Chèvre d'Argent.

"It is a fortress built originally by the Saracens. One might almost say it was sculpted out of the mountain, isn't it? The Normans stormed it on several occasions. There are legends of atrocities and so on. The fortress is, in effect, a village since the many caves beneath and around it have been shaped into dwell-

ings and house a number of peasants, some dependent on the
château and some, like the woman you have noticed, upon their
own industry. The château itself is most interesting, indeed
unique. But not inconvenient. Mr. Oberon has, with perfect tact,
introduced the amenities. We are civilized, as you shall see."

They arrived at a double gate of wrought iron let into the wall
on their left. An iron bell hung beside it. A butler appeared
beyond the doors and opened them. They passed through a
courtyard into a wide hall with deep-set windows through which
a cool ineffectual light was admitted.

Without at first taking any details of this shadowed interior,
Troy received an impression of that particular kind of suavity
that is associated with costliness. The rug under her feet, the
texture and colour of the curtains, the shape of cabinets and
chairs and, above all, a smell which she thought must arise from
the burning sweet-scented oils, all united to give this immediate
reaction. "Mr. Oberon," she thought, "must be immensely rich."
Almost at the same time she saw above the great fireplace a
famous Brueghel which, she remembered, had been sold privately some years ago. It was called: "Consultation of
Sorceresses." An open door showed a stone stairway built inside
the thickness of the wall.

"The stairs," Dr. Baradi said, "are a little difficult. Therefore
we have prepared rooms on this floor."

He pulled back a leather curtain. The men carried Miss
Truebody into a heavily carpeted stone passage hung at intervals
with rugs and lit with electric lights fitted into ancient hanging
lamps, witnesses, Troy supposed, of Mr. Oberon's tact in mod-
ernization. She heard Miss Truebody raise her piping cry of
distress.

Dr. Baradi said: "Perhaps you would be so kind as to assist
her into bed?"

Troy hurried after the stretcher and followed it into a small
bedroom charmingly furnished and provided, she noticed, with
an adjoining bathroom. The two bearers waited with an obliging
air for further instructions. As Baradi had not accompanied
them, Troy supposed that she herself was for the moment in
command. She got Miss Truebody off the stretcher and onto the
bed. The bearers hovered solicitously. She thanked them in her
school-girl French and managed to get them out of the room,
but not before they had persuaded her into the passage, opened a

further door, and exhibited with evident pride a bare freshly scrubbed room with a bare freshly scrubbed table near its window. A woman rose from her knees as the door opened, a scrubbing brush in her hand and a pail beside her. The room reeked of disinfectant. The indoor servant said something about it being *"convenable,"* and the gardener said something about somebody, she thought himself, being *"bien fatigué, infiniment fatigué."* It dawned upon her that they wanted a tip. Poor Troy scuffled in her bag, produced a 500 franc note and gave it to the indoor servant, indicating that they were to share it. They thanked her and, effulgent with smiles, went back to get the luggage. She hurried to Miss Truebody and found her crying feverishly.

Remembering what she could of hospital routine, Troy washed the patient, found a clean nightdress (Miss Truebody wore white locknit nightdresses, sprigged with posies), and got her into bed. It was difficult to make out how much she understood of her situation. Troy wondered if it was the injection of morphine or her condition or her normal habit of mind or all three, that made her so confused and vague. When she settled in bed she began to talk with hectic fluency about herself. It was difficult to understand her as she had frantically waved away the offer of her false teeth. Her father, it seemed, had been a doctor, a widower, living in the Bermudas. She was his only child and had spent her life with him until, a year ago, he had died, leaving her, as she put it, quite comfortably though not well off. She had decided that she could just afford a trip to England and the continent. Her father, she muttered distractedly, had "not kept up," had "lost touch." There had been an unhappy break in the past, she believed, and their relations were never mentioned. Of course there were friends in the Bermudas but not, it appeared, very many or very intimate friends. She rambled on for a little while, continually losing the thread of her narrative and frowning incomprehensibly at nothing. The pupils of her eyes were contracted and her vision seemed to be confused. Presently her voice died away and she dozed uneasily.

Troy stole out and returned to the hall. Alleyn, Ricky and Baradi had gone, but the butler was waiting for her and showed her up the steep flight of stairs in the wall. It seemed to turn about a tower and they passed two landings with doors leading off them. Finally the man opened a larger and heavier door and

Troy was out in the glare of full morning on a canopied
roofgarden hung, as it seemed, in blue space where sky and sea
met in a wide crescent. Not till she advanced some way towards
the balustrade did Cap St. Gilles appear, a sliver of earth
pointing south.

Alleyn and Baradi rose from a breakfast-table near the balustrade. Ricky lay, fast asleep, in a suspended seat under a gay
canopy. The smell of freshly ground coffee and of *brioches* and
croissants reminded Troy that she was hungry.

They sat at the table. It was long, spread with a white cloth
and set for a number of places. Troy was foolishly reminded of
the Mad Hatter's Tea-party. She looked over the parapet and
saw the railroad about eighty feet below her and perhaps a
hundred feet from the base of the Chèvre d'Argent. The walls,
buttressed and pierced with windows, fell away beneath her in a
sickening perspective. Troy had a hatred of heights and drew
back quickly. "Last night," she thought, "I looked into one of
those windows."

Dr. Baradi was assiduous in his attentions and plied her with
coffee. He gazed upon her remorselessly and she sensed Alleyn's
annoyance rising with her own embarrassment. For a moment
she felt weakly inclined to giggle.

Alleyn said: "See here, darling, Dr. Baradi thinks that Miss
Truebody is extremely ill, dangerously so. He thinks we should
let her people know at once."

"She has no people. She's only got acquaintances in the
Bermudas; I asked. There seems to be nobody at all."

Baradi said: "In that case..." and moved his head from side
to side. He turned to Troy and parodied helplessness with his
hands. "So in that direction, we can do nothing."

"The next thing," Alleyn said, speaking directly to his wife,
"is the business of giving an anaesthetic. We could telephone to a
hospital in St. Christophe and try to get someone, but there's
this medical jamboree and in any case it'll mean a delay of some
hours. Or Dr. Baradi can try to get his own anaesthetist to fly
from Paris to the nearest airport. More delay and considerable
expense. The other way is for me to have a shot at it. Should we
take the risk?"

"What," Troy asked, making herself look at him, "do you
think, Dr. Baradi?"

He sat near and a little behind her on the balustrade. His

thighs bulged in their sharkskin trousers. "I think it will be less risky if your husband, who is not unfamiliar with the procedure, gives the anaesthetic. Her condition is not good."

His voice flowed over her shoulder. It was really extraordinary she thought, how he could invest information about peritonitis and ruptured abscesses with such a gross suggestion of flattery. He might have been paying her the most objectionable compliments imaginable.

"Very well," Alleyn said, "that's decided, then. But you'll need other help, won't you?"

"If possible, two persons. And here we encounter a difficulty." He moved round behind Troy but spoke to Alleyn. His manner was now authoritative. "I doubt," he said, "if there is anyone in the house-party who could assist me. It is not every layman who enjoys a visit to an operating theatre. Surgery is not everybody's cup of tea." The colloquialism came oddly from him. "I have spoken to our host, of course. He is not yet stirring. He offers every possible assistance and all the amenities of the château with the reservation that he himself shall not be asked to perform an active part. He is," said Baradi—putting on his sun-glasses—"allergic to blood."

"Indeed," said Alleyn politely.

"The rest of our household—we are seven—" Dr. Baradi explained playfully to Troy, "is not yet awake. Mr. Oberon gave a party here last night. Some friends with a yacht in port. We were immeasurably gay and kept going till five o'clock. Mr. Oberon has a genius for parties and a passion for charades. They were quite wonderful, our charades." Troy was about to give a little ejaculation, which she immediately checked. He beamed at her. "I was cast for one of King Solomon's concubines. And we had the Queen of Sheba, you know. She stabbed Solomon's favourite wife. It was all a little strenuous. I don't think any of my friends will be in good enough form to help us. Indeed, I doubt if any of them, even at the top of his or her form, would care to offer for the role. I don't know if you have met any of them. Grizel Locke, perhaps? The Honourable Grizel Locke?"

The Alleyns said they did not know Miss Locke.

"What about the servants?" Alleyn suggested. Troy was all too easily envisaging Dr. Baradi as one of King Solomon's concubines.

"One of the men is a possibility. He is my personal attendant and valet and is not quite unfamiliar with surgical routine. He will not lose his head. Any of the others would almost certainly be worse than useless. So we need one other, you see."

A silence fell upon them, broken at last by Troy.

"I know," she said, "what Dr. Baradi is going to suggest." Alleyn looked fixedly at her and raised his left eyebrow.

"It's quite out of the question. You well know that you're punctually sick at the sight of blood, my darling."

Troy, who was nothing of the sort, said: "In that case I've no suggestions. Unless you'd like to appeal to cousin Garbel."

There was a moment of silence.

"To whom?" said Baradi softly.

"I'm afraid I was being facetious," Troy mumbled.

Alleyn said: "What about our driver? He seems a hardy, intelligent sort of chap. What would he have to do?"

"Fetch and carry," Dr. Baradi said. He was looking thoughtfully at Troy. "Count sponges. Hand instruments. Clean up. Possibly, in an emergency, play a minor role as unqualified assistant."

"I'll speak to him. If he seems at all possible I'll bring him in to see you. Would you like to stroll back to the car with me, darling?"

"Please don't disturb yourselves," Dr. Baradi begged them. "One of the servants will fetch your man."

Troy knew that her husband was in two minds about this suggestion and also about leaving her to cope with Dr. Baradi. She said: "You go, Rory, will you? I'm longing for my sunglasses and they're locked away in my dressing-case."

She gave him her keys and a ferocious smile. "I think, perhaps, I'll have a look at Miss Truebody," she added.

He grimaced at her and walked out quickly.

Troy went to Ricky. She touched his forehead and found it moist. His sleep was profound and when she opened the front of his shirt he did not stir. She stayed, lightly swinging the seat, and watched him, and she thought with tenderness that he was her defense in a stupid situation which fatigue and a confusion of spirit, brought about by many untoward events, had perhaps created in her imagination. It was ridiculous, she thought, to feel anything but amused by her embarrassment. She knew that Baradi watched her and she turned and faced him.

"If there is anything I can do before I go," she said and kept her voice down because of Ricky, "I hope you'll tell me."

It was a mistake to speak softly. He at once moved towards her and, with an assumption of intimacy, lowered his own voice. "But how helpful!" he said. "So we shall have you with us for a little longer? That is good: though it should not be to perform these unlovely tasks."

"I hope I'm equal to them." She moved away from Ricky and raised her voice. "What are they?"

"She must be prepared for the operation."

He told her what should be done and explained that she would find everything she needed for her purpose in Miss Truebody's bathroom. In giving these specifically clinical instructions, he reverted to his professional manner, but with an air of amusement that she found distastful. When he had finished she said: "Then I'll get her fixed now, shall I?"

"Yes," he agreed, more to himself than to her. "Yes, certainly, we shouldn't delay too long." And seeing a look of preoccupation and responsibility on his face, she left him, disliking him less in that one moment than at any time since they had me. As she went down the stone stairway she thought: "Thank heaven, at least, for the Queen of Sheba."

II

Alleyn found their driver in his vest and trousers on the running-board of the car. A medallion of St. Christopher dangled from a steel chain above the mat of hair on his chest. He was exchanging improper jokes with a young woman and two small boys, who, when he rose to salute his employer, drifted away without embarrassment. He gave Alleyn a look that implied a common understanding of women, and opened the car door.

Alleyn said: "We're not going yet. What is your name?"

"Raoul, Monsieur. Raoul Milano."

"You've been a soldier, perhaps?"

"Yes, Monsieur. I am thirty-three and therefore I have seen some service."

"So your stomach is not easily outraged, then; by a show of blood, for instance? By a formidable wound, shall we say?"

"I was a medical orderly, Monsieur. My stomach also is an old campaigner."

"Excellent! I have a job for you, Raoul. It is to assist Dr. Baradi, the gentleman you have already seen. He is about to remove Mademoiselle's appendix and since we cannot find a second doctor, we must provide unqualified assistants. If you will help us there may be a little reward and certainly there will be much grace in performing this service. What do you say?"

Raoul looked down at his blunt hands and then up at Alleyn: "I say yes, M'sieur. As you suggest, it is an act of grace and in any case one may as well do something."

"Good. Come along, then." Alleyn had found Troy's sunglasses. He and Raoul turned towards the passage, Raoul slinging his coat across his shoulders with the grace of a ballet dancer.

"So you live down in Roqueville?" Alleyn asked.

"In Roqueville, M'sieur. My parents have a little café, not at all smart, but the food is good and I also hire myself out in my car, as you see."

"You've been up to the château before, of course?"

"Certainly. For little expeditions and also to drive guests and sometimes tourists. As a rule Mr. Oberon sends a car for his guests." He waved a hand at a row of garage-doors, incongruously set in a rocky face at the back of the platform. "His cars are magnificent."

Alleyn said: "The Commissaire at the Préfecture sent you to meet us, I think?"

"That is so, M'sieur."

"Did he give you my name?"

"Yes, M'sieur l'Inspector-en-Chef. It is Ahrr-lin. But he said that M'sieur l'Inspecteur-en-Chef would prefer, perhaps, that I did not use his rank."

"I would greatly prefer it, Raoul."

"It is already forgotten, M'sieur."

"Again, good."

They passed the cave-like room, where the woman sat among her figurines. Raoul hailed her in a cheerful manner and she returned his greeting. "You must bring your gentleman in to see my statues," she shouted. He called back over his shoulder: "All in good time, Marie," and added, "She is an artist, that one. Her saints are pretty and of assistance in one's devotions; but then she overcharges ridiculously, which is not so amusing."

He sang a stylish little cadence and tilted up his head. They were walking beneath a part of the Château de la Chèvre d'Argent that straddled the passage-way. "It goes everywhere, this house," he remarked. "One would need a map to find one's way from the kitchen to the best bedroom. Anything might happen."

When they reached the entrance he stood aside and took off his chauffeur's cap. They found Dr. Baradi in the hall. Alleyn told him that Raoul had been a medical orderly and Baradi at once described the duties he would be expected to perform. His manner was cold and uncompromising. Raoul gave him his full attention. He stood easily, his thumbs crooked in his belt. He retained at once his courtesy, his natural grace of posture, and his air of independence.

"Well," Baradi said sharply when he had finished: "Are you capable of this work?"

"I believe so, M'sieur le Docteur."

"If you prove to be satisfactory, you will be given 500 francs. That is extremely generous payment for unskilled work."

"As to payment, M'sieur le Docteur," Raoul said, "I am already employed by this gentleman and consider myself entirely at his disposal. It is at his request that I engage myself in this task."

Baradi raised his eyebrows and looked at Alleyn. "Evidently an original," he said in English. "He seems tolerably intelligent but one never knows. Let us hope that he is at least not too stupid. My man will give him suitable clothes and see that he is clean."

He went to the fireplace and pulled a tapestry bell-rope. "Mrs. Allen," he said, "is most kindly preparing our patient. There is a room at your disposal and I venture to lend you one of my gowns. It will, I'm afraid, be terribly voluminous but perhaps some adjustment can be made. We are involved in compromise, isn't it?"

A man wearing the dress of an Egyptian house-servant came in. Baradi spoke to him in his own language, and then to Raoul in French: "Go with Mahomet and prepare yourself in accordance with his instructions. He speaks French." Raoul acknowledged this direction with something between a bow and a nod. He said to Alleyn: "Monsieur will perhaps excuse me?" and followed the servant, looking about the room with interest as he left it.

Baradi said: "Italian blood there, I think. One comes across these hybrids along the coast. May I show you to my room?"

It was in the same passage as Miss Truebody's, but a little further along it. In Alleyn the trick of quick observation was a professional habit. He saw not only the general sumptuousness of the room but the details also: the Chinese wallpaper, a Wu Tao-tzu scroll, a Ming vase.

"This," Dr. Baradi needlessly explained, "is known as the Chinese room but, as you will observe, Mr. Oberon does not hesitate to introduce modulation. The bureau is by Vernis-Martin."

"A modulation, as you say, but an enchanting one. The cabinet there is a bolder departure. It looks like a Mussonier."

"One of his pupils, I understand. You have a discerning eye. Mr. Oberon will be delighted."

A gown was laid out on the bed. Baradi took it up. "Will you try this? There is an unoccupied room next door with access to a bathroom. You have time for a bath and will, no doubt, be glad to take one. Since morphine has been given there is no immediate urgency, but I should prefer all the same to operate as soon as possible. When you are ready, my own preparations will be complete and we can discuss final arrangements."

Alleyn said: "Dr. Baradi, we haven't said anything about your fee for the operation: indeed, it is neither my business nor my wife's, but I do feel some concern about it. I imagine Miss Truebody will at least be able..."

Baradi held up his hand. "Let us not discuss it," he said. "Let us assume that it is of no great moment."

"If you prefer to do so." Alleyn hesitated and then added: "This is an extraordinary situation. You will, I'm sure, realize that we are reluctant to take such a grave responsibility. Miss Truebody is a complete stranger to us. You yourself must feel it would be much more satisfactory if there was a relation or friend from whom we could get some kind of authority. Especially as her illness is so serious."

"I agree. However, she would undoubtedly die if the operation was not performed and, in my opinion, would be in the gravest danger if it was unduly postponed. As it is, I'm afraid there is a risk, a great risk, that she will not recover. We can," Baradi added, with what Alleyn felt was a genuine, if controlled, anxiety, "only do our best and hope that all may be well."

And on this note Alleyn turned to go. As he was in the

doorway Baradi, with a complete change of manner, said: "Your enchanting wife is with her. Third door on the left. Quite enchanting. Delicious, if you will permit me."

Alleyn looked at him and found what he saw offensive.

"Under these unfortunate circumstances," he said politely, "I can't do anything else."

Evidently Dr. Baradi chose to regard this observation as a pleasantry. He laughed richly. "Delicious!" he repeated, but whether in reference to Alleyn's comment or as a reiterated observation upon Troy it was impossible to determine. Alleyn, who had every reason and no inclination for keeping his temper, walked into the next room.

III

Troy had carried out her instructions and Miss Truebody had slipped again into sleep. The sound of her breathing cut the silence into irregular intervals. Her eyes were not quite closed. Segments of the eyeballs appeared under the pathetic insufficiency of her lashes. Troy was at once unwilling to leave her and anxious to return to Ricky. She heard Alleyn and Dr. Baradi in the passage. Their voices were broken off by a door slam and again there was only Miss Truebody's breathing. Troy waited, hoping that Alleyn knew where she was and would come to her. After what seemed an interminable interval there was a tap at the door. She opened it and he was there in a white gown looking tall, elegant and angry. Troy shut the door behind her and they whispered together in the passage.

"Rum go," he said, "isn't it?"

"Not 'alf. When do you begin?"

"Soon. He's trying to make himself aseptic. A losing battle, I should think."

"Frightful, isn't he?"

"The bottom. I'm sorry, darling, you have to suffer his atrocious gallantries."

"Well, I daresay they're just elaborate Oriental courtesy, or something."

"Elaborate bloody impertinence."

"Never mind, Rory. I'll skip out of his way."

"I shouldn't have brought you to this damn place."

"Fiddle! In any case he's going to be too busy."

"Is she asleep?"

"Sort of. I don't like to leave her, but suppose Ricky should wake?"

"Go up to him. I'll stay with her. Baradi's going to give her an injection before I get going with the ether. And, Troy—"

"Yes?"

"It's important these people don't get a line on who I am."

"I know."

"I haven't told you anything about them, but I think I'll have to come moderately clean when there's a chance. It's a rum setup. I'll get you out of it as soon as possible."

"I'm not worrying now we know about the charades. Funny! You said there might be an explanation, but we never thought of charades, did we?"

"No," Alleyn said, "we didn't, did we?" and suddenly kissed her. "Now, I suppose I'll have to wash again," he added.

Raoul came down the passage with Baradi's servant. They were carrying the improvised stretcher and were dressed in white overalls.

Raoul said: "Madame!" to Troy, and to Alleyn, "It appears, Monsieur, that M. le Docteur orders Mademoiselle to be taken to the operating room. Is that convenient for Monsieur?"

"Of course. We are under Dr. Baradi's orders."

"Authority," Raoul observed, "comes to roost on strange perches, Monsieur."

"That," Alleyn said, "will do."

Raoul grinned and opened the door. They took the stretcher in and laid it on the floor by the bed. When they lifted her down to it, Miss Truebody opened her eyes and said distinctly: "But I would prefer to stay in bed." Raoul deftly tucked blankets under her. She began to wail dismally.

Troy said: "It's all right, dear. You'll be all right," and thought: "But I never call people dear!"

They carried Miss Truebody into the room across the passage and put her on the table by the window. Troy went with them, holding her hand. The window coverings had been removed and a hard glare beat down on the table. The room still

reeked of disinfectant. There was a second table on which a
number of objects were now laid out. Troy, after one glance, did
not look at them again. She held Miss Truebody's hand and
stood between her and the instrument table. A door in the wall
facing her opened and Baradi appeared against a background of
bathroom. He wore his gown and a white cap. Their austerity of
design emphasized the opulence of his nose and eyes and teeth.
He had a hypodermic syringe in his left hand.

"So, after all, you are to assist me?" he murmured to Troy.
But it was obvious that he didn't entertain any such notion.

Still holding the flaccid hand, she said: "I thought perhaps I
should stay with her until..."

"But of course! Please remain a little longer." He began to
give instructions to Alleyn and the two men. He spoke in French
presumably, Troy thought, to spare Miss Truebody's feelings. "I
am left-handed," he said. "If I should ask for anything to be
handed to me you will please remember that. Now, Mr. Allen,
we will show you your equipment, isn't it? Milano!" Raoul
brought a china dish from the instrument table. It had a bottle
and a hand towel on it. Alleyn looked at it and nodded. *"Parfaitement,"* he said.

Baradi took Miss Truebody's other hand and pushed up the
long sleeve of her nightgown. She stared at him and her mouth
worked soundlessly.

Troy saw the needle slide in. The hand she held flickered
momentarily and relaxed.

"It is fortunate," Baradi said as he withdrew the needle, "that
this little Dr. Claudel had Pentothal. A happy coincidence."

He raised Miss Truebody's eyelid. The pupil was out of sight.
"Admirable," he said. "Now, Mr. Allen, we will, in a moment or
two, induce a more profound anaesthesia which you will continue. I shall scrub up and in a few minutes more we begin
operations." He smiled at Troy, who was already on the way to
the door. "One of our party will join you presently on the
roof-garden. Miss Locke; the Honourable Grizel Locke. I believe she has a vogue in England. Quite mad, but utterly charming."

Troy's last impression of the room, a vivid one, was of
Baradi, enormous in his white gown and cap, of Alleyn standing
near the table and smiling at her, of Raoul and the Egyptian

servant waiting near the instruments, and of Miss Truebody's wide-open mouth and of the sound of her breathing. Then the door shut off the picture as abruptly as the tunnel had shut off her earlier glimpse into a room in the Chèvre d'Argent.

"Only *that* time—" Troy told herself, as she made her way back to the roof-garden—"it was only a charade."

III

Morning with Mr. Oberon

I

THE SUN shone full on the roof-garden now, but Ricky was
shielded from it by the canopy of his swinging couch. He was, as
he himself might have said, lavishly asleep. Troy knew he would
stay so for a long time.

The breakfast-table had been cleared and moved to one side
and several more seats like Ricky's had been set out. Troy took
the one nearest to his. When she lifted her feet it swayed gently.
Her head sank back into a heap of cushions. She had slept very
little in the train.

It was quiet on the roof-garden. A few cicadas chittered far
below and once, somewhere a long way away, a car hooted. The
sky, as she looked into it, intensified itself in blueness and
bemused her drowsy senses. Her eyes closed and she felt again
the movement of the train. The sound of the cicadas became a
dismal chattering from Miss Truebody and soared up into noth-
ingness. Presently, Troy, too, was fast asleep.

When she awoke, it was to see a strange lady perched, like
some fantastic fowl, on the balustrade near Ricky's seat. Her
legs, clad in scarlet pedal-pushers, were drawn up to her chin
which was sunk between her knees. Her hands, jewelled and
claw-like, with vermillion talons, clasped her shins, and her toes

protruded from her sandals like branched corals. A scarf was wound around her skull and her eyes were hidden by sun-glasses in an enormous frame below which a formidable nose jutted over a mouth whose natural shape could only be conjectured. When she saw Troy was awake and on her feet she unfolded herself, dropped to the floor, and advanced with a hand extended. She was six feet tall and about forty-five to fifty years old.

"How do you do?" she whispered. "I'm Grizel Locke. I like to be called Sati, though. The Queen of Heaven, you will remember. Please call me Sati. Had a good nap, I hope? I've been looking at your son and wondering if I'd like to have one for myself."

"How do you do?" Troy said without whispering and greatly taken aback. "Do you think you would?"

"Won't he awake? I've got *such* a voice as you can hear when I speak up." Her voice was indeed deep and uncertain like an adolescent boy's. "It's hard to say," she went on. "One might go all possessive and peculiar and, on the other hand, one might get bored and off-load him on repressed governesses. I was off-loaded as a child which, I am told, accounts for almost everything. Do lie down again. You must feel like a boiled owl. So do I. Would you like a drink?"

"No, thank you," Troy said, running her fingers through her short hair.

"Nor would I. What a poor way to begin your holiday. Do you know anyone here?"

"Not really. I've got a distant relation somewhere in the offing but we've never met."

"Perhaps we know them. What name?"

"Garbel. Something to do with a rather rarefied kind of chemistry. I don't suppose you—"

"I'm afraid not," she said quickly. "Has Baradi started on your friend?"

"She's not a friend or even an acquaintance. She's a fellow-traveller."

"How sickening for you," said the lady earnestly.

"I mean, literally," Troy explained. She was indeed feeling like a boiled owl and longed for nothing as much as a bath and solitude.

"Lie down," the lady urged. "Put your boots up. Go to sleep again if you like. I was just going to push ahead with my tanning, only your son distracted my attention."

Troy sat down and as her companion was so insistent she did put her feet up.

"That's right," the lady observed. "I'll blow up my li-low. The servants, alas, have lost the puffer."

She dragged forward a flat rubber mattress. Sitting on the floor she applied her painted mouth to the valve and began to blow. "Uphill work," she gasped a little later, "still, it's an exercise in itself and I daresay will count as such."

When the li-low was inflated she lay face down upon it and untied the painted scarf that was her sole garment. It fell away from a back so thin that it presented, Troy thought, an anatomical subject of considerable interest. The margins of the scapulae shone like plough-shares and the spinal vertebrae looked like those of a flayed snake.

"I've given up oil," the submerged voice explained, "since I became a Child of the Sun. Is there any particular bit that seems undertone, do you consider?"

Troy, looking down upon a uniformly dun-coloured expanse, could make no suggestions and said so.

"I'll give it ten minutes for luck and then toss over the bod," said the voice. "I must say I feel ghastly."

"You had a late night, Dr. Baradi tells us," said Troy, who was making a desperate effort to pull herself together.

"Did we?" The voice became more indistinct, and added something like: "I forgot."

"Charades and everything, he said."

"Did he? Oh. Was I in them?"

"He didn't say particularly," Troy answered.

"I passed," the voice muttered, "utterly and definitely out." Troy had just thought how unattractive such statements always were when she noticed with astonishment that the shoulderblades were quivering as if their owner was convulsed. "I suppose you might call it charades," the lady was heard to say.

Troy was conscious of a rising sense of uneasiness.

"How do you mean?" she asked.

Her companion rolled over. She had taken off her sunglasses. Her eyes were green with pale irises and small pupils.

They were singularly blank in expression. Clad only in her scarlet sans-culotte and head scarf, she was an uncomfortable spectacle.

"The whole thing is," she said rapidly, "I wasn't at the party. I began one of my headaches after luncheon, which was a party in itself and I passed, as I mentioned a moment ago, out. That must have been at about four o'clock, I should think, which is why I am up so early, you know." She yawned suddenly and with gross exaggeration as if her jaws would crack.

"Oh, God," she said, "here I go again!"

Troy's jaws quivered in imitation. "I hope your headache is better," she said.

"Sweet of you. In point of fact it's hideous."

"I'm so sorry."

"I'll have to find Baradi if it goes on. And it will, of course. How long will he be over your fellow-traveller's appendix? Have you seen Ra?"

"I don't think so. I've only seen Dr. Baradi."

"Yes, yes," she said restlessly, and added, "You wouldn't know, of course. I mean Oberon, our Teacher, you know. That's our name for him—Ra. Are you interested in The Truth?"

Troy was too addled with unseasonable sleep and a surfeit of anxiety to hear the capital letters. "I really don't know," she stammered. "In the truth—?"

"Poor sweet, I'm muddling you." She sat up. Troy had a painter's attitude towards the nude but the aspect of this lady, so wildly and so unpleasantly displayed, was distressing and doubly so because Troy couldn't escape the impression that the lady herself was far from unself-conscious. Indeed she kept making tentative clutches at her scarf and looking at Troy as if she felt she ought to apologize for herself. In her embarrassment Troy turned away and looked vaguely at the tower wall which rose above the roof-garden not far from where she sat. It was pierced at ascending intervals by narrow slits. Troy's eyes, glazed with fatigue, stared in aimless fixation at the third slit from the floor level. She listened to a strange exposition on The Truth as understood and venerated by the guests of Mr. Oberon.

"...just a tiny group of Seekers... Children of the Sun in the Outer... Evil exists only in the minds of the earth-bound... goodness is oneness... the great Dark co-exists with the great Light . . ." The phrases disjointed and eked out by ineloquent and unco-ordinated gestures, tripped each other up by the heels. Chichés and aphorisms were tumbled together from the most unlikely sources. One must live dangerously, it appeared, in order to attain merit. Only by encompassing the gamut of earthly experience would one return to the oneness of universal good. One ascended through countless ages by something which the disciple, corkscrewing an unsteady finger in illustrations, called the mystic navel spiral. It all sounded the most dreadful nonsense to poor Troy but she listened politely and, because her companion so clearly expected them, tried to ask one or two intelligent questions. This was a mistake. The lady, squinting earnestly up at her, said abruptly: "You're fey, of course. But you know that, don't you?"

"Indeed, I don't."

"Yes, yes," she persisted, nodding like a mandarin. "Unawakened perhaps, but it's there, oh! so richly. Fey as fey can be."

She yawned again with the same unnatural exaggeration and twisted round to look at the door into the tower.

"He won't be long appearing," she whispered. "It isn't as if he ever touched anything and he's always up for the rites of Ushas. What's the time?"

"Just after ten," said Troy, astonished that it was no later. Ricky, she thought, would sleep for at least another hour, perhaps for two hours. She tried to remember if she had ever heard how long an appendectomy took to perform. She tried to console herself with the thought that there must be a limit to this vigil, that she would not have to listen forever to Grizel Locke's esoteric small-talk, that somewhere down at the Hôtel Royal in Roqueville there was a tiled bathroom and a cool bed, that perhaps Miss Locke would go in search of whatever it was she seemed to await with such impatience, and finally that she herself might, if left alone, sleep away the remainder of this muddled and distressing interlude.

It was at this juncture that something moved behind the slit in the tower wall. Something that tweaked at her attention. She had an impression of hair or fur and thought at first that it was an animal, perhaps a cat. It moved again and was gone, but not before she recognized a human head. She came to the disagreeable conclusion that someone had stood at the slit and listened to their conversation. At that moment she heard steps inside the tower. The door moved.

"Someone's coming!" she cried out in warning. Her companion gave an ejaculation of relief, but made no attempt to resume her garment. "Miss Locke! Do look out!"

"What? Oh! Oh, all right. Only, do call me Sati." She picked up the square of printed silk. Perhaps, Troy thought, there was something in her own face that awakened in Miss Locke a dormant regard for the conventions. Miss Locke blushed and began clumsily to knot the scarf behind her.

But Troy's gaze was upon the man who had come through the tower door onto the roof-garden and was walking towards them. The confusion of spirit that had irked her throughout the morning clarified into one recognizable emotion.

She was frightened.

II

Troy would have been unable to say at that moment why she was afraid of Mr. Oberon. There was nothing in his appearance, one would have thought, to inspire fear. Rather, he had, at first sight, a look of mildness.

Beards, in general, are not rare nowadays though beards like his are perhaps unusual. It was blonde, sparse and silky and divided at the chin which was almost bare. The moustache was a mere shadow at the corners of his mouth, which was fresh in colour. The nose was straight and delicate and the light eyes abnormally large. His hair was parted in the middle and so long that it overhung the collar of his gown. This, and a sort of fragility in the general structure of his head, gave him an air of effeminacy. What was startling and to Troy quite shocking, was the resemblance to Roman Catholic devotional prints such as the "Scared Heart." She was to learn that this resemblance was deliberately cultivated. He wore a white dressing gown to which his extraordinary appearance gave the air of a ceremonial robe.

It seemed incredible that such a being could make normal conversation. Troy would not have been surprised if he had

acknowledged the introduction in Sanskirt. However, he gave
her his hand, which was small and well-formed, and a conventional greeting. He had a singularly musical voice and spoke
without any marked accent, though Troy fancied she heard a
faint American inflection. She said something about his kindness in offering harbourage to Miss Truebody. He smiled gently,
sank on to an Algerian leather seat, drew his feet up under his
gown and placed them, apparently, against his thighs. His hands
fell softly to his lap.

"You have brought," he said, "a gift of great price. We are
grateful."

From the time that they had confronted each other he had
looked fully into Troy's eyes and he continued to do so. It was
not the half-unseeing attention of ordinary courtesy but an
unswerving fixed regard. He seemed to blink less than most
people.

His disciple said: "Dearest Ra, I've got the most monstrous
headache."

"It will pass," he said, still looking at Troy. "You know what
you should do, dear Sati."

"Yes, I do, don't I! But it's so hard sometimes to feel the light.
One gropes and gropes."

"Patience, dear Sati. It will come."

She sat up on her li-low, seized her ankles and with a grunt of
discomfort adjusted the soles of her feet to the inside surface of
her thighs. "Om," she said discontentedly.

Mr. Oberon said to Troy: "We speak of things that are a little
strange to you. Or perhaps they are not altogether strange?"

"Just what *I* thought," the lady began eagerly. "Isn't she *fey*?"
He disregarded her.

"Should I explain that we—my guests here and I—follow
what we believe to be the true Way of Life? Perhaps, up here, in
this ancient house, we have created an atmosphere that to a
visitor is a little overwhelming. Do you feel it so?"

Troy said: "I'm afraid I'm just rather addled with a long
journey, not much sleep, and an anxious time with Miss
Truebody."

"I have been helping her. And, I hope, our friend Baradi."

"Have you?" Troy exclaimed in great surprise. "I thought...?
But how kind of you.... Is... is the operation going well?"

He smiled, showing his perfect teeth. "Again, I do not make

myself clear. I have been with them, not in the body but in the
spirit."

"Oh," mumbled Troy. "I'm sorry."

"Particularly with your friend. This was easy because when
by the will, or, as with her, by the agency of an anaesthetic, the
soul is set free of the body, it may be greatly helped. Hers is a
pure soul. She should be called Miss Truesoul instead of
Truebody." He laughed, a light breathy sound, and showed the
pink interior of his mouth. "But we must not despise the body,"
he said, apparently as an afterthought.

His disciple whispered: "Oh, no! No, indeed! No," and
started to breathe deeply, stopping one nostril with a finger and
expelling her breath with a hissing sound. Troy began to wonder
if Miss Locke was, perhaps, a little mad.

Oberon had shifted his gaze from Troy. His eyes were still
very wide open and quite without expression. He had seen the
sleeping Ricky.

It was with the greatest difficulty that Troy gave her movement towards Ricky a semblance of casualness. Her instinct, she
afterwards told Alleyn, was entirely that of a mother cat. She
leaned over her small son and made a pretence of adjusting the
cushion behind him. She heard Oberon say: "A beautiful child,"
and thought that no matter how odd it might look, she would
stand between Ricky and his eyes until something else diverted
their gaze. But Ricky himself stirred a little, flinging out his arm.
She moved him over with his face away from Oberon. He
murmured: "Mummy?" and she answered: "Yes," and kept her
hand on him until he had fallen back into sleep."

She turned and looked past the ridiculous back of the deep-
breathing disciple to the figure seated in the glare of the sun, and,
being a painter, she recognized, in the midst of her alarm, a
remarkable subject. At the same time it seemed to her that
Oberon and she acknowledged each other as enemies.

This engagement, if it was one, was broken off by the appearance of two more of Mr. Oberon's guests: a tall girl and a lame
young man who were introduced as Ginny Taylor and Robin
Herrington. Both names were familiar to Troy, the girl's as that
of a regular sacrifice on the altars of the glossy weeklies, and the
man's as that of the reputably wildish son of a famous brewer
who was also an indefatigable patron of the fine arts. To Troy
their comparative normality was as a freshening breeze and she

was ready to overlook the shadows under their eyes and their air of unease. They greeted her politely, lowered their voices when they saw Ricky and sat together on one seat, screening him from Mr. Oberon. Troy returned to her former place.

Mr. Oberon was talking. It seemed that he had bought a book in Paris, a newly discovered manuscript, one of those assembled by Roger de Gaignières. Troy knew that he must have paid a fabulous sum for it and, in spite of herself, listened eagerly to a description of the illuminations. He went on to speak of other works: of the calendar of Charles d'Angoulême, of Indian art, and finally of the moderns—Rouault, Picasso and André Derain. "But, of course, André is not a modern. He derives quite blatantly from Rubens. Ask Carbury, when he comes, if I am not right."

Troy's nerves jumped. Could he mean Carbury Glande, a painter whom she knew perfectly well and who would certainly, if he appeared, greet her with feverish effusiveness? Mr. Oberon no longer looked at her or at anyone in particular, yet she had the feeling that he talked at her and he was talking very well. Yes, here was a description of one of Glande's works. "He painted it yesterday from the Saracens' Watchtower: the favourite interplay of lemon and lacquer-red with a single note of magenta, and everything arranged about a central point. The esoteric significance was eloquent and the whole thing quite beautiful." It was undoubtedly Carbury Glande. Surely, surely, the operation must be over and if so, why didn't Alleyn come and take them away? She tried to remember if Carbury Glande knew she was married to a policeman.

Ginny Taylor said: "I wish I knew about Carbury. I can't get anything from his works. I can only say awful Philistinish things such as they look as if they were too easy to do." She glanced in a friendly manner at Troy.

"Do *you* know about modern art?" she asked.

"I'm always ready to learn," Troy hedged with a dexterity born of fright.

"I shall never learn however much I try," sighed Ginny Taylor and suddenly yawned.

The jaws of everyone except Mr. Oberon quivered responsively.

"Lord, I'm sorry," said Ginny, and for some unaccountable reason looked frightened. Robin Herrington touched her hand with the tip of his fingers. "I wonder why they're so infectious," he said. "Sneezes, coughs and yawns. Yawns worst of all. To read about them's enough to set one going."

"Perhaps," Mr. Oberon suggested, "it's another piece of evidence, if a homely one, that separateness is an illusion. Our bodies as well as our souls have reflex actions." And while Troy was still wondering what on earth this might mean his Sati gave a little yelp of agreement.

"True! True!" she cried. She dived, stretched out with her right arm and grasped her toes. At the same time she wound her left arm behind her head and seized her right ear. Having achieved this unlikely posture, she gazed devotedly upon Mr. Oberon. "Is it all right, dearest Ra," she asked, "for me to press quietly on with my Prana and Pranayama?"

"It is well at all times, dear Sati, if the spirit also is attuned."

Troy couldn't resist stealing a glance at Ginny Taylor and Robin Herrington. Was it possible that they found nothing to marvel at in these antics? Ginny was looking doubtfully at Sati, and young Herrington was looking at Ginny as if, Troy thought with relief, he invited her to be amused with him.

"Ginny?" Mr. Oberon said quietly.

The beginning of a smile died on Ginny's lips. "I'm sorry," she said quickly. "Yes, Ra?"

"Have you formed a design for today?"

"No. At least . . . this afternoon . . ."

"I thought, if it suited general arrangements," Robin Herrington said, "that I might ask Ginny to come into Douceville this afternoon. I want her to tell me what colour I should have for new awnings on the after-deck."

But Ginny had got up and walked past Troy to Mr. Oberon. She stood before him white-faced with the dark marks showing under her eyes.

"Are you going, then, to Douceville?" he asked. "You look a little pale, my child. We were so late with our gaieties last night. Should you rest this afternoon?"

He was looking at her as he had looked at Troy.

"I think perhaps I should," she said in a flat voice.

"I, too. The colour of the awnings can wait until the colour of the cheeks is restored. Perhaps Annabella would enjoy a drive to Douceville. Annabella Wells," he explained to Troy, "is with us.

Her latest picture is completed and she is to make a film for Durant Frères in the spring."

Troy was not much interested in the presence of a notoriously erratic if brilliant actress. She had been watching young Herrington, whose brows were drawn together in a scowl. He got up and stood behind Ginny, looking at Oberon over the top of her head. His hands closed and he thrust them into his pockets.

"I thought a drive might be a good idea for Ginny," he said.

But Ginny had sunk down on the end of the li-low at Mr. Oberon's feet. She settled herself there quietly, with an air of obedience. Mr Oberon said to Troy: "Robin has a most wonderful yacht. You must ask him to show it to you." He put his hand on Ginny's head.

"I should be delighted," said Robin and sounded furious. He had turned aside and now added in a loud voice: "Why not this afternoon? I still think Ginny should come to Douceville."

Troy knew that something had happened that was unusual between Mr. Oberon and his guests and that Robin Herrington was frightened as well as angry. She wanted to give him courage. Her heart thumped against her ribs.

In the dead silence they all heard someone come quickly up the stone stairway. When Alleyn opened the door their heads were already turned towards him.

III

He waited for a moment to accustom his eyes to the glare and during that moment he and the five people whose faces were turned toward him were motionless.

One grows scarcely to see one's lifelong companions and it is more difficult to call up the face of one's beloved than that of a mere acquaintance. Troy had never been able to make a memory-drawing of her husband. Yet, at that moment, it was as if a veil of familiarity was withdrawn and she looked at him with fresh perception.

She thought: "I've never been gladder to see him."

"This is my husband," she said.

Mr. Oberon had risen and come forward. He was five inches shorter than Alleyn. For the first time Troy thought him ridiculous as well as disgusting.

He held out his hand. "We're so glad to meet you at last. The news is good?"

"Dr. Baradi will be able to tell you better than I," Alleyn said. "Her condition was pretty bad. He says she will be very ill."

"We shall all help her," Mr. Oberon said, indicating the antic Sati, the bemused Ginny Taylor and the angry-looking Robin Herrington. "We can do so much."

He put his hand on Alleyn's arm and led him forward. The reek of ether accompanied them. Alleyn was introduced to the guests and offered a seat but he said: "If we may, I think perhaps I should see my wife and Ricky on their way back to Roqueville. Our driver is free now and can take them. He will come back for me. We're expecting a rather urgent telephone call at our hotel."

Troy, who dreaded the appearance of Carbury Glande, knew Alleyn had said "my wife" because he didn't want Oberon to learn her name. He had an air of authority that was in itself, she thought, almost a betrayal. She got up quickly and went to Ricky.

"Perhaps," Alleyn said, "I should stay a little longer in case there's any change in her condition. Baradi is going to telephone to St. Christophe for a nurse and, in the meantime, two of your maids will take turns sitting in the room. I'm sure, sir, that if she were able, Miss Truebody would tell you how grateful she is for your hospitality."

"There is no need. She is with us in a very special sense. She is in safe hands. We must send a car for the nurse. There is no train until the evening."

"I'll go," Robin Herrington said. "I'll be there in an hour."

"Robin," Oberon explained lightly, "has driven in the Monte Carlo rally. We must hope that the nurse has iron nerves."

Alleyn said to Robin: "It sounds an admirable idea. Will you suggest it to Dr. Baradi?"

He went to Ricky and lifted him in his arms. Troy gave her hand to Mr. Oberon. His own wrapped itself round hers, tightened, and was suddenly withdrawn. "You must visit us again," he said. "If you are a voyager of the spirit, and I think you are, it might interest you to come to one of our meditations."

"Yes, do come," urged his Sati, who had abandoned her exercises on Alleyn's entrance. "It's madly wonderful. You must. Where are you staying?"

"At the Royal."

"Couldn't be easier. No need to hire a car. The Douceville bus leaves from the corner. Every half-hour. You'll find it perfectly convenient."

Troy was reminded vividly of Mr. Garbel's letters. She murmured something non-committal, said goodbye and went to the door.

"I'll see you out," Robin Herrington offered and took up his heavy walking stick.

As she groped down the darkened stairway she heard their voices rumbling above her. They came slowly; Alleyn because of Ricky and Herrington because of his stiff leg. The sensation of nightmare that threatened without declaring itself mounted in intensity. The stairs seemed endless, yet when she reached the door into the hall she was half-scared of opening it because Carbury Glande might be on the other side. But the hall was untenanted. She hurried through it and out to the courtyard. The iron gates had an elaborate fastening. Troy fumbled with it, dazzled by the glare of sunlight beyond. She pulled at the heavy latch, bruising her fingers. A voice behind her and at her feet said: "Do let me help you."

Carbury Glande must have come up the stairs from beneath the courtyard. His face, on a level with her knees, peered through the interstices of the wrought-iron banister. Recognition dawned on it.

"Can it be Troy?" he exclaimed hoarsely. "But it *is*! Dear heart, how magical and how peculiar. Where *have* you sprung from? And why are you scrabbling away at doors? Has Oberon alarmed you? I may say he petrifies me. What are you up to?"

He had arrived at her level, a short gnarled man whose hair and beard were red and whose face, at the moment, was a dreadful grey. He blinked up at Troy as if he couldn't get her into focus. He was wearing a pair of floral shorts and a magenta shirt.

"I'm not up to anything," said Troy. "In fact, I'm scarcely here at all. We've brought your host a middle-aged spinster with a perforated appendix and now we're on our way."

"Ah, yes. I heard about the spinster. Ali Baradi woke me at cockcrow, full of professional zeal, and asked me if I'd like to thread needles and count sponges. How he dared! Are you going?"

"I must," Troy said. "Do open this damned door for me."

She could hear Alleyn's and Herrington's voice in the hall and the thump of Herrington's stick.

Glande reached for the latch. His hand, stained round the nails with paint, was tremulous. "I am, as you can see, a wreck," he said. "A Homeric party and only four hours' sottish insensitivity in which to recover. Imagine it! There you are."

He opened the doors and winced at the glare outside. "Oberon will be thrilled you're here," he said. "Did you know he bought a thing of yours at the Rond-Point show? It's in the library. 'Boy with a Kite.' He adores it."

"Look here," Troy said hurriedly, "be a good chap and don't tell him I'm me. I've come here for a holiday and I'd so much rather..."

"Well, if you like. Yes, of course. Yes, I understand. And on mature consideration—I fancy this ménage is not entirely your cup of tea. You're almost pathologically normal, aren't you? Forgive me if I bolt back to my burrow, the glare is really more than I can endure. God, somebody's coming?"

He stumbled away from the door. Alleyn, with Ricky in his arms came out of the hall followed by Robin Herrington. Glande ejaculated: "Oh, sorry!" and bolted down the stairs. Herrington scowled after him and said: "That's our tame genius. I'll come to the car, if I may."

As they walked in single file down the steps and past the maker of figurines, Troy had the feeling that Robin wanted to say something to them and didn't know how to begin. They had reached the open platform where Raoul waited by the car before he blurted out:

"I do hope you will let me drive you down, to see the yacht. Both of you, I mean. I mean..." he stopped short. Alleyn said: "That's very nice of you. I hadn't heard about a yacht."

"She's quite fun." He stood there, still with an air of hesitancy. Alleyn shifted Ricky and looked at Troy, who held out her hand to Robin.

"Don't come any further," she said. "Goodbye and thank you."

"Goodbye. If we may, Ginny and I will call at the hotel. It's the Royal, I suppose. I mean, it might amuse you to come for a drive. I mean, if you don't know anybody here..."

"It'd be lovely," Troy temporized, wondering if Alleyn wanted her to accept.

"As a matter of fact," Alleyn said, "we *have* got someone we ought to look up in Roqueville. Do you know anybody about here with the unlikely name of Garbel?"

Robin's jaw dropped. He stared at them with an expression of extraordinary consternation. "I . . . no. We haven't really met any of the local people. No. Well, I mustn't keep you standing in the sun. Goodbye."

And with a precipitancy as marked as his former hesitation, he turned and limped off down the passageway.

"Now what," Troy asked her husband, "in a crazy world, is the significance of that particular bit of lunacy?"

"I've not the beginning of a notion," he said. "But I suggest that when we've got time to think, we call on Mr. Garbel."

IV

The Elusiveness of Mr. Garbel

I

RICKY woke up before they could get him to the car and was bewildered to find himself transported. He was hot, hungry, thirsty and uncomfortable, and he required immediate attention.

While Troy and Alleyn looked helplessly about the open platform Raoul advanced from the car, his face brilliant with understanding. He squatted on his heels beside the flushed and urgent Ricky and addressed him in very simple French which he appeared to understand and to which he readily responded. Marie, of the figurines, Raoul explained to the parents, would offer suitable hospitality and he and Ricky went off together, Ricky glancing up at him with admiration.

"It appears," Alleyn said, "that a French nanny and those bi-weekly conversational tramps with Mademoiselle to the Round Pond have not been unproductive. Our child has the rudiments of the language."

"Mademoiselle," Troy rejoined, "says he's prodigiously quick for his age. An amazing child, she thinks." And she added hotly: "Well, all right, I don't say so to anyone else, do I?"

"My darling, you do not and you shall never say so too often to me. But for the moment let us take our infant phenomenon for granted and look at the situation Chèvre d'Argent. Tell me as quickly as you can, what happened before I cropped up among those cups of tea on the roof-top."

They sat together on the running-board of the car and Troy did her best. "Admirable," he said when she had finished. "I fell in love with you in the first instance because you made such beautiful statements. Now, what do you suppose goes on in that house?"

"Something quite beastly," she said vigorously. "I'm sure of it. Oberon's obviously dishing out to his chums some fantastic hodgepodge of mysticism-cum-religion-cum, I'm very much afraid, eroticism. Grizel Locke attempted a sort of résumé. You never heard such a rigmarole . . . yoga, Nietzsche, black-magic. Voo-doo, I wouldn't be surprised. With Lord knows what fancy touch of their own thrown in. It ought to be merely silly but it's not, its frightening. Grizel Locke, I should say, is potty but the two young ones in any other setting would have struck me as being pleasant children. The boy's obviously in a state about the girl, who seems to be completely in Oberon's toils. It's so fantastic, it isn't true."

"Have you ever heard of the case of Horus and the Swami Vivi Ananda?"

"No."

"They appeared before Curtis Bennett with Edward Carson prosecuting and got swinging sentences for their pains. There's no time to tell you about them now, but you've more or less described their setup and I assure you there's nothing so very unusual about the religio-erotic racket. Oberon's name, by the way, is Albert George Clarkson. He's a millionaire and undoubtedly one of the drug barons. The cult of the Children of the Sun in the Outer is merely a useful sideline and a means, I suspect, of gratifying a particularly nasty personal taste. They suggested as much at the Sûreté though they don't know exactly what goes on among the Sun's Babies. The Sûreté is interested solely in the narcotics side of the show and the Yard's watching it from our end."

"And you?"

"I'm supposed to be the perishing link or something. What about the red-headed gentleman with painty hands and a carryover who was letting you out?"

"He might be serious, Rory. He's Carbury Glande. He paints

those post-surrealist things...witches' sabbaths and mystic unions. You must remember. Rather pretty colour and good design, but a bit nasty in feeling. The thing is, he knows me and although I asked him not to, he'll probably talk."

"Does he know about us?"

"I can't tell. He might."

"Damn!"

"I shouldn't have come, should I? If Glande knows who you are, he won't be able to resist telling them and bang goes your job."

"They didn't give me Glande's name at the Sûreté. He must be a later arrival. Never mind, we'll gamble on his not knowing you made a *mésalliance* with a policeman. Now, listen, my darling, I don't know how long I'll be up here. It may be an hour and it may be twenty-four. Will you settle yourself and Ricky at the Royal and forget about the Chèvre d'Argent? If there's any goat on the premises it will probably be your devoted husband. I'll make what hay I can while the sun shines in the Outer and I'll turn up as soon as maybe. One thing more. Will you try, when you've come to your poor senses, to ring up Mr. Garbel? He may not be on the telephone, of course, but if he is..."

"Lord, yes! Mr. Garbel! Now why, for pity's sake, did Robin Herrington run like a rabbit at the mention of P.E. Garbel? Can cousin Garbel be a drug baron? Or an addict, if it comes to that? It might account for his quaint literary style."

"Have you, by any chance, brought his letters?"

"Only the last, for the sake of his address."

"Hang on to it, I implore you. If he is on the telephone and answers, ask him to luncheon tomorrow and I'll be there. If, by any chance, he turns up before then, find out if he knows any of Oberon's chums and is prepared to talk about them. Here come Raoul and Ricky. Forget about this blasted business, my own true love, and enjoy yourself if you can."

"What about Miss Truebody?"

"Baradi is pretty worried, he says. I'm quite certain he's doing all that can be done for her. He's a kingpin at his job, you know, however much he may stink to high heaven as a chap."

"Shouldn't I wait with her?"

"*No.* Any more of that and I'll begin to think you like having your hand kissed by luscious Oriental gentlemen. Hullo, Rich, ready for your drive?"

Ricky advanced with his hands behind his back and with strides designed to match those of his companion. "Is Raoul driving us?" he asked.

"He is. You and Mummy."

"Good. Daddy, look! Look, Mummy!"

He produced from behind his back a little goat, painted silver grey with one foot upraised and mounted on a base that roughly traced the outlines of the Château de la Chèvre d'Argent. "The old lady made it and Raoul gave it to me," Ricky said. "It's a silver goat and when it's nighttime it makes itself shine. Doesn't it, Raoul? *N'est ce pas, Raoul?*"

"*Oui. Une chèvre d'argent qui s'illumine.*"

"Daddy, isn't Raoul kind?"

Alleyn, a little embarrassed, told Raoul how kind he was and Troy, haltingly, attempted to say that he shouldn't.

Raoul said: "But it is nothing, Madame. If it pleases this young gallant and does not offend Madame, all is well. What are my orders, Monsieur?"

"Will you drive Madame and Ricky to their hotel? Then go to M. le Commissaire at the Préfecture and give him this letter. Tell him that I will call on him as soon as possible. Tell him also about the operation and of course reply to any questions he may ask. Then return here. There is no immediate hurry and you will have time for *déjeuner*. Do not report at the Château but wait here for me. If I haven't turned up by 3:30 you may ask for me at the Château. You will remember that?"

Raoul repeated his instructions. Alleyn looked steadily at him. "Should you be told I am not there, drive to the nearest telephone, ring up the Préfecture and tell M. le Commissaire precisely what has happened. Understood?"

"Well understood, Monsieur."

"Good. One thing more, Raoul. Do you know anyone in Roqueville called Garbel?"

"Garr-bel? No Monsieur. It will be an English person for whom Monsieur enquires?"

"Yes. The address is 16 Rue des Violettes."

Raoul repeated the address. "It is an apartment house, that one. It is true one finds a few English there, for the most part ladies no longer young and with small incomes who do not often engage taxis."

"Ah well," Alleyn said. "No matter."

He took off his hat and kissed his wife. "Have a nice holiday," he said, "and give my love to Mr. Garbel."

"What were you telling Raoul?"

"Wouldn't you like to know! Goodbye, Rick. Take care of your mama, she's a good kind creature and means well."

Ricky grinned. He was quick, when he didn't understand his father's remarks, to catch their intention from the colour of his voice. *"Entendu,"* he said, imitating Raoul, and climbed into the car beside him.

"I suppose I may sit here?" he said airily.

"He *is* a precocious little perisher and no mistake," Alleyn muttered. "Do you suppose it'll all peter out and he'll be a dullard by the time he's eight?"

"A lot of it's purely imitative. It sounds classier than it is. Move up, Ricky, I'm coming in front, too."

Alleyn watched the car drive down the steep lane to the main road. Then he turned back to the Château de la Chèvre d'Argent.

II

On the way back to Roqueville Raoul talked nursery French to Ricky and Troy, pointing out the places of interest: the Alpine monastery where, in the cloisters, one might see many lively pictures executed by the persons of the district whose relations had been saved from abrupt destruction by the intervention of Our Lady of Paysdoux; villages that looked as if they had been thrown against the rocks and had stuck to them; distant prospects of little towns. On a lonely stretch of road, Troy offered him a cigarette and while he lit it he allowed Ricky to steer the scarcely moving car. Ricky's dotage on Raoul intensified with every kilometre they travelled together and Troy's understanding of French improved with astonishing rapidity. Altogether they enjoyed each other's company immensely and the journey seemed a short one. They could scarcely believe that the cluster of yellow and pink buildings that presently appeared beneath them was Roqueville.

Raoul turned aside from the steeply descending road and drove down a narrow side-street past an open market where bunches of dyed immortelles hung shrilly above the stalls and the smells of tuberoses was mingled with the pungency of fruit and vegetables. All the world, Raoul said, was abroad at this hour in the market and he flung loud unembarrassed greetings to many persons of his acquaintance. Troy felt her spirits rising and Ricky dropped into the stillness that with him was a sign of extreme pleasure. He sighed deeply and laid one hand on Raoul's knee and one, clasping his silver goat, on Troy's.

They were in a shadowed street where the houses were washed over with faint candy-pink, lemon and powder-blue. Strings of washing hung from one iron balcony to another. "Rue des Violettes," Raoul said, pointing to the street-sign and presently halted. *"Numéro seize."*

Troy gathered that he offered her an opportunity to call on Mr. Garbel or, if she was not so inclined, to note the whereabouts of his lodging. She could see through the open door into a dim and undistinguished interior. A number of raffish children clustered about the car. They chattered in an incomprehensible patois and stared with an air of hardihood at Ricky, who instantly became stony.

Troy thought Raoul was offering to accompany her into the house, but sensing panic in the breast of her son, she managed to say that she would go in by herself. "I can leave a note," she thought, and said to Ricky: "I won't be a moment. You stay with Raoul, darling."

"O.K.," he agreed, still fully occupied with disregarding the children. He was like a dog who, when addressed by his master, wags his tail but does not lower his hackles. Raoul shouted at the children and made a shooing noise driving them from the car. They retreated a little, skittishly twitting him. He got out and opened the door for Troy, removing his cap as if she were a minor royalty. Impressed by this evidence of prestige, most of the children fell back, though two of the hardier raised a beggar's plaint and were silenced by Raoul.

The door of Number 16 was ajar. Troy pushed it open and crossed a dingy tessellated floor to a lift-well beside which hung a slotted board holding cards, some with printed and some with written names on them. She had begun hunting up and down the board when a voice behind her said: "Madame?"

Troy turned as if she'd been struck. The door of a sort of cubby-hole opposite the lift was held partly open by a grimy and heavily ringed hand. Beyond the hand Troy could see folds of a black satin dress, an iridescence of bead-work and three quarters of a heavy face and piled-up coiffure.

She felt as if she'd been caught doing something shady. Her nursery French deserted her.

"Pardon," she stammered. *"Je désire—je cherche—Monsieur—Garbel—le nom de Garbel."*

The woman said something incomprehensible to Troy, who replied, *"Je ne parle pas français. Malheureusement,"* she added on an afterthought. The woman made a resigned noise and waddled out of her cubby-hole. She was enormously fat and used a walking stick. Her eyes were like black currants sunk in uncooked dough. She prodded with her stick at the top of the board and, strangely familiar in that alien place, a spidery signature in faded ink was exhibited: "P.E. Garbel."

"Ah, merci," Troy cried, but the fat woman shook her head contemptuously and appeared to repeat her former remark. This time Troy caught something like . . . *"Pas chez elle . . . il y a vingt-quatre heures."*

"Not at home?" shouted Troy in English. The woman shrugged heavily and began to walk away. "May I leave a note?" Troy called to her enormous back. *"Puis-je vous donner un billet pour Monsieur?"*

The woman stared at her as if she were mad. Troy scrambled in her bag and produced a notebook and the stub of a BB pencil. Sketches she had made of Ricky in the train fell to the floor. The woman glanced at them with some appearance of interest. Troy wrote: "Called at 11:15. Sorry to have missed you. Hope you can lunch with us at the Royal tomorrow." She signed the note, folded it over and wrote: "M.P.E. Garbel" on the flap. She gave it to the woman (was she a concierge?) and stooped to recover her sketches, aware as she did so, of a dusty skirt, dubious petticoats and broken shoes. When she straightened up it was to find her note displayed with a grey-rimmed sunken finger-nail jabbing at the inscription. "She can't read my writing," Troy thought and pointed first to the card and then to the note, nodding like a mandarin and smiling constrainedly. "Garbel," said Troy, "Gar-r-bel." She remembered about tipping and pressed a 100 franc note into the padded hand. This had an instantaneous effect. The woman coruscated with black unlove-ly smiles. "Mademoiselle," she said, gaily waving the note. "Madame," Troy responded. *"Non, non, non, non, Mademoiselle,"* insisted the woman with an ingratiating leer.

Troy supposed this to be a compliment. She tried to look deprecating, made an ungraphic gesture and beat a retreat.

Ricky and Raoul were in close conversation in the car when she rejoined them. Three of the hard-boiled children were seated on the running-board while the others played leap-frog in an exhibitionist manner up and down the street.

"Darling," Troy said as they drove away, "you speak French much better than I do."

Ricky slewed his eyes round at her. They were a brilliant blue and his lashes, like his hair, were black. *"Naturellement!"* he said.

"Don't be a prig, Ricky," said his mother crossly. "You're much too uppity. I think I must be bringing you up very badly."

"Why?"

"Now then!" Troy warned him.

"Did you see Mr. Garbel, Mummy?"

"No, I left a note."

"Is he coming to see us?"

"I hope so," said Troy and after a moment's thought added: "If he's true."

"If he writes letters to you he must be true," Ricky pointed out. *"Naturellement!"*

Raoul drove them into a little square and pulled up in front of the hotel.

At that moment the concierge at 16 Rue des Violettes, after having sat for ten minutes in morose cogitation, dialled the telephone number of the Chèvre d'Argent.

III

Alleyn and Baradi stood on either side of the bed. The maid, an elderly pinched-looking woman, had withdrawn to the window. The beads of her rosary clicked discreetly through her fingers.

Miss Truebody's face, still without its teeth, seemed to have collapsed about her nose and forehead and to be less than human-sized. Her mouth was a round hole with puckered edges. She was snoring. Each expulsion of her breath blew the margin of the hole outwards and each intake sucked it in so that in a dreadful way her face was busy. Her eyes were incompletely closed and her almost hairless brows drawn together in a meaningless scowl.

"She will be like this for some hours," Baradi said. He drew Miss Truebody's wrist from under the sheet: "I expect no change. She is very ill, but I expect no change for some hours."

"Which sounds," Alleyn said absently, "like a rough sketch for a villanelle."

"You are a poet?"

Alleyn waved a hand: "Shall we say, an undistinguished amateur."

"You underrate yourself, I feel sure," Baradi said, still holding the flaccid wrist. "You publish?"

Alleyn was suddenly tempted to say: "The odd slim vol," but he controlled himself and made a slight modest gesture that was entirely non-committal. Dr. Baradi followed this up with his now familiar comment. "Mr. Oberon," he said, "will be delighted," and added: "He is already greatly moved by your personality and that of your enchanting wife."

"For my part," Alleyn said, "I was enormously impressed with his."

He looked with an air of ardent expectancy into that fleshy mask and could find it in no line or fold that was either stupid or credulous. What was Baradi? Part Egyptian, part French? Wholly Egyptian? Wholly Arab? "Which is the kingpin," Alleyn speculated, "Baradi or Oberon?" Baradi, taking out his watch, looked impassively into Alleyn's face. Then he snapped open his watch and a minute went past, clicked out by the servant's beads.

"Ah, well," Baradi muttered, putting up his watch, "it is as one would expect. Nothing can be done for the time being. This woman will report any change. She is capable and, in the village, has had some experience of sickbed attendance. My man will be able to relieve her. We may have difficulty in securing a trained nurse for tonight, but we shall manage."

He nodded at the woman, who came forward and listened passively to his instructions. They left her, nun-like and watchful, seated by the bed.

"It is eleven o'clock, the hour of meditation," Baradi said as they walked down the passage, "so we must not disturb. There will be something to drink in my room. Will you join me? Your car has not yet returned."

He led the way into the Chinese room where his servant waited behind a table set with Venetian goblets, dishes of olives and sandwiches and something that looked like Turkish Delight. There was also champagne in a silver ice-bucket. Alleyn was almost impervious to irregular hours but the last twenty-four had been exacting, the heat was excessive, and the reek of ether had made him feel squeamish. Lager was his normal choice but champagne would have done very nicely indeed. It was an arid concession to his job that obliged him to say with what he hoped was the right degree of pale complacency: "Will you forgive me if I have water? You see, I've lately become rather interested in a way of life that excludes alcohol."

"But how remarkable. Mr. Oberon will be most interested. Mr. Oberon," Baradi said—signing to the servant that the champagne was to be opened—"is perhaps the greatest living authority on such matters. His design for living transcends many of the ancient cults, drawing from each its purest essence. A remarkable synthesis. But while he himself achieves a perfect balance between austerity and, shall we say, selective enjoyment, he teaches that there is no merit in abstention for the sake of abstention. His disciples are encouraged to experience many pleasures, to choose them with the most exquisite discrimination: 'arrange' them, indeed, as a painter arranges his pictures or a composer traces out the design for a fugue. Only thus, he tells us, may the Ultimate Goal be reached. Only thus may one experience Life to the Full. Believe me, Mr. Alleyn, he would smile at your rejection of this admirable vintage, thinking it is gross an error, if you will forgive me, as over-indulgence. Let me persuade you to change your mind. Besides, you have had a trying experience. You are a little nauseated, I think, by the fumes of ether. Let me, as a doctor," he ended playfully, "insist on a glass of champagne."

Alleyn had taken up a ruby goblet and was looking into it with admiration. "I must say," he said, "this is all most awfully interesting: what you've been saying about Mr. Oberon's teaching, I mean. You make my own fumbling ideas seem pitifully naive." He smiled. "I should adore some champagne from this quite lovely goblet."

He held it out and watched the champagne mount and cream. Baradi was looking at him across the rim of his own glass. One could scarcely, Alleyn thought, imagine a more opulent picture: the corrugations of hair glistened, the eyes were lustrous, the nose over-hung a bubbling field of amber stained with ruby, one could guess at the wide expectant lips.

"To the fullness of life," said Dr. Baradi.

"Yes, indeed," Alleyn rejoined, and they drank.

The champagne was, in fact, admirable.

Alleyn's head was as strong as the next man's but he had had a light breakfast and therefore helped himself freely to the sandwiches, which were delicious. Baradi, always prepared, Alleyn supposed, to experience life to the full, gobbled up the sweetmeats, popping them one after another into his red mouth and abominably washing them down the champagne.

The atmosphere took on a spurious air of unbuttoning, which Alleyn was careful to encourage. So far, he felt tolerably certain, Baradi knew nothing about him, but was nevertheless concerned to place him accurately. The situation was a delicate one. If Alleyn could establish himself as an eager neophyte to the synthetic mysteries preached by Mr. Oberon, he would have taken a useful stop towards the performance of his job. At least he would be able to give an inside report on the domestic setup in the Château de la Chèvre d'Argent. Officers on loan to the Special Branch preserve a strict anonymity and it was unlikely that his name would be known in the drug-racket as an M.I.5. investigator. It might be recognized, however, as that of a detective-officer of the C.I.D. Carbury Glande might respect Troy's request, but if he didn't, it was more than likely that he or one of the others would remember she had married a policeman. Alleyn himself remembered the exuberances of the gossip columnists at the time of their marriage and later, when Troy had held one-man shows or when he had appeared for the police in some much-publicized case. It looked as if he should indeed make what hay he could while the sun shone on the Chèvre d'Argent.

"If Miss Truebody and I get through this party," he thought, "blow me down if I don't take her out and we'll break a bottle of fizz on our own account."

Greatly cheered by this thought, he began to talk about poetry and esoteric writing, speaking of Rabindranath Tagore and the Indian "Tantras," of the "Amanga Ranga" and parts of the Cabala. Baradi listened with every appearance of delight, but Alleyn felt a little as if he were prodding at a particularly resilient mattress. There seemed to be no vulnerable spot and, what was worse, his companion began to exhibit signs of controlled restlessness. It was clear that the champagne was intended for a stirrup cup and that he waited for Alleyn to take his departure. Yet, somewhere, there must be a point of penetration. And remembering with extreme distaste Dr. Baradi's attentions to Troy, Alleyn drivelled hopefully onward, speaking of the secret rites of Eleusis and the cult of Osiris. Something less impersonal at last appeared in Baradi as he listened to these confidences. The folds of flesh running from the corners of his nostrils to those of his mouth became more apparent and he began to look like an Eastern and more fleshy version of Charles II. He went to the bureau by Vernis-Martin, unlocked it, and presently laid before Alleyn a book bound in grey silk on which a design had been painted in violet, green and repellent pink.

"A rare and early edition," he said. "Carbury Glande designed and executed the cover. Do admire it!"

Alleyn opened the book at the page. It was a copy of *The Memoirs of Donatien Alphonse François, Marquis de Sade*.

"A present," said Baradi, "from Mr. Oberon."

It was unnecessary, Alleyn decided, to look any further for the chink in Dr. Baradi's armour.

From this moment, when he set down his empty goblet on the table in Dr. Baradi's room, his visit to the Chèvre d'Argent developed into a covert battle between himself and the doctor. The matter under dispute was Alleyn's departure. He was determined to stay for as long as the semblance of ordinary manners could be preserved. Baradi obviously wanted to get rid of him, but for reasons about which Alleyn could only conjecture, avoided any suggestion of precipitancy. Alleyn felt that his safest line was to continue in the manner of a would-be disciple to the cult of the Children of the Sun. Only thus, he thought, could he avoid planting in Baradi a rising suspicion of his own motives. He must be a bore, a persistent bore, but no more than a bore. And he went gassing on, racking his memory for remnants of esoteric gossip. Baradi spoke of a telephone call. Alleyn talked of telepathic communication. Baradi said that Troy would doubtless be anxious to hear about Miss Truebody;

Alleyn asked if Miss Truebody would not be greatly helped by
the banishment of anxiety from everybody's mind. Baradi mentioned luncheon. Alleyn prattled of the lotus posture. Baradi
said he must not waste any more of Alleyn's time; Alleyn took
his stand on the postulate that time, in the commonly accepted
sense of the word, did not exist. A final skirmish during which an
offer to enquire for Alleyn's car was countered by Rosicru-
cianism and the fiery cross of the Gnostics, ended with Baradi
saying that he would have another look at Miss Truebody and
must then report to Mr. Oberon. He said he would be some time
and begged Alleyn not to feel he must wait for his return. At this
point Baradi's servant reappeared to say a telephone call had
come through for him. Baradi at once remarked that no doubt
Alleyn's car would arrive before he returned. He regretted that
Mr.Oberon's meditation class would still be in progress and
must not be interrupted, and he suggested that Alleyn might care
to wait for his car in the hall or in the library. Alleyn said that he
would very much like to stay where he was and to examine the de
Sade. With a flush of exasperation mounting on his heavy
cheeks, Baradi consented, and went out, followed by his man.

They had turned to the right and gone down the passage to
the hall. The rings on an embossed leather curtain in the entrance clashed as they went through.

Alleyn was already squatting at the Vernis-Martin bureau.

He had the reputation in his department of uncanny accuracy
when a quick search was in question. It's doubtful if he ever
acted more swiftly than now. Baradi had left the bottom drawer
of the bureau open.

It contained half a dozen books, each less notorious if more
infamous than the de Sade, and all on the proscribed list at
Scotland Yard. He lifted them one by one and replaced them.

The next drawer was locked but yielded to the application of
a skeleton-key Alleyn had gleaned from a housebreaker of
virtuosity. It contained three office ledgers and two note-books.
The entries in the first ledger were written in a script that Alleyn
took to be Egyptian but occasionally there appeared proper
names in English characters. Enormous sums of money were
shown in several currencies: piastres, francs, pounds and lire
neatly flanked each other in separate columns. He turned the
pages rapidly, his hearing fixed on the passage outside, his mind
behind his eyes.

Between the first ledger and the second lay a thin quarto volume in violet leather, heavily embossed. The design was tortuous, but Alleyn recognized a pentagram, a triskelion, winged serpents, bulls and a broken cross. Superimposed over the whole was a double-edged sword with formalized flames rising from it in the shape of a raised hand. The covers were mounted with a hasp and lock which he had very little trouble in opening.

Between the covers was a single page of vellum, elaborately illuminated and embellished with a further number of symbolic ornaments. Baradi had been gone three minutes when Alleyn began to read the text:

> Here in the names of Ra and the Sons of Ra and the Daughters of Ra who are also, in the Mystery of the Sun, The Sacred Spouses of Ra, I, about to enter into the Secret Fellowship of Ra, swear before Horus and Osiris, before Annum and Apsis, before the Good and the Evil that are One God, who is both Good and Evil, that I will set a seal upon my lips and eyes and ears and keep forever secret the mysteries and the Sacred Rites of Ra.
>
> I swear that all that passes in this place shall be as if it had never been. If I break this oath in the least degree may my lips be burnt away with the fire that is now set before them. May my eyes be put out with the knife that is now set before them. May my ears be stopped with molten lead. May my entrails rot and my body perish with the disease of the crab. May I desire death before I die and suffer torment for evermore. If I break silence may these things be unto me. I swear by the fire of Ra and the Blade of Ra. So be it.

Alleyn uttered a single violent expletive, relocked the covers and opened the second ledger.

It was inscribed: "Compagnie Chimique des Alpes Maritimes," and contained names, dates and figures in what appeared to be a balance of expenditure and income. Alleyn's attention sharpened. The company seemed to be showing astronomical profits. His fingers, nervous and delicate, leafed through the pages, moving rhythmically.

Then abruptly they were still. Near the bottom of a page, starting out of the unintelligible script and written in a small, rather elaborate handwriting, was a name—P.E. Garbel.

The curtain rings clashed in the passage. He had locked the drawer and with every appearance of avid attention was hanging over the de Sade, when Baradi returned.

IV

Baradi had brought Carbury Glande with him and Alleyn thought he knew why. Glande was introduced and after giving Alleyn a damp runaway handshake, retired into the darker part of the room fingering his beard, and eyed him with an air, half curious, half defensive. Baradi said smoothly that Alleyn had greatly admired the de Sade book-wrapper and would no doubt be delighted to meet the distinguished artist. Alleyn responded with an enthusiasm which he was careful to keep on an amateurish level. He said he wished so much he knew more about the technique of painting. This would do nicely, he thought, if Glande, knowing he was Troy's husband, was still unaware of his job. If, on the other hand, Glande knew he was a detective, Alleyn would have said nothing to suggest that he tried to conceal his occupation. He thought it extremely unlikely that Glande had respected Troy's request for anonymity. No. Almost certainly he had reported that their visitor was Agatha Troy, the distinguished painter of Mr. Oberon's "Boy with a Kite." And then? Either Glande had also told them that her husband was a C.I.D. officer, in which case they would be anxious to find out if his visit was pure coincidence; or else Glande had been able to give little or no information about Alleyn and they merely wondered if he was as ready a subject for skulduggery as he had tried to suggest. A third possibility and one that he couldn't see at all clearly, involved the now highly debatable integrity of P.E. Garbel.

Baradi said that Alleyn's car had not arrived, and with no hint of his former impatience suggested that they show him the library.

It was on the far side of the courtyard. On entering it he was confronted with Troy's "Boy with a Kite." Its vigour and cleanliness struck like a sword-thrust across the airlessness of Mr. Oberon's library. For a second the "Boy" looked with Ricky's eyes at Alleyn.

A sumptuous company of books lined the walls with the

emphasis, as was to be expected, upon mysticism, the occult and Orientalism. Alleyn recognized a number of works that a bookseller's catalogue would have described as rare, curious, and collector's items. Of far greater interest to Alleyn, however, was a large framed drawing that hung in a dark corner of that dark room. It was, he saw, a representation, probably medieval, of the Château de la Chèvre d'Argent and it was part elevation and part plan. After one desirous glance he avoided it. He professed himself fascinated with the books and took them down with ejaculations of interest and delight. Baradi and Glande watched him and listened.

"You are a collector, perhaps, Mr. Allen?" Baradi conjectured.

"Only in a very humble way. I'm afraid my job doesn't provide for the more expensive hobbies."

There was a moment's pause. "Indeed?" Baradi said. "One cannot, alas, choose one's profession. I hope yours is at least congenial."

Alleyn thought: "He's fishing. He doesn't know or he isn't sure." And he said absently, as he turned the pages of a superb Book of the Dead, "I suppose everyone becomes a little bored with his job at times. What a wonderful thing this is, this book. Tell me, Dr. Baradi, as a scientific man—"

Baradi answered his questions. Glande glowered and shuffled impatiently. Alleyn reflected that by this time it was possible that Baradi and Robin Herrington had told Oberon of the Alleyns' enquiries for Mr. Garbel. Did this account for the change in Baradi's attitude? Alleyn was now unable to bore Dr. Baradi.

"It would be interesting," Carbury Glande said in his harsh voice, "to hear what Mr. Alleyn's profession might be. I am passionately interested in the employment of other people."

"Ah, yes," Baradi agreed. "Do you ever play the game of guessing at the occupation of strangers and then proving yourself right or wrong by getting to know them? Come!" he cried with a great show of frankness. "Let us confess, Carbury, we are filled with unseemly curiosity about Mr. Allen. Will he allow us to play our game? Indulge us, my dear Allen. Carbury, what is your guess?"

Glande muttered: "Oh, I plump for one of the colder branches of learning. Philosophy."

"Do you think so? A don, perhaps? And yet there is something that to me suggests that Mr. Alleyn was born under Mars. A soldier. Or, no. I take that back. A diplomat."

"How very perceptive of you," Alleyn exclaimed, looking at him over the Book of the Dead.

"Then I am right?"

"In part, at least. I started in the Diplomatic," said Alleyn truthfully, "but left it at the file-and-corridor stage."

"Really? Then perhaps, I am allowed another guess. No!" he cried after a pause. "I give up. Carbury, what do you say?"

"I? God knows! Perhaps he left the Diplomatic Service under a cloud and went big-game hunting."

"I begin to think you are all psychic in this house," Alleyn said delightedly. "How on earth do you do it?"

"A mighty hunter!" Baradi ejaculated, clapping his hands softly.

"Not at all mighty, I'm afraid, only pathetically persevering."

"Wonderful," Carbury Glande said, drawing his hand across his eyes and suppressing a yawn. "You live in South Kensington, I feel sure, in some magnificently dark apartment from the walls of which glower the glass eyes of monstrous beasts. Horns, snouts, tusks. Coarse hair. Lolling tongues made of a suitable plastic. Quite wonderful."

"But Mr. Allen is a poet and a hunter of rare books as well as of rare beasts. Perhaps," Baradi speculated, "it was during your travels that you became interested in the esoteric?"

Alleyn suppressed a certain weariness of spirit and renewed his raptures. You saw some rum things, he said with an air of simple credulity, in native countries. He had been told and told on good authority—He rambled on, saying that he greatly desired to learn more about the primitive beliefs of ancient races.

"Does your wife accompany you on safari?" Glande asked. "I should have thought—" He stopped short. Alleyn saw a flash of exasperation in Baradi's eyes.

"My wife," Alleyn said lightly, "couldn't approve less of blood sports. She is a painter."

"I am released," Glande cried, "from bondage!" He pointed to the "Boy with a Kite." "*Ecce!*"

"No!" Really, Alleyn thought, Baradi was a considerable actor. Delight and astonishment were admirably suggested. "Not—? Not Agatha Troy? But, my dear Mr. Alleyn, this is quite remarkable. Mr. Oberon will be enchanted."

"I can't wait," Carbury Glande said, "to tell him." He showed his teeth through his moustache. "I'm afraid you're in for a scolding, Alleyn. Troy swore me to secrecy. I may say," he added, "that I knew in a vague way, that she was a wedded woman but she has kept the Mighty Hunter from us." His tongue touched his upper lip. "Understandably, perhaps," he added.

Alleyn thought that nothing would give him more pleasure than to seize Dr. Baradi and Mr. Carbury Glande by the scruffs of their respective necks and crash their heads together.

He said apologetically: "Well, you see, we're on holiday."

"Quite," said Baradi and the conversation languished.

"I think you told us," Baradi said casually, "that you have friends in Roqueville and asked if we knew them. I'm afraid that I've forgotten the name."

"Only one. Garbel."

Baradi's smile looked as if it had been left on his face by an oversight. The red hairs of Glande's beard quivered very slightly as if his jaw was clenched.

"A retired chemist of sorts," Alleyn said.

"Ah, yes! Possibly attached to the monstrous establishment which defaces our lovely olive groves. Monstrous," Baradi added, "aesthetically speaking."

"Quite abominable!" said Glande. His voice cracked and he wetted his lips.

"No doubt admirable from an utilitarian point-of-view. I believe they produce artificial manure in great quantities."

"The place," Glande said, "undoubtedly stinks," and he laughed unevenly.

"Aesthetically?" Alleyn asked.

"Always, aesthetically," said Baradi.

"I noticed the factory on our way up. Perhaps we'd better ask there for our friend."

There was a dead silence.

"I can't think what has become of that man of mine," Alleyn said lightly.

Baradi was suddenly effusive. "But how inconsiderate we are! You, of course, are longing to rejoin your wife. And who can blame you? No woman has the right to be at once so talented and so beautiful. But your car? No doubt, a puncture or perhaps merely our Mediterranean *dolce far niente*. You must allow us to send you down. Robin would, I am sure, be enchanted. Or, if he is engaged in meditation, Mr. Oberon would be delighted to provide a car. How thoughtless we have been!"

This, Alleyn realized, was final. "I wouldn't dream of it," he said. "But I do apologize for being such a pestilent visitor. I've let my ruling passion run away with me and kept you hovering interminably. The car will arrive any moment now, I feel sure, and I particularly want to see the man. If I might just wait here among superb books I shan't feel I'm making a nuisance of myself."

It was a toss-up whether this would work. They wanted, he supposed, to consult together. After a fractional hesitation, Baradi said something about their arrangements for the afternoon. Perhaps, if Mr. Allen would excuse them, they should have a word with Mr. Oberon. There was the business of the nurse—Glande, less adroit, muttered unintelligibly and they went out together.

Alleyn was in front of the plan two seconds after the door had shut behind them.

It was embellished with typical medieval ornaments—a coat of arms, a stylized goat and a great deal of scroll-work. The drawing itself was in two main parts, an elevation, treated as if the entire face of the building had been removed, and a multiple plan of great intricacy. It would have taken an hour to follow out the plan in detail. With a refinement of concentration that Mr. Oberon himself might have envied, Alleyn fastened his attention upon the main outlines of the structural design. The great rooms and principal bedrooms were all, more or less, on the library level. Above this level the Château rose irregularly in a system of connected turrets to the battlements. Below it, the main stairway led down by stages through a maze of rooms that grew progressively smaller until, at a level which must have been below that of the railway, they were no bigger than prison cells and had probably served as such for hundreds of years. A vast incoherent maze that had followed, rather than overcome the contour of the mountain; an architectural compromise, Alleyn murmured, and sharpened his attention upon one room and its relation to the rest.

It was below the library and next to a room that had no outside windows. He marked its position and cast back in his mind to the silhouette of the Château as he had seen it, moonlit, in the early hours of that morning. He noticed that it had a window much longer than it was high and he remembered the shape of the window they had seen.

If it was true that Mr. Oberon and his guest were now occupied, as Baradi had represented, with some kind of esoteric keep-fit exercises on the roof-garden, it might be worth taking a risk. He thought of two or three plausible excuses, took a final look at the plan, slipped out of the library and ran lightly down a continuation of the winding stair that, in its upper reaches, led to the roof-garden.

He passed a landing, a closed door and three narrow windows. The stairs corkscrewed down to a wider landing from which a thickly carpeted passage ran off to the right. Opposite the stairway as a door and, a few steps away, another—the door he sought.

He went up to it and knocked.

There was no answer. He turned the handle delicately. The door opened inwards until there was a wide enough gap for him to look through. He found himself squinting along a wall hung with silk rugs and garnished about midway along with a big prayer wheel. At the far end there was an alcove occupied by an extremely exotic-looking divan. He opened the door fully and walked into the room.

From inside the door his view of Mr. Oberon's room was in part blocked by the back of an enormous looking-glass screwed to the floor at an angle of about 45 degrees to the outside wall. For the moment he didn't move beyond this barrier, but from where he stood, looked at the left-hand end of the room. It was occupied by a sort of altar hung with a stiffly embroidered cloth and garnished with a number of objects: a pentacle in silver, a triskelion in bronze and a large crystal affair resembling a sunburst. Beside the altar was a door, leading, he decided, into the windowless room he had noted on the plan.

He moved forward with the intention of walking round the looking-glass into the far part of the room.

"Bring me the prayer wheel," said a voice beyond the glass. It fetched Alleyn up with the jolt of a punch over the heart. He looked at the door. If the glass had hidden him on his entrance it would mask his exit. He moved towards the door.

"I am at the Third Portal of the Outer and must not uncover my eyes. Do not speak. Bring me the prayer wheel. Put it before me."

Alleyn walked forward.

There, on the other side of the looking-glass facing it and seated on the floor, was Mr. Oberon, stark naked, with the palms of his hands pressed to his eyes. Beyond him was a long window masked by a dyed silk blind, almost transparent, with the design of the sun upon it.

Alleyn took the prayer wheel from the wall. It was an elaborate affair, heavily carved, with many cylinders. He set it before Oberon.

He turned and had reached the door when somebody knocked peremptorily on it. Alleyn stepped back as it was flung open. It actually struck his shoulder. He heard someone go swiftly past and into the room.

Baradi's voice said: "Where are you? Oh, there you are! See here, I've got to talk to you."

He must be behind the glass. Alleyn slipped round the door and darted out. As he ran lightly up the stairs he heard Baradi shut the door.

There was nobody on the top landing. He walked back into the library, having been away from it for five and a half minutes.

He took out his notebook and made a very rough sketch of Mr. Oberon's room, taking particular pains to mark the position of the prayer wheel on the wall. Then he set about memorizing as much of its detail as he had been able to take in. He was still at this employment when the latch turned in the door.

Alleyn pulled out from the nearest shelf a copy of Mr. Montague Summer's major work on witchcraft. He was apparently absorbed in it when a woman came into the library.

He looked up from the book and knew that as far as preserving his anonymity was concerned, he was irrevocably sunk.

"If it's not Roderick Alleyn!" said Annabella Wells.

V

Ricky in Roqueville

I

It was some years ago, in a transatlantic steamer, that Alleyn had met Annabella Wells: the focal point of shipboard gossip to which she had seemed to be perfectly indifferent. She had watched him with undisguised concentration for four hours and had then sent her secretary with an invitation for drinks. She herself drank pretty heavily and, he thought, was probably a drug addict. He had found her an embarrassment and was glad when she suddenly dropped him. Since then she had turned up from time to time as an onlooker at criminal trials where he appeared for the police. She was, she told him, passionately interested in criminology.

In the English theatre her brilliance had been dimmed by her outrageous eccentricities, but in Paris, particularly in the motion-picture studios, she was still one of the great ones. She retained a ravaged sort of beauty and an individuality which would be arresting when the last of her good looks had been rasped away. A formidable woman, and an enchantress still.

She gave him her hand and the inverted and agonized smile for which she was famous. "They said you were a big-game hunter," she said. "I couldn't wait."

"It was nice of them to get that impression."

"An accurate one, after all. Are you on the prowl down here? After some master-felon?"

"I'm on a holiday with my wife and small boy."

"Ah, yes! The beautiful woman who paints famous pictures. I am told by Baradi and Glande that she is beautiful. There is no need to look angry, is there?"

"Did I look angry?"

"You looked as if you were trying not to show a certain uxorious irritation."

"Did I, indeed?" said Alleyn.

"Baradi *is* a bit lush. I will allow and must admit that he's a bit lush. Have you seen Oberon?"

"For a few moments."

"What did you think of *him?*"

"Isn't he your host?"

"Honestly," she said, "you're not true. Much more fabulous, in your way, than Oberon."

"I'm interested in what I have been told of his philosophy."

"So they said. What sort of interest?"

"Personal and academic."

"My interest is personal and unacademic." She opened her cigarette case. Alleyn glanced at the contents. "I see," he said, "that it would be useless to offer you a Capstan."

"Will you have one of these? They're Egyptian. The red won't come off on your lips."

"Thank you. They would be wasted on me." He lit her cigarette. "I wonder," he said, "if I could persuade you to say nothing about my job."

"Darling," she rejoined—she called everyone, "darling"— "you could persuade me to do anything. My trouble was, you wouldn't try. Why do you look at me like that?"

"I was wondering if any dependence could be placed on a heroin addict. Is it heroin?"

"It is. I get it," said Miss Wells, "from America."

"How very tragic."

"Tragic?"

"You weren't taking heroin when you played Hedda Gabler at the Unicorn in '42. Could you give a performance like that now?"

"*Yes,*" she said vehemently.

"But what a pity you don't!"

"My last film is the best thing I've ever done. Everyone says so." She looked at him with hatred. "I can still do it," she said.

"On your good days, perhaps. The studio is less exacting than the theatre. Will the cameras wait when the gallery would boo? I couldn't know less about it."

She walked up to him and struck him across the face with the back of her hand.

"You have deteriorated," said Alleyn.

"Are you mad? What are you up to? Why are you here?"

"I brought a woman who may be dying to your Dr. Baradi. All I want is to go away as I came in—a complete nonentity."

"And you think that by insulting me you'll persuade me to oblige you."

"I think you've already talked to your friends about me and that they've sent you here to find out if you were right."

"You're a very conceited man. Why should I talk about you?"

"Because," Alleyn said, "you're afraid."

"Of you?"

"Specifically. Of me."

"You idiot," she said. "Coming here with a dying spinster and an arty-crafty wife and a dreary little boy! For God's sake, get out and get on with your holiday."

"I should like it above all things."

"Why don't you want them to know who you are?"

"It would quite spoil my holiday."

"Which might mean anything."

"It might."

"Why do you say I'm afraid?"

"You're shaking. That may be a carry-over from alcohol or heroin, or both, but I don't think it is. You're behaving like a frightened woman. You were in a blue funk when you hit me."

"You're saying detestable, unforgivable things to me."

"Have I said anything that is untrue?"

"My life's my own. I've a right to do what I like with it."

"What's happened to your intelligence? You should know perfectly well that this sort of responsibility doesn't end with yourself. What about those two young creatures? The girl?"

"I didn't bring them here."

"No, really," Alleyn said, going to the door, "you're saying such very stupid things. I'll go down to the front and see if my car's come. Goodbye to you."

She followed him and put her hand on his arm. "Look!" she said. "Look at me. I'm terrifying, aren't I? A wreck? But I've still got more than my share of what it takes. Haven't I?"

"For Baradi and his friends?"

"Baradi!" she said contemptuously.

"I really didn't want to insult you with Oberon."

"What do you know about Oberon?"

"I've seen him."

She left her hand on him, but with an air of forgetfulness. A tremor communicated itself to his arm. "You don't know," she said. "You don't know what he's like. Its no good thinking about him in the way you think about other men. There are *hommes fatals,* too, you know. He's terrifying and he's marvellous. You can't understand that, can you?"

"No. To me, if he wasn't disgusting, he'd be ludicrous. A slug of a man."

"Do you believe in hypnotism?"

"Certainly. If the subject is willing."

"Oh," she said hoplessly. "I'm willing enough. Not that it's as simple as hypnotism." She hung her head, looking, with that gesture, like the travesty of a shamed girl. He couldn't hear all she said but caught one phrase: "... wonderful degradation..."

"For God's sake," Alleyn said, "what nonsense is this?"

She frowned and looked at him out of her disastrous eyes. "Could you help me?" she said.

"I have no idea. Probably not."

"I'm in a bad way."

"Yes."

"If I were to keep faith? I don't know what you're up to, but if I were to keep faith and not tell them who you are? Even if it ruined me? Would you think you could help me then?"

"Are you asking me if I could help you to cure yourself of drugging? I couldn't. Only an expert could do that. If you've still got enough character and sense of purpose to keep faith, as you put it, perhaps you should have enough guts to go through with a cure. I don't know."

"I suppose you think I'm trying to bribe you?"

"In a sense—yes."

"Do you know," she said discontentedly, "you're the only man I've ever met—" She stopped and seemed to hesitate. "I can't get this right," she said. "With you it's not an act, is it?"

Alleyn smiled for the first time. "I'm not attempting the

well-known gambit of rudeness introduced with a view to amorous occasions," he said. "Is that what you mean?"

"I suppose it is."

"You should stick to classical drama. Shakespeare's women don't fall for the insult-and-angry-seduction stuff. Sorry. I'm forgetting Richard III."

"Beatrice and Benedick? Petruchio and Katharina?"

"I was excluding comedy."

"How right you were. There's nothing very funny about my situation."

"No, it seems appalling."

"What can I do? Tell me, what I can do?"

"Leave the Chèvre d'Argent today. Now, if you like. I've got a car outside. Go to a doctor in Paris and offer yourself for a cure. Recognize your responsibility and, before further harm can come of this place, tell me or the local commissary or anyone else in a position of authority everything you know about the people here."

"Betray my friends?"

"A meaningless phrase. In protecting them you betray decency itself. Can you think of that child Ginny Taylor and still question what you should do."

She stepped back from him as if he was a physical menace.

"You're not here by accident," she said. "You've planned this visit."

"I could hardly plan a perforated appendix in an unknown maiden lady. The place and all of you speak for yourselves. Yawning your head off because you want your heroin. Pin-point pupils and leathery faces."

She caught her breath in what sounded like a sigh of relief. "Is that all?" she said.

"I really must go. Goodbye."

"I can't do it. I can't do what you ask."

"I'm sorry."

He opened the door. She said: "I won't tell them what you are. But don't come back. Don't come back here. I'm warning you. Don't come back."

"Goodbye," Alleyn said, and without encountering anyone walked out of the house and down the passage-way to the open platform.

Raoul was waiting there with the car.

II

When she returned to the roof-garden, Annabella Wells found the men of the house party waiting for her. Dr. Baradi closed his hand softly round her arm, leading her forward.

"Don't," she said, "you smell of hospitals."

Carbury Glande said: "Annabella, who is he? I mean we all know he's Agatha Troy's husband but, for God's sake, *who* is he?"

"You know as much as I do."

"But you said you'd crossed the Atlantic with him. You said it was a shipboard affair and one knows they don't leave many stones unturned especially in your hands, my angel."

"He was one of my rare failures. He talked of nothing but his wife. He spread her over the Atlantic like an overflow from the Gulf Stream. I gave him up as a bad job. A dull chap, I decided."

"I rather liked him," young Herrington said defiantly.

Mr. Oberon spoke for the first time. "A dangerous man," he said. "Whoever he is and whatever he may be. Under the circumstances, a dangerous man."

Baradi said: "I agree. The enquiry for Garbel is inexplicable."

"Unless they are initiates," Glande said, "and have been given the name."

"They are not initiates," Oberon said.

"No," Baradi agreed.

Young Herrington said explosively: "My God, is there no other way out?"

"Ask yourself," said Glande.

Mr. Oberon rose. "There is no other way," he said tranquilly. "And they must not return. That at least is clear. They must not return."

III

As they drove back to Roqueville, Alleyn said: "You did your job well this morning, Raoul. You are, evidently, a man upon whom one may depend."

"It pleases Monsieur to say so," said Raoul cheerfully. "The Egyptian gentleman is also, it appears, good at his job. In wartime a medical orderly learns to recognize talent, Monsieur. Very often one saw the patients zipped up like a placket-hole. *Paf!* and he's open. *Pan!* and he's shut. But this was different."

"Dr. Baradi is afraid that she may not recover."

"She had not the look of death upon her."

"Can you recognize it?"

"I fancy that I can, Monsieur."

"Did Madame and the small one get safely to their hotel?"

"Safely, Monsieur. On the way we stopped in the Rue des Violettes. Madame inquired for Mr. Garbel."

Alleyn said sharply: "Did she see him?"

"I understand he was not at home, Monsieur."

"Did she leave a message?"

"I believe so, Monsieur. I saw Madame give a note to the concierge."

"I see."

"She is a type, that one," Raoul said thoughtfully.

"The concierge? Do you know her?"

"Yes, Monsieur. In Roqueville all the world knows all the world. She's an original, is old Blanche."

"In what way?"

"*Un article défraîchi.* One imagines she has other interests besides the door-keeping. To be fat is not always to be idle. But the apartments," Raoul added politely, "are perfectly correct." Evidently he felt it would be in bad taste to disparage the address of any friend of the Alleyns.

Alleyn said, choosing his French very carefully: "I am minded to place a great deal of confidence in you, Raoul."

"If Monsieur pleases."

"I think you were more impressed with Mr. Baradi's skill than with his personality."

"That is a fact, Monsieur."

"I also. Have you seen Mr. Oberon?"

"On several occasions."

"What do you think about him?"

"I have no absolute knowledge of his skill, Monsieur, but I think even less of his personality than of the Egyptian's."

"Do you know how he entertains his guests?"

"One hears a little gossip from time to time. Not much, Monsieur. The servants at the Château are for the most part imported and extremely reticent. But there is an under-chambermaid from the Paysdoux, who is not unapproachable. A blonde, which is unusual in the Paysdoux."

"What has the unusual blonde to say about it?"

Raoul did not answer at once and Alleyn turned his head to look at him. He was scowling magnificently.

"I do not approve of what Teresa has to say. Her name, Monsieur, is Teresa. I find what she has to say immensely unpleasing. You see, it's like this, Monsieur. The time has come when I should marry and for one reason or another—one cannot rationalize about these things—my preference is for Teresa. She has got what it takes," Raoul said, using a phrase—*elle a du fond*—which reminded Alleyn of Annabella Wells's desperate claim. "But in a wife," Raoul continued, "one expects certain reticences where other men are in question. I dislike what Teresa tells me of her employer, Monsieur. I particularly dislike her account of a certain incident."

"Am I to hear it?"

"I shall be glad to recount it. It appears, Monsieur, that Teresa's duties are confined to the sweeping of carpets and polishing of floors and that it is not required of her to take *petit déjeuner* to guests or to perform any personal services for them. She is young and inexperienced. And so, one morning, this Egyptian surgeon witnesses Teresa from the rear when she is on her knees polishing. Teresa is as good from behind as she is from in front, Monsieur. And the doctor passes her and pauses to look. Presently he returns with Mr. Oberon and they pause and speak to each other in a foreign language. Next, the *femme de charge* sends for Teresa and she is instructed that she is to serve *petit déjeuner* to this animal Oberon, if Monsieur will overlook the description, in his bedroom and that her wage is to be raised. So Teresa performs this service. On the first morning there is no conversation. On the second he enquires her name. On the third this *vilain coco* asks her if she is not a fine strong girl. On the fourth he talks a lot of *blague* about the spirituality of the body and the non-existence of evil, and on the fifth, when Teresa enters, he is displayed, immodestly clad, before a full-length glass in his salon. I must tell you, Monsieur, that to reach the bedroom, Teresa must first pass through the salon. She is obliged to approach this unseemly animal. He looks at her fixedly and speaks to her in a manner that is irreligious and blasphemous and anathema. Monsieur, Teresa is a good girl. She is frightened, not so much of this animal, she tells me, as of herself because she feels herself to be like a bird when it is held in error by a snake. I have told her she must leave, but she says that the wages are good and they are a large family with sickness and much in debt. Monsieur, I repeat, she is a good girl and it is true she needs the money, but I cannot escape the thought that she is in a kind of bondage from which she cannot summon enough character to escape. And on some mornings, when she goes in, there is nothing to which one could object, but on others he talks and talks and stares and stares at Teresa. So that when I last saw her we quarrelled and I have told her that unless she leaves her job before she is no longer respectable she may look elsewhere for a husband. So she wept and I was discomforted. She is not unique but, there it is, I have a preference for Teresa."

Alleyn thought: "This is the first bit of luck I've had since we got here." He looked up the valley at the glittering works of the Maritime Alps Chemical Company and said: "I think it well to tell you that I am interested professionally in the ménage at the Chèvre d'Argent. If it had not been for the accident of Mademoiselle's illness I should have tried to gain admittance there. M. le Commissaire is also interested. We are colleagues in this affair. You and I agree to forget my rank, Raoul, but for the purposes of this discussion perhaps we should recall it."

"Good, M. l'Inspector-en-Chef."

"There's no reason on earth why you should put yourself out for an English policeman in an affair which, however much it may also concern the French police, hasn't very much to do with you. Apart from Teresa, for whom you have a preference."

"There is always Teresa."

"Are you a discreet man?"

"I don't chatter like a one-eyed magpie, Monsieur."

"I believe you. It is known to the police here and in London that the Chèvre d'Argent is used as a place of distribution in a particularly ugly trade."

"Women, Monsieur?"

"Drugs. Women, it seems, are a purely personal interest. A side-line. I believe neither Dr. Baradi nor Mr. Oberon is a drug addict. They are engaged in the traffic from a business point-of-view. I think that they have cultivated the habit of drug-taking among their guests and are probably using at least one of them as a distributor. Mr. Oberon has also established a cult."

"A cult, Monsieur?"

"A synthetic religion concocted from scraps of mysticism, witchcraft, mythology, Hinduism, Egyptology, what-have-you, with, I very much suspect, a number of particularly revolting fancy touches invented by Mr. Oberon."

"Anathema," Raoul said, "all this is anathema. What do they do?" he added with undisguised interest.

"I don't know exactly but I must, I'm afraid, find out. There have been other cases of this sort. No doubt there are rites. No doubt the women are willing to be drugged."

Raoul said: "It appears that I must be firm with Teresa."

"I should be very firm, Raoul."

"This morning she is in Roqueville at the market. I am to meet her at my parents' restaurant, where I shall introduce a firm note. I am disturbed for her. All this, Monsieur, that you have related is borne out by Teresa. On Thursday nights the local servants and some of the other permanent staff are dismissed. It is on Thursday, therefore, that I escort Teresa to her home up in the Paysdoux where she sleeps the night. She has heard a little gossip, not much, because the servants are discreet, but a little. It appears that there is a ceremony in a room which is kept locked at other times. And on Friday nobody appears until late in the afternoon and then with an air of having a formidable *gueule de bois*. The ladies are strangely behaved on Fridays. It is as if they are half-asleep, Teresa says. And last Friday a young English lady, who has recently arrived, seemed as if she was completely *bouleversée*; dazed, Monsieur," Raoul said, making a graphic gesture with one hand. "In a trance. And also as if she had wept."

"Isn't Teresa frightened by what she sees on Fridays?"

"That is what I find strange, Monsieur. Yes: she says she is frightened, but it is clear to me that she is also excited. That is what troubles me in Teresa."

"Did she tell you where the room is? The room that is unlocked on Thursday nights?"

"It is in the lower part of the Château, Monsieur. Beneath the library, Teresa thinks. Two flights beneath."

"And today is Wednesday."

"Well, Monsieur?"

"I am in need of an assistant."

"Yes, Monsieur?"

"If I asked at the Préfecture they would give me the local gendarme, who is doubtless well-known. Or they would send me a clever man from Paris who as a stranger would be conspicuous. But a man of Roqueville who is well-known and yet is accepted as the friend of one of the maids at the Chèvre d'Argent is not conspicuous if he calls. Do you in fact call often to see Teresa?"

"Often, Monsieur."

"Well, Raoul?"

"Well, Monsieur?"

"Do you care, with M. le Commissaire's permission, to come adventuring with me on Thursday night?"

"Enchanted," said Raoul, gracefully.

"It may not be uneventful, you know. They are a formidable lot, up there."

"That is understood, Monsieur. Again, it will be an act of grace."

"Good. Here is Roqueville. Drive to the hotel, if you please. I shall see Madame and have some luncheon and at three o'clock I shall call on M. le Commissaire. You will be free until then, but leave me a telephone number and your address."

"My parents' restaurant is in the street above that of the hotel. L'Escargot Bienvenu, 20 Rue des Sarrasins. Here is a card, Monsieur, with the telephone number."

"Right."

"My father is a good cook. He has not a great repertoire, but his judgment is sound. Such dishes as he makes he makes well. His *filets mignons* are a speciality of the house, Monsieur, and his sauces are inspired."

"You interest me profoundly. In the days when there was steak in England, one used to dream of *filet mignon* but even then one came to France to eat it."

"Perhaps if Monsieur and Madame find themselves a little weary of the table d'hôte at the Royal they may care to eat cheaply but with satisfaction at L'Escargot Bienvenu."

"An admirable suggestion."

"Of course, we are not at all smart. But good breeding," Raoul said simply, "creates its own background and Monsieur and Madame would not feel out of place. Here is your hotel, Monsieur, and—" His voice changed. "Here is Madame."

Alleyn was out of the car before it stopped. Troy stood in the hotel courtyard with her clasped hands at her lips and a look on her face that he had never seen there before. When he took her arms in his hands he felt her whole body trembling. She tried to speak to him but at first was unable to find her voice. He saw her mouth frame the word "Ricky."

"What is it darling?" he said. "What's the matter with him?"

"He's gone," she said. "They've taken him. They've taken Ricky."

IV

For the rest of their lives they would remember too vividly the seconds in which they stood on the tessellated courtyard of the hotel, plastered by the mid-day sun. Raoul on the footpath watched them and the blank street glared behind him. The air smelt of petrol. There was a smear of magenta bougainvillea on the opposite wall, and in the centre of the street a neat pile of horse-droppings. It was already siesta time and so quiet that they might have been the only people awake in Roqueville.

"I'll keep my head and be sensible," Troy whispered. "Won't I, Rory?"

"Of course. We'll go indoors and you'll tell me about it."

"I want to get into the car and look somewhere for him, but I know that won't do."

"I'll ask Raoul to wait."

He did so. Raoul listened, motionless. When Alleyn had spoken Raoul said, "Tell Madame it will be all right, Monsieur. Things will come right." As they turned away he called his reassurances after them and the sound of his words followed them: *"Les affaires s'arrangeront. Tout ira bien, Madame."*

Inside the hotel it seemed very dark. A porter sat behind a reception desk and an elegantly dressed man stood in the hall wringing his hands.

Troy said: "This is my husband. This is the manager, Rory. He speaks English. I'm sorry, Monsieur, I don't know your name."

"Malaquin, Madame. Mr. Alleyn, I am sure there is some simple explanation—There have been other cases—"

"I'll come and see you, if I may, when I've heard what has happened."

"But of course. *Garçon*—"

The porter, looking ineffably compassionate, took them up in the lift. The stifling journey was interminable.

Troy faced her husband in a large bedroom made less impersonal by the slight but characteristic litter that accompanied her wherever she went. Beyond her was an iron-railed balcony and beyond that the arrogant laundry-blue of the Mediterranean. He pushed a chair up and she took it obediently. He sat on his heels before her and put his hands on the arms of the chair.

"Now, tell me, darling," he said. "I can't do anything until you've told me."

"You were such a lifetime coming."

"I'm here now. Tell me."

"Yes."

She did tell him. She made a great effort to be lucid, frowning when she hesitated or when her voice shook, and always keeping her gaze on him. He had said she was a good witness and now she stuck to the bare bones of her story, but every word was shadowed by a multitude of unspoken terrors.

She said that when they arrived at the hotel Ricky was fretful and white after his interrupted sleep and the excitement of the drive. The manager was attentive and suggested that Ricky could have a tray in their rooms. Tory gave him a bath and put him into pyjamas and dressing-gown and he had his luncheon, falling asleep almost before it was finished. She put him to bed in a dressing-room opening off her own bedroom. She darkened the windows, and seeing him comfortably asleep with his silver goat clutched in his hand, had her bath, changed and lunched in the dining-room of the hotel. When she returned to their room Ricky had gone.

At first she thought that he must have wakened and gone in search of a lavatory or that perhaps he had had one of his panics and was looking for her. It was only after a search of their bathroom and the passages, stairs and such rooms as were open that with mounting anxiety she rang for the chambermaid, and then, as the woman didn't understand English, spoke on the telephone to the manager. M. Malaquin was helpful and expeditious. He said he would at once speak to the servants on duty and report to her. As she put down the receiver Troy looked at the chair across which she had laid Ricky's day clothes ready for his awakening—a yellow shirt and brown linen shorts—and she saw that they were gone.

From that moment she had fought against a surge of terror so imperative that it was accompanied by a physical pain. She ran downstairs and told the manager. The porter and two of the waiters and Troy herself had gone out into the deserted and sweltering streets, Troy running uphill and breathlessly calling Ricky's name. She stopped the few people she met, asking them for a *"petit garçon, mon fils."* The men shrugged, one woman said something that sounded sympathetic. They all shook their heads or made negative gestures with their fingers. Troy found herself in a maze of back streets and stone stairways. She thought she was lost, but looking down a steep alleyway, saw one of the waiters walk across at the lower end and she ran down after him. When she reached the cross-alley she was just in time to see his coat-tails disappear round a further corner. Finally she caught him up. They were back in the little square, and there was the hotel. Her heart rammed against her ribs and she suffered a disgusting sense of constriction in her throat. Sweat poured between her shoulder blades and ran down her forehead into her eyes. She was in a nightmare.

The waiter grimaced. He was idiotically polite and deprecating and he couldn't understand a word that she said. He pursed his lips, bowed and went indoors. She remembered the Commissary of Police and was about to ask the manager to telephone the Préfecture when she heard Raoul's car turn into the street.

Alleyn said: "Right. I'll talk to the Préfecture. But before I do, my dearest dear, will you believe one thing?"

"All right, I'll try."

"Ricky isn't in danger. I'm sure of it."

"But it's true. He's been—it's those people up there—they've kidnapped him, haven't they?"

"It's possible that they've taken a hand. If they have it's because they want to keep me busy. It's also possible, isn't it, that something entered into his head and he got himself up and trotted out."

"He'd never do it, Rory. Never. You know he wouldn't."

"All right. Now, I'll ring the Préfecture. Come on."

He sat her beside him on the bed and kept his arm about her. While he waited for the number he said: "Did you lock the door?"

"No. I didn't like the idea of locking him in. The manager's spoken to the servants. They didn't see anybody. Nobody asked for our room numbers."

"The heavy trunk is still in the hall downstairs and the room numbers chalked on it. What colour are his clothes?"

"Pale yellow shirt and brown shorts."

"Right. We may as well—'*Allo! 'Allo!*...*"

He began to talk into the telephone, keeping his free hand on her shoulder. Troy turned her cheek to it for a moment and then freed herself and went out on the balcony.

The little square—it was called the Place des Sarrasins—was at the top of a hilly street and the greater part of Roqueville lay between it and the sea. The maze of alleys where Troy had lost herself was out of sight behind and above the hotel. As if from a high tower, she looked down into the streets and prayed incoherently that in one of them she would see a tiny figure: Ricky, in his lemon-coloured shirt and brown linen shorts. But all Troy could see was a pattern of stucco and stone, a distant row of carriages whose drivers and horses were snoozing, no doubt, in the shadows, a system of tiled roofs and the paint-like blue of the sea. She looked nearer at hand and there, beneath her, was Raoul Milano's car, seeming like a toy, and Raoul himself, rolling a cigarette. The hotel porter, at that moment, came out and she heard the sound of his voice. Raoul got up and they disappeared beneath her into the hotel.

The tone of Alleyn's voice suggested that he was near the end of his telephone call. She had turned away from her fruitless search of the map-like town and was about to go indoors when out of the tail of her eye she caught a flicker of colour.

It was a flicker of lemon-yellow and brown.

The hot iron of the balcony rail scorched the palms of her hands. She leant far out and stared at a tall building on a higher level than herself, a building that was just in view round the corner of the hotel. It was perhaps a quarter of a mile away and from behind a huddle of intervening roofs, rose up in a series of balconies. It was on the highest of these, behind a blur of iron railings, that she saw her two specks of colour.

"Rory," she cried. "Rory!"

It took several seconds that seemed like as many minutes for Alleyn to find the balcony. "It's Ricky," she said, "isn't it? It must be Ricky." And she ran back into the room, snatched the thin cover from her bed and waved it frantically from the balcony.

"Wait a moment," Alleyn said.

His police case had been brought up to their room and contained a pair of very powerful field glasses. While he focussed them on the distant balcony he said: "Don't be too certain, darling, there may be other small boys in yellow and—no—no, it's Ricky. He's all right. Look."

Troy's eyes were masked with tears of relief. Her hands shook and her fingers were too precipitant with the focussing governors. "I can't do it—I can't see."

"Steady. Wipe your eyes. Here, I will. He's still there. He may have spotted us. Try this way. Kneel down and rest the glasses on the rail. Get each eye right in turn. Quietly does it."

Circles of blurred colour mingled and danced in the two fields of vision. They swam together and clarified. The glasses were in focus now but were trained on some strange blue door, startling in its closeness. She moved them and an ornate gilded steeple was before her with a cross and a clock telling a quarter to two. "I don't know where I am. It's a church. I can't find him."

"You're nearly there. Keep at that level and come round gently." And suddenly Ricky looked through iron rails with vague, not quite frightened eyes whose gaze, while it was directed at her, yet passed beyond her.

"Wave," she said. "Go on waving."

Ricky's strangely impersonal and puzzled face moved a little so that an iron standard partly hid it. His right arm was raised and his hand moved to and fro above the railing.

"He's seen!" she said. "He's waving back."

The glasses slipped a little. The wall of their hotel, out-of-focus and stupid, blotted out her vision. Someone was tapping on the bedroom door behind them.

"*Entrez!*" Alleyn called, and then sharply, "Hullo! Who's that?"

"What? I've lost him."

"A woman came out and led him away. They've gone indoors."

"A woman?"

"Fat and dressed in black."

"Please let's go quickly."

Raoul had come through the bedroom and stood behind them. Alleyn said in French, "Do you see that tall building, just to the left of our wall and to the right of the church? It's pinkish with blue shutters and there's something red on one of the balconies."

"I see it, Monsieur."

"So you know what building it is?"

"I think so, Monsieur. It will be Number 16 in the Rue des Violettes where Madame enquired this morning."

"Troy," Alleyn said. "The Lord knows why, but Ricky's gone to call on Mr. Garbel."

Troy stopped short on her way to the door. "Do you mean...?"

"Raoul says that's the house."

"But—. No," Troy said vigorously. "No, I don't believe it. He wouldn't just get up and go there. Not of his own accord. Not like that. He wouldn't. Come on, Rory."

They were following her when Alleyn said: "When did these flowers come?"

"What flowers? Oh, that. I hadn't noticed it. I don't know. Dr. Baradi, I should think. Please don't let's wait."

An enormous florist's box garnished with a great bow of ribbon lay on the top of a pile of suitcases.

Watched in an agony of impatience by his wife, Alleyn slid a card from under the ribbon and looked at it.

"So sorry," he read, "that I shall be away during your visit. Welcome to Roqueville. P.E. Garbel."

VI

Consultation

I

TROY wouldn't wait for the lift. She ran downstairs with Alleyn and Raoul at her heels. Only the porter was there, sitting at the desk in the hall.

Alleyn said: "This will take thirty seconds, darling. I'm in as much of a hurry as you. Please believe it's important. You can get into the car. Raoul can start the engine." And to the porter he said: "Please telephone this number and give the message I have written on the paper to the person who answers. It is the number of the Préfecture and the message is urgent. It is expected. Were you on duty here when flowers came for Madame?"

"I was on duty when the flowers arrived, Monsieur. It was about an hour ago. I did not know they were for Madame. The woman went straight upstairs without enquiry, as one who knows the way."

"And returned?"

The porter lifted his shoulders. "I did not see her return, Monsieur. No doubt she used the service stairs."

"No doubt," Alleyn said and ran out to the car.

On the way to the Rue des Violettes he said: "I'm going to stop the car a little way from the house, Troy, and I'm going to ask you to wait in it while I go indoors."

"Are you? But why? Ricky's there, isn't he? We saw him."

"Yes, we saw him. But I'm not too keen for other people to see us. Cousin Garbel seems to be known, up at the Chèvre d'Argent."

"But Robin Herrington said he didn't know him and anyway, according to the card on the flowers, Cousin Garbel's gone away. That must be what the concierge was trying to tell me. She said he was *'pas chez elle.'*"

"*'Pas chez soi'* surely?"

"All right. Yes, of course. I couldn't really understand her. I don't understand anything," Troy said desperately. "I just want to get Ricky."

"I know, darling. Not more than I do."

"He didn't look as if he was in one of his panics. Did he?"

"No."

"I expect we'll have a reaction and be furiously snappish with him for frightening us, don't you?"

"We must learn to master our ugly tempers," he said, smiling at her.

"Rory, he will be there still? He won't have gone?"

"It's only ten minutes ago that we saw him on a sixth floor balcony."

"Was she a fat shiny woman who led him in?"

"I hadn't got the glasses. I couldn't spot the shine with the naked eye."

"I didn't like the concierge. Ricky would hate her."

"That is the street, Monsieur," said Raoul. "At the intersection."

"Good. Draw up here by the kerb. I don't want to frighten Madame, but I think all may not be well with the small one whom we have seen on the balcony at Number 16. If anyone were to leave by the back or side of the house, Raoul, would they have to come this way from that narrow side-street and pass this way to get out of Roqueville?"

"This way, Monsieur, either to go east or west out of Roqueville. For the rest there are only other alley-ways with flights of steps that lead nowhere."

"Then if a car should emerge from behind Number 16 perhaps it may come about that you start your car and your engine stalls and you block the way. In apologizing you would no doubt go up to the other car and look inside. And if the small one were

in the car you would not be able to start your own though you
would make a great disturbance by leaning on your horn. And
by that time, Raoul, it is possible that M. le Commissaire will
have arrived in his car. Or that I have come out of Number 16."

"Aren't you going, Rory?"

"At once, darling. All right, Raoul?"

"Perfectly, Monsieur."

Alleyn got out of the car, crossed the intersection, turned
right and entered Number 16.

The hall was dark and deserted. He went at once to the
lift-well, glanced at the index of names and pressed the call-
button.

"Monsieur?" said the concierge, partly opening the door of
her cubby-hole.

Alleyn looked beyond the ringed and grimy hand at one
beady eye, the flange of a flattened nose and half a grape-
coloured mouth.

"Madame," he said politely and turned back to the lift.

"Monsieur desires?"

"The lift, Madame."

"To ascend where, Monsieur?"

"To the sixth floor, Madame."

"To which apartment on the sixth floor?"

"To the principal apartment. With a balcony."

The lift was wheezing its way down.

"Unfortunately," said the concierge, "the tenant is absent on
vacation. Monsieur would care to leave a message?"

"It is the small boy for whom I have called. The small boy
whom Madame has been kind enough to admit to the apartment."

"Monsieur is mistaken. I have admitted no children. The
apartment is locked."

"Can Nature have been so munificent as to lavish upon us a
twin-sister of Madame? If so she has undoubtedly admitted a
small boy to the principal apartment on the sixth floor."

The lift came into sight and stopped. Alleyn opened the door.

"One moment," said the concierge. He paused. Her hand was
withdrawn from the cubby-hole door. She came out, waddling
like a duck and bringing a bunch of keys.

"It is not amusing," she said, "to take a fool's trip. However,
Monsieur shall see for himself."

They went up in the lift. The concierge quivered slightly and gave out the combined odours of uncleanliness, frangipani, garlic and hot satin. On the sixth floor she opened a door opposite the lift, waddled through it and sat down panting and massively triumphant on a high chair in the middle of a neat and ordered room whose French windows gave on to a balcony.

Alleyn completely disregarded the concierge. He stopped short in the entrance of the room and looked swiftly round it at the dressing-table, the shelf above the wash-basin, the gown hanging on the bed-rail and at the three pairs of shoes set out against the wall. He moved to the wardrobe and pulled open the door. Inside it were three sober dresses and a couple of modestly trimmed shraw hats. An envelope was lying on the floor of the wardrobe. He stooped down to look at it. It was a business envelope and bore the legend "Compagnie Chimique des Alpes Maritimes." He read the superscription:

> A Mlle. Penelope E. Garbel,
> 16 Rue des Violettes,
> Roqueville-de-Sud,
> Côte d'Azur

He straightened up, shut the wardrobe door with extreme deliberation and contemplated the concierge, still seated like some obscene goddess, in the middle of the room.

"You disgusting old bag of tripes," Alleyn said thoughtfully in English, "you little know what a fool I've been making of myself."

And he went out to the balcony.

II

He stood where so short a time ago he had seen Ricky stand and looked across the intervening rooftops to one that bore a large sign: Hotel Royal. Troy had left the bed-cover hanging over the rail of their balcony.

"A few minutes ago," Alleyn said, returning to the immovable concierge, "from the Hôtel Royal over there I saw my son who was here, Madame, on this balcony."

"It would require the eyes of a hawk to recognize a little boy at that distance. Monsieur is mistaken."

"It required the aid of binoculars and those I had."

"Possibly the son of the laundress who was on the premises and has now gone."

"I saw you, Madame, take the hand of my son, who like yourself was clearly recognizable, and lead him indoors."

"Monsieur is mistaken. I have not left my office since this morning. Monsieur will be good enough to take his departure. I do not insist," the concierge said magnificently, "upon an apology."

"Perhaps," Alleyn said, taking a mille franc note from his pocket-book, "you will accept this instead."

He stood well away from her, holding it out. The eyes glistened and the painted lips moved, but she did not rise. For perhaps four seconds they confronted each other. Then she said, "If Monsieur will wait downstairs I shall be pleased to join him. I have another room to visit."

Alleyn bowed, stooped and pounced. His hand shot along the floor and under the hem of the heavy skirt. She made a short angry noise and tried to trample on the hand. One of her heels caught his wrist.

"Calm yourself, Madame. My intentions are entirely honourable."

He stepped back neatly and extended his arm, keeping the hand closed.

"A strange egg, Madame Blanche," Alleyn said, "for a respectable hen to lay."

He opened his hand. Across the palm lay a little clay goat, painted silver.

III

From that moment the proceedings in Number 16 Rue des Violettes were remarkable for their unorthodoxy.

Alleyn said: "You have one chance. Where is the boy?"

She closed her eyes and hitched her colossal shoulders up to her earrings.

"Very good," Alleyn said and walked out of the room. She

had left the key in the lock. He turned it and withdrew the bunch.

It did not take long to go through the rest of the building. For the rooms that were unoccupied he found a master-key. As he crossed each threshold he called once: "Ricky?" and then made a rapid search. In the occupied rooms his visits bore the character of a series of disconnected shots on a cinema screen. He exposed in rapid succession persons of different ages taking their siestas in varying degrees of *déshabillé*. On being told that there was no small boy within, he uttered a word of apology and under the dumbfounded gaze of spinsters, elderly gentlemen, married or romantic couples and, in one instance, an outraged Negress of uncertain years, walked in, opened cupboards, looked under and into beds and, with a further apology, walked out again.

The concierge had begun to thump on the door of the principal apartment of the sixth floor.

On the ground floor he found a crisp bright-eyed man with a neat moustache, powerful shoulders and an impressive uniform.

"M. l'Inspecteur-en-Chef, Alleyn? Allow me to introduce myself. Dupont of the Sûreté, at present acting as Commissary at the Préfecture, Roqueville." He spoke fluent English with a marked accent. "So we are already in trouble," she said as they shook hands. "I have spoken to Madame Alleyn and to Milano. And the boy is not yet found?"

Alleyn quickly related what had happened.

"And the woman Blanche? Where is she, my dear Inspecteur-en-Chef?"

"She is locked in the apartment of Miss P.E. Garbel on the sixth floor. The distant thumping which perhaps you can hear is produced by the woman Blanche."

The Commissary smiled all over his face. "And we are reminded how correct is the deportment of Scotland Yard. Let us leave her to her activities and complete the search. As we do so will you perhaps be good enough to continue your report."

Alleyn complied and they embarked on an exploration of the unsavoury private apartments of Madame Blanche. Alleyn checked at a list of telephone numbers and pointed to the third. "The Château Chèvre d'Argent," he said.

"Indeed? Very suggestive," said M. Dupont; and with a startling and incredible echo from Baker Street added, "Pray continue your most interesting narrative while we explore the basement."

But Ricky was not in any room on the ground floor nor in the cellar under the house. "Undoubtedly they have removed him," said Dupont, "when they saw you wave from your balcony. I shall at once warn my confrères in the surrounding districts. There are not many roads out of Roqueville and all cars can be checked. We then proceed with a tactful but thorough investigation of the town. This affair is not without precedent. Have no fear for your small son. He will come to no harm. Excuse me. I shall telephone from the office of the woman Blanche. Will you remain or would you prefer to rejoin Madame?"

"Thank you. I will have a word with her if I may."

"Implore her," M. Dupont said briskly, "to remain calm. The affair will arrange itself. The small one is in no danger." He bowed and went into the cubby-hole. As he went out Alleyn heard the click of a telephone dial.

A police-car was drawn up by the kerb outside Number 16. Alleyn crossed the road to Raoul's car.

There was no need to calm Troy: she was very quiet indeed, and perfectly collected. She looked ill with anxiety but she smiled at him and said: "Bad luck, darling. No sign?"

"Some signs," he said, resting his arms on the door beside her. "Dupont agrees with me that it's an attempt to keep me occupied. He's sure Ricky's all right."

"He *was* there, wasn't he? We did see him?"

Alleyn said: "We did see him," and after a moment's hesitation he took the little silver goat from his pocket. "He left it behind him. Raoul ejaculated: *"La petite chèvre d'argent."*

Troy's lips quivered. She took the goat in her hands and folded it between them. "What do we do now?"

"Dupont is stopping all cars driving out of Roqueville and will order a house-to-house search in the town. He's a good man."

"I'm sure he is," Troy said politely. She looked terrified. "You're not going back to Chèvre d'Argent, are you? You're not going to call their bluff?"

"We're going to take stock." Alleyn closed his hand over hers. "I know one wants to drive off madly in all directions, yelling for Ricky but honestly, darling, that's not the form for this kind of thing. We've *got* to take stock. So far we've scarcely had time to think, much less reason."

"It's just—when he knows he's lost—it's his nightmare—mislaying us."

Two gendarmes, smart in their uniforms and sun-helmets, rode past on bicycles, turned into the Rue des Violettes, dismounted and went into Number 16.

"Dupont's chaps," said Alleyn. "Now we shan't be long. And I have got one bit of news for you. Cousin Garbel is a spinster."

"What on earth do you mean?"

"His name is Penelope and he wears a straw hat trimmed with parma violets."

Troy said: "Don't muddle me, darling. I'm so desperately addled already."

"I'm terribly sorry. It's true. Your correspondent is a woman who has some connection with the chemical works we saw this morning. For reasons I can only guess at, she's let you address her letters as is to a man. How *did* you address them?"

"To M.P.E. Garbel."

"Perhaps she thought you imagined 'M.' to be the correct abbreviation of Mademoiselle?"

Troy shook her head: "It doesn't seem to matter much now, but it's quite incredible. Look: something's beginning to happen."

The little town was waking up. Shop doors opened and proprietors came out in their shirt sleeves scratching their elbows. At the far end of the Rue des Violettes there was an eruption of children's voices and a clatter of shoes on stone. The driver of the police-car outside Number 16 started up his engine and the Commissary came briskly down the steps. He made a crisp signal to the driver, who turned his car, crossed the intersection and finally pulled up in front of Raoul M. Dupont walked across, saluted Troy and addressed himself to Alleyn.

"We commence our search of houses in Roqueville, my dear Inspecteur-en-Chef. The road patrols are installed and a general warning is being issued to my colleagues in the surrounding territory. Between 2:15 by the church clock when you saw your son until the moment when you arrived at these apartments, there was an interval of about ten minutes. If he was removed in an auto it was during those minutes. The patrols were instructed at five minutes to three. Again if he was removed in an auto it has had half an hour's advance and can in that time have gone at the most no further on our roads than fifty kilometres. Outside every town beyond that radius we have posted a patrol and if they have nothing to report we shall search exhaustively within the radius. Madame, it is most fortunate that you saw the small one from your hotel. Thus have you hurled a screwdriver in the factory."

The distracted Troy puzzled over the Commissary's free use of English idiom, but Alleyn gave a sharp exclamation. *"The factory!"* he said. "By the Lord, I wonder."

"Monsieur?"

"My dear Dupont, you have acted with the greatest expedition and judgment. What do you suggest we do now?"

"I am entirely at your disposal, M. l'Inspecteur-en-Chef. May I suggest that perhaps a fuller understanding of the situation—"

"Yes, indeed. Shall we go to our hotel?"

"Enchanted, Monsieur."

"I think," Alleyn said, "that our driver here is very willing to take an active part. He's been extremely helpful already."

"He is a good fellow, this Milano," said Dupont and addressed Raoul in his own language: "See here, my lad, we are making enquiries for the missing boy in Roqueville. If he is anywhere in the town it will be at the house of some associate of the woman Blanche at Number 16. Are you prepared to take a hand?"

Raoul, it appeared, was prepared. "If he is in the town, M. le Commissaire, I shall know it inside an hour."

"Oh, *là-là!*" M. Dupont remarked, "what a song our cock sings."

He scowled playfully at Raoul and opened the doors of the car. Troy and Alleyn were ushered ceremoniously into the police-car and the driver took them back to the hotel.

In their bedroom, which had begun to take on a look of half-real familiarity, Troy and Alleyn filled in the details of their adventure from the time of the first incident in the train until Ricky's disappearance. M. Dupont listened with an air of deference tempered by professional detachment. When they had finished he clapped his knees lightly and made a neat gesture with his thumb and forefinger pressed together.

"Admirable!" he said. "So we are in possession of our facts and now we act in concert, but first I must tell you one little fact that I have in my sleeve. There has been, four weeks ago, a case of child-stealing in the Paysdoux. It was the familiar story. A wealthy family from Lyons. A small one. A flightish nurse.

During the afternoon promenade a young man draws the attention of this sexy nurse. The small one gambols in the gardens by our casino. The nurse and the young man are tête-à-tête upon a seat. Automobile pass to and fro, sometimes stopping. In one are the confederates of the young man. Presently the nurse remembers her duty. The small one is vanished and remains so. Also vanished is the young man. A message is thrown through the hotel window. The small one is to be recovered with five hundred mille francs at a certain time and at a place outside St. Céleste. There are the customary threats in the matter of informing the police. Monsieur Papa, under pressure from Madame Maman, obeys. He is driven to within a short distance of the place. He continues on foot. A car appears. Stops. A man with a handkerchief over his face and a weapon in his hand gets out. Monsieur Papa, again following instructions, places the money under a stone by the road and retires with his hands above his head. The man collects and examines the money and returns to the car. The small one gets out. The car drives away. The small one," said M. Dupont, opening his eyes very wide at Troy, "is not pleased. He wishes to remain with his new acquaintances."

"Oh, *no!*" Troy cried out.

"But yes. He has found them enchanting. Nevertheless he rejoins his family. And now, having facilitated the escape of the cat, Monsieur Papa attempts to close the bag. He informs the police." M. Dupont spread his hands in the classic gesture and waited for his audience-reaction.

"The usual story," Alleyn said.

"M. Dupont," Troy said, "do you think the same men have taken Ricky?"

"No, Madame. I think we are intended to believe it is the same men."

"But why? Why should it not be these people?"

"Because," M. Dupont rejoined, touching his small moustache, "this morning at 7:30 these people were apprehended and are now locked up in the *poste de police* at St. Céleste. Monsieur Papa had the forethought to mark the notes. It was tactfully done. A slight addition to the décor. And the small one gave useful information. The news of the arrest would have appeared in the evening papers but I have forbidden it. The affair was already greatly publicized."

"So our friends," Alleyn suggested, "unaware of the arrest, imitate the performance and hope our reactions will be those of

Monsieur Papa and Madame Maman and that you will turn our attention to St. Céleste."

"But can you be so sure—" Troy began desperately. M. Dupont bent at the waist and gazed respectfully at her. "Ah, Madame," he said, "consider. Consider the facts. At the Château de la Chèvre d'Argent there is a group of persons very highly involved in the drug 'raquette.' By a strange accident your husband already officially interested in these persons, is precipitated into their midst. One, perhaps two of the guests, know who he is. The actress Wells, who is an addict, is sent to make sure. She returns and tell them: 'We entertain, let me inform you, the most distinguished and talented officer of The Scotland Yard. If we do not take some quick steps he will return to enquire for his invalid. It is possible he already suspects.' And it is agreed he must not return. How can he be prevented from doing so? By the apparent kidnapping of his son. This is effected very adroitly. The woman with the bouquet tells the small Ricketts that his mother awaits him at the house she visited this morning. In the meantime a car is on its way from the Château to take them to St. Céleste. He is to be kept in the apartment of Garbel until it comes. The old Blanche takes him there. She omits to lock the doors on to the balcony. He goes out. You see him. He sees you. Blanche observes. He is removed and before you can reach him there the car arrives and he is removed still further."

"Where?"

"If, following the precedent, they go to St. Céleste, they will be halted by our patrols, but I think perhaps they will have thought of that and changed their plans and if so it will not be to St. Céleste."

"I agree," Alleyn said.

"We shall be wiser when their message arrives, as arrive it assuredly will. There is also the matter of this Mademoiselle Garbel whose name is in the books and who has some communication with the Compagnie Chimique des Alpes Maritimes, which may very well be better named the Compagnie pour l'Elaboration de Diacetylmorphine. She is the 'raquette,' no doubt, and you have enquired for her."

"For him. We thought: 'him.'"

"Darling," Alleyn said, "can you remember the letters pretty clearly?"

"No," said poor Troy, "how should I? I only know they were full of dreary information about buses and roads and houses."

"Have you ever checked the relationship?"

"No. He—she—talked about distant cousins who I knew had existed but were nearly all dead."

"Did she ever write about my job?"

"I don't think, directly. I don't think she ever wrote things like 'how awful' or 'how lovely' to be married to a chief detective-inspector. She said things about my showing her letters to my distinguished husband, who would no doubt be interested in their contents."

"And, unmitigated clod that I am, I wasn't. My dear Dupont," Alleyn said, "I've been remarkably stupid. I think this lady has been trying to warn me about the activities of the drug racket in the Paysdoux."

"But I thought," Troy said, "I thought it was beginning to look as if it was she who had taken Ricky. Weren't the flowers a means of getting into our rooms while I was at luncheon? Wasn't the message about being away a blind? Doesn't it took as if she's one of the gang? She knew we were coming here. If she wanted to tell you about the drug racket why did she go away?"

"Why indeed? We don't know why she went away."

"Rory, I don't want to be a horror, but—No," said Troy, "I won't say it."

"I'll say it for you. Why in Heaven's name can't we do something about Ricky instead of sitting here gossiping about Miss Garbel?"

"But, dear Madame," cried M. Dupont, "we *are* doing things about Ricketts. Only—" M. Dupont continued, fortunately mistaking for an agonized sob the snort of hysteria that had escaped Troy—"only by an assemblage of the known facts can we arrive at a rational solution. Moreover, if the former case is to be imitated we shall certainly receive a message and it is important that we are here when it arrives. In the meantime all precautions have been taken. But all!"

"I know," Troy said, "I'm terribly sorry. I know."

"You brought Miss Garbel's last letter, darling. Let's have a look at it."

"I'll get it."

Troy was not very good at keeping things tidy. She had a complicated rummage in her travelling case and handbag before she unearthed the final Garbel letter, which she handed with an anxious look to Alleyn. It was in a crumpled condition and he spread it out on the arm of his chair.

"Here it is," he said, and read aloud.

MY DEAR AGATHA TROY,

I wrote to you on December 17th of last year and hope
that you received my letter and that I may have the pleasure
of hearing from you in the not *too* distant future! I pursue my
usual round of activities. Most of my jaunts take me into the
district lying *west* of Roqueville, a district known as the
Paysdoux (Paysdoux, literally translated, but allowing for
the reversed position of the adjective, means Sweet Country)
though a close acquaintance with some of the inhabitants
might suggest that Pays *Dopes* would be a better title ! ! !
(Forgive the parenthesis and the indifferent and slangy *pun*. I
have never been able to resist an opportunity to play on
words.)

"Hell's boots!" Alleyn said. "Under our very noses! *Pays
Dopes* indeed, District of Dopes and Dope pays." He read on:

As the acquaintances I visit most frequently live some
thirty kilometres (about seventeen miles) away on the western reaches of the Route Maritime I make use of the omnibus, *No. 16,* leaving the Place des Sarrasins at five minutes
past the hour. The fare at the present rate of exchange is
about 1/—English, single, and 1/9 return. I enclose a ticket
which will no doubt be of interest. It is a pleasant drive and
commands a pretty prospect of the Mediterranean on one's
left and on one's right a number of ancient buildings as well
as some evidence of progress, if progress it can be called, in
the presence of a large *chemical* works, in which, owing to
my chosen profession, I have come to take some interest.

"Oh Lord!" Alleyn lamented. "Why didn't I read this before
we left? We have been so bloody superior over this undoubtedly
admirable spinster."

"Please?" said M. Dupont.

"Listen to this, Dupont. Suppose this lady, who is a qualified
chemist, was in the hands of the drug racket. Suppose she
worked for them. Suppose she wanted to let someone in authority in England know what goes on inside the racket. Now. Do

you imagine that there is any reason why she shouldn't write what she knows to this person and put the letter in the post?"

"There is good reason to suppose she might fear to do so, Mr. Chief," rejoined Dupont, who no doubt considered that the time had come for a more familiar mode of address. "As an Englishwoman she is perhaps not quite trusted in the 'raquette.' Her correspondence may be watched. Someone who can read English at the *bureau-de-poste* may be bribed. Perhaps she merely suspects that this may be so. They are thorough, these blackguards. Their net is fine in the mesh."

"So she writes her boring letters and every time she writes, she drops a veiled hint, hoping I may see the letter. The Chèvre d'Argent is about thirty kilometres west on the Route Maritime. She tells us by means of tedious phrases, ferocious puns, and used bus tickets that she is a visitor there. How did she address her letters. Troy?"

"To 'Agatha Troy.' She said in her first letter that she understood that I would prefer to be addressed by my professional name. Like an actress, she added, though not in other respects. With the usual row of ejaculation marks. I don't think she ever used your name. You were always my brilliant and distinguished husband!"

"And is my face red!" said Alleyn. M. Dupont's was puzzled. Alleyn continued reading the letter.

> If ever you and your distinguished husband should visit "these parts"! you may care to take this drive which is full of interesting topographic features that often escape the notion of the *ordinary Tourist*. I fear my own humble account of our local background is a somewhat *Garbelled* (! ! ! !) version and suggest that first-hand observation would be much more rewarding! With kindest regards...

'Really—" Alleyn said, handling the letter back to Troy— "short of cabling: 'Drug barons at work come and catch them' she could scarcely have put it more clearly."

"You didn't read the letters. I only told you about bits of them. I ought to have guessed."

"Well, it's no good blackguarding ourselves. Look here, both of you. Suppose we're on the right track about Miss Garbel. Suppose, for some reason, she's in the racket yet wants to put me wise about it, and has hoped to lure me over here. Why, when

Troy writes and tells her we're coming, does she go away without explanation?"

"And why," Troy interjected, "does she send flowers by someone who used them as a means of kidnapping Ricky and taking him to her flat?"

"The card on the flowers isn't in her writing."

"She might have telephoned the florist."

"Which can be checked," said M. Dupont, "of course. Will you allow me? This, I assume is the bouquet."

He inspected the box of tuberoses. "Ah, yes. Le Pot des Fleurs. May I telephone, Madame?"

While he did so, Troy went out to the balcony and Alleyn, seeing her there, her fingers against her lips in the classic gesture of the anxious woman, joined her and put his arm about her shoulders.

"I'm looking at that other balcony," she said. "It's silly, isn't it? Suppose he came out again. It's like one of those dreams of frustration."

He touched her cheek and she said: "You mustn't be too nice to me."

"Little perisher," Alleyn muttered, "you may depend upon it he's airing his French and saying 'why' with every second breath he draws. Did you know W. S. Gilbert was pinched by bandits when he was a kid?"

"I think I did. Might they have taken him to the Chèvre d'Argent? As a sort of double bluff?"

"I don't think so, my darling. My bet is he's somewhere nearer than that."

"Nearer to Roqueville? Where, Rory, where?"

"It's a guess and an unblushing guess, but—"

M. Dupont came bustling out to the balcony.

"*Alors!*" he began and checked himself. "My dear Monsieur and Madame, we progress a little. Le Pot des Fleurs tells me the flowers were bought and removed by a woman of the servant class, not of the district, who copied the writing on the card from a piece of paper. They do not remember seeing the woman before. We may find she is a maid of the Château, may we not?"

"May we?" said Troy a little desperately.

"But there are better news than these, Madame. The good Raoul Milano has reported to the hotel. It appears that an acquaintance of his, an idle fellow living in the western suburb, has seen a car, a light blue Citroën, at 2:30 P.M. driving out of

Roqueville by the western route. In the car were the driver, a young woman and a small boy dressed in yellow and brown. The man wears a red beret and the woman is bare-headed. The car was impeded for a moment by an omnibus and the acquaintance of Milano heard the small one talking. He spoke in French but childishly and with a little difficulty, using foreign words. He appeared to be making an enquiry. The acquaintance heard him say *'pourquoi'* several times."

"Conclusive," Alleyn said, watching Troy.

She cried out: "Did he seem frightened?"

"Madame, no. It appears that Milano made the same enquiry. The acquaintance said the small one seemed exigent. The actual phrase," M. Dupont said, turning to Alleyn, "was: '*Il semblait être impatient de comprendre quelque chose'!*"

"He was impatient to understand something," Troy ejaculated, "is that it?"

"*Mais oui, Madame,*" said Dupont and added a playful compliment in French to the effect that Troy evidently spoke the language as if she were born to it. Troy failed to understand a word of this and gazed anxiously at him. He continued in English. "Now, between Roqueville and the point where the nearest patrol on the western route is posted there are three deviations: all turning inland. Two are merely rural lanes. The third is a road that leads to a monastery and also—" Here M. Dupont raised his forefinger and looked roguish.

"And also," Alleyn said, "to the Factory of the Maritime Alps Chemical Company."

"*Parfaitement!*" said M. Dupont.

IV

"And you think he's there!" Troy cried out. "But why? Why take him there?"

Alleyn said: "As I see it, and I don't pretend, Lord knows, to see at all clearly, this might be the story. Oberon & Co. have a strong interest in the factory but they don't realize we know it. Baradi and your painting chum Glande were at great pains to deplore the factory: to repudiate the factory as an excrescence in the landscape. But we suspect it probably houses the most impudent manufactory of hyoscine in Europe and we know Oberon's concerned in the traffic. All right. They realize we've seen Ricky on the balcony of Number 16 and have called in the police. If Blanche has succeeded in getting herself out of durance vile she's told them all about it. They've lost their start. They daren't risk taking Ricky to St. Céleste, as they originally planned. What are they to do with him? It would be easy and safe to house him in one of the offices at the factory and have him looked after. You must remember that nobody up at the Château knows that he understand a certain amount of French."

"The people who've got him will have found that out by now."

"And also that his French doesn't go beyond the nursery stage. They may have told him that we've gone back to look after Miss Truebody and have arranged for him to be minded until we are free. I think they may have meant to keep him at Number 16 while we went haring off to St. Céleste. *La Belle Blanche* (damn her eyes) probably rang up and said we'd spotted him on the balcony and they thought up the factory in a hurry."

"Could they depend on our going to St. Céleste? Just on the strength of our probably getting to hear about the other kidnapping?"

"No," said Alleyn and Dupont together.

"Then—I don't understand."

"Madame," said Dupont, "there is no doubt that you shall be directed, if not to a place near St. Céleste, at least to some other place along the eastern route. To some place as far as possible from the true whereabouts of Ricketts."

"Directed?"

"There will be a little note or a little telephone message. Always remember they fashion themselves on the pattern of the former affair, being in ignorance of this morning's arrest."

"It all sounds so terribly like guesswork," Troy said after a moment. "Please, what do we do?"

Alleyn looked at Dupont, whose eyebrows rose portentously. "It is a little difficult," he said. "From the point-of-view of my department, it is a delicate situation. We are not yet ready to bring an accusation against the organization behind the factory. When we are ready, Madame, it will be a very big matter, a matter not only for the department but for the police forces of several nations, for the International Police and for the United Nations Organization itself."

Troy suddenly had a nightmarish vision of Ricky in his lemon shirt and brown shorts abandoned to a labyrinth of departmental corridors.

Watching her, Alleyn said: "So that we mustn't suggest, you see, that we are interested in anything but Ricky."

"Which, God knows, I'm not," said Troy.

"Ah, Madame," Dupont said, "I too am a parent." And to Troy's intense embarrassment he kissed her hand.

"It seems to me," Alleyn said, "that the best way would be for your department, my dear Dupont, to make a great show of watching the eastern route and the country round St. Céleste and for us to make an equally great show of driving in a panic-stricken manner about the countryside. Indeed, it occurs to me that I might very well help matters by ringing up the Château and *registering* panic. What do you think?"

Dupont made a tight purse of his mouth, drew his brows together, looked pretty sharply at Alleyn and then lightly clapped his hands together.

"In effect," he said, "why not?"

Alleyn went to the telephone. "Baradi, I fancy," he said thoughtfully, and after a moment's consideration: "Yes, I think it had better be Baradi."

He dialled the hotel office and gave the number. While he waited he grimaced at Troy: "Celebrated imitation about to begin. You will notice that I have nothing in my mouth."

They could hear the bell ringing, up at the Chèvre d'Argent.

"'*Allo, 'allo!*" Alleyn began in a high voice and broke into a spate of indifferent French. Was that the Chèvre d'Argent? Could he speak to Dr. Baradi? It was extremely urgent. He gave his name. They heard the telephone quack: "*Un moment, Monsieur.*" He grinned at Troy and covered the receiver with his hand. "Let's hope they have to wake him up," he said. "Give me a cigarette, darling."

But before he could light it Baradi had come to the telephone. Alleyn's deep voice was pitched six tones above its normal range and sounded as if it was only just under control. He began speaking in French, corrected himself, apologized and started again in English. "Do forgive me," he said, "for bothering you again. The truth is, we are in trouble here. I know it sounds ridiculous but *has* my small boy by any chance turned up at the Château? Yes. Yes, we've lost him. We thought there might be the chance—there are buses, they say—and we're at our wits' end. No, I was afraid not. It's just that my wife is quite frantic. Yes. Yes, I know. Yes, so we've been told. Yes, I've seen the police but you know what they're like." Alleyn turned towards M. Dupont, who immediately put on a heroic look. "They're the same wherever you go, red-tape and inactivity. Most unsatisfactory." M. Dupont bowed. "Yes, if it's the same blackguards we shall be told what we have to do. No, no, I refuse to take any risks of that sort. Somehow or another I'll raise the money but it won't be easy with the restrictions." Alleyn pressed his lips together. His long fingers blanched as they tightened round the receiver. "Would you really?" he said and the colour of his voice, its diffidence and its hesitancy, so much at variance with the look in his eyes, gave him the uncanny air of a ventriloquist. "Would you really? I say, that's *most* awfully kind of you both. I'll tell my wife. It'll be a great relief to her to know—yes, well I ought to have said something about that, only I'm so damnably worried—I'm afraid we shan't be able to do anything about Miss Truebody until we've found Ricky. I am taking my wife to St. Céleste, if that's where—yes, probably this afternoon if—I don't think we'll feel very like coming back after what's happened, but of course—Is she? Oh, dear! I'm very sorry. That's very good of him. I *am* sorry. Well, if you really don't mind. I'm afraid I'm not much use. Thank you. Yes. Well, goodbye."

He hung up the receiver. His face was white.

"He offers every possible help," he said, "financial and otherwise, and is sure Mr. Oberon will be immeasurably distressed. He has now, no doubt, gone away to enjoy a belly laugh at our expense. It is going to be difficult to keep one's self-control over Messrs. Oberon and Baradi."

"I believe you," said M. Dupont.

"Rory, you're certain now, in your own mind, aren't you?"

"Yes. He didn't utter a word that was inconsistent with genuine concern and helpfulness, but I'm certain in my own mind."

"Why?"

"One gets a sixth sense about that sort of bluff. And I think he made a slip. He said: 'Of course you can do nothing definite until those scoundrels ring you up.'"

M. Dupont cried, "Ahah!"

"But you said to him," Troy objected, "that we would be told what to do."

"'Would be *told* what to do!' Exactly. In the other case the kidnappers' instructions came by letter. Why should Baradi think that this time they would telephone?"

As if in answer, the bedroom telephone buzzed twice.

"This will be it," said Alleyn and took up the receiver.

VII

Sound of Ricky

I

ALLEYN was used to anonymous calls on the telephone. There was a quality of voice that he had learned to recognize as common to them all. Though this new voice spoke in French it held the familiar tang of artifice. He nodded to Dupont, who at once darted out of the room.

The voice said: "M. Allen?"

"C'est Allen qui parle."

"Bien. Écoutez. A sept heures demain soir, presentez-vous à pied et tout seul, vis-à-vis du pavillon de chasse en ruines, il y a sept kilomètres vers le midi du village St. Céleste-des-Alpes. Apportez avec vous cent mille francs en billets de cent. N'avertissez-pas la police, ou le petit apprendra bien les consequences. Compris?"

Alleyn repeated it in stumbling French, as slowly as possible and with as many mistakes as he dared to introduce. He wanted to give Dupont time. The voice grew impatient in correction. Alleyn, however, repeated his instructions for the third time and began to expostulate in English. *"Plus rien à dire,"* said the voice and rang off.

Alleyn turned to Troy. "Did you understand?" he asked.

"I don't know. I think so."

"Well, it's all right, my dearest. It's as we thought. Tomorrow evening outside a village called St. Céleste-des-Alpes with a hundred quid in my hand. The village, no doubt, will be somewhere above St. Céleste."

"You didn't recognize the voice?"

"It wasn't Baradi or Oberon. It wasn't young Herrington. I wouldn't swear it wasn't Carbury Glande, who was croaking with hangover this morning and might have recovered by now. And I would by no means swear that it wasn't Baradi's servant, whom I've only heard utter about six phrases in Egyptian but who certainly understands French. There was a bit of an accent and I didn't think it sounded local."

Dupont tapped and entered. "Any luck?" Alleyn said.

"Of a kind. I rang the *centrale* and was answered by an imbecile but the call has been traced. And to where do you suppose?"

"Number 16, Rue des Violettes?"

"Precisely!"

"Fair enough," Alleyn said. "It must be their town office."

"I also rang the Préfecture. No reports have come in from the patrols. What was the exact telephone message, if you please?"

Alleyn told him in French, wrapping up the threats to Ricky in words that were outside Troy's vocabulary.

"The same formula," Dupont said, "as in the reported version of the former affair. My dear Mr. Chief and Madame, it seems that we should now pursue our hunch."

"To the chemical works?"

"Certainly."

"Thank God!" Troy ejaculated.

"All the same," Alleyn said, "it's tricky. As soon as we get there the gaff is blown. The Château, having been informed that the telephone message went through, will wait for us to go to St. Céleste. When we turn up at the factory, the factory will ring the Château. Tricky! How far away is St. Céleste?"

"About seventy kilometres."

"Is it possible to start off on the eastern route and come around to the factory by a detour? Behind Roqueville?"

M. Dupont frowned. "There are some mountain lanes," he said. "Little more than passages for goats and cattle but of a width that is possible."

"Possible for Raoul who is, I have noticed, a good driver."

"He will tell us, at least. He is beneath."

"Good." Alleyn turned to his wife. "See here, darling. Will you go down and ask Raoul to fill up his tank—*faire plein d'essence* will be all right—and ask him to come back as soon as he's done it. Will you then ask for the manager and tell him we're going to St. Céleste, but would like to leave our heavy luggage here and keep our rooms. Perhaps you should offer to pay a week in advance. Here's some money. I'll bring down a couple of suitcases and join you in the hall. All right?"

"All right. *Voulez-vous*," Troy said anxiously, "*faire plein d'essence et revenez ici*. O.K.?"

"O.K."

When she had gone Alleyn said, "Dupont, I wanted a word with you. You can see what a hellish business this is for me, can't you? I know damn well how important it is not to let our investigation go off like a damp squib. I realize, nobody better, that a premature inquiry at the factory might prejudice a very big coup. I'm here on a job and my job is with the police of your country and my own. In a way it's the most critical assignment I've ever had."

"And for me, also."

"But the boy's my boy and his mother's my wife. It looked perfectly safe to bring them here and they gave me admirable cover, but as things have turned out, I shouldn't have brought them. But for the unfortunate Miss Truebody, of course, it *would* have been all right."

"And she, too, provided admirable cover. An unquestioned entrée."

"Not for long, however. What I'm trying to say is this: I've fogged out a scheme of approach. I realize that in suggesting it I'm influenced by an almost overwhelming anxiety about Ricky. I'll be glad if you tell me at once if you think it impracticable and, from the police angle, unwise."

Dupont said: "M. l'Inspecteur-en-Chef, I understand the difficulty and respect, very much, your delicacy. I shall be honoured to advise."

"Thank you. Here goes, then. It's essential that we arouse no suspicion of our professional interest in the factory. It's highly probable that the key men up there have already been informed from the Château of my real identity. There's a chance, I suppose, that Annabella Wells has kept her promise, but it's a poor chance. After all, if these people don't know who I am why should they kidnap Ricky? All right. We make a show of leaving this hotel and taking the eastern route for St. Céleste. That will satisfy anybody who may be watching us at this end. We take to the hills and double back to the factory. By this time, you, with a suitable complement of officers, are on your way there. I go in and ask for Ricky. I am excitable and agitated. They say he's not there. I insist that I've unimpeachable evidence that he is there. I demand to see the manager. I produce Raoul, who says he took his girl for a drive and saw a car with Ricky in it turn in at the factory gates. They stick to their guns. I make a hell of a row. I tell them I've applied to you. You arrive with a carload of men. You take the manager aside and tell him I am a V.I.P. on holiday."

"Comment? V.I.P.?"

"A very important person. You see it's extremely awkward. That you think the boy's been kidnapped and that it's just possible one of their workmen has been bribed to hide him. You'll say I'll make things very hot for you at the Sûreté if you don't put on a show of searching for Ricky. You produce a *mandat de perquisition*. You are terribly apologetic and very bored with me, but you say that unfortunately you have no alternative. As a matter of form you must search the factory. Now, what does the manager do?"

Dupont's sharp eyebrows were raised to the limit. Beneath them his round eyes stared with glazed impartiality at nothing in particular. His arms were folded. Alleyn waited.

"In effect," Dupont said at last, "he sends his secretary to investigate. The secretary returns with Ricketts and there are a great many apologies. The manager assures me that there will be an exhaustive enquiry and appropriate dismissals."

"What do you say to this?"

"Ah," said Dupont, suddenly lowering his eyebrows and unfolding his arms. "That is more difficult."

"Do I perhaps intervene? Having clasped my son to my bosom and taken him out with his mother to the car, thus giving the manager an opportunity to attempt bribery at a high level, do I not return and take it as matter of course that you consider this an admirable opportunity to pursue your search for the kidnappers?"

Dupont's smile irradiated his face. "It is possible," he said. "It is conceivable."

"Finally, my dear Dupont, can we act along these lines or any other that suggest themselves without arousing the smallest suspicion that we are interested in anything but the recovery of the child?"

"The word of operation is indeed 'act.' From your performance on the telephone, Mr. Chief, I can have no misgivings about your own performance. And for myself"—here Dupont tapped his chest, touched his moustache and gave Alleyn an indescribably roguish glance—"I believe I shall do well enough."

They stood up. Alleyn put his police bag inside a large suitcase. After looking at the chaos within Troy's partly unpacked luggage, he decided on two cases. He also collected their overcoats and Ricky's.

"Shall we about it?" he asked.

"*En avant, alors!*" said Dupont.

II

Mr. Oberon looked down at the figure on the bed. "Quite peaceful," he said. "Isn't it strange?"

"The teeth," Baradi pointed out, "make a great difference."

"There is a certain amount of discolouration."

"Hypostatic staining. The climate."

"Then there is every reason," Mr Oberon observed with satisfaction, "for an immediate funeral."

"Certainly."

"If they have in fact gone off to St. Céleste they cannot return until the day after tomorrow."

"If, on the other hand, this new man at the Préfecture is intelligent, which Allen says is not the case, they may pick up some information."

"Let us—" Mr. Oberon suggested as he absentmindedly rearranged the sprigged locknit nightgown which was pinned down by crossed hands to the rigid bosom—"let us suppose the worst. They recover the child," he raised his hand. "Yes, yes, it is unlikely, but suppose it happens. They call to enquire. They ask to see her."

The two men were silent for a time. "Very well," Baradi said. "So they see her. She will not be a pretty sight, but they see her."

Mr. Oberon was suddenly inspired. "There must be flowers,"

he ejaculated. "Masses and masses of flowers. A nest. A coverlet all of flowers, smelling like incense. Tuberoses," he cried softly clapping his hands together. "They will be entirely appropriate. I shall order them. Tuberoses! And orchids."

III

The eastern route followed the seaboard for three miles out of Roqueville and then turned slightly inland. At this point a country road branched off it to the left. Raoul took the road which mounted into the hills by a series of hairpin bends. They climbed out of soft coastal air and entered a region of mountain freshness. A light breeze passed like a hand through the olive groves and sent spirals of ruddy dust across the road. The seaboard with its fringe of meretricious architecture had dwindled into an incident, while the sea and sky and warm earth widely enlarged themselves.

The road, turning about the contour of the hills, was littered with rock and scarred by wheel tracks. Sometimes it became a ledge traversing the face of sheer cliffs, and in normal times Troy, who disliked heights, would have feared these passages. Now she dreaded them merely because they had to be taken slowly.

"How long," she asked, "will it be, do you suppose?"

"Roqueville's down there a little ahead of us. We'll pass above it in a few minutes. I gather we now cast back into the mountains for about the same distance as we've travelled already and then work round to a junction with the main road to the factory. Sorry about these corners, darling," Alleyn said as they edged round a bend that looked like a take-off into space. "Are you minding it very much?"

"Only because it's slow. Raoul's a good driver, isn't he?"

"Very good indeed. Could you bear it if I told you about this job? I think perhaps I ought to, but it'll be a bit dreary."

"Yes," Troy said. "I'd like that. The drearier the better because I'll have to concentrate."

"Well, you know it's to do with the illicit drug trade, but I don't suppose you know much about the trade itself. By and large it's probably the worst thing apart from war that's happened to human beings in modern times. Before the 1914 war the nation most troubled by the opium racket had begun to do something about it. There was a Shanghai conference and a Hague Convention. Both were cautious tentative shows. None of the nations came to them with a clean record and all the delegates were embarrassed by murky backgrounds in which production, manufacture and distribution involved the revenue both of states and highly placed individuals. Dost thou attend me?"

"Sir," said Troy, "most heedfully."

They exchanged the complacent glance of persons who recognize each other's quotations.

"At the Hague Convention they did get round to making one or two conservative decisions but before they were ratified the war came along and the whole thing lapsed. After the peace the traffic was stepped up most murderously. It's really impossible to exaggerate the scandal of those years. At the top end were nations getting a fat revenue out of the sale of opium and its derivatives. An investigator said at one stage that half Europe was being poisoned to bolster up the domestic policy of Bulgaria. The goings-on were fantastic. Chargés d'affaires smuggled heroin in their diplomatic baggage. Drug barons built works all over Europe. Diacetylmorphine, which is heroin to you, was brewed on the Champs Élysées. Highly qualified chemists were offered princely salaries to work in drug factories and a great number of them fell for it. Many of the smartest and most fashionable people in European society lived on the trade: murderers, if the word has any meaning. At the other end of the stick were the street pedlars, at the foot of Nurse Cavell's statue among other places, and the addicts. The addicts were killing themselves in studies, studios, dressing-rooms, brothels, boudoirs and garrets; young intellectuals and young misfits were ruining themselves by the score. Girls were kept going by their *souteneurs* with shots of the stuff. And so on. Thou attendest not."

"Oh, good sir, I do."

"I pray thee, mark me. At the Peace Conference this revolting baby was handed over to the League of Nations, who appointed an Advisory Committee who began the first determined assault on the thing. The international police came in, various bodies were set up and a bit of real progress was made. Only a bit.

Factories pulled down in Turkey were rebuilt in Bulgaria. Big centralized industries were busted only to reappear like crops of small ulcers in other places. But something was attempted and a certain amount was achieved by 1939."

"Oh, dear! History at it again?"

'More or less. The difference lies in the fact that this time the preliminary work had been done and the machinery for investigation partly set up. But the Second World War did its stuff and everything lapsed. U.N.O. doesn't start from scratch in the way that the League did. But it faces the old situation and it's still up against the Big Boys. The police still catch the sprats at the customs counter and miss the mackerels in high places. The factories have again moved: from Bulgaria into post-war Italy and from post-war Italy, it appears, into the Paysdoux of Southern France. And the Big Boys have moved with them. Particularly Dr. Baradi and Mr. Oberon."

"Are they really big?"

"Not among the tops, perhaps. There we climb into very rarefied altitudes and by as hazardous a road as this one. But Oberon and Baradi are certainly in the mackerel class. Oberon, I regret to tell you, is a British subject at the moment although he began in the Middle East where he ran a quack religion of a dubious sort and got six months for his pains. He came to us by way of Portugal and Egypt. In Portugal he practiced the same game during the war and made his first connection with the dope trade. In Egypt he was stepped up in the racket and made the acquaintance of his chum Baradi. By that time he'd acquired large sums of money. Two fortunes fell into his lap from rich disciples in Lisbon—middle-aged women, who became Daughters of the Sun or something, remade their wills and died shortly afterwards."

"Oh, Lord!"

"You may well say so. Baradi's a different story. Baradi was a really brilliant medical student who trained in Paris and has become one of the leading surgeons of his time. He had some sort of entrée to court circles in Cairo and, thanks to his skill and charms, any number of useful connections in France. *You* may not think him very delicious but it appears that a great many women do. He got in with the Boys in Paris and Egypt and is known to be a trafficker in a big way. It's his money and Oberon's that's behind the Chemical Company of the Maritime

Alps. That's as much as the combined efforts of the international police, the Sûreté and the Yard have gleaned about Baradi and Oberon, and it's on that information I'm meant to act."

"And is Ricky a spanner in the works?"

"He may be a spanner in their works, my pretty. He gives us an excuse for getting into the factory. They may have played into our hands when they took Ricky into the factory."

"*If* they took him there," Troy said under her breath.

"If they drove beyond the turn-off to the factory the patrols would have got them. Of course he may be maddening the monks in the monastery further up."

"Mightn't the car have pushed on and come round by this appalling route?"

"The patrols on the eastern route will get it if it did and there are no fresh tyre tracks."

"It's so strange," Troy said, "to hear you doing your stuff."

Raoul humoured the car down a steep incline and past a pink-washed hovel overhanging the cliff. A peasant stood in the doorway. At Alleyn's suggestion Raoul called to him.

"*Hé* friend! Any other driver come this way today?"

"*Pas un de si bête!*"

"That was: 'no such fool,' wasn't it?" Troy asked.

"It was."

"I couldn't agree more."

They bumped and sidled on for some time without further conversation. Raoul sang. The sky was a deeper blue and the Mediterranean, now almost purple, made unexpected gestures between the tops of hills. Troy and Alleyn each thought privately how much, in spite of the road, they would have enjoyed themselves if Ricky had been with them.

Presently Raoul, speaking slowly out of politeness to Troy, pointed to a valley they were about to enter.

"The Monastery Road. M'sieur—Madame. We descend."

They did so, precipitately. The roofs of the Monastery of Our Lady of Paysdoux appeared, tranquil and modest, folded in a confluence of olive groves. As they came into the lower valley they looked down on an open place where a few cars were parked and where visitors to the cloisters moved in and out of long shadows. The car dived down behind the monastery, turned and ran out into the head of a good sealed road. "The factory," Raoul said, "is round the next bend. Beyond, Monsieur can see the main road and away to the right is the headland with the tunnel that comes out by the Château de la Chèvre d'Argent."

"Is there a place lower down and out of sight of the factory where we can watch the main road on the Roqueville side?"

"Yes, Monsieur. As one approaches the bend."

"Let us stop there for a moment."

"Good, Monsieur."

Raoul's point of observation turned out to be a pleasant one overlooking the sea and commanding a full view of the main road as it came through the hills from Roqueville. He ran the car to the outer margin of their road and stopped. Alleyn looked at his watch. "A quarter past four. The works shut down at five. I hope Dupont's punctual. We'll have a final check. Raoul first, darling, if you don't mind. See how much you can follow and keep your eye on the main road for the police car. *Alors,* Raoul."

Raoul turned to listen. He had taken off his chauffeur's cap, and his head, seen in profile against the Homeric blue of the Mediterranean, took on classic air. Its colour was a modulation of the tawny earth. Grape-like curls clustered behind his small ears, his mouth was fresh, reflected light bloomed on his cheekbones and his eyes held a look of untroubled acceptance. It was a beautiful head, and Troy thought: "When we're out of this nightmare I shall want to paint it."

Alleyn was saying: ". . . so you will remain at first in the car. After a time I may fetch or send for you. If I do you will come into the office and tell a fairy story. It will be to this effect . . ."

Raoul listened impassively, his eyes on the distant road. When Alleyn had done, Raoul made a squaring movement with his shoulders, blew out his cheeks into a mock-truculent grimace and intimated that he was ready for anything.

"Now, darling," Alleyn said, "do you think you can come in with me and keep all thought of our inside information out of your mind? You know only this: Ricky has been kidnapped and Raoul has seen him being driven into the factory. I'm going to have a shot at the general manager, who is called Callard. We don't know much about him. He's a Parisian who worked in the States for a firm that was probably implicated in the racket and he speaks English. Any of the others we may run into may also speak English. We'll assume, whatever we find, that they understand it. So don't say anything to me that they shouldn't hear.

On the other hand, you can with advantage keep up an agitated chorus. I shall speak bad French. We don't know what may develop so we'll have to keep our heads and ride the skids as we meet them. How do you feel about it?"

"Should I be a brave little woman biting on the bullet or should I go in, boots and all, and rave?"

"Rave if you feel like it, my treasure. They'll probably expect it."

"I daresay a Spartan mother would seem more British in their eyes or is that a contradiction in terms? Oh, Rory!" Troy said in a low voice. "It's so grotesque. Here we are half-crazy with anxiety and we have to put on a sort of anxiety act. It's—it's a cruel thing, isn't it?"

"It'll be all right," Alleyn said. "It *is* cruel but it'll be all right. I promise. You'll be as right as a bank whatever you do. Hallo, there's Dupont."

A car had appeared on the main road from Roqueville.

"M. le Commissaire," said Raoul, and flicked his headlamps on and off. The police car, tiny in the distance, winked briefly in response.

"We're off," said Alleyn.

IV

The entrance hall of the factory was impressive. The décor was carried out in obscured glass, chromium and plastic and was beautifully lit. In the centre was a sculptured figure, modern in treatment, suggestive of some beneficent though pinheaded being, who drew strength from the earth itself. Two flights of curved stairs led airily to remote galleries. There was an imposing office on the left. Double doors at the centre back and a series of single doors in the right wall all bore legends in chromium letters. The front wall was plate glass and commanded a fine view of the valley and the sea.

Beyond a curved counter in the outer office a girl sat over a ledger. When she saw Alleyn and Troy she rose and stationed herself behind a chromium notice on the counter: *Renseignements.*

"Monsieur?" asked the girl. "Madame?"

Alleyn, without checking his stride, said: "Don't disarrange yourself, Mademoiselle," and made for the central doors.

The girl raised her voice: "One moment, Monsieur, whom does Monsieur wish to see?"

"M. Callard, le Controleur."

The girl pushed a bell on her desk. Before Alleyn could reach the double doors they opened and a commissionaire came through. Alleyn turned to the desk.

"Monsieur has an appointment?" asked the girl.

"No," Alleyn said, "but it is a matter of extreme urgency. I must see M. Callard, Mademoiselle."

The girl was afraid that M. Callard saw nobody without an appointment. Troy observed that her husband was making his usual impression on the girl, who touched her hair, settled her shoulders and gave him a look.

Troy said in a high voice: "Darling, what's she saying? Has she seen him?"

The girl just glanced at Troy and then opened her eyes at Alleyn. "Perhaps I can be of assistance to Monsieur?" she suggested.

Alleyn leaned over the counter and haltingly asked her if by any chance she had seen a little boy in brown shorts and a yellow shirt. The question seemed to astonish her. She made an incredulous sound and repeated it to the commissionaire, who merely hitched up his shoulders. They had not seen any little boys, she said. Little boys were not permitted on the premises.

Alleyn stumbled about with his French and asked the girl if she spoke English. She said that unfortunately she did not.

"Mademoiselle," Alleyn said to Troy, "doesn't speak English. I think she says M. Callard won't see us. And she says she doesn't know anything about Ricky."

Troy said: "But we know he's here. We must see the manager. Tell her we must."

This time the girl didn't so much as glance at Troy. With a petunia-tipped finger and thumb she removed a particle of mascara from her lashes and discreetly rearranged her figure for Alleyn to admire. She said it was too bad that she couldn't do anything for him. She thought he had better understand this and said that at any other time she might do a lot. She reacted with a facial expression which corresponded, Troy thought, with the "haughty little *moue*" so much admired by Edwardian novelists.

He said: "Mademoiselle, will you have the kindness of an angel? Will you take a little message to M. Callard?" She hesitated and he added in English: "And do you know that there is a large and I believe poisonous spider on your neck?"

She flashed a smile at him. "Monsieur makes a *grivoiserie* at my expense. He says naughty things in English, I believe, 'to pull a carrot at me.'"

"Doesn't speak English," Alleyn said to Troy without moving his eyes from the girl. He took out his pocket-book, wrote a brief message and slid it across the counter with a five hundred franc note underneath. He playfully lifted the girl's hand and closed it over both.

"Well, I must say!" said Troy, and she thought how strange it was that she could be civilized and amused and perhaps a little annoyed at this incident.

With an air that contrived to suggest that Alleyn as well as being a shameless flirt was also a gentleman, the girl moved back from the counter, glanced through the plate-glass windows of the main office where a number of typists and two clerks looked on with undisguised curiosity, seemed to change her mind, and came out by way of a gate at the top of the counter and walked with short steps to the double doors. The commissionaire opened them for her. They looked impassively at each other. She passed through and he followed her.

Alleyn said: "She's taking my note to the boss. It ought to surprise him. By all the rules he should have been rung up and told we're on the road to St. Céleste."

"Will he see us?"

"I don't see how he can refuse."

While they waited, Troy looked at the spidery stairs, the blind doors and the distant galleries. "If he should appear!" she thought. "If there could be another flash of yellow and brown." She began to imagine how it would be when they found Ricky. Would his face be white with smudges under the eyes? Would he cry in the stifled inarticulate fashion that always gripped her heart in a stricture? Would he shout and run to her? Or, by a merciful chance, would he behave like the other boy and want to stay with his terrible new friends? She thought: "It's unlucky to anticipate. He may not be here at all. It may be a false scent. If we don't find him before tonight I think I shall crack up."

She knew Alleyn's mind followed hers as closely as one mind

can follow another, and she knew that as far as one human being can find solace in another she found solace in him, but she suffered, nevertheless, a great loneliness of spirit. She turned to him and saw compassion and anger in his eyes.

"If anything could make me want more to get these gentlemen," he said, "it would be this. We'll get them, Troy."

"Oh, yes," she said. "I expect you will."

"Ricky's here. I know it in my bones. I promise you."

The girl came back through the double doors. She was very formal.

"Monsieur Callard will see Monsieur and Madame," she said. The commissionaire waited on the far side, holding one door open. As Alleyn stood aside for Troy to go through, the girl moved nearer to him. Her back was turned to the commissionaire. Her eyes made a sign of assent.

He murmured: "And I may understand—what, Mademoiselle?"

"What Monsieur pleases," she said, and minced back to the desk.

Alleyn caught Troy up and took her arm in his hand. The commissionaire was several paces ahead. "Either that girl's given me the tip that Ricky's here," Alleyn muttered, "or she's the smartest job off the skids in the Maritime Alps."

"What did she say?"

"Nothing. Just gave the go-ahead signal."

"Good Lord! Or did it mean Ricky?"

"It'd better mean Ricky," Alleyn said grimly.

They were in an inner hall, heavily carpeted and furnished with modern wall-tables and chairs. They passed two doors and were led to a third in the end wall. The commissionaire opened it and went in. They heard a murmur of voices. He returned and asked them to enter.

A woman with blue hair and magnificent poise rose from a typewriter. *"Bon jour, Monsieur et Madame,"* she said. *"Entrez, s'il vous plaît."* She opened another door. *"Monsieur et Madame Alleyn,"* she announced.

"Come right in!" invited a voice in hearty American. "C'm on! Come right in."

V

M. Callard was a fat man with black eyebrows and bluish chops. He was not a particularly evil-looking man: rather one would have said that there was something meretricious about him. His mouth looked as if it had been disciplined by meaningless smiles and his eyes seemed to assume rather than possess an air of concentration. He was handsomely dressed and smelt of expensive cigars. His English was fluent and falsely Americanized with occasional phrases and inflections that made it clear he wasn't speaking his native tongue.

"Well, well, well," he said, pulling himself up from his chair and extending his hand. The other held Alleyn's note. "Very pleased to meet you, Mr.—I just can't quite get the signature."

"Alleyn."

"Mr. Alleyn."

"This is my wife."

"Mrs. Alleyn," said M. Callard, bowing. "Now, let's sit down, shall we, and get acquainted. What's all this I hear about Junior?"

Alleyn said: "I wouldn't have bothered you if we hadn't by chance heard that our small boy who went missing early this afternoon, had, Heaven knows how, turned up at your works. In your office they didn't seem to know anything about him and our French doesn't go very far. It's a great help that your English is so good. Isn't it, darling?" he said to Troy.

"Indeed, yes. M. Callard, I can't tell you how anxious we are. He just disappeared from our hotel. He's only six and it's so dreadful—"

To her horror Troy heard her voice tremble. She was silent.

"Now, that's just too bad," M. Callard said. "And what makes you think he's turned up in this part of the world?"

"By an extraordinary chance," Alleyn said, "the man we've engaged to drive us took his car up this road earlier this afternoon and he saw Ricky in another car with a man and woman. They turned in at the entrance to your works. We don't pretend to understand all this, but you can imagine how relieved we are to know he's all right."

133

M. Callard sat with a half smile on his mouth, looking at Alleyn's left ear. "Well," he said, "I don't pretend to understand it either. Nobody's told me anything. But we'll soon find out."

He bore down with a pale thumb on his desk bell. The blue-haired secretary came in and he spoke to her in French.

"It appears," he said, "that Monsieur and Madame have been given information by their chauffeur that their little boy who has disappeared was seen in an auto somewhere on our premises. Please make full enquiries, Mademoiselle, in all departments."

"At once, Monsieur le Directeur," said the secretary and went out.

M. Callard offered Troy a cigarette and Alleyn a cigar, both of which were refused. He seemed mysteriously to expand. "Maybe," he said, "you folks are not aware there's a gang of kidnappers at work along this territory. Child-kidnappers."

Alleyn at once broke into a not too coherent and angry dissertation on child-kidnappers and the inefficiency of the police. M. Callard listened with an air of indulgence. He had taken a cigar and he rolled it continuously between his thumb and fingers, which were flattish and backed with an unusual amount of hair. This movement was curiously disturbing. But he listened with perfect courtesy to Alleyn and every now and then made sympathetic noises. There was, however, a certain quality in his stillness which Alleyn recognized. M. Callard was listening to him with only part of his attention. With far closer concentration he listened for something outside the room: and for this, Alleyn thought, he listened so far in vain.

The secretary came back alone.

She told M. Callard that in no department of the works nor among the gardens outside had anyone seen a small boy. Troy only understood the tenor of this speech. Alleyn, who had perfectly understood the whole of it, asked to have it translated. M. Callard obliged, the secretary withdrew, and the temper of the interview hardened. Alleyn got up and moved to the desk. His hand rested on the top of a sound system apparatus. Troy found herself looking at the row of switches and the loud-speaker and at the good hand above them.

Alleyn said he was not satisfied with the secretary's report. M. Callard said he was sorry but evidently there had been some mistake. Troy, taking her cue from him, let something of her anxiety and anger escape. M. Callard received her outburst with

odious compassion and said it was quite understandable that she
was not just 100 per cent reasonable. He rose, but before his
thumb could reach the bell-push Alleyn said that he must ask
him to listen to the account given by their chauffeur.

"I'm sure that when you hear the man you will understand
why we are so insistent," Alleyn said. And before Callard could
do anything to stop him he went out leaving Troy to hold, as it
were, the gate open for his return.

Callard made a fat, wholly Latin gesture, and flopped back
into his chair. "My dear lady," he said, "this good man of yours
is just a little difficult. Certainly I'll listen to your chauffeur who
is, no doubt, one of the local peasants. I know how they are
around here. They say what they figure you want them to say
and they don't worry about facts: it's not conscious lying, it's just
that they come that way. They're just naturally obliging. Now,
your husband's French isn't so hot and my guess is, he's got this
guy a little bit wrong. We'll soon find out if I'm correct. Pardon
me if I make a call. This is a busy time with us and right now I'm
snowed under."

Having done his best to make Troy thoroughly uncomfortable he put through a call on his telephone, speaking such rapid
French that she scarcely understood a word of what he said. He
had just hung up the receiver when something clicked. This
sound was followed by a sense of movement and space beyond
the office. M. Callard glanced at the switchboard on his desk
and said: *"Ah?"* A disembodied voice spoke in mid-air.

*"Monsieur le Directeur? Le service de transport avise qu'il est
incapable d'expédier la marchandise."*

"Qu'est ce qu'il se passe?"

"Rue barrée!"

"Bien. Prenez garde. Remettez la marchandise à sa place."

"Bien. Monsieur," said the voice. The box clicked and the
outside world was shut off.

"My, oh my," sighed M. Callard, "the troubles I have!" He
opened a ledger on his desk and ran his flattened forefinger
down the page.

Troy thought distractedly that perhaps he was right about
Raoul and then, catching herself up, remembered that Raoul
had in fact never seen the car drive in at the factory gates with
Ricky and a man and woman in it, that they were bluffing and
that perhaps all Alleyn's and Dupont's theories were awry.

Perhaps this inhuman building had never contained her little son. Perhaps it was idle to torture herself by thinking of him: near at hand yet hopelessly withheld.

M. Callard looked at a platinum mounted wristwatch and then at Troy, and sighed again. "He's trying to shame me out of his office," she thought and she said boldly: "Please don't let me interrupt your work." He glanced at her with a smile from which he seemed to make no effort to exclude the venom.

"My work requires the closest concentration, Madame," said M. Callard.

"Sickening for you," said Troy.

Alleyn came back with Raoul at his heels. Through the door Troy caught a glimpse of the blue-haired secretary, half-risen from her desk, expostulation frozen on her face. Raoul shut the door.

"This is Milano, M. Callard," Alleyn said. "He will tell you what he saw. If I have misunderstood him you will be able to correct me. He doesn't speak English."

Raoul stood before the desk and looked about him with the same air of interest and ease that had irritated Dr. Baradi. His gaze fell for a moment on the sound system apparatus and then moved to M. Callard's face.

"Well, my friend," said M. Callard in rapid French. "What's the tarradiddle Monsieur thinks you've told him?"

"I think Monsieur understood what I told him," Raoul said cheerfully and even more rapidly. "I spoke slowly and what I said, with all respect, was no tarradiddle. With Monsieur's permission I will repeat it. Early this afternoon, I do not know the exact time, I drove my young lady along the road to the factory. I parked my car and we climbed a little way up the hillside opposite the gates. From here we observed a car come up from the main road. In it were a man and a woman and the small son of Madame and Monsieur who is called Riki. This little Monsieur Riki was removed from the car and taken into the factory. That is all, Monsieur le Directeur."

M. Callard's eyelids were half-closed. His cigar rolled to and fro between his fingers and thumb.

"So. You see a little boy and a man and a woman. Let me tell you that early this afternoon a friend of my works-superintendent visited the factory with his wife and boy and that undoubtedly it was this boy whom you saw."

"With respect, what is the make of the car of the friend of Monsieur's works-superintendent?"

"I do not concern myself with the cars of my employees' acquaintances."

"Or with the age and appearance of their children, Monsieur?"

"Precisely."

"This was a light blue Citroën, 1946, Monsieur, and the boy was Riki, the son of Monsieur and Madame, a young gentleman whom I know well. He was not two hundred yards away and was speaking his bizarre French, the French of an English child. His face was as unmistakable," said Raoul, looking full into M. Callard's face, "as Monsieur's own. It was Riki."

M. Callard turned to Alleyn: "How much of all that did you get?" he asked.

Alleyn said: "Not a great deal. When he talks to us he talks slowly. But I'm sure—"

"Pardon me," M. Callard said, and turned smilingly to Raoul.

"My friend," he said, "You are undoubtedly a conscientious man. But I assure you that you are making a mistake. Mistakes can cost a lot of money. On the other hand, they sometimes yield a profit. As much, for the sake of argument, as five thousand francs. Do you follow me?"

"No, Monsieur."

"Are you sure? Perhaps—" suggested M. Callard thrusting his unoccupied hand casually into his breast pocket—"when we are alone I may have an opportunity to make my meaning plainer and more acceptable."

"I regret. I shall still be unable to follow it," Raoul said.

M. Callard drew a large handkerchief from his breast pocket and dabbed his lips with it. *"Sacré nigaud,"* he said pleasantly and shot a venomous glance at Raoul before turning to Troy and Alleyn.

"My dear good people," he said expansively, "I'm afraid this boy has kidded you along quite a bit. He admits that he did not get a good look at the child. He was up on the hillside with a dame and his attention was—well, now," said M. Callard smirking at Troy, "shall we say, kind of semi-detached. It's what I thought. He's told you what he figures you'd like to be told and if you ask him again he'll roll out the same tale all over."

"I'm afraid I don't believe that," said Alleyn.

"I'm afraid you don't have an alternative," said M. Callard. He turned on Raoul. *"Fichez-moi le camp,"* he said toughly.

"What's that?" Alleyn demanded.

"I've told him to get out."

"Vous permettez, Madame, Monsieur?" Raoul asked and placed himself between the two men with his back to M. Callard.

"What?" Alleyn said. He winked at Raoul. Raoul responded with an ineffable grimace. "What? Oh, all right. *All right. Oui. Allez."*

With a bow to Troy and another that was rather less respectful than a nod to M. Callard, Raoul went out. Alleyn walked up to the desk and took up his former position.

"I'm not satisfied," he said.

"That's too bad."

"I must ask you to let me search this building."

"You!" said M. Callard and laughed. "Pardon my mirth but I guess there'd be two of you gone missing if you tried that one. This is quite a building, Mr.—" he glanced again at Alleyn's note—"Mr. Alleyn."

"If it's as big as all that your secretary's enquiries were too brief to be effective. I don't believe any enquiries have been made."

"Look!" M. Callard said, and smacked the top of his desk with a flat palm. "This sound system operates throughout these works. I can speak to every department or all departments together. We don't have to go round on a hiking trip when we make general enquiries. Now!"

"Thank you," Alleyn said and his hand darted over the switchboard. There was a click. *"Ricky!"* he shouted, and Troy cried out: *"Ricky!* Are you there? *Ricky!"*

And as if they had conjured it from the outer reaches of space a small voice said excitedly: "They've come! *Mummy!"*

A protesting outcry was cut off as M. Callard struck at Alleyn's hand with a heavy paper knife. At the same moment M. Dupont walked into the room.

VIII

Ricky Regained

I

Troy could scarcely endure the scene that followed and very nearly lost control of herself. She couldn't understand a word of what was said. Alleyn held her by the arm and kept saying: "In a minute, darling. He'll be here in a minute. He's all right. Hold on. He's all right."

Dupont and Callard were behaving like Frenchmen in English farces. Callard, especially, kept giving shrugs that began in his middle and surged up to his ears. His synthetic Americanisms fell away and when he threw a sentence in English at Troy or at Alleyn he spoke it like a Frenchman. He shouted to Alleyn: "If I lose my temper it is natural. I apologize. I knew nothing. It was the fault of my staff. There will be extensive dismissals. I am the victim of circumstances. I regret that I struck you."

He pounded his desk bell and shouted orders into the sound system. Voices from the other places said in mid-air: "*Immédiatement, M. le Directeur.*" "*Tout de suite, Monsieur.*" "*Parfaitement, M. le Directeur.*" The secretary ran in at a high-heeled double and set up a gabble of protest which was cut short by Dupont. She teetered out again and could be heard yelping down her own sound system.

With one part of her mind Troy thought of the door and how

it must soon open for Ricky and with another part she thought it was unlucky to anticipate this event and that the door would open for the secretary or a stranger and, so complicated were her thoughts, she also wondered if, when she saw Ricky, he would have a blank look of panic in his eyes, or if he would cry or be casually pleased, or if these speculations too were unlucky and he wouldn't come at all.

Stifled and terrified, she turned on Dupont and Callard and cried out: "Please speak English. You both can. Where is he? Why doesn't he come?"

"Madame," said Dupont gently, "he is here."

He had come in as she turned away from the door.

The secretary was behind him. She gave his shoulder a little push and he made a fastidious movement away from her and into the room. Troy knew that if she spoke her voice would shake. She held out her hand.

"Hallo, Rick," Alleyn said. "Sorry we've muddled you about."

"You have, rather," Ricky said. He saw Dupont and Callard. "How do you do," he said. He looked at Troy and his lip trembled. He ran savagely into her arms and fastened himself upon her. His fierce hard little body was rammed against hers, his arms gripped her neck and his face burrowed into it. His heart thumped piston-like at her breast.

"We'll take him out to the car," Alleyn said.

Troy rose, holding Ricky with his legs locked about her waist. Alleyn steadied her and they went out through the secretary's room and the lobby and the entrance hall to where Raoul waited in the sunshine.

II

When they approached the car Ricky released his hold on his mother as abruptly as he had imposed it. She put him down and he walked a little distance from her. He acknowledged Raoul's greeting with an uncertain nod and stood with his back turned to them, apparently looking at M. Dupont's car which was occupied by three policemen.

Alleyn murmured: "He'll get over it all right. Don't worry."

"He thinks we've let him down. He's lost his sense of security."

"We can do something about that. He's puzzled. Give him a moment and then I'll try."

He went over to the police car.

"I suppose," Ricky said to nobody in particular, "Daddy's not going away again."

Troy moved close to him. "No, darling, I don't think so. Not far anyway. He's on a job, though, helping the French police."

"Are those French policemen?"

"Yes. And the man you saw in that place is a French detective."

"As good as Daddy?"

"I don't expect quite as good but good all the same. He helped us find you."

Ricky said: "Why did you let me be got lost?"

"Because," Troy explained with a dryness in her throat, "Daddy didn't know about it. As soon as he knew, it was all right, and you weren't lost any more. We came straight up here and got you."

The three policemen were out of the car and listening ceremoniously to Alleyn. Ricky watched them. Raoul, standing by his own car, whistled a lively air and rolled a cigarette.

"Let's go and sit with Raoul, shall we," Troy suggested, "until Daddy's ready to come home with us?"

Ricky looked miserably at Raoul and away again. "He might be cross of me," he muttered.

"*Raoul* cross with you, darling? *No*. Why?"

"Because—because—I—lost—I lost—"

"No, you didn't!" Troy cried. "We found it. Wait a moment." She rooted in her bag. "Look."

She held out the little silver goat. Ricky's face was transfused with a flush of relief. He took the goat carefully into his square hands. "He's the nicest thing I've ever had," he said. "He shines in the night. *Il s'illume*. Raoul and the lady said he does."

"Has he got a name?"

"His name's Goat," Ricky said.

He walked over to the car. Raoul opened the door and Ricky got into the front seat casually displaying the goat.

"*C'est ça*," Raoul said comfortably. He glanced down at Ricky, nodded three times with an air of sagacity, and lit his cigarette. Ricky shoved one hand in the pocket of his shorts and leaned back. "Coming, Mum?" he asked.

Troy got in beside him. Alleyn called Raoul, who swept off his chauffeur's cap to Troy and excused himself.

"What's going to happen?" Ricky asked.

"I think Daddy's got a job for them. He'll come and tell us in a minute."

"Could we keep Raoul?"

"While we are here I think we can."

"I daresay he wouldn't like to live with us always."

"Well, his family lives here. I expect he likes being with them."

"I do think he's nice, however. Do you?"

"Very," Troy said warmly. "Look, there he goes with the policemen."

M. Dupont had appeared in the factory entrance. He made a crisp signal. Raoul and the three policemen walked across and followed him into the factory. Alleyn came to the car and leaned over the door. He pulled Ricky's forelock and said: "How's the new policeman?" Ricky blinked at him.

"Why?" he asked.

"I think you've helped us to catch up with some bad lots."

"Why?"

"Well, because they thought we'd be so busy looking for you we wouldn't have time for them. But, sucks to them, we didn't lose you and do you know why?"

"Why?"

"Because you waved from the balcony and dropped your silver goat and that was a clue and because you called out to us and we knew you were there. Pretty good."

Ricky was silent.

Troy said: "Jolly good, helping Daddy like that."

Ricky was turned away from her. She could see the charming back of his neck and the curve of his cheek. He hunched his shoulders and tucked in his chin.

"Was the fat, black smelly lady a bad lot?" he asked in a casual tone.

"Not much good," Alleyn said.

"Where is she?"

"Oh, I shut her up. She's a silly old thing, really. Better, shut up."

"Was the other one a bad lot?"

"Which one?"

"The Nanny."

Alleyn and Troy looked at each other over his head.

"The one who fetched you from the hotel?" Alleyn asked.

"Yes, the new Nanny."

"Oh, *that* one. Hadn't she got a red hat or something?"

"She hadn't got a hat. She'd got a moustache."

"Really? Was her dress red perhaps?"

"No. Black with kind of whitey blobs."

"Did you like her?"

"Not extra much. Quite, though. She wasn't bad. I didn't think I had to have a Nan over here."

"Well, you needn't. She was a mistake. We won't have her."

"Anyway, she shouldn't have left me there with the fat lady, should she, Daddy?"

"No." Alleyn reached over the door and took the goat. He held it up admiring it. "Nice, isn't it?" he said. "Did she speak English, that Nanny?"

"Not properly. A bit. The man didn't."

"The driver?"

"'M."

"Was he a chauffeur like Raoul?"

"No. He had funny teeth. Sort of black. Funny sort of driver for a person to have. He didn't have a cap like Raoul or anything. Just a red beret and no coat and he wasn't very clean either. He's Mr. Garbel's driver, only Mr. Garbel's a *Mademoiselle* and not a Mr."

"*Is* he? How d'you know?"

"May I have Goat again, please? Because the Nanny said you were waiting for me in Mademoiselle Garbel's room. Only you weren't. And because Mademoiselle Garbel rang up. The lady in the goat shop has got other people that light themselves at night too. Saints and shepherds and angels and Jesus. Pretty decent."

"I'll have a look next time I'm there. When did Miss Garbel ring up, Rick?"

"When I was in her room. The fat lady told the Nanny. They didn't know about me understanding which was sucks to them."

"What did the fat lady say?"

"'*Mademoiselle Garbel a téléphoné.*' Easy!"

"What did she telephone about, do you know?"

"Me. She said they were to take me away and they told me you would be up here. Only—"

Ricky stopped short and looked wooden. He had turned rather white.

"Only—?" Alleyn said and then after a moment: "Never mind. I think I know. They went away to talk on the telphone and you went out on the balcony. And you saw Mummy and me waving on our balcony and you didn't know quite what was up with everybody. Was it like that?"

"A bit."

"Muddly?"

"A bit," Ricky said tremulously.

"I know. We were muddled too. Then that fat old thing came out and took you away, didn't she?"

Ricky leaned back against his mother. Troy slipped her arm round him and her hand protected his two hands and the silver goat. He looked at his father and his lip trembled.

"It was beastly," he said. "She was beastly." And then in a most desolate voice: "They took me away. I was all by myself for ages in there. They said you'd be up here and you weren't. You weren't here at all." And he burst into a passion of sobs, his tear-drenched face turned in bewilderment to Alleyn. His precocity fell away from him: he was a child who had not long ago been a baby.

"It's all right, old boy," Alleyn said, "it was only a sort of have. They're silly bad lots and we're going to stop their nonsense. We wouldn't have been able to if you hadn't helped."

Troy said: "Daddy *did* come, darling. He'll always come. We both will."

"Well, anyway," Ricky sobbed, "another time you'd jolly well better be a bit quicker."

A whistle at the back of the factory gave three short shrieks. Ricky shuddered, covered his ears and flung himself at Troy.

"I'll have to go in," Alleyn said. He closed his hand on Ricky's shoulder and held it for a moment. "You're safe, Rick," he said, "you're safe as houses."

"O.K.," Ricky said in a stifled voice. He slewed his head around and looked at his father out of the corner of his eyes.

"Do you think in a minute or two you could help us again? Do you think you could come in with me to the hall in there and tell me if you can see that old Nanny and Mr. Garbel's driver?"

"Oh, *nc*, Rory," Troy murmured. "Not now!"

"Well, of course, Rick needn't if he'd hate it, but it'd be helping the police quite a lot."

Ricky had stopped crying. A dry sob shook him but he said: "Would you be there? And Mummy?"

"We'll be there."

Alleyn reached over, picked up Troy's gloves from the floor of the car and put them in his pocket.

"Hi!" Troy said. "What's that for?"

"'To be worn in my beaver and borne in the van,'" he quoted, "or something like that. If Raoul or Dupont or I come out and wave will you and Ricky come in? There'll be a lot of people there, Rick, and I just want you to look at 'em and tell me if you can see that Nanny and the driver. O.K.?"

"O.K.," Ricky said in a small voice.

"Good for you, old boy."

He saw the anxious tenderness in Troy's eyes and added: "Be kind enough, both of you, to look upon me as a tower of dubious strength."

Troy managed to grin at him. "We have every confidence," she said, "in our wonderful police."

"Like hell!" Alleyn said and went back to the factory.

III

He found a sort of comic-opera scene in full swing in the central hall. Employees of all conditions were swarming down the curved stairs and through the doors: men in working overalls, in the white coat of the laboratory, in the black jacket of bureaucracy; women equally varied in attire and age: all of them looking in veiled annoyance at their watches. A loudspeaker bellowed continually:

"'Allo, 'allo, Messieurs et Dames, faites attention, s'il vous plaît. Tous les employés, ayez la bonté de vous rendre immédiatement au grand vestibule. 'Allo, 'allo."

M. Dupont stood in a commanding position on the base of the statue and M. Callard, looking sulky, stood at a little distance below him. A few paces distant, Raoul, composed and god-like in his simplicity, surveyed the milling chorus. The gendarmes were nowhere to be seen.

Alleyn made his way to Dupont, who was obviously in high

fettle and, as actors say, well inside the skin of his part. He addressed Alleyn in English with exactly the right mixture of deference and veiled irritability. Callard listened moodily.

"Ah, Monsieur! You see we make great efforts to clear up this little affair. The entire staff is summoned by Monsieur le Directeur. We question everybody. This fellow of yours is invited to examine the persons. You are invited to bring the little boy, also to examine. Monsieur le Directeur is most anxious to assist. He is immeasurably distressed, is it not, Monsieur le directeur?"

"That's right," said M. Callard without enthusiasm.

Alleyn said with a show of huffiness that he was glad to hear that they recognized their responsibilities. M. Dupont bent down as if to soothe him and he murmured: "Keep going as long as you can. Spin it out."

"To the last thread."

Alleyn made his way to Raoul and was able to mutter: "Ricky describes the driver as a man with black teeth, a red beret, as your friend observed, and no jacket. The woman has a moustache, is bareheaded and wears a black dress with a whitish pattern. If you see a man and woman answering to that description you may announce that they resemble the persons in the car."

Raoul was silent. Alleyn was surpised to see that his face, usually a ready mirror of his emotions, had gone blank. The loud-speaker kept up its persistent demands. The hall was filling rapidly.

"Well, Raoul?"

"Would Monsieur describe again the young woman and the man?"

Alleyn did so. "If there are any such persons present you may pretend to recognize them, but not with positive determination. The general appearance, you may say, is similar. Then we may be obliged to bring Ricky in to see if he identifies them."

Raoul made a singular little noise in his throat. His lips moved. Alleyn saw rather than heard his response.

"Bien, Monsieur," he said.

"M. Dupont will address the staff when they are assembled. He will speak at some length. I shall not be present. He will continue proceedings until I return. Your *soi-distant* identification will then take place. *Au 'voir, Raoul."*

"'Voir, Monsieur."

Alleyn edged through the crowd and round the wall of the room to the double doors. The commissionaire stood near them and eyed him dubiously. Alleyn looked across the sea of heads and caught the notice of M. Dupont, who at once held up his hand. *"Attention!"* he shouted. *"Approchez-vous davantage, je vous en prie."* The crowd closed in on him, and Alleyn, left on the margin, slipped through the doors.

He had at the most fifteen minutes in which to work. The secretary's office was open, but the door into M. Callard's room was, as he had anticipated, locked. It responded to his manipulation and he relocked it behind him. He went to the desk and turned on the general inter-communication switch in the sound system releasing the vague rumour of a not quite silent crowd and the voice of M. Dupont embarked on an elaborate exposé of child-kidnapping on the Mediterranean coast.

Perhaps, Alleyn thought, at this rate he would have a little longer than he had hoped. If he could find a single piece of evidence, enough to ensure the success of a surprise investigation by the French police, he would be satisfied. He looked at the filing cabinet against the walls. The drawers had independent keyholes but the first fifteen were unlocked. He tried them and shoved them back without looking inside. The sixteenth, marked with the letter P, was locked. He got it open. Inside he found a number of the usual folders each headed with its appropriate legend: *Produits chimiques en commande; Peron et Cie; Plastiques,* and so on. He went through the first of these, memorizing one or two names of drugs he had been told to look out for. Peron et Cie was on the suspect list at the Sûreté and a glance at the correspondence showed a close business relationship between the two firms. He flipped over the next six folders and came to the last which was headed: *Particulier à M. Callard. Secret et confidentiel.*

It contained rough notes, memoranda and a number of letters, and Alleyn would have given years of routine plodding for the right to put the least of them into his pocket. He found letters from distributors in New York, Cairo, London, Paris and Istanbul, letters that set out modes of conveyance, suggested suitable contacts, gave details of the methods used by other illicit traders and warnings of leakage. He found a list of the guests at the Chèvre d'Argent with Robin Herrington's name scored under a query beside it.

"*Cette pratique abominable,*" boomed the voice of M. Dupont, warming to its subject, "*cette tache indéracinable sur l'honneur de notre communauté—*"

"Boy," Alleyn muttered in the manner of M. Callard, "you said it."

He laid on the desk a letter from a wholesale firm dealing in cosmetics in Chicago. It suggested quite blandly that *Crème Veloutée* in tubes might be a suitable mode of conveyance for diacetylmorphine and complained that the last consignment of calamine lotion had been tampered with in transit and had proved on opening to contain noting but lotion. It suggested that a certain customs official had set up in business on his own account and had better be dealt with pretty smartly.

Alleyn unshipped from his breast pocket a minute and immensely expensive camera. Groaning to himself he switched on M. Callard's fluorescent lights.

"*—et, Messieurs, Dames,*" thundered the voice of M. Dupont, "*parmi vous, ici, ici, dans cette usine, ce crime dégoûtant a élevé sa tête hideuse.*"

Alleyn took four photographs of the letter, replaced it in the folder in its file, relocked the drawer and stowed away his Lilliputian camera. Then, with an ear to M. Dupont, who had evidently arrived at the point where he could not prolong the cackle but must come to the 'osses, Alleyn made notes, lest he should forget them, of points from the other documents. He returned his notebook to his pocket, switched off the loudspeaker and turned to the door.

He found himself face-to-face with M. Callard.

"And what the hell," M. Callard asked rawly, "do you think you are doing?"

Alleyn took Troy's gloves from his pocket. "My wife left these in your office. I hope you don't mind."

"She did not and I do. I locked this office."

"If you did someone obviously unlocked it. Perhaps your secretary came back for something."

"She did not," said M. Callard punctually. He advanced a step. "Who the hell are you?"

"You know very well who I am. My boy was kidnapped and brought into your premises. You denied it until you were forced to give him up. Your behavior is extremely suspicious, M. Callard, and I shall take the matter up with the appropriate authorities in Paris. I have never," continued Alleyn, who had decided to lose his temper, "heard such damned impudence in my life! I was prepared to give you the benefit of the doubt but in view of your extraordinary behavior I am forced to suspect that you are implicated personally in this business. And in the former affair of child-stealing. Undoubtedly in the former affair."

M. Callard began to shout in French, but Alleyn shouted him down. "You are a child-kidnapper, M. Callard. You speak English like an American. No doubt you have been to America where child-kidnapping is a common racket."

"Sacré nom d'un chien—"

"It's no use talking jargon to me, I don't understand a bloody word of it. Stand aside and let me out."

M. Callard's face was not an expressive one, but Alleyn thought he read incredulity and perhaps relief in it.

"You broke into my office," M. Callard insisted.

"I did nothing of the sort. Why the hell should I? And pray what have you got in your office," Alleyn asked as if on a sudden inspiration, "to make you so damned touchy about it? Ransom money?"

"Imbécile! Sale cochon!"

"Oh, get to hell!" Alleyn said, and advanced upon him. He stood, irresolute, and Alleyn with an expert movement neatly shouldered him aside and went back to the hall.

IV

Dupont saw him come in. Dupont, Alleyn considered, was magnificent. He must have had an appalling job spinning out a short announcement into a fifteen-minute harangue, but he wore the air of an orator in the first flush of his eloquence.

His gaze swept over Alleyn, and round his audience.

"Eh bien, Messieurs, Dames, chacun à sa tâche, Defilez, s'il vous plaît, devant cette statue. . . . Rappelez-vous de mes instructions. Milano!"

He signalled magnificently to Raoul, who stationed himself below him, at the base of the statue. Raoul was pale and stood rigid like a man who faces an ordeal. M. Callard appeared through the double doors and watched with a leaden face.

The gendarmes, who had also reappeared, set about the
crowd in a business-like manner, herding it to one side and then
sending it across in single file in front of Raoul. Alleyn adopted a
consequential air and bustled over to Dupont.

"What's all this, Monsieur?" he asked querulously. "Is it an
identification parade? Why haven't I been informed of the procedure?"

Dupont bent in a placatory manner towards him and Alleyn
muttered: "Enough to justify a search," and then shouted: "I
have a right to know what steps are being taken in this affair."

Dupont spread his blunt hands over Alleyn as if he were
blessing him.

"Calm yourself, Monsieur. Everything arranges itself," he
said magnificently and added in French for the benefit of the
crowd: "The gentleman is naturally overwrought. Proceed, if
you please."

Black-coated senior executive officers and white-coated
chemists advanced, turned and straggled past with dead-pan
faces. They were followed by clerks, assistant stenographers and
laboratory assistants. One or two looked at Raoul, but by far the
greater number kept on without turning their heads. When they
had gone past, the gendarmes directed them to the top of the hall
where they formed up into lines.

Alleyn watched the thinning ranks of those who were yet to
come. At the back, sticking together, were a number of what he
supposed to be the lesser fry: cleaners, van-drivers, workers
from the canteen and porters. In a group of women he caught
sight of one a little taller than the rest. She stood with her back
towards the statue and at first he could see only a mass of bronze
hair with straggling tendrils against the opulent curve of a full
neck. Presently her neighbor gave her a nudge and for a moment
she turned. Alleyn saw the satin skin and liquid eyes of a Murillo
peasant. She had a brilliant mouth and had caught her under-lip
between her teeth. Above her upper lip was a pencilling of hair.

Her face flashed into sight and was at once turned away again
with a movement that thrust up her shoulder. It was clad in a
black material spattered with a whitish-grey pattern.

Behind the girls was a group of four or five men in labourer's
clothes: boiler-men, perhaps, or outside hands. As the girls hung
back, the gendarme in charge of this group sent the men forward. They edged self-consciously past the girls and slouched

towards Raoul. The third was a thick-set fellow wearing a tight-fitting short-sleeved vest and carrying a red beret. He walked hard on the heels of the men in front of him and kept his eyes on the ground. He had two long red scratches on the cheek nearest to Raoul. As he passed by, Alleyn looked at Raoul, who swallowed painfully and muttered: *"Voici le type."*

Dupont raised an eyebrow. The gendarme at the top of the room moved out quietly and stationed himself near the men. The girls came forward one by one and Alleyn still watched Raoul. The girl in the black dress with the whitish-grey pattern advanced, turned and went past with averted head. Raoul was silent.

Alleyn moved close to Dupont. "Keep your eye on that girl, Dupont. I think she's our bird."

"Indeed? Milano has not identified her."

"I think Ricky will."

Watched by the completely silent crowd, Alleyn went out of the hall and, standing in the sunshine, waved to Troy. She and Ricky got out of the car and, hand-in-hand, came towards him.

"Come on, Rick," he said, "let's see if you can find the driver and the Nanny. If you do we'll go and call on the goatshop lady again. What do you say?"

He hoisted his little son across his shoulders and, holding his ankles in either hand, turned him towards the steps.

"Coming, Mum?" Ricky asked.

"Rather! Try and stop me."

"Strike up the band," Alleyn said. "Here comes the Alleyn family on parade."

He heard his son give a doubtful chuckle. A small hand was laid against his cheek. "Good old horse," Ricky said courageously and in an uncertain falsetto: "How many miles to Babylon?"

"Five score and ten," Alleyn and Troy chanted and she linked her arm through his.

They marched up the steps and into the hall.

The crowd was still herded at one end of the great room and had broken into a subdued chattering. One of the gendarmes stood near the man Raoul had identified. Another had moved round behind the crowd to a group of girls. Alleyn saw the back of that startlingly bronze head of hair and the curve of the opulent neck. M. Callard had not moved. M. Dupont had come down from his eminence and Raoul stood by himself behind the statue, looking at his own feet.

"Ah-ha!" cried M. Dupont, advancing with an air of camaraderie, "so here is Ricketts."

He reached up his hand. Ricky stooped uncertainly from his father's shoulders to put his own in it.

"This is Ricky," Alleyn said, "M. Dupont, Ricky, Superintendent of Police in Roqueville. M. Dupont speaks English."

"How do you do, sir," said Ricky in his company voice.

M. Dupont threw a complimentary glance at Troy.

"So we have an assistant," he said. "This is splendid. I leave the formalities to you, M. Alleyn."

"Just have a look at all these people, Rick," Alleyn said, "and tell us if you can find the driver and the Nanny who brought you up here."

Troy and Dupont looked at Ricky. Raoul, behind the statue, continued to look at his boots. Ricky, wearing the blank expression he reserved for strangers, surveyed the crowd. His attention came to halt on the thick-set fellow in the short-sleeved jersey. Dupont and Troy watched him.

"Mum?" said Ricky.

"Hallo?"

Ricky whispered something inaudible and nodded violently.

"Tell Daddy."

Rick stooped his head and breathed noisily into his father's ear.

"O.K.," Alleyn said. "Sure?"

"'M."

"Tell M. Dupont."

"Monsieur, voici le chauffeur."

"Montrez avec le doigt, mon brave," said M. Dupont.

"Point him out, Rick," said Alleyn.

Ricky had been instructed by his French Nanny that it was rude to point. He turned pink in the face and made a rapid gesture, shooting out his finger at the man. The man drew back his upper lip and bared a row of blackened teeth. The first gendarme shoved in beside him. The crowed stirred and shifted.

"Bravo," said M. Dupont.

"Now the Nanny," Alleyn said. "Can you see her?"

There was a long pause. Ricky, looking at the group of girls at the back, said: "There's someone that hasn't turned around."

M. Dupont shouted: *"Présentez-vous de face, tout le monde!"*

The second gendarme pushed through the group of girls. They melted away to either side as if an invisible wedge had been driven through them. The impulse communicated itself to their neighbours: the gap widened and stretched, opening out as Alleyn carried Ricky towards it. Finally Ricky, on his father's shoulders, looked up an exaggerated perspective to where the girl stood with her back to them, her hands clasped across the nape of her neck as if to protect it from a blow. The gendarme took her by the arm, turned her, and held down the hands that now struggled to reach her face. She and Ricky looked at each other.

"Hallo, Teresa," said Ricky.

V

Two cars drove down the Roqueville road. In the first was M. Callard and two policemen and in the second, a blue Citroën, were its owner and a third policeman. The staff of the factory had gone. M. Dupont was busy in M. Callard's office and a fourth gendarme stood, lonely and important, in the empty hall. Troy had taken Ricky, who had begun to be very pleased with himself, to Raoul's car. Alleyn, Raoul and Teresa sat on an ornamental garden seat in the factory grounds. Teresa wept and Raoul gave her cause to do so.

"Infamous girl," Raoul said, "to what sink of depravity have you retired? I think of your perfidy," he went on, "and I spit."

He rose, retired a few paces, spat and returned. "I compare your behaviour," he continued, "to its disadvantage with that of Herod, the Anti-Christ who slit the throats of first-born innocents. Ricky is an innocent and also, Monsieur will correct me if I speak in error, a first-born. He is, moreover, the son of Monsieur, my employer, who, as you observe, can find no words to express his loathing of the fallen woman with whom he finds himself in occupation of this contaminated piece of garden furniture."

"Spare me," Teresa sobbed. "I can explain myself."

Raoul bent down in order to place his exquisite but distorted
face close to hers. "Female ravisher of infants," he apos-
trophized. "Trafficker in unmentionable vices. Associate of per-
verts."

"You insult me," Teresa sobbed. She rallied slightly. "You
also lie like a brigand. The Holy Virgin is my witness."

"She blushes to hear you. Answer me." Raoul shouted and
made a complicated gesture a few inches from her eyes. "Did you
not steal the child? Answer!"

"Where there is no intention, there is no sin," Teresa bawled,
taking her stand on dogma. "I am as pure as the child himself. If
anything, purer. They told me his papa wished me to call for
him."

"Who told you?"

"Monsieur," said Teresa, changing colour.

"Monsieur Goat! Monsieur Filth! In a word, Monsieur
Oberon."

"It is a lie," Teresa repeated but rather vaguely. She turned
her sumptuous and tear-blubbered face to Alleyn. "I appeal to
Monsieur who is an English nobleman and will not spit upon the
good name of a virtuous girl. I throw myself at his feet and
implore him to hear me."

Raoul also turned to Alleyn and spread his hands out in a
gesture of ineffable poignancy.

"If Monsieur pleases," he said, making Alleyn a present of
the whole situation.

"Yes," Alleyn said. "Yes. Well now—"

He looked from one grand-opera countenance to the other.
Teresa gazed at him with nerveless compliance, Raoul with
grandeur and a sort of gloomy sympathy. Alleyn got up and
stood over the girl.

"Now, see here, Teresa," he began. Raoul took a respectful
step backwards. "It appears that you have behaved very
foolishly for a long time and you are a fortunate girl to have
come out of it without involving yourself in disaster."

"Undoubtedly," Teresa said with a hint of complacency, "I
am under the protection of Our Lady of Paysdoux for whom I
have a special devotion."

"Which you atrociously abuse," Raoul remarked to the landscape.

"Be that as it may," Alleyn hurriedly intervened. "It's time
you pulled yourself together and tried to make amends for all the

harm you have done. I think you must know very well that your employer at the Château is a bad man. In your heart you know it, don't you, Teresa?"

Teresa placed her hand on her classic bosom. "In my heart, Monsieur, I am troubled to suffocation in his presence. It is in my soul that I find him impure."

"Well, wherever it is, you are perfectly correct. He is a criminal who is wanted by the police of several countries. He has made fools of many silly girls before you. You're lucky not to be in gaol, Teresa. M. le Commissaire would undoubtedly have locked you up if I had not asked him to give you a chance to redeem yourself."

Teresa opened her mouth and let out an appropriate wail.

"To such deplorable depths have you reduced yourself," said Raoul, who had apparently assumed the maddening role of chorus. "And me!" he pointed out.

"However," Alleyn went on, "we have decided to give you this chance. On condition, Teresa, that you answer truthfully any questions I ask you."

"The Holy Virgin is my witness—" Teresa began.

"There are also other less distinguished witnesses," said Raoul. "In effect, there is the child-thief Georges Martel with whom you conspired and who is probably your paramour."

"It is a lie."

"How," Alleyn asked, "did it come about that you took Ricky from the hotel?"

"I was in Roqueville. I go to the market for the *femme de charge*. At one o'clock following my custom I visited the restaurant of the parents of Raoul, who is killing me with cruelty," Teresa explained, throwing a poignant glance at her fiancé. "There is a message for me to telephone the Château. I do so. I am told to wait as Monsieur wishes to speak to me. I do so. My heart churns in my bosom because that unfortunately is the effect Monsieur has upon it: it is not a pleasurable sensation."

"Tell that one in another place," Raoul advised.

"I swear it. Monsieur instructs me: there is a little boy at the Hotel Royal who is the son of his dear friends, Monsieur and Madame *Alleyn*. He plans with Monsieur *Alleyn* a little trick upon Madame, a drollery, a *blague*. They have *nounou* for the child and while they are here I am to be presented by Monsieur as a *nounou* and I am to receive extra salary."

"More atrocity," said Raoul. "How much?"

"Monsieur did not specify. He said an increase. And he instructs me to go to Le Pot des Fleurs and purchase turberoses. He tells me, spelling it out, the message I am to write. I have learned a little English from the servants of English guests at the Château so I understand. The flowers are from Mademoiselle Garbel who is at present at the Château."

"Is she, by Heaven!" Alleyn ejaculated. "Have you seen her?"

"Often, Monsieur. She is often there."

"What does she look like?"

"Like an Englishwoman. All Englishwomen with the exception, no doubt, of Madame, the wife of Monsieur, have teeth like mares and no *poitrine*. So, also, Mademoiselle Garbel."

"Go on, Teresa."

"In order that the drollery shall succeed, I am to go to the hotel while Madame is at *déjeuner*. I shall have the tuberoses and if without enquiry I can ascertain the apartments of Monsieur and Madame I am to go there. If I am questioned I am to say I am the new *nounou* and go up to the *appartements*. I am to remove the little one by the service stairs. Outside Georges Martel, who is nothing to me, waits in his auto. And from that point Georges will command the proceedings!"

"And that's what you did? No doubt you saw the number of the *appartement* on the luggage in the hall."

"Yes, Monsieur."

"And then?"

"Georges drives us to 16 Rue des Violettes where the concierge tells me she will take the little boy to the *appartement* of Mademoiselle Garbel where his father awaits him. I am to stay in the auto in the back-street with Georges. Presently the concierge returns with the little boy. She says to Georges that the affair is in the water as the parents have seen the boy. She says that the orders are to drive at once to the factory. Georges protests: 'Is it not to St. Céleste?' She says: 'No, at once, quickly to the factory.' The little boy is angry and perhaps frightened and he shouts in French and in English that his papa and mama are not in a factory but in their hotel. But Georges uses blasphemous language and drives quickly away. And Monsieur will, I entreat, believe me when I tell him I regretted then very much everything that had happened. I was afraid. Georges would tell me nothing except to keep my mouth sewn up. So I see that I am involved in wickedness and I say several decades of the rosary and try to make amusements for the little boy who is angry and frightened and weeps for the loss of a statue bought from Marie of the Chèvre d'Argent. I think also of Raoul," said Teresa.

"It's easy to see," Raoul observed, "that in the matter of intelligence you have not invented the explosive." But he was visibly affected, nevertheless. "You should have known at once that it was a lot of *blague* about the *nounou.*"

"And when you got to the factory?" Alleyn asked.

"Georges took the little boy inside. He then returned alone and we drove round to the garages at the back. I tried to run away and when he grasped my arms I inflicted some formidable scratches on his face. But he threw me a smack on the ear and told me Monsieur Oberon would put me under a malediction."

"When he emerges from gaol," Raoul said thoughtfully, "I shall make a meat *pâté* of Georges. He is already fried."

"And then, Teresa?"

"I was frightened again, Monsieur, not of Georges but of what Monsieur Oberon might do to me. And presently the whistle blew and a loud-speaker summoned everybody to the hall. And Georges said we should clear out. He walked a little way and peeped round the corner and came back saying there were gendarmes at the gates and we must conceal ourselves. But one of the gendarmes came into the garage and said we must go into the hall. And when we arrived Georges left me saying: 'Get out, don't hang round my heels.' So I went to some of the girls I knew and when I heard the announcement of Monsieur le Commissaire and saw Raoul and they said Raoul had seen me: Oh, Monsieur, judge of my feelings! Because, say what you will, Raoul is the friend of my heart and if he no longer loves me I am desolate."

"You are as silly as a foot," said Raoul, greatly moved, "but it is true that I love you."

"Ah!" said Teresa simply. *"Quelle extase!"*

"And upon that note," said Alleyn, "we may return to Roqueville and make our plans."

IX

Dinner at Roqueville

I

ON the return journey Alleyn and Troy sat in the back seat with Ricky between them. Teresa, who was to be given a lift to the nearest bus stop, sat in the front by Raoul. She leaned against him in a luxury of reconciliation, every now and then twisting herself sideways in order to gaze into his face. Ricky, who suffered from an emotional hangover and was, therefore, inclined to be querulous and in any case considered Raoul his especial property, looked at these manifestations with distaste.

"Why does she do that?" he asked fretfully. "Isn't she silly? Does Raoul like her?"

"Yes," said Troy, hugging him.

"I bet he doesn't really."

"They are engaged to be married," said Troy, "I think."

"You and Mummy are married, aren't you, Daddy?"

"Yes."

"Well, Mummy doesn't do it."

"True," said Alleyn, who was in good spirits, "but I should like it if she did."

"Ooh, Daddy, you would *not*."

Teresa wound her arm round Raoul's neck.

"Je t'adore!" she crooned.

"Oh, gosh!" said Ricky and shut his eyes.

"All the same," Alleyn said, "we'll have to call a halt to her raptures." He leaned forward. "Raoul, shall we stop for a moment? If Teresa misses her bus you may drive her back from Roqueville."

"Monsieur, may I suggest that we drive direct to Roqueville where, if Monsieur and Madame please, my parents will be enchanted to invite them to an *apéritif* or, if preferred, a glass of good wine, and perhaps an early but well-considered dinner. The afternoon has been fatiguing. Monsieur has not eaten, I think, since morning and Madam and Monsieur Ricky may be glad to dine early. Teresa is, no doubt, not expected at the house of infamy, being, as they will suppose, engaged in the abduction of Ricky and in any case I do not permit her to return."

Teresa made a complicated noise, partly protesting but mostly acquiescent. She essayed to tuck one of Raoul's curls under his cap.

Ricky, with his eyes still shut, said: "Is Raoul asking us to tea, Daddy? May we go? Just us however," he added pointedly.

"We shall all go," Alleyn said, "including Teresa. Unless, Troy darling, you'd rather take Ricky straight to the hotel."

Ricky opened his eyes. "Please not, Mummy. Please let's go with Raoul."

"All right, my mammet. How kind of Raoul."

So Alleyn thanked Raoul and accepted his invitation, and as they had arrived at the only stretch of straight road on their journey Raoul passed his right arm round Teresa and broke into song.

They drove on through an evening drenched in a sunset that dyed their faces and hands crimson and closely resembled the coloured postcards that are sold on the Mediterranean coast. Two police-cars passed them with a great sounding of horns and Alleyn told Troy that M. Dupont had sent for extra men to effect a search of the factory. "It was too good an opening to miss," he said. "He'll certainly find enough evidence to throw a spanner through the plate glass and thanks for the greater part, let's face it, to young Rick."

"What have I done, Daddy?"

"Well, you mustn't buck too much about it but by being a good boy and not making a fuss when you were a bit frightened you've helped us to shut up that factory back there and stop everybody's nonsense."

"Lavish!" said Ricky.

"Not bad. And now you can pipe down for a bit while I talk to Mummy."

Ricky looked thoughtfully at his father, got down from his seat and placed himself between Alleyn's knees. He then aimed a blow with his fist at Alleyn's chest and followed it up with a tackle. Alleyn picked him up. "Pipe down, now," he said, and Ricky, suddenly quiescent, lay against his father and tried to hide his goat from the light in the hope that it would illuminate itself.

"The next thing," Alleyn said to Troy, "is to tackle our acquaintance of this morning. And from this point onwards, my girl, you fade, graciously but inexorabley, *out*. You succour your young, reside in your classy pub, and if your muse grows exigent you go out with Raoul and your young and paint pretty peeps of the bay, glimpsed between sprays of bougainvillea."

"And do we get any pretty peeps of you?"

"I expect to be busyish. Would you rather move on to St. Céleste or back to St. Christophe? Does this place stink for you, after today?"

"I don't think so. We know the real kidnappers are in jug, don't we? And I imagine the last thing Oberon and Co. will try on is another shot at the same game."

"The very last. After tomorrow night," Alleyn said, "I hope they will have no chance of trying anything on except the fruitless contemplation of their past infamies and whatever garments they are allowed to wear in the local lock-up."

"Really? A coup in the offing?"

"With any luck. But see here, Troy, if you're going to feel at all jumpy we'll pack you both off to—well, home, if necessary."

"I don't want to go home," Ricky said from inside Alleyn's jacket. "I think Goat's beginning to illumine himself, Daddy."

"Good. What about Troy?"

"I'd rather stay, Rory. Indeed, if it wasn't for the young, and yet I suppose because of him, I'd rather muck in on the job. I'm getting a first hand look at the criminal classes and it's surprising how uncivilized it makes one feel."

Alleyn glanced at the now hazardously entwined couple in the front seat. He adjusted Ricky and flung an arm round Troy.

"A fat lot they know about it," he muttered.

As the car slipped down the familiar entry into Roqueville he said: "And how would you muck in, may I ask?"

"I might say I wanted to do a portrait of Oberon in the lotus bud position and thus by easy degrees become a Daughter of the Sun."

"Like hell, you might."

"Anyway, let's stay if only to meet Cousin Garbel."

She felt Alleyn's arm harden. Like Teresa, she turned to look at her man.

"Rory," she said, "did you believe Baradi's story about the charades?"

"Did you?"

"I thought I did. I wanted to. Now, I don't think I do."

"Nor do I," Alleyn said.

"*On arrive*," said Raoul, turning into a narrow street. "*Voici L'Escargot Bienvenu.*"

II

It was, as Raoul had said, an unpretentious restaurant. They entered through a *portière* of wooden beads into a white-washed room with fresh window curtains and nine tables. A serving counter ran along one side and on it stood baskets of fresh fruit, of bread and of *langoustes* bedded in water-cress. Bottles of wine and polished glasses filled the shelves behind the counter and an open door led into an inner room where a voice was announcing the weather forecast in French. There were no customers in the restaurant, and Raoul, having drawn out three chairs and seated his guests, placed his arm about Teresa's waist and led her into the inner room.

"Maman! Papa!" he shouted.

An excited babble broke out in the background.

"Come to think of it," Alleyn said, "I'm damned hungry. Raoul told me his papa was particularly good with steak. *Filet mignon?* What do you think?"

"Are we going to be allowed to pay?"

"No. Which means that good or bad we'll have to come back for more. But my bet is, it'll be good."

The hubbub in the background came closer, and Raoul reappeared accompanied by a magnificent Italian father and a plump French mother, both of whom he introduced with cere- mony. Everybody was very polite, Ricky was made much of and a bottle of extremely good sherry was opened. Ricky was given grenadine. Healths were drunk, Teresa giggled modestly in the background. M. Milano made a short but succinct speech in which he said he understood that Monsieur and Madame Ahlaine had been instrumental in saving Teresa from a fate that was worse than death and had thus preserved the honour of both families and made possible an alliance that was the dearest wish of their hearts. It was also, other things being equal, a desirable match from the practical point of view. Teresa and Raoul listened without embarrassment and with the detachment of connoisseurs. M. Milano then begged that he and Madame might be excused as they believed they were to have the great pleasure of serving an early dinner and must therefore make a little preparation with which Teresa would no doubt be pleased to assist. They withdrew. Teresa embraced Raoul with passionate enthusiasm and followed them.

Alleyn said: "Bring a chair, Raoul. We have much to say to each other."

"Monsieur," Raoul said without moving, "no mention has been made of my neglect of duty this afternoon. I mean, Monsieur, my failure, which was deliberate, to identify Teresa."

"I have decided to overlook it. The circumstances were extraordinary."

"That is true, Monsieur. Nevertheless, the incident had the effect of incensing me against Teresa who, foolish as she is, has yet got something which caused me to betray my duty. That is why I spoke a little sharply to Teresa. With results," he added, "that are, as Monsieur may have noticed, not undesirable."

"I have noticed. Sit down, Raoul."

Raoul bowed and sat down. Madame Milano, beaming and business-like, returned with a book in her hands. It was a shabby large book with a carefully mended binding. She laid it on the table in front of Ricky.

"When my son was no larger than this little Monsieur," she said, "it afforded him much amusement."

"*Merci,* Madame," Ricky said, eyeing it.

Troy and Alleyn also thanked her. She made a deprecating face and bustled away. Ricky opened the book. It was a tale of heroic and fabulous adventures enchantingly illustrated with coloured lithographs. Ricky honoured it with the silence he reserved for special occasions. He removed himself and the book

to another table. "Coming, Mum?" he said and Troy joined him.
Alleyn looked at the two dark heads bent together over the book
and for a moment or two he was lost in abstraction. He heard
Raoul catch his breath in a vocal sigh, a sound partly affirmative, partly envious. Alleyn looked at him.

"Monsieur is fortunate," Raoul said simply.

"I believe you," Alleyn muttered. "And now, Raoul, we make
a plan. Earlier today, and I must say it feels more like last week,
you said you were willing to join in an enterprise that may be a
little hazardous: an enterprise that involves an unsolicited visit
to the Chèvre d'Argent on Thursday night."

"I remember, Monsieur."

"Are you still of the same mind?"

"If possible, I feel an increase of enthusiasm."

"Good, now, listen. It is evident that there is a close liaison
between the persons at the Château and those at the factory.
Tonight the commissary will conduct an official search of the
factory and he will find documentary evidence of the collabora-
tion. It is also probable that he will find quantities of illicitly
manufactured heroin. It is not certain whether he will find direct
and conclusive evidence of sufficient weight to warrant an arrest
of Mr. Oberon and Dr. Baradi and their associates. Therefore, it
would be of great assistance if they could be arrested for some
other offense and could be held while further investigations were
made."

"There is no doubt, Monsieur, that their sins are not confined
to contraband."

"I agree."

"They are capable of all."

"Not only capable but culpable! I think," Alleyn said, "that
one of them is a murderer."

Raoul narrowed his eyes. His stained mechanic's hands lying
on the table, flexed and then stretched.

"Monsieur speaks with confidence," he said.

"I ought to," Alleyn said drily, "considering that I saw the
crime."

"You—"

"Through a train window." And Alleyn described the circumstances.

"Bizarre," Raoul commented, summing up the incident.
"And the criminal, Monsieur?"

"Impossible to say. I had the impression of a man or woman in a white gown with a cowl or hood. The right arm was raised and held a weapon. The face was undistinguishable although there was a strong light thrown from the side. The weapon was a knife of some sort."

"The animal," said Raoul, who had settled upon this form of reference for M. Oberon, "displays himself in a white robe."

"Yes."

"And the victim was a woman, Monsieur?"

"A woman. Also, I should say, wearing some loose-fitting garment. One saw only a shape against a window blind and then for a second, against the window itself. The man, if it was a man, had already struck and had withdrawn the weapon which he held aloft. The impression was melodramatic," he added, almost to himself. "Over-dramatic. One might have believed it was a charade."

"A charade, Monsieur?"

"Dr. Baradi offered the information that there were charades last night. It appears that someone played the part of the Queen of Sheba stabbing King Solomon's principal wife. He himself enacted a concubine."

"Obviously he is not merely a satyr but also a perverted being—a distortion of nature. Only such a being could invent such a disgusting lie."

While he grinned at Raoul's scandalized sophistry Alleyn wondered at the ease with which they talked to each other. And, being a modest man, he found himself ashamed. Why, in Heaven's name, he thought, should he not find it good to talk to Raoul, who had an admirable mind and a simple approach? He thought: "We understand so little of our fellow creatures. Somewhere in Raoul there is a limitation but when it comes to the Oberons and Baradis he, probably by virtue of his limitation, is likely to be a much more useful judge than..."

"The Queen of Sheba," Raoul fumed, "is a Biblical personage. She was the *chère amie* of the Lord's anointed. To murder he adds a blasphemy which has not even the merit of being true. Unfortunately he is left-handed," he added in a tone of acute disappointment.

"Exactly! Moreover he offered this information," Alleyn pointed out. "One must remember the circumstances. The scene, real or simulated, reached its climax as the train drew up and stopped. The blind was released as the woman fell against it. And the man, not necessarily Oberon or Baradi, you know, saw other windows—those of the train."

"So knowing Monsieur must have been in the train and awake, since he was to alight at Roqueville, this blasphemer produces his lies."

"It might well be so. M. Dupont and I both incline to think so. Now, you see, don't you, that if murder *was* done in that room in the early hours of this morning, we have great cause to revisit the Château. Not only to arrest a killer but to discover why he killed. Not only to arrest a purveyor of drugs who has caused many deaths but to discover his associates. And not only for these reasons but also to learn, if we can, what happens in the locked room on Thursday nights. For all these reasons, Raoul, it seems imperative that we visit the Château."

"Well, Monsieur."

"Two courses suggest themselves. I may return openly to enquire after the health of Mademoiselle Truebody. If I do this I shall have to admit that Ricky has been found."

"They will have learned as much from the man Callard, Monsieur."

"I am not so sure. This afternoon M. Dupont ordered that all outward calls from the factory should be blocked at central and that the Château should be cut off. At the Château they will be extremely anxious to avoid any sign that they are in touch with the factory. They will, of course, question Teresa, to whom we must give instructions. If I pursue our first course I shall tell the story of the finding of Ricky to Mr. Oberon and his guests and I shall utter many maledictions against Callard as a child-kidnapper. And, having seen Miss Truebody, I must appear to go away and somehow or another remain. I've no idea how this can be done. Perhaps, if one had a colleague within the place one might manage it. The alternative is for me, and you, Raoul, to go secretly to the Château. To do this we would again need a colleague who would admit and conceal us."

Raoul put his head on one side with the air of a collector examining a doubtful treasure. "Monsieur refers, of course, to Teresa," he said.

"I do."

"Teresa," Raoul continued anxiously, "has not displayed herself to advantage this afternoon. She was *bouleversée* and therefore behaved foolishly. Nevertheless, she is normally a girl of spirit. She is also at the present time desirous of reestablishing herself in my heart. Possibly I have been too lenient with her but one inclines to leniency where one's affections are engaged. I have, as Monsieur knows, forbidden her return to this temple of shame. Nevertheless, where the cause is just and with the protection of Our Lady of Paysdoux (about whose patronage Teresa is so unbecomingly cocksure), there can be no sin."

"I take it," Alleyn said, "that you withdraw your objection?"

"Yes, Monsieur. Not without misgivings because Teresa is dear to me and, say what you like, it is no place for one's girl."

"Judging by the lacerations in Georges Martel's face, Teresa is able to defend herself on occasion."

"True," Raoul agreed, cheering up. "She has enterprise."

"Suppose we talk to her about it?"

"I will produce her."

Raoul went out to the kitchen.

"Hallo, you two," Alleyn said.

"Hallo, yourself," Troy said.

"Daddy, this is a lavish book. I can read it better than Mummy."

"Don't buck," Alleyn said automatically.

"Have you sent Raoul to get that nanny-person? Teresa?"

"Yes."

"Why?"

"We've got a job for her."

"*Not* minding me?"

"No, no. Nothing to do with you, old boy."

"Well, good, anyway," said Ricky returning to his book.

Raoul came back with Teresa, who now wore an apron and seemed to be in remarkably high spirits. On Alleyn's invitation she sat down using, however, the very edge of her chair. Alleyn told her briefly what he wanted her to do. Raoul folded his arms and scowled thoughtfully at the tablecloth.

"You see, Teresa," Alleyn said, "these are bad men and also unfortunately extremely clever men. They think they've made a fool of you as they have of a great many other silly girls. The thing is—are you ready to help Raoul and me and the police of your own country to put a stop to their wickedness?"

"Ah, yes, Monsieur," said Teresa cheerfully. "I now perceive my duty and with the help of Raoul and the holy saints, dedicate myself to the cause."

"Good. Do you think you can keep your head and behave

sensibly and with address if an emergency should arise?"

Teresa gazed at him and said that she thought she could.

"Very well. Now, tell me: were you on duty last evening?"

"Yes, Monsieur. During the dinner I helped the housemaids go round the bedrooms and then I worked in the kitchen."

"Was there a party?"

"A party? Well, Monsieur, there was the new guest, Mlle. Wells, who is an actress. And after dinner there was a gathering of all the guests in the private apartments of M. Oberon. I know this because I heard the butler say that Monsieur wished it made ready for a special welcome for Mlle. Wells. And this morning," said Teresa, looking prim, "Jeanne Barre, who is an under-housemaid, said that Mlle. Locke, the English noblewoman, must have taken too much wine because her door was locked with a notice not to disturb and this is always a sign she has been indiscreet."

"I see. Tell me, Teresa: have you ever seen into the room that is only opened on Thursday night?"

"Yes, Monsieur. On Thursday morning I dust this room and on Fridays it is my duty to clean it."

"Where is it exactly?"

"It is down the stairs, three flights, from the vestibule, and beneath the library. It is next to the private apartments of M. Oberon."

"Has it many windows?"

"It has no windows, Monsieur. It is in a very old part of the Château."

"And M. Oberon's rooms?"

"Oh, yes, Monsieur. The salon has a window which is covered always by a white blind with a painting of the sun because Monsieur dislikes a brilliant light, so it is always closed. But Monsieur has nevertheless a great lamp fashioned like the sun and many strange ornaments and a strange wheel which Monsieur treasures and a magnificent bed and in the salon a rich divan," said Teresa, warming to her subject, "and an enormous mirror where—" There she stopped short and blushed.

"Continue," Raoul ordered, with a face of thunder.

"Where once when I took in *petit déjeuner* I saw Monsieur contemplating himself in a state of nature."

Alleyn, with an eye on Raoul, said hurriedly, "Will you

describe the room that you clean?"

Raoul reached across the table and moved his forefinger to and fro in front of his beloved's nose. "Choose your words, my treasure," he urged. "Invent nothing. Accuracy is all."

"Yes, indeed it is," said Alleyn heartily.

Thus warned, Teresa looked self-consciously at her folded hands and with a slightly sanctimonious air began her recital.

"If you please, Monsieur, it is a large room and at first I thought perhaps it was a chapel."

"*A chapel?*" Alleyn exclaimed. Raoul made a composite noise suggestive of angry incredulity.

"Yes, Monsieur. I thought perhaps it was reserved for the private devotions of M. Oberon and his friends. Because at one side is a raised place with a table like the holy altar, covered in a cloth which is woven in a rich pattern with gold and silver and jewels. But although one saw the holy cross, there were other things in the pattern that one does not see in altar cloths."

"The hoof prints of anathema!" Raoul ejaculated.

"Go on, Teresa," said Alleyn.

"And on the table there was something that was also covered with an embroidered cloth."

"What was that, do you suppose?"

Teresa's white eyelids were raised. She gave Alleyn the glance of a cunning child.

"Monsieur must not think badly of me if I tell him I raised the cloth and looked. Because I wanted to see if it was a holy relic."

"And was it?"

"No, Monsieur. At first I thought it was a big monstrance made of glass. Only it was not a monstrance although in shape it resembled a great sun and inside the sun a holy cross broken and a figure like this."

With a sort of disgusted incredulity Alleyn watched her trace with her finger on the table, a pentagram. Raoul groaned heavily.

"And it was, as I saw when I looked more closely, Monsieur, a great lamp because there were many, many electric bulbs behind it and behind the sun at the back was a bigger electric bulb than I have ever seen before. So I dropped the heavy cloth over it and wondered."

"What else did you see?"

"There was nothing else in the room, Monsieur. No chairs or any furniture or anything. The walls were covered with black velvet and there were no pictures."

"Any doors, other than the one leading from Mr. Oberon's room?"

"Yes, Monsieur. There was a door in the wall opposite the table. I didn't notice it the first time I cleaned the room because it is covered like the walls and had no handle. But the second time it was open and I was told to clean the little room beyond."

"What was it like, this room?"

"On the floor there were many black velvet cushions and one large one like the mattress for a divan. And the walls here also were covered in black velvet and there was a black velvet curtain behind which were hanging a great number of white robes such as the robe Monsieur wears and one black velvet robe. And on the table there were many candles in black candlesticks which I had to clean. There was also a door from the passage into this little room."

"Nastier and nastier," Alleyn muttered in English.

"I beg Monsieur's pardon?"

"Nothing. And this was the only other door into the big room?"

"No, Monsieur, there was another, very small like a trap-door behind the table, painted with signs like the signs on the sunlamp and on the floor."

"There were signs on the floor?"

"Yes, Monsieur. I had been told to clean the floor, Monsieur. It is a beautiful floor with a pattern made of many pieces of stone and the pattern is the same as the other." Her finger traced the pentagram again. "And when I came to clean it, Monsieur, I knew the room was not a chapel."

"Why?"

"Because the floor in front of the table was as dirty as a farmyard," said Teresa. "It was like our yard at my home in the Paysdoux. There had been an animal in the room."

"An animal!" Raoul ejaculated. "I believe you! And what sort of animal?"

"That was easy to see," said Teresa simply. "It was a goat."

III

Alleyn decided finally that the following evening he and Raoul would call at the Chèvre d'Argent. He would arrive after the hour of six when, according to Teresa, the entire household would have retired for something known as private meditation, but which was supposed by Teresa to be a sound sleep. It was unusual at this time for anyone to appear, and indeed again, according to Teresa, a rule of silence and solitude was imposed from six until nine by Mr. Oberon. On Thursdays there was no dinner, but Teresa understood that there was a very late supper at which the guests were served by the Egyptian servant only. Teresa herself was dismissed with the other servants as soon as their late afternoon and early evening tasks were executed. If they didn't encounter any member of the household on their way through the tunnel Alleyn and Raoul were to go past the main entrance and down a flight of steps to a little-used door through which Teresa would admit them. No attention would be paid to Raoul if he was seen by any other servants who might still be about, and if Alleyn kept in the background it might be possible to suggest that he was a relative from Marseilles. "A distinguished relative," Raoul amended, "seeing that in appearance and in speech Monsieur is clearly of a superior class."

Teresa would then conceal Alleyn and Raoul in her own room where, with any luck, she would have already secreted two of the white robes. She was pretty certain there were many more in the little ante-room than would be needed by M. Oberon's guests. It would be tolerably easy when she cleaned this room to remove them under cover of the laundry it was her duty to collect from the bedrooms.

"Is it not as I have said, Monsieur?" Raoul remarked, indicated his fiancée. "She is not without enterprise, is Teresa?" Teresa looked modestly at Alleyn and passionately at Raoul.

If all went well, up to this point, Teresa would have done as much as could be expected of her. She would take her departure as usual and could either wait in Raoul's car or catch the evening bus to her home in Paysdoux. It should be possible for Alleyn and Raoul to pass through the house without attracting attention. The cowls of their robes would be drawn over their heads and it might be supposed if they were seen that they were belated guests or even early arrivals for the ceremony. Teresa had heard that occasionally there were extra people on Thursday nights, people staying in Roqueville or in St. Christophe.

And then? "Then," Alleyn said, "it will be up to us, Raoul."

The alternative to this plan was tricky. If he was spotted on his way into the Chèvre d'Argent, Alleyn would put a bold face on it and say that he had come to see Miss Truebody. No doubt Baradi would be summoned from his private meditation and Alleyn would have to act upon the situations as they arose. Raoul would still call on Teresa and hide in her room.

"All right," Alleyn said. "That's as far as we need go. Now Teresa, this evening you will return to the Château and Mr. Oberon will no doubt question you about today's proceedings. You will tell him exactly what happened at the factory, up to and after the identification parade. You will tell him that Ricky identified you. Then, you will say, the police made you come back to Roqueville and asked you many questions, accusing you of complicity in the former kidnapping affair and asking who were your colleagues in that business. You will say that you told the police you know nothing: that Georges Martel offered you a little money to fetch the boy and beyond that you know nothing at all. This is important, Teresa. Repeat it, please."

Teresa folded her hands and repeated it, prompted without necessity by Raoul.

"Excellent," Alleyn said. "And you will, of course, have had no conversation with me. Perhaps it will be well to say, if you are asked, that you returned to Roqueville in Raoul's car. You may have been seen doing so. But you will say that Madame and I were so overjoyed on recovering our son that we had nothing to say except that no doubt the police would deal with you."

"Yes, Monsieur."

"Have courage, my little one," Raoul admonished her. "Lie no more than is necessary, you understand, but when you do lie, lie like a brigand. It is in the cause of the angels."

"Upon whose protection and of that of Our Lady of Paysdoux," Teresa neatly interpolated, "I hurl myself."

"Do so."

Teresa rose and made a convent-child's bob. Raoul also asked to be excused. As they went together to the door, Alleyn said: "By the way, did you hear tomorrow's weather forecast for the district?"

"Yes, Monsieur. It is for thunderstorms. There are electrical disturbances."

"Indeed? How very apropos. Thank you, Raoul."

"Monsieur," said Raoul obligingly and withdrew his beloved into the inner room.

Alleyn rejoined his family. "Did you get much of that?" he asked.

"I've reached exhaustion point for French," Troy said. "I can't even try to listen. And Ricky, as you see, is otherwise engaged."

Ricky looked up from a brilliant picture of two knights engaged in single combat. "I bet there'll be a wallop when they crash," he said. "Whang! I daresay I'd be able to read this pretty soon if we stayed here. I can read a bit, can't I, Mummy?"

"English, you can."

"I know. So don't you daresay I could, French, Daddy?"

"I wouldn't put it past you. Did you know what we were talking about, just now?"

"I wasn't listening much." Ricky lowered his voice to a polite whisper. "If it isn't a rude question," he said, "when's dinner?"

"Soon. Pipe down, now. I want to talk to Mummy."

"O.K. What are you going to do in Teresa's bedroom tomorrow night, Daddy?"

"I must say I should like to be associated with that enquiry," said Troy warmly.

"I am changing there for a party."

"Who's having a party?" Ricky demanded.

"A silver goat. I rather think he lights himself up."

The door opened. Teresa came in with a tray.

IV

The dinner was superb, the *filets mignons* particularly being inspired. When it was finished the Alleyns invited the Milanos to join them for *fines* and M. Milano produced a bottle of distinguished cognac. The atmosphere was gay and *comme il faut*. Presently the regular clientele of the house began to come in:

quiet middle-class people who greeted Madame Milano and took down their own table-napkins from hooks above their special places. A game of draughts was begun at the corner table. Troy, who had enjoyed herself enormously but was in a trance of fatigue, said she thought that they should go. Elaborate leave-takings were begun. Ricky, full of vegetables and rich gravy and sticky with grenadine, yawned happily and bestowed a smile of enchanting sweetness upon Madame Milano.

"Mille remerciements, chère Madame," he said, stumbling a little over the long word, *"de mon beau repas,"* and held out his hand. Madame made a complicated, motherly, bustling movement and ejaculated, *"Ah, mon Dieu, quel amour d'enfant!"* There followed a great shaking of hands and interchange of compliments and the Alleyns took their departure on the crest of the wave.

Raoul drove them back to their hotel where, regrettably, a great fuss was again made over Ricky, who began to show infantile signs of vainglory and struck an attitude before M. Malaquin, the proprietor, shouting: "Kidnappers! Huh! Easy!" and was applauded by the hall porter.

Alleyn said: "That's more than enough from you, my friend," picked his son up and bore him into the lift. Troy followed wearily, saying: "Don't be an ass, Ricky darling." When they got upstairs Ricky, who had been making tentative sounds of defiance, became quiet. When he was ready for bed he turned white and said he wouldn't sleep in "that room." His parents exchanged the look that recognizes a dilemma. Troy muttered: "It *is* trying him a bit high, isn't it?" Alleyn locked the outer door of Ricky's room and took him into the passage to show him that it couldn't be opened. They returned, leaving the door between the two rooms open. Ricky hung back. He had shadows under his eyes and looked exhausted and miserable. "Why can't Daddy go in there?" he asked angrily.

Alleyn thought a moment and then said: "I can of course, and you can be with Mummy."

"Please," Ricky said. "Please."

"Well, I must say that's a bit more civil. Look here, old boy, will you lend me your goat to keep me company? I want to see if it really does light itself up."

"Yes, of course he will," said Troy with an attempt at maternal prompting, "which," she thought, "I should find perfectly maddening if I were Ricky."

Ricky said: "I want to be in here with Mummy and I want Goat to be here too. Please," he added.

"All right," Alleyn said. "You won't see him light himself up, of course, because Mummy will want her lamp on for some time, won't you, darling?"

"For ages and ages," Troy, who desired nothing less, agreed.

Ricky said: "Please take him in there and tell me if he illumines." He fished his silver goat out of the bosom of his yellow shirt. Alleyn took it into the next room, put it on the bedside table, shut the door and turned out the lights.

He sat on the bed staring into the dark and thinking of the events of the long day and of Troy and Ricky, and presently a familiar experience revisited him. He seemed to see himself for the first time, a stranger, a being divorced from experience, a chrysalis from which his spirit had escaped and which it now looked upon, he thought, with astonishment as a soul might look after death at its late housing. He thought: "I suppose Oberon imagines he's got all this sort of thing taped. Raoul and Teresa too, after *their* fashion and belief. But I have never found an answer." The illusion, if it were an illusion and he was never certain about this, could be dismissed, but he held to it still and in a little while he found he was looking at a fluorescence, a glimmer of something, no more than a bat-light. It grew into a shape. It was Ricky's little figurine faithfully illuminating itself in the dark. And Ricky's voice, still rather fretful, brought Alleyn back to himself.

"Daddy!" he was shouting. "Is he doing it? *Daddy!*"

"Yes," Alleyn called, rousing himself, "he's doing it. Come and see. But shut the door after you or you'll spoil it."

There was a pause. A blade of light appeared and widened. He saw Ricky come in, a tiny figure in pyjamas. "Shut the door, Ricky," Alleyn repeated, "and wait a moment. If you come to me, you'll see."

The room was dark again.

"If you'd go on talking, however," Ricky's voice said, very small and polite, "I'd find you."

Alleyn went on talking and Ricky found him. He stood between his father's knees and watched the goat shining. "He honestly is silver," he said. "It's all true." He leaned back against his father, smelling of soap, and laid his relaxed hand on Alleyn's. Alleyn lifted him on to his knee. "I'm fizzily and 'motionly zausted," Ricky said in a drawling voice.

"What in the world does that mean?"

"It's what Mademoiselle says I am when I'm overtired." He yawned cosily. "I'll look at Goat a bit more and then I daresay...." His voice trailed into silence.

Alleyn could hear Troy moving about quietly in the next room. He waited until Ricky was breathing deeply and then put him to bed. The door opened and Troy stood there listening. Alleyn joined her. "He's off," he said and watched while she went to see for herself. They left the door open.

"I don't know whether that was sound child-psychiatry or a barefaced cheat," Alleyn said, "but it's settled his troubles. I don't think he'll be frightened of his bedroom now."

"Suppose he wakes and gets a panic, poor sweet."

"He won't. He'll see his precious goat and go to sleep again. What about you?"

"I'm practically snoring on my feet."

"Fizzily and 'motionly zausted?"

"Did he say that?"

"Queer little bloke that he is, he did. Shall I stay with you, too, until you go to sleep?"

"But—what about you?"

"I'm going up to the factory. Dupont's still there and Raoul's hiring me his car."

"Rory, you can't. You must be dead."

"Not a bit of it. The night's young and it'll be tactful to show up. Besides I've got to make arrangements for tomorrow."

"I don't know how you do it."

"Of course you don't my darling. You're not a cop."

She tried to protest but was so bemused with sleepiness that her voice trailed away as Ricky's had done. By the time Alleyn had washed and found himself an overcoat, Troy too was in bed and fast asleep. He turned off the lights and slipped out of the room.

Left to itself, the little silver goat glowed steadfastly through the night.

X

Thunder in the Air

I

ALLEYN left word at the office that he might be late coming in and said that unless he himself rang up no telephone calls were to be put through to Troy. Anybody who rang was to be asked to leave a message. It was nine o'clock.

The porter opened the doors and Alleyn ran down the steps to Raoul's car. There was another car drawn up beside it, a long and stylish racing model with a G.B. plate. The driver leaned out and said cautiously: "Hallo, sir."

It was Robin Herrington.

"Hullo," Alleyn said.

"I'm on my way back actually, from Douceville. As a matter of fact I was just coming in on the chance of having a word with you," Herrington said rapidly, and in a muted voice. "I'm sorry you're going out. I mean, I don't suppose you could give me five minutes. Sorry not to get out, but as a matter of fact I sort of thought—It wouldn't take long. Perhaps I could drive you to wherever you're going and then I wouldn't waste your time. Sort of."

"Thank you, I've got a car but I'll give you five minutes with pleasure. Shall I join you?"

"Frightfully nice of you, sir. Yes, please do."

Alleyn walked round and climbed in.

"It won't take five minutes," Herrington said nervously and was then silent.

"How," Alleyn asked after waiting for some moments, "is Miss Truebody?" Robin shuffled his feet. "Pretty bad," he said. "She was when I left. Pretty bad, actually."

Alleyn waited again and was suddenly offered a drink. His companion opened a door and a miniature cocktail cabinet lit itself up.

"No, thank you," Alleyn said. "What's up?"

"I will, if you don't mind. A very small one." He gave himself a tot of neat brandy and swallowed half of it. "It's about Ginny," he said.

"Oh!"

"As a matter of fact, I'm rather worried about her, which may sound a bit funny."

"Not very."

"Oh. Well, you see, she's so terrifyingly young, Ginny. She's only nineteen. And, as a matter of fact, I don't think this is a madly appropriate setting for her." Alleyn was silent and after a further pause Robin went on, "I don't know if you've any idea what sort of background Ginny's got. Her people were killed when she was a kid. In the blitz. She was trapped with them and hauled out somehow, which rocked her a good deal at the time and actually hasn't exactly worn off even now. She's rather been nobody's baby. Her guardian's a pretty odd old number. More interested in marmosets and miniatures than children, really. He's her great uncle."

"You don't mean Mr. Penderby Locke?" Alleyn said, recognizing this unusual combination of hobbies.

"Yes, that's right. He's quite famous on his own pitch, I understand, but he couldn't have been less interested in Ginny."

"Then—Miss Taylor is related to Miss Grizel Locke who, I think, is Penderby Locke's sister, isn't she?"

"Is she? I don't know. Yes, I think she must be," Robin said, shooting out the words quickly and hurrying on. "The thing is, Ginny just sort of grew up rather much under her own steam. She was sent to a French family and they weren't much cop, I gather, and then she came back to England and somebody brought her out and she got in with a pretty vivid set and had a miserable love affair with a poor type of chap and felt life wasn't as gay as it's cracked up to be. And this affair busted up when they were staying with some of his chums at Cannes and Ginny felt what was the good of anything anyway, and I must say I know what that's like."

"She arrived at this philosophy in Cannes?"

"Yes. And she met Baradi and Oberon there. And I was there too, as it happened," said Robin with a change of voice. "So we were both asked to come on here. About a fortnight ago."

"I see. And then?"

"Well, it's a dimmish sort of thing to talk about one's hosts, but I don't think it was a particularly good thing, her coming. I mean it's all right for oneself."

"Is it?"

"Well, I don't know. Just to do once and—and perhaps not do again. Quite amusing, really," said Robin miserably. "I mean, I'm not madly zealous about being a Child of the Sun. I just thought it might be fun. Of a sort. I mean, one knows one's way about."

"One would, I should think, need to."

"Ginny doesn't," Robin said.

"No?"

"She thinks she does, poor sweet, but actually she hasn't a clue when it comes to—well, to this sort of party, you know."

"What sort of party?"

Robin pushed his glass back and shut the cupboard with a bang. "You saw, didn't you, sir?"

"I believe Dr. Baradi is a very good surgeon. I only met the others for a few moments, you know."

"Yes, but—well, you know Annabella Wells, don't you? She said so."

"We crossed the Atlantic in the same ship. There were some five hundred other passengers."

"I'd have thought she'd have shown up if there'd been five million," Robin said with feeling. Alleyn glanced at his watch. "I'm sorry, I'm not exactly pressing ahead with this," Robin said.

"Don't you think you'd better tell me what you want me to do?"

"It sounds so odd. Mrs. Alleyn will think it such cheek."

"Troy? How can it concern her?"

"I—well, I was wondering if Mrs. Alleyn would ask Ginny to dinner tomorrow night."

"Why tomorrow night, particularly?"

Robin muttered: "There's going to be a sort of party up there. I'd rather Ginny was out of it."

"Would she be rather out of it?"

"Hell!" Robin shouted. "She would if she were herself. My God, she would!"

"And what exactly," Alleyn asked, "do you mean by that?"

Robin hit the wheel of his car with his clenched fist and said almost inaudibly: "He's got hold of her. Oberon. She thinks he's the bottom when she's not—it's just one of those bloody things."

"Well," Alleyn said, "we'd be delighted if Miss Taylor would dine with us but don't you think she'll find the invitation rather odd? After all, we've scarcely met her. She'll probably refuse."

"I'd thought of that," Robin said eagerly. "I know. But I thought if I could get her to come for a run in the car, I'd suggest we called on Mrs. Alleyn. Ginny liked Mrs. Alleyn awfully. And you, sir, if I may say so. Ginny's interested in art and all that and she was quite thrilled when she knew Mrs. Alleyn was Agatha Troy. So I thought if we might we could call about cocktail time and I'd say I'd got to go somewhere to see about something for the yacht or something and then I could ring up from somewhere and say I'd broken down."

"She would then take a taxi back to the Chèvre d'Argent."

Robin gulped. "Yes, I know," he said. "But—well, I thought perhaps by that time Mrs. Allen might have sort of talked to her and got her to see. Sort of."

"But why doesn't Miss Locke talk to her? Surely, as her aunt—What's the matter?"

Robin had made a violent ejaculation. He mumbled incoherently: "Not that sort. I've told you. They didn't care about Ginny."

Alleyn was silent for a minute.

"I know it's a hell of a lot to ask," Robin said desperately.

"I think it is," Alleyn said, "when you are so obviously leaving most of the facts out of your story."

"I don't know what you mean."

"You are asking us to behave in a difficult and extremely odd manner. You want us, in effect, to kidnap Miss Taylor. We have had," Alleyn said, "our bellyful of kidnapping, this afternoon. I suppose you heard about Ricky."

Robin made an inarticulate noise that sounded rather like a groan. "I know. Yes. We did hear. I'm awfully sorry. It must be terribly worrying."

"And how," Alleyn asked, "did you hear about it?" and would have given a good deal to have had a clear view of Robin's face.

"Well, I—well, we rang up the hotel this afternoon."

"I thought you said you had been to Douceville all the afternoon."

"Hell!"

"I think you must have known much earlier that Ricky was kidnapped, didn't you?"

"Look here, sir, I don't know what to say."

"I'll tell you. If you want me to help you with this child, Ginny, and I believe you do, you will answer, fully and truthfully, specific questions that I shall put to you. If you don't want to answer, we'll say goodnight and forget we had this conversation. But don't lie. I shall know," Alley said mildly, "if you lie."

Robin waited for a moment and then said: "Please go ahead."

"Right. What precisely do you expect to happen at this party?"

A car came down the square. Its headlights shone momentarily on Robin's face. It looked very young and frightened, like the face of a sixth-form boy in serious trouble with his tutor. The car turned and they were in the dark again.

Robin said: "It's a regular thing. They have it on Thursday nights. It's a sort of cult. They call it the Rites of the Children of the Sun in the Outer and Oberon's the sort of high priest. You have to swear not to talk about it. I've sworn. I can't talk. But it ends pretty hectically. And tomorrow Ginny—I've heard them—Ginny's cast for—the leading part."

"And beforehand?"

"Well—it's different from ordinary nights. There's no dinner. We go to our rooms until the Rites begin at eleven. We're meant not to speak to each other or anything."

"Oh, there are drinks. And so on."

"What does 'so on' mean?" Robin was silent. "Do you take drugs? Reefers? Snow?"

"What makes you think that?"

"Come on. Which is it?"

"Reefers mostly. There's food when we smoke. There has to be. I don't know if they are the usual kind. Oberon doesn't smoke. I don't think Baradi does."

"Are they traffickers?"

"I don't know much about them."

"Do you know that much?"

"I should think they might be."

"Have they asked you to take a hand?"

"Look," Robin said, "I'm sorry but I've got to say it. I don't know much about you either, sir. I mean, I don't know that you won't—" He had turned his head and Alleyn knew he was peering at him.

"Inform the police?" Alleyn suggested.

"Well—you might."

"Come: you don't, as you say, know me. Yet you've elected to ask me to rescue this wretched child from the clutches of your friends. You can't have it both ways."

"You don't know," Robin said. "You don't know how tricky it all is. If they thought I'd talked to you!"

"What would they do?"

"Nothing!" Robin cried in a hurry. "Nothing! Only I've accepted, as one says, their hospitality."

"You *have* got your values muddled, haven't you?"

"Have I? I daresay I have."

"Tell me this. Has anything happened recently—I mean within the last twenty-four hours—to precipitate the situation?"

Robin said: "Who are you?"

"My dear chap, I don't need to be a thought-reader to see there's a certain urgency behind all this preamble."

"I suppose not. I'm sorry. I'm afraid I can't answer any more questions. Only—only, for God's sake, sir, will you do something about Ginny?"

"I'll make a bargain with you. I gather that you want to remove the child without giving a previous warning to the house party."

"That's it, sir. Yes."

"All right. *Can* you persuade her, in fact, to drive into Roqueville at six o'clock?"

"I don't know. I was gambling on it. If *he's* not about, I might. She—I think she is quite fond of me," Robin said humbly, "when he's not there to bitch it all up."

"Failing a drive, could you get her to walk down to the car park?"

"I might do that. She wants to buy one of old Marie's silver goats."

"Would it help to tell her we had rung up and asked if she

would choose a set of the figures for Ricky? Aren't there groups of them for Christmas? Cribs?"

"That might work. She'd like to do that."

"All right. Have your car waiting and get her to walk on to the park. Suggest you drive down to our hotel with the figures."

"You know, sir, I believe that'd do it."

"Good. Having got her in the car it's up to you to keep her away from the Château. Take her to see Troy by all means. But I doubt if you'll get her to stay to dinner. You may have to stage a breakdown on a lonely road. I don't know. Use your initiative. Block up the air vent in your petrol cap. One thing more. Baradi, or someone, said something about a uniform of sorts that you all wear on occasion."

"That's right. It's called the mantle of the sun. We wear them about the house and—and always on Thursday nights."

"Is it the white thing Oberon had on this morning?"

"Yes. A sort of glorified monk's affair with a hood."

"Could you bring two of them with you?"

Robin turned his head and peered at Alleyn in astonishment. "I suppose I could."

"Put them in your car during the day."

"I don't see—"

"I'm sure you don't. Two of your own will do, if you have two. You needn't worry about bringing Miss Taylor's gown specifically."

"Hers!" Robin cried out. "Bring hers! But that's the whole thing! Tomorrow night they'll make Ginny wear the Black Robe."

"Then you must bring a black robe," Alleyn said.

II

On Thursday evening the Côte d'Azur, inclined always to the theatrical, became melodramatic and, true to the weather report, staged a thunderstorm.

"It's going to rain," a voice croaked from the balustrade of the Chèvre d'Argent. "Listen! Thunder!"

Far to southward the heavens muttered an affirmative.

Carbury Glande looked at the brilliantly-clad figure perched, knees to chin, on the balustrade. It mingled with a hanging swag of bougainvillea. "One sees a voice rather than a person. You look like some fabulous bird, dear Sati," he said. "If I didn't feel so ghastly I'd like to paint you."

"Rumble, mumble, jumble and clatter," said the other, absorbed in delighted anticipation. "And then the rains. That's the way it goes." She pursed her lips out and, drawing in air with the smoke, took a long puff at an attenuated cigarette.

Baradi walked over to her and removed the cigarette. "Against the rules," he said. "Everything in its appointed time. You're over-excited." He threw the cigarette away and returned to his chair.

A whiteness flickered above the horizon and was followed after a pause by a tinny rattle.

"We do this sort of thing much better at the Comédie Française," Annabella Wells paraphrased, twisting her mouth in self-contempt.

Baradi leaned forward until his nose was placed in surrealistic association with her ear. Beneath the nose his moustache shifted as if it had a life of its own and beneath the moustache his lips pouted and writhed in almost soundless articulation. Annabella Wells's expression did not change. She nodded slightly. His face hung for a moment above her neck and then he leaned back in his chair.

Above the blacked Mediterranean the sky splintered with forked lightning.

"One. Two. Three. Four," the hoarse voice counted to an accompaniment of clapping hands. The other guests ejaculated under a canopy of thunder.

"You always have to count," the voice explained when it could be heard again.

"The thing I really hate," Ginny Taylor said rapidly, "is not the thunder or lightning but the pauses between bouts. Like this one."

"Come indoors," Robin Herrington said. "You don't have to stay out here."

"It's a kind of dare I have with myself."

"Learning to be brave?" Annabella Wells asked with a curious inflexion in her voice.

"Ginny will have the courage of a lioness," said Baradi, "and the fire of a phoenix."

Annabella got up with an abrupt expert movement and walked over to the balustrade. Baradi followed her. Ginny pushed her hair back from her forehead and looked quickly at Robin and away again. He moved nearer to her. She turned away to the far end of the roof-garden. Robin hovered uncertainly. The other four guests had drawn closer together. Carbury Glande half-closed his eyes and peered at the cloud-blocked sky and dismal sea. "Gloriously ominous," he said, "and quite unpaintable. Which is such a good thing."

The pause was not really one of silence. It was dramatized by minor noises, themselves uncannily portentous. Mr. Oberon's canary, for instance, hopped scratchily from cage-floor to perch and back again. A cicada had forgotten to stop chirruping in the motionless cactus slopes that Mr. Oberon called his *jardin exotique*. Down in the servants' quarters a woman laughed, and many kilometres away, towards Douceville, a train shrieked effeminately. Still, beside the threat of thunder, these desultory sounds added up to silence.

Glande, with an eye on Ginny, muttered: "I damned well think we need something. After all—" He swallowed. "After everything. It's nervy work waiting." His voice shot up into falsetto. "I don't pretend to be phlegmatic. I'm a bloody artist, I am."

Baradi said: "Keep your voice down. You certainly have a flair for the appropriate adjective," and laughed softly.

Glande fingered his lips and stared at Baradi. "How you can!" he whispered.

Annabella, looking out to sea, said: "Keep your hand to the plough, Carbury dear. You've put it there. No looking back."

"*I'm* on your side," announced the voice from the balustrade. "Look what I am doing for you all."

From her remote station Ginny said: "I can't stand this."

"Well, don't," Robin said quietly. "Old Marie asked me to tell you there's only one of the big silver goats left. Why not dodge down before the rain and get it? In the passage you won't see if there's lightning. Come on."

Ginny looked at Baradi. He caught her glance and walked across to her. "What is it?" he said.

"I thought I might go to old Marie's shop," Ginny said. "It's away from the storm."

"Why not?" he said. "What a good idea."

"I thought I might," Ginny repeated doubtfully.

For a split second lightning wrote itself across the sky in livid calligraphy. The voice on the balustrade had counted two when the heavens crashed together in a monstrous report. Ginny's mouth was wide open. She ran into the tower and Robin followed her.

The initial clap was succeeded by a prolonged rattle and an ambiguous omnipotent muttering. Above this rumpus Glande could be heard saying: "What I mean to say: do we know we can trust them? After all, they're comparative strangers and I must say I don't like the boy's manner."

Baradi, who was watching Annabella Wells, said: "There's no need to disturb yourself on their account. Robin is much too heavily involved and as for Ginny, can we not leave her safely to Ra? In any case, she knows nothing."

"The boy does. He might blurt out something to those other two—Troy and her bloody high-hat husband."

"If Mr. and Mrs. Allen should arrive there need be no meeting."

"How do you know they don't suspect something already?"

"I have told you. The girl Teresa reports that having recovered the boy, they have retired to their hotel in high glee."

"There was a bungle over the kid. There might be another bungle. Suppose Allen hangs about like he did last time asking damn-fool esoteric questions?"

"They were not as silly as you think, my dear Carbury. The man is an intelligent man. He behaved intelligently during the operation. He would make a good anaesthetist."

"Well—there you are!"

"Please don't panic. He is both intelligent and inquisitive. That is why we thought it better to remove him, if possible, to St. Céleste, until the Truebody has been disposed of." Baradi's teeth gleamed under his moustache.

"I can see no cause for amusement."

"Can you not? You must cultivate a taste for irony. Annabella," Baradi continued, looking at her motionless figure against the steel-dark sky, "Annabella tells us that Mr. Allen, as far as she knows, is the person he appears to be: a dilettante with a taste for mysticism, curious literature and big-game hunting. The latter, I may add, in the generally accepted sense of the expression."

"Oh, for God's sake!" Glande cried out. The voice from the

balustrade broke into undisciplined laughter. "Shut up!" he shouted. "Shut up, Sati! You of all people to laugh. It's so damned undignified. Remember who you are!"

"Yes, Grizel dear," Annabella Wells said, "pray do remember that."

It had grown so dark that the lightning darted white on their faces. They saw one another momentarily as if by a flash-lamp, each wearing a look of fixity. The thunder-clap followed at once. One might have imagined the heavens had burst outward like a gas-filled cylinder.

Mr. Oberon, wearing his hooded gown, stepped out of the tower door and contemplated his followers.

"*Cher maître*," shouted Baradi, waving his hand, "you come most carefully upon your hour. What an entrance! Superb!"

The volley rolled away into silence. Mr. Oberon moved forward and, really as if he had induced it, rain struck down in an abrupt deluge.

"You will get wet, dear Sati," said Mr. Oberon.

Glande said: "What's happened?"

They all drew near to Mr. Oberon. The rain made a frightful din, pelting like bullets on water and earth and stone and on the canvas awning above their heads. Landscape and seascape were alive with its noise. The four guests, with the anxious air of people who are hard-of-hearing, inclined their heads towards their host.

"What's happened?" Glande repeated, but with a subdued and more deferential manner.

"All is well. It is arranged for tomorrow afternoon. An Anglican ceremony," said Oberon, smiling slightly. "I have spoken to the—should I call him priest? I was obliged to call on him. The telephone is still out of order. He is a dull man but very obliging. A private funeral, of course."

"But the other business—the permit or whatever it is?"

"I've already explained," Baradi cut in irritably, "that my authority as a medical man is perfectly adequate. The appropriate official will be happy to receive me tomorrow when the necessary formalities will be completed."

"Poor old Truebody," said Annabella Wells.

"The name is, by the way, to be Halebory. Pronounced Harber. So English."

"They'll want to see the passport," Glande said instantly.

"They shall see it. It has received expert attention."

"Sati," said Mr. Oberon gently, "you have been smoking, I think."

"Dearest Ra, only the least puff."

"Yet, there is our rule. Not until tonight."

"I was upset. It's so difficult. Please forgive me. Please."

Mr. Oberon looked blankly at her. "You will go to your room and make an exercise. The exercise of the Name. You will light your candle and looking at the flame without blinking you will repeat one hundred times: 'I am Sati who am Grizel Locke!' Then you will remain without moving until it is time for the Rites. So."

She touched her forehead and lips and chest with a jerky movement of her hand and went at once.

"Where is Ginny?" Mr. Oberon asked.

"She was nervous," said Baradi. "The storm upset her. She went down to the shop where one buys those rather vulgar figurines."

"And Robin?"

"He went with her," said Annabella loudly.

Mr. Oberon's mouth parted to show his teeth. "She must rest," he said. "You are, of course, all very careful to say nothing of an agitating nature in front of her. She knows the lady has died as the result of a perforated appendix. Unfortunately it was unavoidable that she should be told so much. There must be no further disturbance. When she returns send her to her room. It is the time of meditation. She is to remain in her room until it is time for the Rites. There she will find the gift of enlightenment."

He moved to the tower door. The rain drummed on the awning above their heads but they heard him repeat: "She must rest," before he went indoors.

III

Old Marie's shop was a cave sunk in the face of the hill and protected at its open end by the Chèvre d'Argent, which at this point straddled the passage. Ginny and Robin were thus hidden from the lightning and even the thunder sounded less formidable in there. The walls of the cave had been hewn out in shelves and

on these stood Marie's figurines. She herself sat at a table over
an oil lamp and wheezed out praises of her wares.

"She's got lots of goats," Ginny pointed out, speaking English.

"Cunning old cup-of-tea," Robin said. "Thought you needed
gingering up, I suppose. By the way," he added, "Miss Troy or
Mrs. Allen or whatever she should be called, wanted a set of
nativity figures—don't you call it a crib?—for the little boy.
Marie wasn't here when they left yesterday. I promised I'd get
one and take it down this afternoon. How awful! I entirely
forgot."

"Robin! How could you! And they'll want it more than ever
after losing him like that."

"She thought perhaps you wouldn't mind choosing one."

"Of course I will," Ginny said, and began to inspect the
groups of naïve little figures.

Old Marie shouted: "Look, Mademoiselle, the Holy Child
illuminates himself. And the beasts! One would say the she-ass
almost burst herself with good milk. And the lamb is infinitely
touching. And the ridiculous price! I cannot bring myself to
charge more. It is an act of piety on my part."

Robin bought a large silver goat and Ginny bought the
grandest of the cribs. "Let's take it down now," he said. "The
storm's nearly over, I'm sure, and the car's out. It'd save my
conscience. Do come, Ginny."

She raised her troubled face and looked at him. "I don't
know," she said, "I suppose—I don't know."

"We shan't be half-an-hour. Come on."

He took her by the arm and hurried her into the passage-way.
They ran into a world of rain, Ginny protesting and Robin
shouting encouragement. With the help of his stick he broke into
quite a lively sort of canter. "Do be careful!" Ginny cried. "Your
dot-and-go-one leg!"

"Dot-and-go-run, you mean. Come on."

Their faces streamed with cool water and they laughed without cause.

"It's better out here," Robin said. "Isn't it, Ginny?"

The car stood out on the platform like a rock in a waterfall.
He bundled her into it. "You look like—you look as you're
meant to look," he said. "It's better outside. Say it's better,
Ginny."

"I don't know what's come over you," Ginny said, pressing her hands to her rain-blinded face.

"I've got out. We've both got out." He scrambled in beside her and peered into the trough behind the driver's seat. "What are you doing?" Ginny asked hysterically. "What's happened? We've gone mad. What are you looking for?"

"Nothing. A parcel for my tailor. It's gone. Who cares! Away we go."

He started up his engine. Water splashed up like wings on either side and cascaded across the windscreen. They roared down the steep incline and turned left above the tunnel and over the high headland, on the road to Roqueville.

High up in the hills on their vantage point in the factory road, Alleyn and Raoul waited in Raoul's car.

"In five minutes," Alleyn said, "it will be dark."

"I shall still know the car, Monsieur."

"And I. The rain's lifting a little."

"It will stop before the light goes, I think."

"How tall are you, Raoul?"

"One mètre, sixty, Monsieur."

"About five foot eight," Alleyn muttered, "and the girl's tall. It ought to be all right. Where was the car exactly?"

"Standing out on the platform, Monsieur. The parcel was in the trough behind the driver's seat."

"He's stuck to his word so far, at least. Where did you put the note?"

"On the driver's seat, Monsieur. He could not fail to see it."

But Robin, driving in a state of strange exhilaration towards Roqueville, sat on the disregarded note and wondered if it was by accident or intention that Ginny leaned a little towards him.

"It will be fine on the other side of the hill," he shouted. "What do you bet?"

"It couldn't be."

"You'll see. You'll see. You'll jolly well see."

"Robin, what *has* come over you?"

"I'll tell you when we get to Roqueville. There you are! What did I say?"

They drove down the mountain-side into a translucent dusk, rain-washed and fragrant.

"There they go," Alleyn said and turned his field glasses on the tiny car. "She's with him. He's brought it off. So far."

"And now, Monsieur?"

Alleyn watched the car diminish. Just before it turned the point of a distant headland, Robin switched on his lamps. Alleyn lowered the glasses. "It is almost lighting-up time, Raoul. We wait a little longer. They turned as if by a shared consent and looked to the west where, above and beyond the tunnelled hill, the turrets of the Chèvre d'Argent stood black against a darkling sky.

Presently, out on Cap St. Gilles pricks of yellow began to appear. The window of a cottage in the valley showed red. Behind them the factory presented a dark front to the dusk, but higher up in its folded hills the monastery of Our Lady of Paysdoux was alive with glowing lights.

"They are late with their lamps at the Chèvre d'Argent," said Raoul.

"Which is not surprising," Alleyn rejoined. "Seeing that Monsieur le Commissaire has arranged that their electrical service is disconnected. The thunderstorm will have lent a happy note of credibility to the occurrence. The telephone also is still disconnected." He used his field glasses. "Yes," he said, "they are lighting candles. Start up your engine, Raoul. It is time to be off."

IV

"You disturb yourself without cause," Baradi said. "She is buying herself a silver goat. Why not? It is a good omen."

"Already she's been away half-an-hour."

"She had gone for a walk, no doubt."

"With him."

"Again, why not? The infatuation is entirely on one side. Let it alone."

"I am unusually interested and therefore nervous," said Mr. Oberon. "It means more to me, this time, than ever before and besides the whole circumstance is extraordinary. The mystic association. The blood-sacrifice and then, while the victim is still here, the other, the living sacrifice. It is unique."

Baradi looked at him with curiosity. "Tell me," he said, "how much of all this"—he made a comprehensive gesture—"means anything to you? I mean I can understand the, what shall I call it, the factual pleasure. That is a great deal. I envy you your flair. But the esoteric window-dressing—is it possible that for you—?" He paused. Mr. Oberon's face was as empty as a mask. He touched his lips with the tip of his tongue.

He said: "Wherein, if not in my belief, do you suppose the secret of my flair is to be found? I am what I am and I go back to beyond the dawn. I was the King of the Wood."

Baradi examined his own shapely hands. "Ah, yes?" he said politely. "A fascinating theory."

"You think me a poseur?"

"No, no. On the contrary. It is only as a practical man I am concerned with the hazards of the situation. You, I gather, though you have every cause, are not at all anxious on that account? The Truebody situation, I mean?"

"I find it immeasurably stimulating."

"Indeed," said Baradi drily.

"Only the absence of the girl disturbs me. It is almost dark. Turn on the light."

Baradi reached out his hand to the switch. There was a click.

"No lights, it seems," he said and opened the door. "No lights anywhere. There must be a fuse."

"How can she be walking in the dark? And with a cripple like Robin? It is preposterous."

"The British do these things."

"I am British. I have my passport. Telephone the bureau in Roqueville."

"The telephone is still out of order."

"We must have light."

"It may be a fault in the house. The servants will attend to it. One moment."

He lifted the receiver from Mr. Oberon's telephone. A voice answered.

"What is the matter with the lights?" Baradi asked.

"We cannot make out, Monsieur. There is no fault here. Perhaps the storm has brought down the lines."

"Nothing but trouble. And the telephone? Can one telephone yet to Roqueville?"

"No, Monsieur. The centrale sent up a man. The fault is not in the Château. They are investigating. They will ring through when the line is clear."

"Since yesterday afternoon we have been without the telephone. Unparalleled incompetence!" Baradi ejaculated. "Have Mr. Herrington and Mlle. Taylor returned?"

"I will enquire, Monsieur."

"Do so, and ring Mr. Oberon's apartments if they are in."

He clapped down the receiver. "I am uneasy," he said. "It has happened at a most tiresome moment. We have only the girl Teresa's account of the affair at the factory. No doubt she is speaking the truth. Having found the boy, they are satisfied. All the same it is not too amusing, having had the police in the factory."

"Callard will have handled them with discretion."

"No doubt. The driver, Georges Martel, however, will be examined by the police."

"Can he be trusted?"

"He has too much at stake to be anything but dependable. We pay him very highly. Also he has his story. He was rung up by an unknown client purporting to be the boy's father. He took the job in good faith and merely asked the girl Teresa to accompany him. They know nothing. The police will at once suspect the former kidnappers. Nevertheless, I wish we had not attempted the affair with the boy."

"One wanted to rid oneself of the parents."

"Exactly. Of the father. If circumstances were different," Baradi said softly, "I should not be nearly so interested in ridding myself of Mama. Women!" he ejaculated sententiously.

"Woman!" Mr. Oberon echoed with an inexplicable laugh and added immediately: "All the same I am getting abominably anxious. I don't trust him. And then, the light! Suppose it doesn't come on again before the Rites. How shall we manage?"

"Something can be done with car batteries, I think, and a soldering iron. Mahomet is ingenious in such matters. I shall speak to him in a moment."

Baradi walked over to the window and pulled back the silk blind. "It is quite dark." The blind shot up with a whirr and click.

"It really is much too quick on the trigger," he observed.

Mr. Oberon said loudly: "Don't do that! You exacerbate my nerves. Pull it down. Tie it down."

And while Baradi busied himself with the blind he added: "I shall send out. My temper is rising and that is dangerous. I must not become angry. If his car his gone I shall send after it."

"I strongly suggest you do nothing of the sort. It would be an unnecessary and foolish move. She will return. Surely you have not lost your flair."

Mr. Oberon, in the darkness, said: "You are right. She will return. She must."

"As for your rising temper," said Baradi, "you had better subdue it. It is dangerous."

XI

P. E. Garbel

I

RAOUL slowed down at a point above the entrance to the tunnel.

"Where should we leave the car, Monsieur?"

"There's a recess off the road, on the far side, near the tunnel and well under the lee of the hill. Pull in there."

The silhouette of the Chèvre d'Argent showed black above the hills against a clearing but still stormy sky. A wind had risen and cloud-rack scurried across a brilliant display of stars.

"Gothic in spirit," Alleyn muttered, "if not in design."

The road turned the headland. Raoul dropped to a crawl and switched off his lights. Alleyn used a pocket torch. When they came down to the level of the tunnel exit he got out and guided Raoul into a recess hard by the stone facing.

Raoul dragged out a marketing basket from which the inter-mingled smells of cabbage, garlic and flowers rose incongruously on the rain-sweetened air.

"Have you hidden the cloaks underneath?" Alleyn asked him.

"Yes, Monsieur. It was an excellent notion. It is not unusual for me to present myself with such gear. The aunt of Teresa is a market-gardener."

"Good. We'll smell like two helpings of a particularly exotic soup."

"Monsieur?"

"No matter. Now, Raoul, to make certain we understand each other will you repeat the instructions?"

"Very well, Monsieur. We go together to the servants' entrance. If, by mischance, we encounter anybody on the way who recognizes Monsieur, Monsieur will at once say he has come to enquire for the sick Mademoiselle. I will continue on and will wait for Monsieur at the servants' entrance. If Monsieur, on arriving there, is recognized by one of the servants who may not yet have left, he will say he has been waiting for me and is angry. He will say he wishes to speak to Teresa about the stealing of Riki. If, on the other hand, all goes well and we reach the servants' quarters together and unchallenged, we go at once to Teresa's room. Monsieur is seen but not recognized, he is introduced as the intellectual cousin of Teresa who has been to England, working in a bank, and has greatly improved his social status, and again we retire quickly to Teresa's room before the Egyptian valet or the butler can encounter Monsieur. In either case, Teresa is to give a message saying it has come by a peasant on a bicycle. It is to say that Mr. Herrington's car has broken down but that Miss Taylor and he will arrive in time for the party. Finally, if Monsieur does not come at all, I wait an hour then go to seek for him."

"And if something we have not in the least anticipated turns up?"

Raoul laughed softly in the dark: "One must then use one's wits, Monsieur."

"Good, shall we start?"

They walked together up the steep incline to the platform.

A goods train came puffing up from Douceville. The glow from the engine slid across the lower walls and bastions of the Chèvre d'Argent. Behind the silk blind a dim light burned: a much fainter light than the one they had seen from the window of their own train. Higher up, at odd intervals in that vast façade, other windows glowed or flickered where candles had been placed or were carried from one room to another.

The train tooted and clanked into the tunnel.

It was quite cold on the platform. A mountain breeze cut across it and lent credibility to the turned-up collar of Alleyn's raincoat and the scarf across his mouth. The passage was almost pitch dark but they thought it better not to use a torch. They slipped and stumbled on wet and uneven steps. The glow from old Marie's door was a guide. As they passed by she shouted from behind the oil-lamp: "Hola, there! Is it still raining?"

Raoul said quietly: "The stars are out. Good night, Marie," and they hurried into the shadows. They heard her shouting jovially after them: "Give her something to keep out the cold."

"She speaks of Teresa," Raoul whispered primly. "There is a hint of vulgarity in Marie."

Alleyn stifled a laugh. They groped their way round a bend in the passage, brushing their hands against damp stone. Presently an elegant design of interlaced rosettes appeared against a background of reflected warmth. It was the wrought-iron gate of the Chèvre d'Argent.

"As quick as we dare," Alleyn whispered.

The passage glinted wet before the doorway. The soles of his shoes were like glass. He poised himself and moved lightly forward. As he entered the patch of light he heard a slither and an oath. Raoul hurtled against him, throwing him off his balance. He clung to the gate while Raoul, in a wild attempt to recover himself, clutched at the nearest object.

It was the iron bell-pull.

The bell gave tongue with a violence that was refracted intolerably by the stone walls.

Three cabbages rolled down the steps. Raoul by some desperate effort still clung to the basket with one hand and to the bell-pull with the other.

"Monsieur! Monsieur!" he stammered.

"Go on," Alleyn said. *"Go on!"*

Raoul let go the bell-pull and a single note fell inconsequently across the still-echoing clangour. He plunged forward and was lost in shadow.

Alleyn turned to face the door.

"Why, if it's not Mr. Alleyn!" said Mr. Oberon.

II

He stood on the far side of the door with his back to a lighted candelabrum that had been set down on a chest in the entry. Little could be seen of him but his shape, enveloped in his white gown with the hood drawn over his head. He moved towards the door and his hands emerged and grasped two of the iron bars.

Alleyn said: "I'm afraid we made an appalling din. My chauffeur slipped and grabbed your bell-pull."

"Your chauffeur?"

"He's taken himself off. I fancy he knows one of your maids. He had some message for her, it seems."

Mr. Oberon said, as if to explain his presence at the door: "I am waiting for someone. Have you seen—" He paused and shifted his hands on the bars. His voice sounded out of focus. "Perhaps you met Ginny. Ginny Taylor? And Robin Herrington? We are a little anxious about them."

"No," Alleyn said. "I didn't see them. I came to ask about Miss Truebody."

Mr. Oberon didn't move. Alleyn peered at him. "How is she?" he asked.

Mr. Oberon said abruptly: "Our telephone has been out of order since yesterday afternoon. Do forgive me. I am a little anxious, you know."

"How is Miss Truebody?"

"Alas, she is dead," said Mr. Oberon.

They faced each other like actors in some medieval prison scene. The shadow of twisted iron was thrown across Alleyn's face and chest.

"Perhaps," Alleyn said, "I may come in for a moment."

"But, of course. How dreadful of me! We are all so distressed. Mahomet!"

Evidently the Egyptian servant had been waiting in the main hall. He unlocked the door, opened and stood aside. When Alleyn had come in he relocked the door.

With the air of having arrived at a decision, Mr. Oberon led the way into the great hall. Mahomet came behind them bringing the candelabrum, which he set down on a distant table. In that vast interior it served rather to emphasize the dark than relieve it.

"Monsieur," said Mahomet in French, "may I speak?"

"Well?"

"There is a message brought by a peasant from Mr. Herrington. He has had trouble with his auto. He is getting a taxi. He and Mlle. Taylor will arrive in time for the ceremony."

"Ah!" It was a long-drawn out sigh. "Who took the message?"

"The girl Teresa, who was on her way to catch the omnibus. The peasant would not wait so the girl returned with the message. Miss Taylor also sent a message. It was that Monsieur must not trouble himself. She will not fail the ceremony. She will go immediately to her room."

"Is all prepared?"

"All is prepared, Monsieur."

Mr. Oberon raised his hand in dismissal. Mahomet moved away into the shadows. Alleyn listened for the rattle of curtain rings but there was no other sound than that of Mr. Oberon's uneven breathing. "Forgive me again," he said, coming closer to Alleyn. "As you heard it was news of our young people."

"I'm afraid my French is too rudimentary for anything but the most childish phrases."

"Indeed? It appears they have had a breakdown but all is now well."

Alleyn said: "When did Miss Truebody die?"

"Ah, yes. We are so sorry. Yesterday afternoon. We tried to get you at the hotel, of course, but were told that you had gone to St. Céleste for a few days."

"We changed our plans," Alleyn said. "May I speak to Dr. Baradi?"

"To Ali? I am not sure—I will enquire—Mahomet!"

"Monsieur?" said a voice in the shadows.

"Tell your master that the English visitor is here. Tell him the visitor knows that his compatriot has left us."

"Monsieur."

The curtain rings jangled together.

"He will see if our friend is at home."

"I feel," Alleyn said, "that I should do everything that can be done. In a way she is our responsibility."

"That is quite wonderful of you, Mr. Allen," said Mr. Oberon, who seemed to have made a return to his normal form. "But I already sensed in you a rare and beautiful spirit. Still, you need not distress yourself. We felt it our privilege to speed this soul to its new life. The interment is tomorrow at three o'clock. Anglican. I shall, however, conduct a little valedictory ceremony here."

The curtain rings clashed again. Alleyn saw a large whiteness move towards them.

"Mr. Allen?" said Baradi, looming up on the far side of the candelabrum. He wore a white robe and his face was a blackness within the hood. "I am so glad you've come. We were puzzled what to do when we heard you had gone to St. Céleste."

"Fortunately there was no occasion. We ran Ricky to earth, I'm glad to say."

They both made enthusiastic noises. They were rejoiced. An atrocious affair. Where had he been found?

"In the chemical factory, of all places," Alleyn said. "The police think the kidnappers must have got cold feet and dumped him there." He allowed their ejaculations a decent margin and then said: "About poor Miss Truebody—"

"Yes, about her," Baradi began crisply. "I'm sorry it happened as it did. I can assure you that it would have made no difference if there had been a hospital with an entire corps of trained nurses and surgeons. And certainly, may I add, she could not have had a more efficient anaesthetist. But, as you know, peritonitis was greatly advanced. Her condition steadily deteriorated. The heart, by the way, was not in good trim. Valvular trouble. She died at 4:28 yesterday afternoon without recovering consciousness. We found her address in her passport. I have made a report which I shall send to the suitable authorities in the Bermudas. Her effects, of course, will be returned to her home there. I understand there are no near relatives. I have completed the necessary formalities here. I should have preferred, under the circumstances, to have asked a brother medico to look at her, but it appears they are all in conclave at St. Christophe."

"I expect I should write to—well, to somebody."

"By all means. Enclose a letter with my report. The authorities in the Bermudas will see that it reaches the lawyer or whoever is in charge of her affairs."

"I think perhaps—one has a feeling of responsibility—I think perhaps I should see her."

There was an infinitesimal pause.

"Of course," Baradi said. "If you wish, of course, I must warn you that the climatic conditions and those of her illness and death have considerably accelerated the usual postmortem changes."

"We have done what we could," Mr. Oberon said. "Tuberoses and orchids."

"How very kind. If it's not troubling you too much."

There was a further slight pause. Baradi said: "Of course," again and clapped his hands. "No electricity," he explained. "So provoking." The servant reappeared, carrying a single candle. Baradi spoke to him in their own language and took the candle from him. "I'll go with you," he said. "We have moved her into a room outside the main part of the Château. It is quite suitable and cooler."

With this grisly little announcement he led Alleyn down the now familiar corridor past the operating room and into a much narrower side-passage that ended in a flight of descending steps and a door. This, in turn, opened on a further reach of the outside passageway. The night air smelled freshly after the incense-tained house. They turned left and walked a short distance down the uneven steps. Alleyn thought that they could not be far from the servants' entrance.

Baradi stopped at a deeply recessed doorway and asked Alleyn to hold the candle. Alleyn produced his torch and switched it on. It shone into Baradi's face.

"Ah!" he said blinking, "that will be better. Thank you." He set down the candle. It flickered and guttered in the draught. He thrust his hand under his gown and produced a heavily furnished key-ring that might have hung from the girdle of a medieval gaoler. Alleyn turned his light on it and Baradi selected a great key with a wrought-iron loop. He stopped to fit it in a key-hole placed low in the door. His wide sleeves drooped from his arms, his hood fell over his face, and his shadow, grotesque and distorted, sprawled down the steps beyond him.

"If you would lend me your torch," he said. "It is a little awkward, this lock."

Alleyn gave him his torch. The shadow darted across the passage and reared itself up the opposite wall. After some fumbling, the key was engaged and noisily turned. Baradi shoved at the door and with a grind of its hinges it opened suddenly inwards and he fell forward with it, dropping the torch, nose first, on the stone threshold. There was a tinkle of glass and they were left with with the guttering candle.

"*Ah, sacré nom d'un chien!*" Baradi ejaculated. "My dear Mr. Allen, what have I done!"

Alleyn said: "Be careful of the broken glass."

"I am wearing sandals. But how careless! I am so sorry."

"Never mind. The passage seems to be unlucky for us this evening. Let's hope there's not a third mishap. Don't give it another thought. Shall we go in?" Alleyn laid down his walking-stick and took up the candle and the broken torch. They went in, Baradi shutting the door with a heave and a weighty slam.

It seemed to be a small room with whitewashed stone walls and a shuttered window. Candlelight wavered over a bank of flowers. A coffin stood in the middle on trestles. The mingled odours of death and tuberoses were horrible.

"I hope you are not over-sensitive," Baradi said. "We have done our best. Mr. Oberon was most particular, but—well—as you see—"

Alleyn saw. The lid of the coffin had been left far enough withdrawn to expose the head of its inhabitant, which was literally bedded in orchids. A white veil of coarse net lay over the face, but it did little to soften the inexorable indignities of death.

"The teeth," said Baradi, "make a difference, don't they?"

Looking at them Alleyn was reminded of Teresa's generality to the effect that all English spinsters have teeth like mares. This lonely spinster's dentist had evidently subscribed to Teresa's opinion and Alleyn saw the other stigmata of her kind: the small mole, the lines and pouches, the pathetic tufts of grey hair from which the skin had receded.

He backed away. "I thought it better to see her," he said, and his voice was constrained and thin. "In case there should be any question of identification."

"Much better. Are you all right? For the layman it is not a pleasant experience."

Alleyn said: "I find it quite appalling. Shall we go? I'm afraid I—" His voice faded. He turned away with a violent movement and at the same time jerked his handkerchief. It flapped across the candle flame and extinguished it.

In the malodorous dark Baradi cursed unintelligibly. Alleyn gabbled: "The door, for God's sake, where is the door? I'm going to be sick." He lurched against Baradi and sent him staggering to the far end of the room. He drop-kicked the candlestick in the opposite direction. His hands were on the coffin. His left hand discovered the edge of the lid, slid under it, explored a soft material, a tight band and the surface beneath. His fingers, inquisitive and thrusting, found what they sought.

"I can't stand this!" he choked out. "The door!"

Baradi was now swearing in French. *"Idiot!"* he was saying. *"Maladroit, imbécile!"*

Alleyn made retching noises. He found his way unerringly to

the door and dragged it open. A pale lessening of the dark was
admitted. He staggered out into the passage-way and rested
against the stone wall. Baradi came after him and dragged the
door shut. Alleyn heard him turn the key in the lock.

"That was not an amusing interlude," Baradi said. "I warned
you it would not be pleasant."

Alleyn had his handkerchief pressed to his mouth. He said
indistinctly: "I'm sorry. I didn't realize—I'll be all right."

"Of course you will," Baradi snapped at him. "So shall I when
my bruises wear off."

"Please don't let me keep you. Fresh air. I'll go back to the
car. Thank you: I'm sorry."

Apparently Baradi had regained his temper. He said: "It is
undoubtedly the best thing you can do. I recommend a hot bath,
a stiff drink, two aspirins and bed. If you're sure you're all right
and can find your way back—"

"Yes, yes. It's passing off."

"Then if you will excuse me. I am already late. Good night,
Mr. Alleyn."

Alleyn, over his handkerchief, watched Baradi return up the
steps, open the side-door and disappear into the house. He
waited for some minutes, accustoming his eyes to the night.

"Somehow," he thought, "I must get a wash," and he wiped
his left hand vigorously on his handkerchief which he then threw
into the shadows.

But he did not wipe away the memory of a not very large
cavity under the left breast of a sprigged locknit nightgown.

III

He had been right about the nearness of the servants' entrance. The stone passage-way dipped, turned and came to an
end by a sort of open pent-house. Alleyn had to grope his way
down steps, but the non-darkness that is starlight had filtered
into the purlieus of the Chèvre d'Argent and glistened faintly on
ledges and wet stone. He paused for a moment and looked back
and upwards. The great mass of stone and rock made a black
hole in the spangled heavens. The passage-way had emerged
from beneath a bridge-like extension of the house. This linked

the seaward portion with what he imagined must be the original
fortress, deep inside the cliff-face. Alleyn moved into an inky-
dark recess. A light had appeared on the bridge.

It was carried by the Egyptian servant, who appeared to have
something else, possibly a tray, in his hand. He was followed by
Baradi. Unmistakably it was Baradi. The servant turned and his
torchlight flickered across the dark face. The doctor no longer
wore his robe. Something that looked like a smooth cord hung
round his neck. They moved on and were lost inside the house.
Alleyn gave a little grunt of satisfaction and continued on his
way.

A lantern with a stub of candle in it hung by a half-open door
and threw a yellow pool on the flat surface beneath.

"Monsieur?" a voice whispered.

"Raoul?"

"Oui, Monsieur. Tout va bien. Allons.

Raoul slid out of the penthouse. Alleyn's wrist was grasped.
He moved into the pool of light. Raoul pushed the door open
with his foot. They entered a stone corridor, passed two closed
doors and turned right. Raoul tapped with his finger-tips on a
third door. Teresa opened it and admitted them.

It was a small neat bedroom, smelling a little fusty. One of old
Marie's Madonnas, neatly inscribed: "Notre Dame de
Paysdoux" stood on a corner shelf with a stool before it. Dusty
paper flowers, candles and a photograph of Teresa in her confir-
mation dress, with folded hands and upturned eyes, completed
the décor. A sacred print, looking dreadfully like Mr. Oberon,
hung nearby. Across the bed were disposed two white gowns. A
washstand with a jug and basin stood in a further corner.

Teresa, looking both nervous and complacent, pushed forward her only chair.

Alleyn said: "It is possible to wash one's hands, Teresa? A
little water and some soap?"

"I will slip out for some warm water, Monsieur. It is quite
safe to do so. Monsieur will forgive me. I had forgotten. The
English always wish to wash themselves."

Alleyn did not correct this aphorism. When she had gone he
said: "Well, Raoul?"

"The servants have gone out, Monsieur, with the exception
of the Egyptian, who is occupied downstairs. The guests are in

their rooms. It is unlikely that they will emerge before the ceremony." He extended his hands, palms upwards. "Monsieur, how much mischief have I made by my imbecility?"

Alleyn said: "Well, Raoul, you certainly rang the bell," and then seeing his companion's bewilderment and distress, added: "It was not so bad after all. It worked out rather well. Dr. Baradi and I have visited the body of a murdered woman."

"Indeed, Monsieur?"

"It lies among orchids in a handsome coffin in a room across the passage of entrance. The coffin, as M. le Commissaire had already ascertained, arrived this morning from an undertaker in Roqueville."

"But Monsieur—"

"There is a wound, covered by a surgical dressing, under the left breast."

"Teresa has told me that the English lady died."

"Here *is* Teresa," Alleyn said and held up his hand.

While he washed he questioned Teresa about Miss Truebody.

"Teresa, in what room of the house did the English lady die? Was it where we put her after the operation?"

"No, Monsieur. She was moved at once from there. The Egyptian and the porter carried her to a room upstairs in the Saracen's watch-tower. It is not often used. She was taken there because it would be quieter, Monsieur."

"I'll be bound she was," Alleyn muttered. He dried his hands and began to outline a further plan of action. "Last night," he said, "I learned from Mr. Herrington a little more than Teresa perhaps may know, of the normal procedure on Thursday nights. At eleven o'clock a bell is rung. The guests then emerge from their rooms wearing their robes which have been laid out for them. They go in silence to the ceremony known as the Rites of the Children of the Sun. First they enter the small ante-room where each takes up a lighted candle. They then go into the main room and stay there until after midnight. Supper is served in Mr. Oberon's salon. The whole affair may go on, after a fashion, until five o'clock in the morning."

Teresa drew in her breath with an excited hiss.

"Now it is my intention to witness this affair. To that end I propose that you, Raoul, and I replace Miss Taylor and Mr.

Herrington, who will not be there. Electricity will not be restored in the Château tonight and by candlelight we have at least a chance of remaining unrecognized."

Teresa made a little gesture. "If Monsieur pleases," she said.

"Well, Teresa?"

"The Egyptian has brought in iron boxes from Mr. Oberon's auto and a great deal of electrical cord and a soldering iron; he has arranged that the sun lamp in the room of ceremonies shall be lighted."

"Indeed? How very ingenious of him."

"Monsieur," Raoul said, eyeing the gowns on the bed, "is it your intention that I make myself to pass for a lady?"

Teresa cackled and clapped her hand over her mouth.

"Exactly so," said Alleyn. "You are about the same height as Miss Taylor. In the black gown with the hood drawn over your face and hands—by the way, you too must wash your hands—hidden in the sleeves, you should, with luck, pass muster. You have small feet. Perhaps you may be able to wear Miss Taylor's slippers."

"Ah, mon Dieu, quelle blague!"

"Comport yourself with propriety, Teresa, Monsieur is speaking."

"If you cannot manage this I have bought a pair of black slippers which will have to do instead."

"And my costume, Monsieur?" Raoul asked, indicating with an expressive gesture his stained singlet, his greenish black trousers and his mackintosh hitched over his shoulders.

"I understand that, apart from the gown and slippers there is no costume at all."

"Ah, mon Dieu, en voilà une affaire!"

"Teresa! Attention!"

"However, the gown is voluminous. For propriety's sake, Raoul, you may retain your vest and underpants. In any case you must be careful to conceal your legs which, no doubt, are unmistakably masculine."

"They are superb," said Teresa. "But undoubtedly masculine."

"It seems to me," continued Alleyn, who had become quite used to the peculiarities of conversation with Raoul and Teresa, "that our first difficulty is the problem of getting from here to the respective rooms of Mr. Herrington and Miss Taylor. Teresa, I see, has brought two white gowns. Mr. Herrington has provided us with a white and a black one. Miss Taylor would have appeared in black tonight. Therefore, you must put on the black, Raoul, and I shall wear the longest of the white. Teresa must tell us where these rooms are. If the Egyptian or any of the guests should see us on our way to them we must hope they will observe the rule of silence which is enforced before the ceremony and pay no attention. It will be best if we can find our way without candles. Once inside our rooms we remain there until we hear the bell. How close, Teresa, are these rooms to the room where the ceremony is held? The room you described to me yesterday."

"The young lady's is nearby, Monsieur. It is therefore close also to the apartment of Mr. Oberon."

"In that case, Raoul, when you hear the bell, go at once to the ante-room. Take a candle and, by the communicating door, go into the ceremonial room. There will be five or six black cushions on the floor and a large black divan. If there are six cushions, yours will be apart from the others. If there are five, your position will be on the divan. I am only guessing at this. One thing I do know—the rule of silence will be observed until the actual ceremony begins. If you are in the wrong position it will be attributed, with luck, to stage-fright and somebody will put you right. Where is Mr. Herrington's room, Teresa?"

"It is off the landing, Monsieur, going down to the lower storey where the ceremonies are held."

"And the other guests?"

"They are in the higher parts of the Château, Monsieur. Across the outside passage and beyond it."

"Do you know the room of Miss Grizel Locke?"

"Yes, Monsieur."

"Have you seen her today?"

"Not since two days ago, Monsieur, but that is not unusual. As I have informed Monsieur, it is the lady's habit to keep to her room and leave a notice that she must not be disturbed."

"I see. Now, if I leave Mr. Herrington's room on the first stroke of the bell, I should arrive hard on your heels, Raoul, and in advance of the others. I may even go in a little earlier." He looked at his watch. "It is half-past-seven. Let us put on our gowns. Then, Teresa, you must go out and, if possible, discover the whereabouts of the Egyptian."

"Monsieur, he was summoned by M. Baradi before you came

in. I heard him speaking on the house telephone."

"Let us hope the doctor keeps his man with him for some time. Now then, Raoul. On with the motley!"

The gowns proved to be amply made, wrapping across under their girdles. The hoods would come well forward and, when the head was bent, completely exclude any normal lighting from the face. "But it will be a different story if one holds a lighted candle," Alleyn said. "We must not be seen with our candles in our hands."

He had bought for Raoul a pair of feminine sandals, black and elegant with highish heels. Raoul said he thought they would fit admirably. With a grimace of humorous resignation he washed his small, beautiful and very dirty feet and then fitted them into the sandals. *"Oh, là, là!"* he said, "one must be an acrobat, it appears." And for the diversion of Teresa he minced to and fro, wagging his hips and making unseemly gestures. Teresa crammed her fists in her mouth and was consumed with merriment. *"Ah, mon Dieu,"* she gasped punctually, *"quel drôle de type!"*

Alleyn wondered rather desperately if he was dealing with children or merely with the celebrated latin *joie de vivre*. He called them to order and they were at once as solemn as owls.

"Teresa," he said, "you will go a little ahead of us with your candle. Go straight through the house and down the stairs to the landing beneath the library. If you see anybody, blow your nose loudly."

"Have you a handkerchief, my jewel?"

"No."

"Accept mine," said Raoul, offering her a dubious rag.

"If anybody speaks to you and, perhaps, asks you why you are still on the premises, say that you missed your bus because of the message about Miss Taylor. If it is necessary, you must say you are going to her room to do some little act of service that you had forgotten and that you will leave to catch the later bus. If it is possible, in this event, Raoul and I will conceal ourselves until the coast is clear. If this is not possible, we will behave as Mr. Herrington and Miss Taylor would behave under the rule of silence. You will continue to Miss Taylor's room, open the door for Raoul and go in for a moment, but only for a moment. Then, Teresa, I have another task for you," continued Alleyn, feeling for the second time in two days that he had become as big a bore as Prospero. Teresa, however, was a complacent Ariel and merely gazed submissively upon him.

"You will find Mr. Oberon and will tell him that Miss Taylor has returned and asks to be allowed her private meditation alone in her room until the ceremony. That is very important."

"Ah, Monsieur, if he were not so troubling to my soul!"

"If you value my esteem, Teresa—" Raoul began.

"Yes, yes, Monsieur," said Teresa in a hurry, "I am resolved! I will face it."

"Good. Having given this message, come and report to me. After that your tasks for the night are finished. You will catch the late bus for your home in the Paysdoux. Heaven will reward you and I shall not forget you. Is all that clear, Teresa?"

Teresa repeated it all.

"Good. Now, Raoul, we may not have a chance to speak to each other again. Do as I have said. You are enacting the role of a frightened yet fascinated girl who is under the rule of silence. What will happen during the ceremony I cannot tell you. Mr. Herrington could not be persuaded to confide more than you already know. You can only try to behave as the others do. If there is a crisis I shall deal with it. You will probably see and hear much that will shock and anger you. However beastly the behaviour of these people, you must control yourself. Have you ever heard of the Augean Stables?"

"No, Monsieur."

"They were filthy and were cleansed. It was a heroic task. Now, when you get to Miss Taylor's room you will find a robe, like the one you are wearing, laid out for her. If there is no difference you need not change. I don't think you need try to wear her shoes but if there is anything else set out for her— gloves perhaps—you must wear whatever it may be. One thing more. There may be cigarettes in Miss Taylor's room. Don't smoke them. If cigarettes are given to us during the ceremony we must pretend to smoke. Like this."

Alleyn pouted his lips as if to whistle, held a cigarette in the gap between them and drew in audibly. "They will be drugged cigarettes. Air and smoke will be inhaled together. Keep your thumb over the end like this and you will be safe. That's all. A great deal depends upon us, Raoul. There have been many girls before Miss Taylor who have become the guests of Mr. Oberon. I think perhaps of all evil-doers, his kind are the worst. Monsieur le Commissaire and I are asking much of you."

Raoul, perched on his high heels and peering out of the black hood, said: "Monsieur l'Inspecteur-en-Chef, in the army one learns to recognize authority. I recognize it in you, Monsieur, and I shall serve it to the best of my ability."

Alleyn was acutely embarrassed and more than a little touched by this speech. He said: "Thank you. Then we must all do our best. Shall we set about it? Now, Teresa, as quietly as you can unless you meet anybody, and then—boldly. Off you go."

"Courage, my beloved. Courage and good sense."

Teresa bestowed a melting glance upon Raoul, opened the door and, after a preliminary look down the passage, took up her candle and went out. Alleyn followed with his walking-stick in his hand and Raoul, clicking his high heels and taking small steps, brought up the rear.

Down in Roqueville Troy absent-mindedly arranged little figures round a crib and pondered on the failure of her session with Ginny and Robin. She heard again Ginny's desperate protest: "I don't want to, I don't want to but I must. I've taken the oath. Dreadful things will happen if I don't go back."

"You don't really believe that," Robin had said and she had cried out: " *You've* sworn and *you* won't tell. If we don't believe, why don't we tell?"

Suddenly, with something of Ricky's abandon, she had flung her arms round Troy. "If you could help," she had stammered, "but you can't; you can't!" And she had run out of the room like a frightened animal. Robin, limping after her, had turned at the door.

"It's all right," he had said. "Mrs. Allen, it's all right. She won't go back."

There was a tidily arranged pile of illustrated papers in the private sitting-room where they had had their drinks. Troy found herself idly turning the pages of the top one. Photographs of sunbathers and race-goers flipped over under her abstracted gaze. Dresses by Dior and dresses by Fath, Prince Aly Khan leading in his father's horse, the new ballet at the Marigny—"*Les invités réunis pour quelques jours au Château de la Chèvre d'Argent. De gauche à droite: l'Hôte, M. Oberon; Mlle. Imogen Taylor, M. Carbury Glande, Dr. Baradi, M. Robin Herrington et la Hon. Grizel Locke*—" Troy's attention was arrested and then transfixed. It was a clear photograph taken on the roof-garden. There they were, perfectly recognizable, all except Grizel Locke.

The photograph of Grizel Locke was that of a short, lean woman with the face of a complete stranger.

IV

Robin was driving up a rough lane into the hills with Ginny beside him saying feverishly: "You're sure this is a shorter way? It's a quarter to eight, Robin! Robin, you're sure?"

He thought: "The tank was half-full. How long will it take for half a tank of air to be exhausted?"

"There's tons of time," he said, "and I'm quite sure." As he turned the next corner the engine missed and then stopped. Robin crammed on his brakes.

Looking at Ginny's blank face he thought: "Now, we're for it. It's tonight or nevermore for Ginny and me."

Dupont, waiting under the stars on the platform outside the Chèvre d'Argent, looked at his watch. It was a quarter to eight. He sighed and settled himself inside his coat. He expected a long vigil.

V

Teresa's candle bobbed ahead. Sometimes it vanished round corners, sometimes dipped or ascended as she arrived at steps and sometimes it was stationary for a moment as she stopped and listened. Presently they were on familiar ground. Forward, on their left, was the operating room: opposite this, the room where Miss Truebody had waited. Nearer, on their right, a thin blade of light across the carpet indicated the door into Baradi's room. Teresa's hand, dramatized by candlelight, shielded the flame. Beyond her, the curtain at the end of the passage was faintly defined against some further diffusion of light.

She passed Baradi's room. Alleyn and Raoul approached it. Alleyn held up a warning hand. He halted and then crept for-

ward. His ear was at the door. Beyond it, like erring souls,
Baradi and his servant were talking together in their own language.

Alleyn and Raoul moved on. Teresa had come to the curtain.
They saw her lift it and a triangle of warmth appeared. Her
candle sank to the floor. The foot of the curtain was raised and
the candle, followed by the doubled-up shape of Teresa, disappeared beneath it.

"Good girl," Alleyn thought, "she's remembered the rings."

He followed quickly. He was tall enough to reach the rings
and hold the top of the curtain to the rail while he raised the skirt
for Raoul to pass through.

Now Raoul was in the great hall where the candellabrum still
burned on the central table. Teresa had already passed into the
entrance lobby. Alleyn still held the curtain in his hand when
Teresa blew her nose.

He slipped back behind the curtain, leaving a peephole for
himself. He saw Raoul hesitate and then move forward until his
back was to the light and he saw a white-robed figure that might
have been himself come in from the lobby. Looking beyond the
six burning candles he watched the two figures confront each
other. The white hood was thrust back and Carbury Glande's
red beard jutted out. Alleyn heard him mutter:

"Well, thank God for you, anyway. You *have* put him in a
tizzy! What happened?"

The black cowl moved slightly from side to side. The head
was bent.

"Oh, *all* right!" Glande said pettishly. "What a stickler you
are, to be sure!"

The white figure crossed the end of the hall and disappeared
up the stairway.

Raoul moved on into the lobby and Alleyn came out of cover
and followed him. When he entered the lobby, Alleyn went to
the carved chest that stood against the back wall. It was there
that the Egyptian servant had put the key of the wrought-iron
door. Alleyn found the key and through the grill tossed it out of
reach into the outside passage-way.

From the lobby, the staircase wound downstairs. Teresa's
candle, out of sight and sinking, threw up her own travelling
shadow and that of Raoul. Alleyn followed them, but they
moved faster than he and he was left to grope his way down in a

kind of twilight. He had completed three descending spirals when he arrived at the landing. The door he had noticed on his previous visit was not open and beyond it was a bedroom with a light burning before a looking-glass. This, evidently, was Robin Herrington's room. Alleyn went in. On the inside door-handle hung a notice: "*Heure de Méditation. Ne dérangez pas.*" He hung it outside and shut the door.

The room had the smell and sensation of luxury that were characteristic of the Chèvre d'Argent. A white robe, like his own, was laid out together with silk shorts and shirt and a pair of white sandals. Alleyn changed quickly. On a table near the bed was a silver box, an ashtray, an elaborate lighter and, incongruously, a large covered dish which, on examination, proved to contain a sumptuous assortment of hors d'oeuvres and savouries. In the box were three cigarettes: long, thin and straw-coloured. He took one up, smelt it, broke it across and put the two halves in his case. He held a second to his candle, kept it going by returning it continuously to the flame and, as it was consumed, broke the ash into the tray.

"Three of those," he thought, "and young Herrington's values would be as cockeyed as one of Carbury Glande's abstracts."

There was the lightest of taps on the door. It opened slightly. "Monsieur?" whispered Teresa.

He let her in.

"Monsieur, it is to tell you that I have executed your order. I have spoken to M. Oberon. Tonight he was not as formerly he has been. He was not interested in me, but all the same he was excited. One would have thought he was intoxicated, Monsieur, but he does not take wine."

"You gave the message?"

"Yes, Monsieur. He listened eagerly and questioned me, saying: 'Have you seen her?' and I thought best, with the permission of the saints, to say 'yes.'"

"Quite so, Teresa."

"He then asked me if Mademoiselle Taylor was quite well and I said she was and then if she seemed happy and I said: 'Yes, she seemed pleased and excited,' because that is how one is, Monsieur, when one keeps an appointment. And I repeated that Mademoiselle had asked to be alone and he said: 'Of course, of course. It is essential,' as if to himself. And he was staring in a strange manner as if I was not there and so I left him. And although I was frightened, Monsieur, I was not troubled as formerly by M. Oberon because Raoul is the friend of my bosom and to him I will be constant."

"I should certainly stick to that, if I were you. You are a good girl, Teresa, and now you must catch your bus. Tomorrow you shall choose a fine present against your wedding-day."

"Ah, Monsieur!" Teresa exclaimed and neatly sketching ineffable astonishment and delight, she slipped out of the room.

It was now eight o'clock. Alleyn settled down to his vigil. He thought of poor Miss Truebody and of the four remaining guests and Mr. Oberon, each in his or her room, and each, he believed, oppressed by an almost intolerable sense of approaching climax. He wondered if Robin Herrington had followed his advice about blocking the vent in the cap on his petrol tank and he wondered if Troy had had any success in breaking down Ginny's enthralment.

He turned over in his mind all he had read of that curious expression of human credulity called magic. As it happened he had been obliged on a former case to dig up evidence of esoteric ritual and had become fascinated by its witness to man's industry in the pursuit of a chimera. Hundreds and hundreds of otherwise intelligent men, he found, had subjected themselves throughout the centuries to the boredom of memorizing and reciting senseless formulae, to the indignity of unspeakable practices and to the threat of the most ghastly reprisals. Through age after age men and women had starved, frightened and exhausted themselves, had got themselves racked, broken and burned, had delivered themselves up to what they believed to be the threat of eternal damnation and all without any firsthand evidence of the smallest success. Age after age the Oberons and Baradis had battened on this unquenchable credulity, had traced their pentagrams, muttered their interminable spells, performed their gruelling ceremonies and taken their toll. And at the same time, he reflected, the Oberons (never the Baradis) had ended by falling into their own traps. The hysteria they induced was refracted upon themselves. Beyond the reek of ceremonial smoke they too began to look for the terrifying reward.

He wondered to what class of adept Oberon belonged. There was a definite hierarchy. There had always been practitioners

who, however misguided, could not be accused of charlatanism.
To this day, he believed, such beings existed, continuing their
barren search for a talisman, for a philosopher's stone, for
power and for easy money.

Magical rituals from the dawn of time had taken on the
imprint of their several ages. From the scope and dignity of the
Atkadian Inscriptions to the magnificence of the Graeco-
Egyptian Papyri, from the pious Jewish mysteries to the
squalors, brutalities and sheer silliness of the German pseudo-
Faustian cults. From the Necromancer of the Coliseum to the
surprisingly fresh folklorishness of the English genre: each had
its peculiar character and its own formula of frustration. And
alongside the direct line like a bastard brother ran the cult of
Satanism, the imbecile horrors of the Black Mass, the Amatory
Mass and the Mortuary Mass.

If Oberon had read all the books in his own library he had a
pretty sound knowledge of these rituals together with a generous
helping of Hinduism, Voodoo and Polynesian mythology: a
wide field from which to concoct a ceremony for the downfall of
Ginny Taylor and her predecessors. Alleyn fancied that the
orthodox forms would not be followed. The oath of silence he
had read in Baradi's room was certainly original. "If it's the
Amatory Mass as practised by Madame de Montespan," he
thought, "poor old Raoul's sunk from the word go." And he
began to wonder what he should to if this particular crisis arose.

He spent the rest of his vigil eating the savouries that had no
doubt been provided to satisfy the hunger of the reefer addict
and smoking his own cigarettes. He checked over the possibili-
ties of disaster and found them many and formidable. "All the
same," he thought, "it's worth it. And if the worst comes to the
worst we can always—"

Somebody was scratching at his door.

He ground out his cigarette, extinguished his candle and
seated himself on the floor with his back to the door and his legs
folded Oberon-wise under his gown. He was facing the dressing-
table with its large tilted looking-glass. The scratching persisted
and turned into a feather-light tattoo of finger-tips. He kept his
gaze on that part of the darkness where he knew the looking-
glass must be. He heard a fumbling and a slight rap and guessed
that the notice had been moved from the door-handle. A vertical
sliver of light appeared. He watched the reflection of the opening

door and of the white-robed candle-bearer. He caught a glimpse,
under the hood, of a long face with a beaked nose. Robed like
that she seemed incredibly tall: no longer the figure of fantasy
that she had presented yesterday in pedal-pushers and scarf and
yet, unmistakably, the same woman. The door was shut. He bent
his head and looked from under his brows at the reflexion of the
woman, who advanced so close that he could hear her breathing
behind him.

"I know it's against the Rule," she whispered, "I've got to
speak to you."

He made no sign.

"I don't know what they'll do to me if they find out but I'm
actually past caring!" In the glass he saw her put the candle on
the table. "Have you smoked?" she said. "If you have I suppose
it's no good. I haven't." He heard her sit heavily in the chair.
"Well," she whispered almost cosily, "it's about Ginny. You've
never seen an initiation, have you? I mean of that sort. You
might at least nod or shake your head."

Alleyn shook his head.

"I thought not. You've got to stop her doing it. She's fond of
you, you may depend upon it. If it was not for *him* she'd be in
love, like any other nice girl, with you. And you're fond of her. I
know. I've watched. Well, you've got to stop it. She's a thoroughly nice girl," the prim whisper insisted, "and you're still a
splendid young fellow. Tell her she mustn't."

Alleyn's shoulders rose in an exaggerated shrug.

"Oh, *don't!*" The whisper broke into a vocal protest. "If you
only knew how I've been watching you both. If you only knew
what I'm risking. Why, if you tell on me I don't know what they
won't do. Murder me, as likely as not. It wouldn't be the first
time unless you believe she killed herself, and I certainly don't."

The voice stopped. Alleyn waited.

"One way or another," the voice said quite loudly, "you've
got to give me a sign."

He raised his hand and made the Italian negative sign with his
finger.

"You won't! You mean you'll let it happen. To Ginny? In
front of everybody? Oh, dear me!" The voice sighed out most
lamentably. "Oh, dear, dear me, it's enough to break one's
heart!" There was a further silence. Alleyn thought: "The time's
going by: we haven't much longer. If she'd just say one thing!"

The voice said strongly, as if its owner had taken fresh courage: "Very well. I shall speak to her. It won't do any good. I look at you and I ask myself what sort of creature you are. I look—"

She broke off. She had moved her candle so that its reflexion in the glass was thrown back upon Alleyn. He sat frozen.

"Who are you?" the voice demanded strongly. "You're not Robin Herrington."

She was behind him. She jerked the hood back from his head and they stared at each other in the looking-glass.

"And you're not Grizel Locke," Alleyn said. He got up, faced her and held out his hand. "Miss P.E. Garbel, I presume," he said gently.

XII

Eclipse of the Sun

I

"THEN you guessed!" said Miss Garbel, clinging to his hand and shaking it up and down as if it were a sort of talisman. "How did you guess? How did you get here? What's happening?"

Alleyn said: "We've got twenty-five minutes before that damn bell goes. Don't let's squander them. I wasn't sure. Yesterday morning, when you talked like one of your letters, I wondered."

"I couldn't let either of you know who I was. Oberon was watching. They all were. I thought the remark about the Douceville bus might catch your attention."

"I didn't dare ask outright, of course. Now, tell me. Grizel Locke's dead, isn't she?"

"Yes; small hours of yesterday morning. We were told an overdose of self-administered heroin. *I* think—murdered."

"Why was she murdered?"

"*I* think, because she protested about Ginny. Ginny's her niece. *I* think she may have threatened them with exposure."

"Who killed her?"

"I haven't an idea. Oh, not a notion!"

"What exactly were you told?"

"That if it was found out we'd all be in trouble. That the

whole thing would be discovered: the trade in diacetylmorphine, the connection with the factory—have you discovered about the factory?—everything, they said, would come out and we'd all be arrested and the Bristish subjects would be extradited and tried and imprisoned. Then, it appears, you rang up about Miss Truebody. Baradi saw it as a chance to dispose of poor Grizel Locke. She would be buried, you see, and you would be told it was Miss Truebody. Then later on when you were out of the way and Miss Truebody was well, a made-up name would be put over the grave. Baradi said that if anybody could save Miss Truebody's life, he could. I'm guessing at how much you know. Stop me if I'm not clear. And then you or your wife asked about 'Cousin Garbel.' You can imagine how that shocked them! I was there, you see. I'm their liason with the factory. I work at the factory. I'll tell you why and how if we've time. Of course I guessed who you were, but I told them I hadn't a notion. I said I supposed you must be some unknown people with an introduction or something. They were terribly suspicious. They said I must see you both and find out what you were doing, and why you'd asked about me. Then Baradi said it would be better if I didn't present myself as me. And then they said I must pretend to be Grizel Locke so that if there was ever an enquiry or trouble, you and Cousin Aggie—"

"*Who!*" Alleyn ejaculated.

"Your wife, you know. She was called Agatha after my second cousin, once—"

"Yes, yes. Sorry. I call her Troy."

"Really? Quaint! I've formed the habit of thinking of her as Cousin Aggie. Well, the plan was that I'd be introduced to you as Grizel Locke and I should tell them afterwards if I recognized you or knew anything about you. They made me wear Grizel's clothes and paint my face, in case you'd heard about her or would be asked about her afterwards. And then, tomorrow, after the funeral we are meant to meet again and I'm to say I'm leaving for a trip to Budapest. If possible, you are to see me go. So that if a hue-and-cry goes out for Grizel Locke, you will support the story that she's left for Hungary. I'm to go as far as Marseilles and stay there until you're both out of the way. The factory has extensive connections in Marseilles. At the same time we're to give out that I, as myself, you know, have gone on holiday. How much longer have we got?"

"Twenty-one minutes."

"I've time, at least, to tell you quickly that whatever you're planning you mustn't depend too much upon me. You see, I'm one of them."

"You mean," Alleyn said, "you've formed the habit—?"

"I'm fifty. Sixteen years ago I was a good analytical chemist but terribly poor. They offered me a job on a wonderful salary. Research. They started me off in New York, and after the war they brought me over here. At first I thought it was all right and then gradually I discovered what was happening. They handled me on orthodox lines. A man, very attractive, and parties. I was always plain and he was experienced and charming. He started me on marihuana—reefers, you know—and I've never been able to break off. They see to it I get just enough to keep me going. They get me up here and make me nervous and then give me cigarettes. I'm very useful to them. When I smoke I get very silly. I hear myself saying things that fill me with bitter shame. But when I've got the craving to smoke and when *he's* given me cigarettes, I—well, you've seen. It wasn't all play-acting when I pretended to be Grizel Locke. We all get like that with Oberon. He has a genius for defilement."

"Why did you write as you did to Troy? I must tell you that we didn't realize what you were up to until yesterday."

"I was afraid you wouldn't. But I daren't be explicit. Their surveillance is terribly thorough and my letters might have been opened. They weren't, as turned out, otherwise you would have been recognized as my correspondent. I wrote—"

The voice, half vocal, half whispering, faltered. She pushed back her hood and tilted her tragic-comic face towards Alleyn's. "I began to write because of the girls like Ginny. You've seen me and you've seen Annabella Wells—frightful, aren't we? Grizel Locke was the same. Drug-soaked old horrors. We're what happens to the Ginnys. And there are lots and lots of Ginnys: bomb-children I call 'em. No moral stamina and no nervous reserve. Parents killed within the child's memory and experience. Sense of insecurity and impending disaster. The poor ones with jobs have the best chance. But the others—the rich Ginnys—if they run into our sort of set—whoof! And once they're made Daughters of the Sun it's the end of them. Too ashamed to look back or up or anywhere but at him. So when I saw in the English papers that my clever kinswoman had married *you,* I thought: 'I'll do it. I haven't the nerve or self-control to fight on my own but I'll try and hint.' So I did. I was a little surprised when Cousin Aggie replied as if to a man, but I did not correct her. Her mistake gave me a foolish sense of security. How long, now?"

"Just over seventeen minutes. Listen! Herrington and Ginny won't come back tonight. My chauffeur and I are replacing them. Can we get away with it? What happens in the ceremony?"

She had been talking eagerly and quickly, watching him with a bird-like attentiveness. Now it was as if his question touched her with acid. She actually threw up her hands in a self-protective movement and shrank away from him.

"I can't tell you. I've taken an oath of silence."

"All that dagger and fire and molten lead nonsense?"

"You can't know! How do you know? Who's broken faith?"

"Nobody. I hoped you might."

"Never!"

"A silly gimcrack rigmarole. Based on infamy."

"It's no good. I told you. I'm no good."

"My man's about Ginny's height and he's wearing the black robe. Has he a chance of getting by?"

"Not to the end. Of course not." She caught her breath in something that might have been a sob or a wretched giggle. "How can you dream of it?"

"Will anybody be asked to take this oath—alone?"

"No—I can tell you nothing—but—he—no. Why are you doing this?"

"We think the ceremony may give us an opportunity for an arrest on a minor charge. Not only that—" Alleyn hesitated. "I feel as you do," he said hurriedly, "about this wretched child. For one thing she's English and there's a double sense of responsibility. At the same time I'm not here to do rescue work, particularly if it prejudices the success of my job. What's more, if Oberon and Baradi suspect that this child and young Herrington have done a bolt, they'll also suspect a betrayal. They'll have the machinery for meeting such a crisis. All evidence of their interest in the racket will be destroyed and they'll shoot the moon. Whereas, if, by good luck, we can diddle them into thinking Ginny Taylor and Robin Herrington have returned to their unspeakable fold we may learn enough, here, tonight to warrant an arrest. We can then hold the principals, question the smaller fry and search the whole place."

"I'm small fry. How do you know I won't warn them?"

"I've heard you plead for Ginny."

"You've told me she's safe," whimpered Miss Garbel. She bit her finger-tips and looked at him out of the corner of her pale eyes. "That's all I wanted. You ask me to bring ruin on myself. I've warned you. I'm no good. I've no integrity left. In a minute I must smoke and then I'll be hopeless. You ask too much."

Alleyn said: "You're a braver woman than you admit. You've tried for months to get me here, knowing that if I succeed your job will be gone and you will have to break yourself of your drug. You risked trying to tip me off yesterday morning and you risked coming to plead with young Herrington here tonight. You're a woman of science with judgement and curiosity and a proper scepticism. You know, positively, that this silly oath of silence was taken under the influence of your drug, that the threats it carries are meaningless, that it's your clear duty to abandon it. I think you will believe me when I say that if you keep faith with us tonight you will have our full protection afterwards."

"You can't protect me," she said, "from myself."

"We can try. Come! Having gone so far, why not all the way?"

"I'm so frightened," said Miss Garbel. "You can't think. So dreadfully frightened."

She clasped her claw-like hands together. Alleyn covered them with his own. "All right," he said. "Never mind. You've done a lot. I won't ask you to tell me about the rites. Don't go to the ceremony. Can you send a message?"

"I must go. There must be seven."

"One for each point of the pentagram, with Oberon and the Black Robe in the middle?"

"Did *they* tell you? Ginny and Robin? They wouldn't dare."

"Call it a guess. Before we separate I'm going to ask you to make one promise tonight. Shall we say for Grizel Locke's sake? Don't smoke so much marihuana that you may lose control of yourself and perhaps betray us."

"I shan't betray you. I *can* promise that. I don't promise not to smoke and I implore you to depend on me for nothing more than this. I won't give you away."

"Thank you a thousand times, my dear cousin-by-marriage. Before the night is over I shall ask if I may call you Penelope."

"Naturally you may. In my bad moments," said poor Miss

Garbel, "I have often cheered myself up by thinking of you both as Cousins Roddy and Aggie."

"Have you really?" Alleyn murmured and was saved from the the necessity of further comment by the sound of a cascade of bells.

Miss Garbel was thrown into a great state of perturbation by the bells which, to Alleyn, were reminiscent of the dinner chimes that tinkle through the corridors of ocean liners.

"There!" she ejaculated with a sort of wretched triumph. "The Temple bells! And here we are in somebody else's room and goodness *knows* what will become of us."

"I'll see if the coast's clear," Alleyn said. He took up his stick and then opened the door. The smell of incense hung thick on the air. Evidently candles had been lit on the lower landing. The stair-well sank into reflected light through which there rose whorls and spirals of scented smoke. As he watched, a shadow came up from below and the sound of bells grew louder. It was the Egyptian servant. Alleyn watched the distorted image of his tarboosh travel up the curved wall followed by that of his body and of his hands bearing the chime of bells. Alleyn stood firm, leaning on his stick with his hood over his face. The Egyptian followed his own shadow upstairs, ringing his little carillon. He crossed the landing, made a salutation as he passed Alleyn and continued on his way upstairs.

Alleyn looked back into the room. Miss Garbel stood there, biting her knuckles. He went to her.

"It's all right," he said. "You can go down. If you feel *very* brave and venturesome keep as close as you dare to the Black Robe and if he looks like he's making a mistake try and stop him. He only speaks French. Now, you'd better go."

She shook her head two or three times. Then, with an incredible suggestion of conventional leave-taking she began to settle herself inside her robe. She actually held out her hand.

"Goodbye. I'm sorry I'm not a braver woman," she said.

"You've been very brave for a long time and I'm exceedingly grateful," Alleyn said.

He watched her go and after giving her about thirty seconds, blew out the candle and followed her.

II

The stairs turned three times about the tower before he came limping to the bottom landing. Here a lighted candelabrum stood near a door: the door he had noticed yesterday morning. Now it was open. The air was dense with the reek of incense so that each candle flame blossomed in a nimbus. His feet sank into the deep carpet and dimly he could make out the door into Oberon's room and the vista of wall-tapestries, receding into a passage.

Through the open door he saw four separate candlesticks, each with a lighted black candle. This, then, was the ante-room. Alleyn went in. The black velvet walls absorbed light and an incense burner hanging from the ceiling further obscured it. He could make out a partly opened curtain and behind this a rack of hanging robes. He could not be sure he was alone. Limping carefully, he made for the candles and took one up.

Remembering what Teresa had told him, he turned to the right and with his free hand explored the wall. The velvet surface was disagreeable to his touch. He moved along still pressing it and in a moment it yielded. He had found the swing-door into the temple.

There was an unwholesomeness about the silent obedience of the velvet door. It was as if everyday objects had begun to change their values. He followed his hand and walked, as it seemed, through the retreating wall into the temple.

At first he was aware only of two candle flames below the level of his knees and some distance ahead, six glowing braziers. Then he saw a white robe, squatting not far from a candle and then a black robe, near a second flame. He felt the tessellated floor under his feet and, using his stick, tapped his way across. "All the same," he thought, "young Herrington's stick is rubbershod."

By the light of his own candle he made out the shape of the giant pentagram in the mosaic of the floor. It had been let into the pavement and was traced in some substance that acted as a reflector. The five-pointed star was enclosed in a double circle and he saw that at each of the points there was a smaller circle

and in this a black cushion and a brazier filled with glowing
embers. It was on one of these cushions that the white robe
squatted. He drew close to it. A recognizable hand crept out
from under the sleeve. It was Miss Garbel's. He turned to the
centre of the pentagram. Raoul was holding his candle under his
own face. His hands and arms were gloved in black. He was
seated, cross-legged on a black divan and in front of him was a
brazier.

Alleyn murmured: "The lady behind you and to your right is
not unfriendly. She knows who you are."

Raoul signalled an assent.

"Depend on me for nothing—nothing," admonished a ghost-
whisper in French and then added in a sort of frenzy, "Not there!
Not in the middle. Not yet. Like me. *There!*"

"Quick, Raoul. *There!*"

Raoul darted into the point of the pentagram in front of Miss
Garbel's. He put down his candle on the floor and pulled forward his hood.

Alleyn moved to the encircled point opposite Miss Garbel's.
He had seated himself on the cushion before his brazier and had
laid down his stick and candle when a light danced across the
facets of the pentagram. He sensed, rather than heard, the
entrance of a new figure. It passed so close that he recognized
Annabella Wells's scent. She moved into the encircled point on
his right and seated herself facing outwards as he did. At the
same time there was a new glint of candlelight and the sound of a
subsidence behind and to the left of Alleyn. In a moment or two
a figure, unmistakably Baradi's, swept round the pentagram and
entered it between Annabella and Raoul. Alleyn guessed he had
taken up his position at the centre. At the same time the bells
cascaded close at hand. "Here we go," he thought.

The five candles and six braziers furnished light enough for
him to get a fitful impression of the preposterous scene. By
turning his head slightly and slewing round his eyes, he could see
the neighbouring points of the great pentagonal star, each protected by its circle and each containing its solitary figure, seated
before a brazier and facing outward. Outside the pentagram and
facing the points occupied by Annabella and Raoul was the
altar. Alleyn could see the glint of metal in the embroidered
cloth and quite distinctly, could make out the shape of the great
crystal sun-burst standing in the middle.

The sound of bells came close and then stopped. A door opened in the wall beside the altar and the Egyptian servant walked through. He wore only a loin cloth and the squarish head-dress of antiquity. Before each of the initiates he set down a little box. "More reefers," thought Alleyn, keeping his head down. "Damned awkward if he wants to light them for us."

But the Egyptian made no attempt to do so. He moved away and out of the tail of his eye, Alleyn saw Annabella Wells reached out to her brazier, take a pair of tongs and light her cigarette with a piece of charcoal. Alleyn found that his brazier, too, was provided with tongs.

Because of the form of the pentagram the occupants of the five points all had their backs turned to Baradi and their shoulders to each other. If Baradi was on his feet he would have a sort of aerial survey of their backs. If he was seated on the divan he would have a still less rewarding view. Alleyn reached out for a cigarette, hid it inside his robe and produced one of his own. This he lit with a coal from the brazier. He wondered if it had occurred to Raoul to employ the same ruse.

Little spires of smoke began to rise from the five points of the star. The Egyptian had retired to a dark corner beyond the altar and presently began to strike a drum and play a meandering air on some reed instrument. To Alleyn the scene was preposterous and phony. He remembered Troy's comment on the incident of the train window: hadn't she compared it to bad cinematography? Even the ritual, for what it was worth, was bogus: a vamped-up synthesis, he thought, of several magic formulae. The reedy phrase trickled on like a tourist-class advertisement for Cairo, the drum throbbed and presently he sensed a stir of excitement among the initiates. The Egyptian began to chant and to increase the pace and volume of his drumming. Drum and voice achieved a sort of crescendo at the peak of which a second voice entered with a long vibrant call, startling in its unexpectedness. It was Baradi's.

From that moment it was impossible altogether to dismiss the Rites of the Sun as cheap or ridiculous. No doubt they were both but they were also alarming.

Alleyn supposed that Baradi spoke Egyptian and that his chant was one of the set invocations of ritual magic. He thought he recognized the characteristic repetition of names: "O Oualb-paga! O Kammara! O Kamalo! O Karhenmou! O Amagaa! O

Thoth! O Anubis!" The drum thumped imperatively. Small feral
noises came from the points of the pentagram. Behind Alleyn,
Carbury Glande began to beat with his palm on the floor. The
other initiates followed, Alleyn with them. The Egyptian left his
drum and running about the pentagram, threw incense on the
braziers. Columns of heavily scented smoke arose amid sharp
cries from the initiates. A gong crashed and there was immediate
silence.

It was startling, after the long exhortations in an incomprehensible tongue to hear Baradi cry in a loud voice: "Children of
the Sun in the Outer, turn inward, now turn in. Silence, silence,
silence, symbol of the imperishable god protect us, silence. Turn
inward now, turn in."

This injunction was taken literally by the initiates who reversed their positions on the cushions and thus faced Baradi and
the centre of the pentagram. Looking across, diagonally, to the
Black Robe, Alleyn saw that Raoul had not moved. The exhortations, being in English, had meant nothing to him. Alleyn
dared not look up at Baradi. He could see his feet and his white
robe, up to his knees. Between drifts of incense he caught sight of
the other initiates, all waiting. It seemed as if an age went by
before the Black Robe rose, turned and reseated itself. He saw
Baradi's feet shift and his robe swing as he faced the alter.

Baradi intoned in a loud voice: "Here in the Names of Ra and
Of the Sons of Ra—"

It was the oath Alleyn had read. Baradi gave it out phrase by
phrase and the initiates repeated it after him. Alleyn spoke on
the top register of his very deep voice. Raoul, of course, said
nothing. Miss Garbel's thin pipe was unmistakable. Annabella's
trained and vibrant voice rang out loudly. Carbury Glande's
sounded uncoordinated and hysterical.

"If I break this oath in the least degree," Baradi dictated and
was echoed, "may my lips be burned with the fire that is now set
before them." He gestured over his brazier. A tongue of flame
darted up from it.

"May my eyes be put out by the knife that is now set before
them."

With a suddenness that was extraordinarily unnerving, five
daggers dropped from the ceiling and checked with a jerk before
the five initiates; faces. A sixth, bigger, fell in front of Baradi,
who seized and flourished it. The others hung glittering in the

flamelight of the brazier. The women gave little whimpering febrile cries.

The oath of silence was taken through to its abominable conclusion. The flame subsided, the smaller daggers were drawn up to the ceiling, presumably by the Egyptian. The initiates turned outward again and Baradi settled down to a further exhortation, this time in English.

It was the blackest possible kind of affair, quite short and entirely infamous. Baradi demanded darkness and the initiates put out their candles. Alleyn dared not look at Raoul, but knew by the delayed flicker of light that he was a little slow with this. Then Baradi urged first of all the necessity of experiencing something called "the caress of the left hand of perfection" and went on to particularize in terms that would have appalled anyone who was not an alienist or a member of Mr. Oberon's chosen circle. The Egyptian had returned to his reed and drum and the merciless repetition of a single phrase had its own effect. Baradi began to pour out a stream of names: Greek, Jewish, Egyptian: Pan, Enlil, Elohim, Ra, Anubis, Seti, Adonis, Ra, Silenus, Ereschigal, Tetragrammaton, Ra. The recurrent "Ra" was presently taken up by the initiates, who began to bark it out with an enthusiasm, Alleyn thought, only to be equalled by the organized cheers of an American ball game.

"There are two signs," Baradi intoned. "There is the Sign of the Sun, Ra" ("Ra," barked the initiates), "and there is the sign of the Goat, Pan. And between the Sun and the Goat runs the endless cycle of the senses. Ra."

"Ra!"

"We demand a sign."

"We demand a sign."

"What shall the sign be?"

"The sign of the goat which is also the sign of the Sun which is also the sign of Ra."

"Let the goat come forth which is the Sun which is Ra."

"Ra!"

The drumming was increased to a frenzy. The initiates beat on the floor and clapped. Baradi must have thrown more incense on his brazier: the air was thick with billowing fumes. Alleyn could scarcely make out the shape of the altar. Now Baradi must be striking cymbals together.

The din was intolerable. The initiates, antic figures, half-masked by whorls of smoke, seemed to have gone down on all fours and to be flinging their hands high as they slapped the floor and cried out. Baradi broke into a chant, possibly in his own language, interspersed with further strings of names—Pan, Hylaesos, Lupercus, Silenos, Faunus—names that were caught up and shouted in a fury of abandon by the other voices. Alleyn, shouting with the rest, edged round on his knees, until he could look across the pentagram to Raoul. In the glow of the braziers he could just make out the black crouching figure and the black gloved hands rising and falling like drumsticks.

"A Sign, a Sign, let there be a Sign!"

"It comes."

"It comes."

"It is here."

Again the well-staged crescendo that ended, this time, in a deafening crash of cymbals followed by a dead silence.

And across that silence: bathetic, ridiculous and disturbing, broke the unmistakable bleat of a billy goat.

The smoke eddied and swirled, and there, on the altar for all the world like one of old Marie's statuettes, it appeared, horned and shining, a silver goat whose hide glittered through the smoke. It opened its mouth sideways and superciliously bleated. Its pale eyes stared and it stamped and tossed its head.

"It's been shoved up there from the back," Alleyn thought. "They've treated it with flourescent paint. *Ça s'illumine.*"

Baradi was speaking again.

"Prepare, prepare," he chanted. "The Sign is the Shadow of the Substance. The Goat-god is the precursor of the Man-god. The Man-god is the Bridegroom. He is the Spouse. He is Life. He is the Sun. Ra!"

There was a blare of light, for perhaps a second literally blinding in its intensity. "Flash-powder," thought Alleyn. "The Egyptian must be remarkably busy." When his eyes had adjusted themselves, the goat had disappeared and in its place the sun-burst blazed on the altar. "Car batteries," thought Alleyn, "perhaps. Flex soldered at the terminals. Well done, Mahomet or somebody."

"Ra! Ra! Ra!" the initiates ejaculated with Baradi as their cheerleader.

The door to the left of the altar had opened. It admitted a naked man.

He advanced through wreaths of incense and stood before the blazing sun-burst. It was, of course, Mr. Oberon.

III

Of the remainder of the ceremony, as far as he witnessed it, Alleyn afterwards prepared an official report. Neither this, nor a manual called *The Book of Ra,* which contained the text of the ritual, has ever been made public. Indeed, they have been stowed away in the archives of Scotland Yard where they occupy a place of infamy rivalling that of the *Book of Horus and the Swami Viva Ananda.* There are duplicates at the Sûreté. In the trial they were not put in as primary evidence, and the judge, after a distasteful glance, said that he saw no reason why the jury should be troubled to look at them.

For purposes of this narrative it need only be said that with the appearance of Oberon, naked, in the role of Ra or Horus, or both, the Rites took on the character of unbridled Phallicism. He stood on some raised place before the blazing sun-burst, holding a dagger in both hands. More incense burners were set reeking at his feet, and there he was, the nearest approach, Alleyn afterwards maintained, that he had ever seen, to a purely evil being.

His entry stung the initiates into their pitch of frenzy. Incredible phrases were chanted, indescribable gestures were performed. The final crescendo of that scandalous affair rocketed up to its point of climax. For the last time the Egyptian's drum rolled and Baradi clashed his cymbals. For the last time pandemonium gave place to silence.

Oberon came down from his eminence and walked towards the encircled pentagram. His feet slapped the tessellated pavement. His hair, lit from behind, was a nimbus about his head. He entered the pentagram and the initiates turned inwards, crouching beastily at the points. Oberon placed himself at the centre. Baradi spoke.

"Horus who is Savitar who is Baldur who is Ra. The Light, The Beginning and The End, The Life, The Source and The Fulfilment. Choose, now, Lord, O choose."

Oberon extended his arm and pointed his dagger at Raoul.

Baradi went to Raoul. He held out his hand. In the capricious glare from the sun-burst Alleyn could see Raoul on his knees, his shadow thrown before him towards Oberon's feet. His face was deeply hidden in his hood. Alleyn saw the gloved hand and arm reach out. Baradi took the hand. He passed Raoul across him with a dancer's gesture.

Raoul now faced Oberon.

Somewhere in the shadows the Egyptian servant cried out shrilly.

Baradi's dark hands, themselves seeming gloved, closed on the shoulders of Raoul's robe. Suddenly, with a flourish, and to a roll of the drum, he swept it free of its wearer. "Behold!" he shouted: "The Bride!"

And then, in the glare from the sun-burst, where, like an illustration from La Vie Parisienne, Mr. Oberon's victim should have been discovered; there stood Raoul in his underpants, black slippers and Ginny Taylor's gloves.

A complete surprise is often something of an anti-climax and so, for a moment or two, was this. It is possible that Annabella Wells and Carbury Glande were too fuddled with marihuana to get an immediate reaction. Miss Garbel, of course, had been prepared. As for Oberon and Baradi, they faced each other across the preposterous Thing they had unveiled and their respective jaws dropped like those of a pair of simultaneous comedians. Raoul himself merely cast a scandalized glance at Oberon and uttered in a loud apocalyptic voice the single word: "*Anathema!*"

It was then that Miss Garbel erupted in a single hoot of hysteria. It escaped from her and was at once cut off by her own hand clapped across her mouth. She squatted, heaving, in the corner of the pentacle, her terrified eyes staring over her knuckles at Baradi.

Baradi, in an unrecognizable voice and an unconscious quotation, said: "Which of you has done this?"

Oberon gave a bubbling cry: "I am betrayed!"

Raoul, hearing his voice, repeated: "Anathema!" and made the sign of the cross.

Oberon dragged Miss Garbel to her feet. He held her with his right hand; in his left was the dagger. She chattered in his face: "You can't! You can't! I'm protected. You can't!"

Alleyn advanced until he was quite close to them. Glande and Annabella Wells were on their feet.

"Is this your doing?" Oberon demanded, lowering his face to Miss Garbel's.

"Not mine!" she chattered. "Not this time. Not mine!"

He flung her off. Baradi turned on Raoul.

"Well!" Baradi said in French, "so I know you, now. Where's your master?"

"Occupy yourself with your own affairs, Monsieur."

"We are lost!" Oberon cried out in English.

His hand moved. The knife glinted.

"Alors, Raoul!" said Alleyn.

Raoul stooped and ran. He ran out of the pentacle and across the floor. The Egyptian darted out and was knocked sideways. His head struck the corner of the altar and he lay still. Raoul sped through the open door into Oberon's room. Oberon followed him. Alleyn followed Oberon and caught him up on the far side of the great looking-glass. He seized his right hand as it was raised. "Not this time," Alleyn grunted and jerked his arm. The dagger flew from Oberon's hand and splintered the great glass. At the same moment Raoul kicked. Oberon gave a scream of pain, staggered across the room and lurched against the window. With a whirr and a clatter the blind flew up and Oberon sank on the floor moaning. Alleyn turned to find Baradi facing him with the knife in his left hand.

"You," Baradi said. "I might have guessed. *You!*"

IV

From the moment that the affair began, as it were, to wind itself up in Oberon's room, it became a straightout conflict between Alleyn and Baradi. Alleyn had guessed that it would be so. Even while he sweated to remember his police training in unarmed combat he found time to consider that Oberon, naked and despicable, had at last become a negligible element. Alleyn was even aware of Carbury Glande and Annabella Wells teetering uncertainly in the doorway, and of Miss Garbel, who hovered like a spinsterly half-back on the edge of the scrimmage.

But chiefly he was aware of Baradi's dark infuriated body, smelling of sandalwood and sweat, and of the knowledge that he himself was the fitter man. They struggled together ridiculously and ominously, looking, in their white robes, like a couple of frenzied monks. There was, for Alleyn, a sort of pleasure in this fight. "I needn't worry. For once, I needn't worry," he thought. "For once the final arbitrament is as simple as this. I'm fitter than he is."

And when Raoul, absurd in his underpants and long gloves, suddenly hurled himself at Baradi and brought him down with a crash, Alleyn was conscious of a sort of irritation. He looked across the floor and saw that Raoul's foot, in its ridiculous sandal, had pinned down Baradi's left wrist. He saw Baradi's fingers uncurl from the knife-handle. He shoved free, landed a short-arm jab on the point of Baradi's jaw and felt him go soft. They had brought down the prayer wheel in their struggle. Alleyn reached for it and flung it at the window. It crashed through and he heard it fall with the broken glass on the railway line below. Oberon screamed out an oath. Alleyn fetched his breath and blew with all the wind he had on M. Dupont's police whistle. It trilled shrilly, like a toy, and was answered and echoed and answered again outside.

"The house is surrounded," Alleyn said, looking at Glande and Oberon. "I have a police authority. Anyone trying violence or flight will be dealt with out-of-hand. Stay where you are, all of you."

The glare from the sun-burst streamed through the doorway on clouds of incense. Alleyn bound Baradi's arms behind his back with the cord of his gown. Raoul tied his ankles together with the long gloves. Baradi's head lolled drunkenly and he made uncouth noises.

"I want to make a statement," Oberon said shrilly. "I am a British subject. I have my passport. I offer myself for Queen's evidence. I have my passport."

Annabella Wells, standing in the doorway, began to laugh. Carbury Glande said: "Shut up, for God's sake. This is IT."

Abruptly the room was lit. Wall-lamps, a bedside lamp and a standard lamp all came to life. By normal standards it was not a brilliant illumination, but it had the effect of reducing that unlikely interior to an embarrassing state of anti-climax. Glande, Annabella Wells and poor Miss Garbel, huddled in their robes, looked dishevelled and ineffectual. Baradi had a trickle of blood running from his nose into his moustache. The Egyptian servant staggered into the doorway, holding his head in his hands and wearing the foolish expression of a punch-happy pugilist. Oberon, standing before the cracked looking-glass as no doubt he had often done before: Oberon, naked, untactfully lit, was so repellent a sight that Alleyn threw the cover of the divan at him.

"You unspeakable monstrosity," he said, "get behind that."

"I offer a full statement. I am the victim of Dr. Baradi. I claim protection."

Baradi opened his eyes and shook the blood from his moustache.

"I challenge your authority," he said, blinking at Alleyn.

"Alleyn. Chief Detective-Inspector, C.I.D., New Scotland Yard. On loan to the Sûreté. My card and my authority are in my coat-pocket and my coat's in young Herrington's room."

Baradi twisted his head to look at Annabella. "Did you know this?" he demanded.

"Yes, darling," she said.

"You little—"

"Is that Gyppo for what, darling?"

"In a moment," Alleyn said, "the Commissioner of Police will be here and you will be formally arrested and charged. I don't know that I'm obliged to give you the customary warning but the habit's irresistible. Anything you say—"

Baradi and Annabella entirely disregarded him.

"*Why* didn't you tell me who he was?" Baradi said, *"Why?"*

"He asked me not to. He's got something. I didn't know he was here tonight. I didn't think he'd come back."

"Liar!"

"As you choose, my sweet."

"—may be used in evidence."

"You can't charge *me* with anything," Carbury Glande said. "I am an artist. I've formed the habit of smoking and I come to France to do it. I'm not mixed up in anything. If I hadn't had my smokes tonight I'd bloody well fight you."

"Nonsense," said Alleyn.

"I desire to make a statement," said Oberon, who was now wrapped in crimson satin and sitting on the divan.

"I wish to speak to you alone, Mr. Alleyn," said Baradi.

"All in good time."

"Garbel!" Baradi ejaculated.

"Shall I answer him, Roddy dear?"

"If you want to, Cousin Penelope."

"*Cousin!*" Mr. Oberon shouted.

"Only by marriage. I informed you," Miss Garbel reminded him, "of the relationship. And I think it only right to tell you that if it hadn't been for all the Ginnys—"

"My God," Carbury Glande shouted, "where are Ginny and Robin?"

"Ginny!" Oberon cried out. "Where is Ginny?"

"I hope!" rejoined Miss Garbel, "in no place so unsanctified where such as thou mayst find her.' The quotation, cousin, is from *Macbeth*."

"And couldn't be more appropriate," murmured Alleyn, bowing to her. He sat down at Mr. Oberon's desk and drew a sheet of paper towards him.

"This woman," Baradi said to Alleyn, "is not in her right mind. I tell you this professionally. She has been under my observation for some time. In my considered opinion she is unable to distinguish between fact and fantasy. If you base your preposterous behavior on any statement of hers—"

"Which I don't, you know."

"I am an Egyptian subject. I claim privilege. And I warn you, that if you hold me, you'll precipitate a political incident."

"My dear M. l'Inspecteur-en-Chef," said M. Dupont, coming in from the passage, "do forgive me if I am a little unpunctual."

"On the contrary, my dear M. le Commissaire, you come most punctually upon your cue."

M. Dupont shook hands with Alleyn. He was in tremendous form, shining with leather and wax and metal: gloved, holstered and batoned. Three lesser officers appeared inside the door.

"And these," said M. Dupont, touching his moustache and glancing round the room, "are the personages. You charge them?"

"For the moment, with conspiracy."

"I am a naturalized British subject. I offer myself as Queen's evidence. I charge Dr. Ali Baradi with murder."

Baradi turned his head and in his own language shot a stream of very raw-sounding phrases at his late partner.

"All these matters," said M. Dupont, "will be dealt with in an appropriate manner. In the meantime, Messieurs et Dames, it is required that you accompany my officers to the *Poste de Police* in Roqueville where an accusation will be formally laid." He nodded to his men, who advanced with a play of handcuffs.

Annabella Wells held her robe about her with one practiced hand and swept back her hair with the other. She addressed herself in French to Dupont.

"M. le Commissaire, do you recognize me?"

"Perfectly, Madame. Madame is the actress Annabella Wells."

"Monsieur, you are a man of the world. You will understand that I find myself in a predicament."

"It is not necessary to be a man of the world to discover your predicament, Madame. It is enough to be a policeman. If Madame would care to make some adjustment to her toilette—a walking costume, perhaps—I shall be delighted to arrange the facilities. There is a *femme-agent de police* in attendance."

She looked at him for a moment, seemed to hesitate, and then turned on Alleyn.

"What are you going to do with me?" she said. "You've trapped me finely, haven't you? What a fool I was! Yesterday morning I might have guessed. And I kept faith! I didn't tell them what you were. God, *what* a fool!"

"It's probably the only really sensible thing you've done since you came here. Don't regret it."

"Is it wishful thinking or do I seem to catch the suggestion that I may be given a chance?"

"Give yourself a chance, why not?"

"Ah," she said, shaking her head. "That'll be the day, won't it?"

She grinned at him and moved over to the door where Raoul waited. Raoul stared at her with a kind of incredulity. He had kicked off his sandals and wore only his pants and his St. Christopher medal and, thus arrayed, contrived to look god-like.

"What a charmer!" she said in English. "Aren't you?"

"*Madame?*"

"*Quel charmeur vous êtes!*"

"*Madame!*"

She asked him how old he was and if he had seen many of her films. He said he believed he had seen them all. Was he a cinephile, then? "*Madame,*" Raoul said, "*Je suis un fervent—de vous!*"

"When they let me out of gaol," Annabella promised, "I shall send you a photograph."

The wreckage of her beauty spoke through the ruin of her make-up. She made a good exit.

"Ah, Monsieur," said Raoul. "What a tragedy! And yet it is the art that counts and she is still an artist."

This observation went unregarded. They could hear Annabella in conversation with the *femme-agent* in the passage outside.

"My dear Dupont," Alleyn murmured, "may I suggest that in respect of this woman we make no arrest. I feel certain that she will be of much greater value as a free informant. Keep her under observation, of course, but for the moment, at least—"

"But, of course, my dear Alleyn," M. Dupont rejoined, taking the final plunge into intimacy. "I understand perfectly, but perfectly."

Alleyn was not quite sure what Dupont understood so perfectly but thought it better merely to thank him. He said: "There is a great deal to be explained. May we get rid of the men first?"

Dupont's policemen had taken charge of the four men. Oberon, still wrapped in crimson satin, was huddled on his bed. His floss-like hair hung in strands over his face. Above the silky divided beard the naked mouth was partly open. The eyes stared, apparently without curiosity, at Alleyn.

Dupont's men had lifted Baradi from the floor, seated him on the divan and pulled his white robe about him. His legs had been unbound, but he was now handcuffed. He, too, watched Alleyn, but sombrely, with attentiveness and speculation.

Carbury Glande stood nearby, biting his nails. The Egyptian servant flashed winning smiles at anybody who happened to look at him. Miss Garbel sat at the desk with an air of readiness, like an eccentrically uniformed secretary.

Dupont glanced at the men. "You will proceed under detention to the *Commissariat de Police* at Roqueville. M. l'Inspecteur-en-Chef and I will later conduct an interrogation. The matter of your nationalities and the possibility of extradition will be considered. And now—forward."

Oberon said: "A robe. I demand a robe."

"Look here, Alleyn," Glande said, "what's going to be done about me? I'm harmless, I tell you. For God's sake tell him to let me get some clothes on."

"Your clothes'll be sent after you and you'll get no more and

no less than was coming to you," Alleyn said. "In the interest of
decency, my dear Dupont, Mr. Oberon should, perhaps, be
given a garment of some sort."

Dupont spoke to one of his men, who opened a cupboard-
door and brought out a white robe.

"If," Miss Garbel said delicately, "I might be excused. Of
course, I don't know—?" She looked enquiringly from Alleyn to
Dupont.

"This is Miss Garbel, Dupont, of whom I have told you."

"Truly? Not, as I supposed, the Honourable Locke?"

"Miss Locke has been murdered. She was stabbed through
the heart at five thirty-eight yesterday morning in this room. Her
body is in a coffin in a room on the other side of the passage-of-
entry. Dr. Baradi was good enough to show it to me."

Baradi clasped his manacled hands together and brought
them down savagely on his knees. The steel must have cut and
bruised him, but he gave no sign.

Glande cried out: "Murdered! My God, they told us she'd
given herself an overdose."

"Then the—pardon me, Mademoiselle, if I express it a little
crudely—the third English spinster, my dear Inspecteur-en-
Chef? The Miss Truebody?"

"Is to the best of my belief recovering from her operation in a
room beyond a bridge across the passage-of-entry."

Baradi got clumsily to his feet. He faced the great cheval-
glass. He said something in his own language. As he spoke,
through the broken window, came the effeminate shriek of a
train whistle followed by the labouring up-hill clank of the train
itself. Alleyn held up his hand and they were all still and looked
through the broken window. Alleyn himself stood beside
Baradi, facing the looking-glass, which was at an angle to the
window. Baradi made to move but Alleyn put his hand on him
and he stood still, as if transfixed. In the great glass they both
saw the reflection of the engine pass by and then the carriages,
some of them lit and some in darkness. The train dragged to a
standstill. In the last carriage a lighted window, which was
opposite their own window, was unshuttered. They could see
two men playing cards. The men looked up. Their faces were
startled.

Alleyn said: "Look, Baradi. Look in the glass. The angle of

incidence is always equal to the angle of refraction, isn't it? We see their reflexion and they see ours. They see you in your white robe. They see your handcuffs. Look, Baradi!"

He had taken a paper-knife from the desk. He raised it in his left hand as if to stab Baradi.

The men in the carriage were agitated. Their images in the glass talked excitedly and gestured. Then, suddenly, they were jerked sideways and in the glass was only the reflexion of the wall and the broken window and the night outside.

"Yesterday morning, at five thirty-eight, I was in a railway carriage out there," Alleyn said. "I saw Grizel Locke fall against the blind and when the blind shot up I saw a man with a dark face and a knife in his right hand. He stood in such a position that the prayer wheel showed over his shoulder and I now know that I saw, not a man, but his reflexion in that glass and I know he stood where you stand and that he was a left-handed man. I know that he was you, Baradi."

"And really, my dear Dupont—" Alleyn said a little later, when the police-car had removed the four men and the two ladies had gone away to change—"really, this is all one has to say about the case. When I saw the room yesterday morning I realized what had happened. There was this enormous cheval-glass screwed into the floor at an angle of about forty-five degrees to the window. To anybody looking in from outside it must completely exclude the right-hand section of the room. And yet, I saw a man, apparently *in* the right-hand section of the room. He must, therefore, have been an image in the glass of a man in the left-hand section of the room. To clinch it, I saw part of the prayer wheel near the right shoulder of the image. Now, if you sit in a railway-carriage outside that window, you will, I think, see part of the prayer wheel, or rather, since I chucked the prayer wheel through the window, you will see part of its trace on the faded wall, just to your left of the glass. The stabber, it was clear, must be a left-handed man and Baradi is the only left-handed man we have. I was puzzled that his face was more shadowed than the direction of the light seemed to warrant. It is, of course, a dark face."

"It is perfectly clear," Dupont said, "thought the verdict is not to be decided in advance. The motive was fear, of course."

"Fear of exposure. Miss Garbel believes that Grizel Locke was horrified when her young niece turned up at the Chèvre d'Argent. It became obvious that Ginny Taylor was destined to play the major role, opposite Oberon, in these unspeakable Rites. The day before yesterday it was announced that she would wear the Black Robe tonight. My guess is that Grizel Locke, herself the victim of the extremes of mood that agonize all drug-addicts, brooded on the affair and became frantic with—with what emotion? Remorse? Anxiety? Shame?"

"But jealousy? She is, after all, about to become the supplanted mistress, is she not? Always an unpopular assignment."

"Perhaps she was moved by all of these emotions. Perhaps, after a sleepless night or—God knows—a night of pleading, she threatened to expose the drug racket if Oberon persisted with Ginny Taylor. Oberon, finding her intractable, summoned Baradi. She threatened both of them. The scene rose to a climax. Perhaps—is it too wild a guess?—she hears the train coming and threatens to scream out their infamy from the window. Baradi reverts to type and uses a knife, probably one of the symbolic knives with which they frighten the initiates. She falls against the blind and it flies up. There, outside, is the train with a dimly lighted compartment opposite their own window. And, between the light and the window of the compartment is the shape of a man—myself."

Dupont lightly struck his hands together. "A pretty situation, in effect!"

"He no sooner takes it in than it is over. The train enters the tunnel and Baradi and Oberon are left with Grizel Locke's body on their hands. And within an hour I ring up about Miss Truebody. And by the way, I suggest we visit Miss Truebody. Here comes Miss Garbel who, I daresay, will show us to her room."

Miss Garbel appeared, scarcely recognizable, wearing an unsmart coat and skirt and no make-up. It was impossible to believe this was the woman who, an hour ago, had lent herself to the Rites of the Children of the Sun and who, yesterday morning, had appeared in pedal-pushers and a scarf on the roof-garden. Dupont looked at her with astonishment. She was very tremulous and obviously distressed. She went to the point, however, with the odd directness that Alleyn was learning to expect from her.

"You are yourself again, I see," he said.

"Alas, yes! Or not, of course altogether, alas. It is nice not having to pretend to be poor Grizel any more but, as you noticed, I found it only too easy, at certain times, to let myself go. I sometimes think it is a peculiar property of marihuana to reduce all its victims to a common denominator. When we are 'high,' as poor Grizel used to call it, we all behave rather in her manner. I am badly in need of a smoke now, after all the upset, which is why I'm so shaky, you know."

"I expect you'd like to go back to your own room in the Rue des Violettes. We'll take you there."

"I would like it of all things, but I think I should stay to look after our patient. I've been doing quite a bit of the nursing— Mahomet and I took it in turns with one of the maids. Under the doctor's instructions, of course. Would you like to see her?"

"Indeed, we should. It's going to be difficult to cope with Miss Truebody. Of course, they never sent for a nurse?"

"No, no! Too dangerous, by far. But I assure you every care has been taken of the poor thing."

"I'll bet it has. They didn't want two bodies on their hands. M. le Commissaire has arranged for a doctor and a nurse to come up by the night train from St. Christophe. In the meantime, shall we visit her?"

Miss Garbel led the way up to the front landing. M. Dupont indicated the wrought-iron door. "We discovered the key, my dear Alleyn," he said gaily. "An excellent move!" They climbed to the roof-garden and thence though a labyrinth of rooms to one of the bridge-like extensions that straddled the outside passage-way.

They were half-way across this bridge when their attention was caught by the sound of voices and of boots on the cobblestones below.

From the balustrade they looked down into a scene that might have been devised by a film director. The sides of the house fell away from moon-patched shadow into a deep blackness. At one point a pool of light from an open door lay across the passage-way. Into this light moved an incongruous company of foreshortened figures: the Egyptian servant, Baradi and Oberon in their white robes, Carbury Glande bareheaded and in shorts, and six gendarmes in uniform. They shifted in and out of the light, a curious pattern of heads and shoulders.

"*Alors*," said Dupont, looking down at them: "*Bon débarras!*"

His voice echoed stonily in the passage. One of the white

hoods was tilted backwards. The face inside it was thus exposed to the light but, being itself dark, seemed still to be in shadow. Alleyn and Baradi looked at each other. With a peck of his head Baradi spat into the night.

"Pas de ça!" said one of the gendarmes and turned Baradi about. It was then seen that he was handcuffed to his companion.

"Mr. Oberon," Alleyn said, "will be delighted."

The procession moved off with a hollow clatter down the passage. Raoul appeared in the doorway, rolling a cigarette, and watched them go.

Miss Garbel made a curious and desolate sound but immediately afterwards said brightly: "Shall we—?" and led them indoors.

"Here we are!" she said and tapped. A door was opened by the woman Alleyn had already seen at Miss Truebody's bedside.

"These are the friends of Mademoiselle," said Miss Garbel. "Is she awake?"

"She is awake but M. le Docteur left orders, Mademoiselle, that no one—" She saw Dupont's uniform and her voice faded.

"M. le Docteur," said Miss Garbel, "has reconsidered his order."

The woman stood aside and they went into the room. Dupont stayed by the door but Alleyn walked over to the bed. There, on the pillow, was the smooth, blunt and singularly hairless face he had remembered. She looked at him and smiled and this time she was wearing her teeth. They made a great difference.

"Why, it's Mr. Alleyn," she murmured in a thread-like voice. "How kind!"

"You're getting along splendidly," Alleyn said. "I won't tire you now, but if there is anything you want you'll let us know."

"Nothing. Much better. The doctor—too kind."

"There will be another doctor tomorrow and a new nurse to help these."

"Not—? But—Dr. Baradi—?"

"He has been obliged to go away," Alleyn said, "on a case of some urgency."

"Oh." She closed her eyes.

Alleyn and Dupont went outside. Miss Garbel came to the door.

"If you don't want me," she said, "I'll stay and take my turn.

I'm all right, you know. Quite reliable until morning."

"And always," he rejoined warmly.

"Ah," she said, shaking her head. "That's another story."

She showed them where a stairway ran down to ground level and she peered after them, smiling and nodding over the banister.

"We must pay one more visit," Alleyn said.

"The third English spinster," Dupont agreed. He seemed to have a sort of relish for this phrase.

But when they stood in the whitewashed room and the raw light from an unshaded lamp now shone dreadfully on what was left of Grizel Locke, he looked thoughtful and said: "All three, each after her own fashion, may be said to have served the cause of justice."

"This one," Alleyn said drily, "may be said to have died for it."

V

It was a quarter past two when Grizel Locke was carried in her coffin down to a mortuary van that shone glossily in the moonlight. Two hours later Alleyn and Dupont walked out of the Château de la Chèvre d'Argent. They left two men on guard and with Raoul went down the passage-way to the open platform. It was flooded in moonlight. The Mediterranean glittered down below and the hills reared themselves up fabulously against the stars. Robin Herrington's rakish car was parked at the edge of the platform.

Alleyn said: "These are our chickens come home to roost."

"Ah!" said M. Dupont cosily. "It is a night for love."

"Nevertheless, if you will excuse me—"

"But, of course!"

Alleyn, whistling tunelessly and tactfully, went over to the car. Robin was in the driver's seat with Ginny beside him. Her head was on his shoulder. He showed no particular surprise at seeing Alleyn.

"Good morning," Alleyn said. "So you had a breakdown."

"We did, sir, but we think we're under our own steam again."

"I'm glad to hear it. You will find the Chèvre d'Argent rather empty. Here's my card. The gendarme at the door will let you in.

If you'd rather collect your possessions and come back to Roqueville, I expect we could get rooms for you both at the Royal."

He waited for an answer but it was perfectly clear to him that although they smiled and nodded brightly they had not taken in a word of his little speech.

Robin said: "Ginny's going to marry me."

"I hope you will both be *very* happy."

"We think of beginning again in one of the Dominions."

"The Dominions are, on the whole, both tolerant and helpful."

Ginny, speaking for the first time, said: "Will you please thank Mrs. Alleyn? She sort of did the trick."

"I shall. She'll be delighted to hear it." He looked at them for a moment and they beamed back at him. "You'll be all right," he said. "Get a tough job and forget you've had bad dreams. I'm sure it will work out."

They smiled and nodded.

"I'll have to ask you to come and see me later in the morning. At the Préfecture at eleven?"

"Thank you," they said vaguely. Ginny said: "You can't think how happy we are, all of a sudden. And just imagine, I was furious when the car broke down! And yet, if it hadn't, we might never have found out."

"Strange coincidence," said Alleyn, looking at Robin. And seeing that they were incapable of coming out of the moonlight he said: "Good morning and good luck to you both," and left them to themselves.

On the way down to Roqueville he and Dupont discussed the probable development of the case. "Oberon," Alleyn said, "has gone to pieces, as you see. He will try and buy his way out with information."

"Callard also is prepared to upset the peas. But thanks to your admirable handling of the case we shall be able to dispense with such aids, and Oberon, I trust, will be tried with Baradi."

"Of the pair, Oberon is undoubtedly the more revolting," Alleyn said thoughtfully. "I wonder how many deaths could be laid at the door of those two. I don't know how you feel about it, Dupont, but I put their sort at the top of the criminal list. If they hadn't directly killed poor Grizel, by God, they'd still be mass murderers."

"Undoubtedly," said Dupont, stifling a yawn. "I imagine we

take statements from the painter, the actress Wells and the two young ones and let it go at that. They may be more useful running free. Particularly if they return to the habit."

"The young ones won't. I'm sure of that. As for the others: there are cures."

In the front seat, Raoul, influenced no doubt by the moonlight and by his glimpse of Ginny and Robin, began to sing: *"La nuit est faite pour l'amour."*

"Raoul," Alleyn said in French for his benefit, "did a good job of work tonight, didn't he?"

"Not so bad, not so bad. We shall have you in the service yet, my friend," said Dupont. He leaned forward and struck Raoul lightly on the shoulder.

"No, M. le Commissaire, it is not my *métier*. I am about to settle with Teresa. And yet, if M. l'Inspecteur-en-Chef Alleyn should come back one day, who knows?"

They drove through the sleeping town to the little Square des Sarracins and put Alleyn down at the hotel.

Troy was fast asleep, with Ricky curled in beside her. The little silver goat illuminated himself on the bedside table. The French windows were wide open and Alleyn went out for a moment on the balcony. To the east the stars had turned pale and the first dawn cock was crowing in the hills above Roqueville.

NGAIO MARSH

America's most prominent mystery writer living today!
"She writes better than Christie ever did."
—*The New York Times*

A CLUTCH OF CONSTABLES   (03858-0—$1.75)

COLOUR SCHEME   (03859-9—$1.75)

DEAD WATER   (03857-2—$1.75)

DEATH AND THE BAR   (03491-7—$1.50)

DEATH IN ECSTASY   (03644-8—$1.50)

DIED IN THE WOOL   (03860-2—$1.75)

ENTER A MURDERER   (04300-2—$1.75)

FINAL CURTAIN   (03490-9—$1.50)

LAST DITCH   (03676-6—$1.75)

SCALES OF JUSTICE   (03551-4—$1.50)

A WREATH FOR RIVERA   (03856-4—$1.75)

Send for a list of all our books in print.

These books are available at your local bookstore, or send price indicated plus 30¢ for postage and handling. If more than four books are ordered, only $1.00 is necessary for postage. Allow three weeks for delivery. Send orders to:

Berkley Book Mailing Service
P.O. Box 690
Rockville Centre, New York 11570

"WE ONLY HAVE ONE TEXAS"

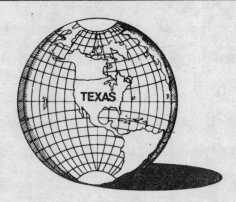

People ask if there is really an energy crisis. Look at it this way. World oil consumption is 60 million barrels per day and is growing 5 percent each year. This means the world must find three million barrels of new oil production each day. Three million barrels per day is the amount of oil produced in Texas as its peak was 5 years ago. The problem is that it is not going to be easy to find a Texas-sized new oil supply every year, year after year. In just a few years, it may be impossible to balance demand and supply of oil unless we start conserving oil today. So next time someone asks: "is there really an energy crisis?" Tell them: "yes, we only have one Texas."

ENERGY CONSERVATION -
IT'S YOUR CHANCE TO SAVE, AMERICA

Department of Energy, Washington, D.C.